When THE TOWNSMAN was first published by The John Day Company and became a selection of the Literary Guild, it was widely acclaimed by the critics and quickly became a best seller. The author's name, John Sedges, was admittedly a pseudonym.

Who was John Sedges? At last we know that John Sedges was Pearl S. Buck, one of America's best-loved authors and the only American woman ever to be awarded the Nobel Prize for Literature. In a special preface to this book she tells why she used a pseudonym and why John Sedges has at last become Pearl S. Buck.

THE TOWNSMAN
was originally published by The John Day Company, Inc.

Other books by Pearl S. Buck

The Angry Wife
A Bridge for Passing
Come, My Beloved
Command the Morning
Death in the Castle
Dragon Seed
The Exile
Fighting Angel
God's Men
The Good Earth
The Hidden Flower
Imperial Woman
Kinfolk
Letter from Peking
The Living Reed
The Long Love
The Mother
My Several Worlds
Pavilion of Women
Peony
Portrait of a Marriage
The Time Is Noon

Published by Pocket Books

 *Are there paperbound books you want
but cannot find in your retail stores?*

Pearl S. BUCK

The Townsman

PUBLISHED BY POCKET BOOKS NEW YORK

THE TOWNSMAN

John Day edition published May, 1945

A *Pocket Book* edition
1st printing .... June, 1958
5th printing .... September, 1969

This *Pocket Book* edition includes every word
contained in the original, higher-priced edition. It is printed
from brand-new plates made from completely reset, clear, easy-to-read
type. *Pocket Book* editions are published by Pocket Books, a division
of Simon & Schuster, Inc., 630 Fifth Avenue, New York, N.Y. 10020.
Trademarks registered in the United States and other countries.

Foreword

Some years ago I woke one morning to find myself strangely oppressed. I felt suddenly that I was no longer a free individual. I had been cast in a mold. I had written so many books about Chinese people that I had become known as a writer only about China. This was natural enough and nobody's fault. When I began to write I knew no people intimately except the Chinese. My entire life had been spent in China and beyond that in Asia. In midstream, however, I had transferred myself to the West and to my own country, the United States. Soon, since any writer writes out of his everyday environment, I began, however tentatively, to write about American people. I became thereby someone else.

This someone else, who now was also I—for the old self, the Asian self, continued to exist and will always continue—was, I repeat, oppressed. The oppression was the result of a determination on the part of my readers, sometimes loving, sometimes critical, to insist that there must be no other me than the one they had always known; that is to say, the Asian me. But here was the new American me, eager to explore and adventure among my own people. To provide freedom for this American me, pseudonymity was the answer. The writer must have a new name. I chose the name of John Sedges, a simple one, and masculine because men have fewer handicaps in our society than women have, in writing as well as in other professions.

My first John Sedges novel was *The Townsman*. It is a long

book, a story of the West, Kansas in scene, to which state I had made many quiet visits. I was pleased when Kansans praised its authenticity. Its hero is a modest fellow who refuses to ride wild horses, be a cowboy, shoot pistols into the air, kill his enemies, find gold in any hills, destroy Indians, or even get drunk. He is content merely to become the solid founder of a city. The novel was well received by critics and sold to some tens of thousands of readers. It thus proved itself as a successful first novel by an unknown writer.

Four other novels were published under the name John Sedges, and guesses became rampant as to the author. No secrets in this world are kept forever. Somebody always knows and tells. And my two selves were beginning to merge. I was by now at home in my own country, my roots were digging deep, and I was becoming increasingly familiar with my own people. The protection of John Sedges was neither so necessary nor so effective as it had been. In Europe the John Sedges novels were openly sold as Pearl Buck books. I was moving toward freedom. The shield was no longer useful.

So John Sedges has served his purpose and may now be discarded and laid away in the silver foil of memory. I declare my independence and my determination to write as I please in a free country, choosing my material as I find it. People are people whether in Asia or America, as everybody knows or ought to know, and for me the scene is merely the background for human antics. Readers will still be the critics, of course, but I shall hope and strive to please and to amuse. Why else should books be written?

—PEARL S. BUCK

Part One

I

FROM THE WINDOW OF HIS ROOM IN THE ATTIC JONATHAN Goodliffe could see, if the day were fair, the white sails of ships upon the Irish Sea. The day must be translucently fair, the sky blue and not washed with the pale English mists, so that the sea could be deep blue beneath it, and then the sun could glitter upon the sails. This was his judgment of the day.

The cottage was near enough to the city of Blackpool for him to have walked there to the seacoast if he liked, for he was fifteen years old. His brother Edward, three years older than he, had a job in a ship's chandlery and walked home from there often enough on a Sunday, or even on a weekday in the evening. But he and Jonathan were different. Edward as a boy could put his hoe down any day in the middle of the afternoon and without a word go away. Jonathan could not. He must stay until the work he had allotted for himself was done, and by then it was always evening. He could have gone to Blackpool in the evening, but he had seen how his mother fretted because Edward went too often in the years when he was at home, and now he had not the heart to add to her trouble. So after his supper he helped with the dishes, and then sat down in the sitting room with her and the younger children. Sometimes he read aloud to her, if his father were not there, and sometimes he played games with the children until they went to bed, and then talked with her, trying to think of what might interest her.

There were four of these children younger than himself. He

3

knew his mother had not wanted the last one, though never had she said one word to him about the children she had. So far as he might have known from her, the child was simply there one day. She was so dainty in her speech, so shy, so small and exquisite in her person, that these great children she bore one after the other seemed to have nothing to do with her. He was glad she did not speak of them. He could pretend they had nothing to do with her, though he was fond of them, too. But so sensitive was he to every look in her delicate face that it seemed to him he could feel the very instant when her being began to divide itself. He could feel her spirit, half-distressed, half-withdrawn, as her body set upon its task again. When this had happened the last time, he had gone quickly upstairs to his room and burst into tears. He had cried silently and deeply for a few moments, without knowing why. While he was crying he heard her step coming slowly up the stairs, and he rushed to draw the wooden bar across his door. She shook the door a little when she found it locked.

"I want to make your bed, Jonathan!" she cried through the crack.

"I'm washin' myself," he called back.

"Whatever fer now, after breakfast?" she cried, amazed.

"I scamped it afore," he answered shortly.

He heard her breathe. "Well, I never!"

"Go on," he shouted. "I'll do my own bed today."

She did not answer, and after a moment he heard her go down again. But her coming had startled him out of weeping. He went to the window and stood looking out, and at that moment the last shreds of the morning mist faded, and suddenly he saw the small flecks of white which were the sails of ships upon the Irish Sea. The very sight of them quieted him, as they always did. He was thankful again that, when he and Edward divided the attic, he had chosen this side for himself. It had been an accident. No one knew that from this window the ships could be seen. He had been excited when he saw them first, and not for days had he happened to see them. . . .

"Come down out of there, Jonathan!" his father roared at him from the garden patch below. "Whatever are you thinkin' to be idlin' this time of day and all the work waitin'?"

He turned away from the window, sick at the very sight of his father this morning, and rushed downstairs. In the kitchen his mother was moving slowly about the dishes. She looked up when he came in, and he saw she had been crying, too. He longed to hug her, but this he had not done for too long. His father had stopped it.

"Have done with kissin' and huggin' your mother, you great lads," he had ordered his two older sons. "It fair makes me sick to see it."

"Shame on you, Clyde Goodliffe!" his mother had cried, and her fair skin had turned crimson under her yellow hair. But neither Jonathan nor Edward had kissed her from that day.

Less than ever could he kiss her now, though he did not know why. She was always beautiful to him, and now touching as she stood beside the sink, so small in her little blue cotton frock. He was not tall for his age, but already he was taller than she was.

"I'm goin' to plant some of them flowerin' peas for you, Mother," he blurted.

"Those," she said gently, "not them." But she corrected him so gently that he did not mind. He was even glad to be corrected for something. It made her seem more usual to him.

"Those," he repeated obediently. She had been a teacher in a board school before she was married, and she knew about words.

"I'll be glad to have them, son," she said quietly. "They're pretty, if what I hear of them be true."

She smiled, and suddenly he choked.

"Oh, Mother—" he muttered. She turned and looked at him. And she flew to him, and he put his arms around her and was near crying again.

"Let me help you," he muttered. "Let me do the heavy work. You just call me, Mother. I'm goin' to stay around the house more."

"You're my good boy," she whispered.

They hugged each other hard. It was such comfort to feel her in his arms. But her little shoulder blades were sharp.

"You're thin, aren't you, Mother?" he asked anxiously.

She drew back at this. "Not more than common," she said. She put back a loosened lock of her straight golden hair, and suddenly they were both shy.

"Well, eat your food, Mother, do," he said sternly.

"Aye—yes, I will," she promised. She was back at the sink again, her eyes turned away.

He had gone on to school. But he knew, and she felt his knowledge. All during the long months he had done all he could to lift heavy things and hang the clothes on the line, and every morning he spread his own bed before he came downstairs. And sometimes he was afraid of himself because he hated his father so heartily.

Yet when Maggie was born he was fond of her. He was always fond of them, after they were born. He had been fond of Jamie first because it was a pleasure to have a brother younger than he so that he need not be Edward's only younger brother, and then he was fond of Jamie because he was so full of jokes and laughing. And then Ruth was born, and he was fond of her because she was his first sister. And Arthur was delicate from the day of his birth, and at three was still delicate, so that one could not but grow fond of him because he was so patient and good. And Maggie was soon eight months old, and he was fond of her because she was so hearty and independent and because she was not pretty like Ruth, and so needed his fondness the more.

"A homely woman!" his mother sighed. "She'll have to be made up to somehow, for she'll have a hard row to hoe. God send she's smart!"

Maggie was smart enough for anybody. At four months she had two solid strong white teeth, at five she sat alone, and now at eight months she could walk from chair to table and clamor for bits from Jonathan's plate at mealtimes. He fed her secretly, proud of her ability to eat anything.

"You'll give her the colic, sure!" his mother cried.

But nothing gave her colic. Looking into her round, plain, healthy little face, doomed to freckles, he felt his heart grow hot with the soft warmth which rushed out of it always for his mother and the younger children. He and they were the real family, he sometimes felt. His father and Edward did not seem to belong to them.

And yet neither he nor the younger children possessed the power to disturb his mother that his father did. Years ago he had learned when he came into the house to fear, to pause and listen to whether the house was silent or whether he heard his father shouting, arguing, stamping up and down the bedroom above the small parlor of which his mother was so proud. He could never quite hear what his father was actually saying when he went into his chilly little attic room. But he always went in and stood shivering and listening to the bumbling roar of his father's voice.

He could not hear his mother at all. The walls of the cottage were of stone, old and thick, and plastered again and again by many hands, and the ceiling was close. If the house had been that one in Blackpool which he could only vaguely remember, it would have been easy to hear anything. Yet all he could remember of that house was hearing his mother cry out when Jamie was being born. Perhaps there had never been a quarrel about leaving Blackpool, but he seemed to remember a quarrel between his father and mother about it. His mother had hated the port and the coarse sailors sauntering into the little shop she kept so clean and neat. Wherever they moved she always opened a little shop somehow, in one of the rooms. Her father had kept a draper's shop and was well-to-do in a small way, so that she had gone to school until she was seventeen and then had taught for three years.

It was in her father's shop that she had met Clyde Goodliffe. Then he had been a salesman for dry goods, and old Mr. Layton had wanted him in the shop after they were married, since he had two girls and no son. But it had not lasted. His Aunt Myra could not abide his father, his mother said. There had been a tremendous quarrel, he knew, and then his father had done something else.

His father had done almost everything. They were all used to his beginning one of his lordly tales of a wonderful happening by his smacking his lips and saying. "It was when I was a journeyman once that I saw the most wonderful, fearful sight. . . ." Or he said, "Once when I was in the candle and coal business, a chap thought he'd be smarter than I was. . . ."

But for the last ten years they had lived in this house. Clyde Goodliffe had come and gone; had rented this land and that, and given it up in disgust because it was too wet or too dry, too stony or too mucky; had sold one thing and another or nothing; but his mother had kept them all firmly in this low whitewashed cottage that was home. It stood on the side of a hill above the village of Dentwater, and the kitchen garden sloped up the hill in the back, so that Jamie, digging potatoes, tried to roll them into the kitchen door. In the front she had her flowers, and on the other side of their bit of land was the village street. Beyond Dentwater the hill flattened, then went rolling on into the levels around Blackpool.

This home Jonathan loved. It troubled him continually and sometimes in the night frightened him to think he must leave it because he was growing. Plenty of boys left home at fifteen.

"Why for should I be feedin' a lad of fifteen?" his father grumbled.

"Give him another year at school till he's sixteen," his mother begged. "He's as good as a girl in the house and a wonder to help in the shop. And Edward's enough in that filthy Blackpool."

"Money idn't to be found in a hole like Dentwater, though," his father shouted.

"Money idn't to be found anywhere, Clyde," his mother replied with a gentle firmness. "It's got to be made."

All his heart moved to his mother. But between these two who were his parents, Jonathan Goodliffe had long since learned to keep silence, because he knew, somehow, that in spite of all their quarreling, they loved each other, and this love shut him out from between them. However much his mother loved him, she loved his father more. The consciousness of it kept Jonathan humbled and quiet, and whatever he did for his mother was never quite enough.

On the thirteenth of January in the year 1866, at half past four in the afternoon, he was coming home from the village school cold and hungry for tea. If his father were not home, he and his mother and the small ones would have their tea about the kitchen hearth. All day long in the damp chill of the schoolroom he had been imagining that hour before the fire, his knees hot, his face burning, his hands and feet warm at last, and he drinking hot tea. If his father were home, tea would be set out on the table, and he would have to take his place there and listen to his father's boisterous talk.

He plodded steadily down the cobbled street, holding an umbrella against the windy drizzle. It was already dark, and the twenty-odd cottages of Dentwater were lit as though night had fallen. One by one the four older pupils of the school had stopped at these cottages until only Archie Bainter, a boy a little younger than he, was with him. Then Archie stopped, too.

"Well, here I be, Jonathan," Archie said as a light grew out of the mist.

"So you be," Jonathan answered. "I'll be seein' you tomorrow, Archie."

"Well, maybe you will and maybe you won't," Archie said solemnly.

"Where'll you be goin'?" Jonathan asked, amazed. He paused under the umbrella to stare into the vagueness of Archie's face.

"I'm sick of school," Archie said.

"We're all that, I reckon," Jonathan said soberly.

"Yes, but I'm goin' to rid myself of it," Archie said.

"Runnin' away to America?" Jonathan teased him. He laughed when he spoke. It was the word for ridicule in Dentwater. "Oh, run away to Ameriky!" people roared at each other, meaning the utmost folly.

"I dunno." Archie said sullenly. "But I'm agoin'."

"I'm goin', too—but home," Jonathan rejoined. "I've a good tea waitin', and I'm froze."

He went on, forgetting Archie's childishness. Archie Bainter was always in trouble at the school. "For shame to you, Archie Bainter!" the master cried at him only this afternoon. "A great lad that ought to be a sign and sample to the younger ones! If it wasn't that they are dismissed earlier than you, I'd feel called to punish you before them to teach them what happens to lads in school that don't study their lessons and read wicked yellow-covered books inside their geographies!"

He had held up between his thumb and forefinger the yellow book. "American trash!" he had snorted.

But there were no younger children after three o'clock, only the four of them being coached for the examinations. If Jonathan passed the examinations, he could go on to be a teacher. That was his private hope. He wanted to go on, maybe even to London University, and be some day headmaster of a school. His mother knew—no one else.

"*Hic—haec—hoc—huius—huius—huius—*" he muttered. He should have begun Latin long ago, but they did not teach it in the village school. Mr Hopkins, the master, was teaching him every day between-times, as he could. He should have told Mr. Hopkins long ago he was going to be a teacher. But it had seemed presumptuous, and he had not done it. Some day when Mr. Hopkins was old he maybe would have this very school—or a better one. And he would live with his mother at home. By that time he'd have done all she wanted done, like a bit of porch put on the south, glassed in, where she could keep her flowers in winter.

He turned in at the little gate, and from the low-set windows candlelight gleamed softly through the fringing mist. Now, if only his father were not at home, he'd tell his mother what Mr. Hopkins said today about his Latin, how he said, "You learn so uncommonly fast, young man, it's a downright shame I have to spend hours on a lot of numskulls and let a lad like you have the minutes. But 'tis the educational system we labor under."

And then he gave up every hope. He heard his father's voice resounding through the room as he opened the door.

"I say to Ameriky I'm goin', and so I be agoin'!"

He shut the door quietly. Nobody noticed him. They were all staring at his father, who was standing in the middle of the kitchen. He had a loaf of bread against his chest and was cutting a great slab from it. Edward was there, too, leaning against the small wooden mantel behind the stove, his hands in his pockets, his mouth pursed under his young moustache. The children were at the table, eating buttered bread and drinking their mugs of milk and water. But Jonathan looked at his mother. She was sitting at the table with the baby Maggie at her breast; and her face, turned toward his father, was white and woeful.

"Oh, Clyde!" she whispered. "You'd never go off to America!"

"Why not?" Clyde Goodliffe retorted. "I been hearin' of it. It's the on'y place now on God's earth a man can hope to get land for himself. Here in this danged England you've to be born with land under your feet, else you go tiddlin' along the rest of your days. I'm sick of puttin' my back and my blood into land for another man."

"A lot you put into it!" she cried, goaded. "A great big lazy chap, allays at Blackpool where you've no reason to be, and the land waitin' to be tended!"

"Ah-ha, but 'twas at Blackpool I heard of this!" he said triumphantly. He put down the loaf now and smeared butter upon the slice he had sawed. "Listen, Mary, you get on a boat—"

"Not free, I'll lay," she broke in, but he scorned to notice this.

"And you sail away to New York, see, and then you go part by train—well, maybe all the way by train—to Kansas. Kansas is the country for us. The soil's that thick and black there's no plumbin' it—and it's free—or all but. They want enterprisers there—chaps with large minds that'll build the country big. England's a tiddlin' place."

"England'll treat you fair if you treat it fair," his wife broke in.

Clyde Goodliffe banged the flat of his hand on the table so hard that the thick dishes jumped.

"I'm goin' to Ameriky," he said sternly. "I've signed papers to go. And you're all goin' with me. The man asks me, 'Have you help?' and I sayed, 'I have—three on 'em.' And he sayed, 'Good—it's a country where the more sons a man has, the better!'"

"I'm not goin'," Edward said in his hard voice. He was a square young man called handsome by his fellows because he was fair-haired and his skin ruddy.

"You'll go if I say it," his father shouted, turning on him.

"Not I, Father," Edward said. "I'm doin' well in my job, and Millie Turner and I are engaged. I was goin' to tell you tonight, Mother."

"You and Millie— Well, I never, Eddie!" his mother cried. She was diverted by this news, and her look on Edward was surprised and full of simple admiration.

Nothing else, Jonathan knew, could have staved off his father except this news. Old Mr. Turner owned the best ships' chandler's shop in Blackpool and the one in which Edward worked.

"I knew you were doin' wonderful well, Ed," his father said, amazed, "but not so well as that."

Edward grinned complacently. "Look to the top while you're lookin', says I," he replied. "So I popped the question last night, and she took me."

"Well, may God bless me," Clyde Goodliffe roared. "Why, bring 'er along, lad, and we'll start a ship's chandlery in Kansas!"

"But it ain't by the sea, is it, Father?" Jonathan put in.

His father stopped drinking and looked struck. "Dang it," he said, "it's in the middle of Ameriky!"

"So a man would be a fool to go if he was me," Edward said triumphantly.

"He would be a fool if he was anyone," his mother retorted. "And you, too, Clyde, if you leave the land you've lost money on five years runnin' and this year the first, after all the manurin' and tillin', that it has brought us in a bit."

"Rented land!" Clyde Goodliffe muttered. He was pulling at the loaf of bread again, tearing off great snags of the crust and wiping them in the butter before he put them in his mouth.

"Land's worth what you get off it," his wife replied. "And what about my shop and the cottage and the garden— Oh, Clyde!" She broke down into weeping; and Maggie, solemnly watching all this, began to roar. Jonathan, leaning with his back against the door, came forward and took her from his mother's knees.

"There now, lass," he soothed her. "Come to Jonnie. Here, Ruthie, give 'er a sup of your milk and water."

He put Ruth's half-empty mug to the baby's lips and silenced her.

But there was no way of silencing his mother's weeping. They were used to it, and yet they would never grow used to it. The children hung their heads miserably and tried to go on eating and drinking. Ruth held a lump of bread and butter in her cheek and could not swallow it, and tears came welling into her large hazel-brown eyes. Pale little Arthur shrank smaller in his chair, and only Jamie seemed unmoved. He kept his eyes down and went on chewing steadily.

His wife's tears always made Clyde sweat with rage. The dampness sprang out now on his forehead, and he leaped up and threw the loaf on the floor.

"Dang the last lot of you!" he shouted. "You're allays holdin' a man down with your bits of shops and your talk of a man ought to do this and do that until I'm fair crazy, like a boat tied to a rock. Stay with your tiddlin' shops! I'm goin' to Ameriky if I live a lone man the rest of my days!"

He kicked the loaf across the kitchen and stalked out of the door and slammed it so that lime flew from the whitewashed walls around it.

Behind him they sat exactly as they were, except that the mother stopped weeping. She turned her head away from them and wiped her eyes on her apron. Then after a few seconds she went and picked up the loaf and dusted it with her hands and put it on the table. No one spoke. She stroked back her hair, her hands trembling. Then she sat down again and put out her arms.

"Give me the baby, Jonathan," she said.

He set Maggie upon her knees and, bending over her, saw that the cup upon the table beside her was unused.

"Shall I pour your tea now, Mother?" he asked.

"Yes, please, Jonathan," she replied in a quivering voice.

He poured her cup and then his own, and they sat, a sober little group, in the quiet kitchen. The kettle on the stove began suddenly to sing, and the yellow cat, asleep underneath the oven, came out stretching itself and yawning.

"When will you be countin' on marryin' Millie, Edward?" his mother asked.

"I dunno, Mother," he replied. "I said, 'Name the day, Millie,' but she says, 'Oh, it's early for that, Eddie.' But I count on summer, maybe."

"There's no use in waitin' when the girl's as much a prize as Millie is," his mother agreed.

She was almost herself again, and the children began to come out from their shadow. Arthur drank his milk, and Jamie spread jam upon a fresh slice of bread, and Ruth jumped from her seat and ran over to her mother and squeezed the baby heartily.

"Oh, you're a sweet tiddlin' thing!" she cried, and skipped away to a corner where she kept her dolls.

"Where'll you be livin', Edward?" his mother inquired.

"I'll move into old Turner's house," Edward said solemnly.

"You'll never!" his mother cried.

"He wants it and so does the old lady," Edward replied. "Millie bein' their only, they won't hear to aught else."

"It's a handsome place," Jonathan said respectfully.

"You're wise not to give in to your father," his mother said.

"Don't you give in to him neither, Mother," Edward told her. He rose as he spoke. "Must be goin', I reckon," he said. "Millie's waitin'." He began putting on his reefer coat. Outside, the twilight had thickened into night. "Hope you don't think I was too rough, Mother. But you see how silly 'twould be for me with my chances to go off to Ameriky."

"I do see it, Edward," his mother answered. She was

sopping bits of dry bread in her milky tea and feeding the baby.

Edward bent and kissed her on the cheek and then kissed the baby.

"Well, good-by, all of you," he said. He stood, his hand on the door. "Shall you be givin' in to 'im, Mother?" he asked.

His mother lifted tragic eyes. "How do I know what to do with him?" she replied. "I only know when I think of leavin' England I feel myself sick inside. 'Twould be bad enough to leave Dentwater and this bit of a place I've held together for home for all of you. But to leave England!" She bit her lip and shook her head, and tears gathered again in her blue eyes as she went back to feeding Maggie.

And Jonathan, watching her, for the first time saw the full meaning of what might come. To be leaving England! He had never thought of such horror. To leave England was to leave all that was life and home and place in the world.

"I'd advise you stay by your own mind, Mother," Edward said.

"There's more to things than that," his mother said sadly.

"I reckon there is," he admitted. He hesitated awkwardly. "Well, good-by all—till next time," he said and went out.

Left behind with his mother, Jonathan resolved to ask her nothing. How could she know what to do? How could any of them know what to do? He wiped Arthur's mouth and untied his bib, and the child slipped down. Jamie was already behind the stove with his ship.

Suddenly his mother looked up. "Draw back the curtains, son," she said. "Your father will be comin' home after his rage. He always does, though he'll be late, maybe. And set the candle on the sill."

He drew back the brown homespun curtains as far as he could, and then, after an instant, he set the lighted candle upon the deep stone sill.

✾ 2 ✾

THEY WERE GOING TO AMERICA. JONATHAN KNEW WHEN
he came down to breakfast in the morning that they were
going. Night had done it again. There was some strange
power in the night. He had seen it work before to change his
father from anger into good temper and his mother from
rebellion into acquiescence. When he had gone upstairs last
night, the candle still burning in the window, he had been
troubled. If only night were not ahead! His mother had
seemed quite calm all evening, though his father had not
come back. The children were in bed, and she sat stitching on
a shirt. He had wanted to sit with her and read aloud to her
after he had finished his lessons. She was fond of having him
read to her, but tonight she put him off.

"Better go to bed, Jonathan," she said. "It's late."

"It's late for you, too," he objected.

"Aye, but it's my duty to sit up for 'im," she replied.

He looked at her. Her small, fine-featured face looked
composed and firm again. He leaned and kissed her cheek and
went up the narrow stair, hung like a ladder against the wall.
He might have been tempted to trust her if there had not been
night ahead, he thought, and sighed, being bewildered by what
he did not understand.

He always gets around her by somehow I don't know, he
thought sadly, and lay awake a long time after that, the
bedcovers drawn decently up to his chin, and the close ceiling
near enough above his head to reach if he put his hand up to
touch it.

And then in the morning he did not need to hear his father's loud and cheerful voice to know the night had worked once more as he had feared. He had overslept himself a little, so that when he hastened down the stove was already hot, and the kettle on, and his mother setting the breakfast table. Near the stove his father was shaving himself before a milky mirror and talking as he shaved, and around the room the children were dressing themselves. Only Maggie sat upon a rag mat on the floor, still as she had been lifted from bed, sucking a crust and watching them all with sharp bright eyes.

"Hey there, Jonnie!" his father called to him. He stretched his jaw as he scraped at it. "Lend a hand to Artie's boots, will ye, lad? He's been hollerin' against the laces. I can't abide lacin' their boots—there's no end to 'em on such a lot as I have. Well, when we get to Ameriky they can all go barefoot. The sun's that warm over there, they tell me."

So he knew. He stooped and laced Arthur's small patched boots, and Ruth stood waiting to have her pinafore buttoned.

"Wash them a bit before they eat, Jonathan," his mother bade him. "The kettle water's hot."

"Yes, Mother," he said.

He waited until his father had finished with the pottery basin and then emptied it outside the door. It was still dark outside, and the air was raw. He shut the door quickly and, filling the basin, washed one face after another of the row before him. They were all good children except Jamie.

"I'm washed," Jamie said briefly.

"You're not," Jonathan said sternly.

"I am, too—I washed in Father's water," Jamie said doggedly.

Jonathan seized him firmly, his head under his arm, and scrubbed his face.

"Then you'd best be washed once more," he said.

"Gently, Jonathan," his mother called.

"Kick him, Jamie!" his father cried, and roared when Jamie let out his foot and kicked at Jonathan's shins.

"For shame, Clyde!" his mother said. "Jamie, you should thank your brother. Come and sit down to your porridge, all of you."

It was like every other morning and yet like none other. Jonathan finished his breakfast and washed his bowl and spoon and set it away on the shelf as he always did and put on his coat and cap and his brown knit muffler and took up his books. He had said nothing to anyone, though all through the meal his father had been gabbling about what he would do. Through the wall he put up by long habit against his father, he heard only fragments of the boasting, windy voice.

"A thousand acres . . . You don't manure, you just toss in your seed. . . . A handful of folk to a land ten times the size of England . . . I s'll build you a house, lass, that's a dook's castle to this 'un. . . . The Indians are driven off, I tell you—it's not like it was—the land belongs to English folk now, like us. . . ."

"I'm off now, Mother," Jonathan said at the door, and waited for her answering look.

"Good-by, son," she said.

But her mind was not on him this morning, and he saw it and went lonely away, trudging through the gray streets into the chill lantern-lit schoolroom. Mr. Hopkins was there already, setting a problem in square white figures upon the black-painted wall.

"Good morning, Jonathan Goodliffe," he said briskly. "You're here fine and early. There'll be time for the fifth declension before the rest of them come in."

Jonathan put his books down upon his desk.

"I doubt there's any good in my goin' on with Latin, sir," he said.

Mr. Hopkins turned upon him, astonished, the round lump of chalk in his hand.

"What's that?" he asked sharply.

"We're goin' to America," Jonathan told him.

"America!" Mr. Hopkins repeated. "Whatever for?"

Jonathan shook his head. "I don't know, sir," he said.

Mr. Hopkins took off his glasses with one hand. "Why, I never heard of anybody goin' from these parts!" he said earnestly. "From Cornwall, yes, they're poor enough to go anywhere, and the Scotch and Irish—why shouldn't they go to get away from what they've got? But here—it's folly! You poor lad, Jonathan Goodliffe! No, you're right. What'll the savages over there be wanting with Latin?"

Jonathan felt his throat swell. He could not speak.

"Well, I never!" Mr. Hopkins said slowly and, putting on his glasses, stared at Jonathan so severely that he felt weak and sat down and began studying furiously.

The morning dragged its length along to noon, and he went

home to dinner. But there he found his father not at home and his mother unexpectedly cheerful.

"We don't have to go for a year, Jonathan," she told him the moment he came in the door. "That is, you and me and the children don't. Your father's goin' first. If he likes it when the year's up, we'll come along to him. If he don't, he can come back to us. I stuck out for that," she added triumphantly.

They looked at each other.

"Mother!" he cried, and suddenly she began to laugh, and he laughed with her.

"A year!" she said mischievously. "When did he ever like anything as long as a year?"

It was reprieve and all but final pardon from a sentence.

"Then I'll go back to Latin," he said joyously. "Mr. Hopkins said as how savages wouldn't need it."

"And I shall go on with the garden," she said. "I was countin' on a new rosebush or two this year. Last night I thought 'twas no use. But today when he said he'd leave us behind a year, I said, 'Then I'll get the rosebushes from the vicar's wife, after all.'"

She looked years younger than she had at breakfast. She was a small, cheerful, chirping little creature upon whom sadness always sat foolishly. But joy became her. Her blue eyes shone, and her cheeks were pink, and she ran about the kitchen putting the meal on the table.

"Mother!" Jonathan cried at her again, and when she looked at him in astonishment as childlike as Maggie's, he rushed to her and threw his arms about her and could not speak.

A year, he was thinking, a whole year, he and she and the children!

"There!" she said, pushing him away. "Let be, Jonathan. Sit and eat your meat."

Her practical, reasonable voice, clear and soft, seemed on the instant to set the world secure again and drive away the huge dark continent of the unknown, and he sat down and ate heartily.

The new year began the day his father left them. Clyde Goodliffe could not do quickly enough whatever he had decided upon. He had the furious determination of the impatient and variable man. Within twelve days he was ready to sail for America. The only stumbling block had been the twenty acres of land he rented from three different men. He wanted to give it up, leaving the winter wheat in which much of it stood in lieu of rent.

"Tidn't as if I was goin' to be here to harvest it," he said.

But Jonathan had seen his mother's wish to keep the land. "Land is easy to be rid of and hard to get back again," she had said.

"I'll never be wantin' them bits of acres back again," Clyde shouted back with contempt. "Why, twenty acres don't make a kitchen garden in Kansas!"

"What you'll do with more I don't know," she retorted, "seein' that twenty's been too much for you here."

"Tiddlin' English land," he sneered, "allays awantin' manure and lime and stuff put in it!"

"I'll take care of it," Jonathan said. He had never done all the work alone before, but now he felt he could. With his father gone, he would work twice as hard for them all, and what he did not know he could ask of his neighbors.

"I want to be rid of the rent," his father said shortly.

"I'll make the shop pay for it," his mother broke in. "It does seem right-down folly for us to give up what was just beginnin' to pay. Stands to reason there'll be good crops this year after the bad ones."

"It's been a good winter with snow and all," Jonathan said earnestly.

"Have it your own way, then, so long as my money don't go for it," Clyde retorted. "I got to put by enough to bring over the lot of you by next year's spring."

His dark eyes grew mischievously tender. " 'Twould be a wonderful good chance for a man to free himself from a burden of worry and trouble and start out new. What'd you do, lass, if I let old England have you and said good-by for good 'n' all?"

"I'd be glad enough to be rid of you," his wife retorted, "if that's the way you feel."

He threw back his head until they could see his hairy throat, and gave his bellow of laughter.

"Danged if I'm not fond of you and all your brats," he shouted, and tumbled her head in his two hands like a ball until she cried, laughing and protesting, "Clyde—Clyde—let me be—I'm all dizzy!"

Jonathan slipped out into the yard. He was suddenly sick. He could not bear the sight of his mother's smooth blond head rolling between his father's big hairy hands.

He's so cruel rough with her! he thought passionately. His chest heaved, and he wanted to weep. Why doesn't she stop him? he thought furiously. He needed to do something hard and immediate and driving, and he stooped and began pushing and pulling at the big square stone that made the upper of the two steps down from door to path.

The door opened, and his father stood ready to come out.

"What're you doin', you daft boy?" he demanded.

Jonathan, on his knees in the mud, looked up at him.

"I'm makin' these steps straight," he said sullenly. "They've been crooked this long while."

"I haven't seen 'em crooked," his father said gaily. He stepped down and went to the gate. "Allays settin' somethin' right, you be!" He went down the street, whistling.

He's goin' to the public house again, Jonathan thought bitterly, and then was no happier for knowing he was unjust. His father was not a drunkard and did not spend much time with drinking men. That was the trouble with him, Jonathan thought. There was nothing you could lay a finger on. He had no real wickedness. It would have been easier if he had. He longed for his father to be a downright plain bad man like Archie's father, who drank and when he was drunk beat his wife.

If I saw my dad lay a hand on my mother to hurt her! Jonathan thought savagely. But, no, his father kicked the furniture, and he could throw a loaf of bread or a plate across a room; but he beat not even one of the children. And on the same day when he was lowering and quarrelsome and angry about one thing after another, he could stop everything to pour a saucer of milk for the cat and set it under the stove. A mixed-up, trying sort of man, Jonathan thought with frequent gloom. Today, as he watched his father go toward Blackpool, he added, "Allays thinkin' too big about what isn't there, and never seein' what's under his nose to be done!"

If it weren't for him, her son, what would become of his mother with a man like that?

And yet on the day when his two older sons went to Blackpool to bid Clyde Goodliffe good-by, it was a sorrowful day for them all in its strange way. He had found a berth to work his way on a freight ship sailing from Liverpool to New York.

"Never tell me it don't pay to hang about the town a bit, lass," he said to his wife. "That is, if you're a clever chap, like me."

From Blackpool he was going on a coal ship free because the captain was a man he knew. At the cottage his wife had cried quietly now and then while she packed his bag, until he looked at her with impatience in his eyes.

"Give over, Mary—do! S'all I carry the memory of you weepin' and wailin' all the months I'm to be away? You'll be safe from me for a year. Think about that and dry up, lass. Ain't that a comfort? For a year you can sleep safe in your bed and not wake up to worry whether you're goin' to have a baby or not!"

"Oh, Clyde!" She was so shocked that she stopped crying.

"You've thought of it, I lay," he said, his eyes dancing. He seized her and rubbed her cheek with his. "Own up to yourself, now, lass."

"I will not!" she cried.

"Then ye have," he said, laughing.

"If I have, it's not to say I won't long for you," she said. "Oh, Clyde, dear lad!"

She threw down the coat she held in her hand and curled against him in the sweet way she had. She did not do it often now. But when she did, it caught hold of him just as it always had.

"Don't look at another woman, Clyde!" she begged him in a tight little whisper.

"Never fear, Mary!" he whispered to her.

"You'll come back if you don't like it, won't ye, Clyde?" she begged. "You wouldn't be proud and stick to America just to be stubborn, would you? And make us all give up England if America isn't what you think it is?"

"If it ain't better than I think it is, even, I'll come back," he told her.

And then he had kissed her hard twice and then again, and she picked up the coat and put it in the bag. They went downstairs, and he kissed the younger children and pulled

Jamie's nose, "for extra," he said, because Jamie was his pet, and they stood watching him go with the two big ones, Edward on one side of him and Jonathan on the other, carrying his bags.

"Here, you lummoxes," he had said, "it'll be the last time for many a month."

They picked up the bags, Edward the smaller one, and Jonathan, always silent, the heavy sack. Down the street before the road went over the hill, Clyde stopped, turned, and waved both arms to the little group in the door; and Mary's apron waved like a flag in reply. Then he went on again, his thick boots clumping the cobbled street. What he was thinking his sons did not know. But when they were down the shallow hill and out of sight of Dentwater, and there was only the low-lying Blackpool ahead, he began to talk, not of them, but of America.

"I'm free inside for the first time in my life," he said in his harsh, loud voice. "Smothered I've been in this little bit of an old country. There's been no room here for a hundred year, I'll lay. A new country is the country for men and lads." He remembered then that Edward was not coming. "Don't you shut yourself to coming, Edward," he said to his oldest son. "Send I find everything goin' big, I'll let you know, and you can set up one way or 'nother, you and Millie, and whatever children are yours. I aim to begin big. That's the secret in Ameriky, they tells me. Everybody begins big. The little 'uns are lost."

He took off his cap, and the wind lifted his rough black hair from his forehead that was low and square. His high cheekbones were red, and his full lips pressed together with unusual firmness. None of his sons had the largeness of his build. The fineness of their mother had tempered his share in them. Edward was as near his father's height as he would ever be, and he was three inches shorter.

"Jamie'll beat me, and the only one to do it," Clyde always said. But Jamie was only a small freckle-faced boy now.

"It's a wunnerful good thing I'm doin' for you all," he went on. The road was muddy, but he went tramping through it. "You'll live to thank the day I was bold enough to see it and make up my mind to do the big thing."

They were going over the long flats now, and Blackpool lay ahead, dark against a windy gray sea. It was February, and they had not seen the sun in a month. There was no sun today, but the air was not cold as they walked. A carter came by. His cart was empty, and it was drawn by two great sluggish gray horses. He pulled up.

"Want a ride?" he inquired. He peered down at them from under a rusty felt hat, and his face was narrow and askew.

"We do," Clyde said gladly. He was beginning to feel embarrassed by the long walk with his sons. He was not used to being with them alone. They climbed in, bags and all.

"Leavin' for somewhere?" the carter inquired affably. Seen now face to face, it was apparent that his jaw had once been dislocated and never set properly. But one saw such faces in Blackpool.

"Goin' to Ameriky," Clyde answered proudly.

The carter whistled. "A long way," he said. He looked at Edward. "You goin'?" he asked.

"No," Edward said coldly. He sat on the side of the cart carefully to save his clothing from coal dust.

"You?" the carter asked Jonathan.

"I—don't know." Jonathan faltered and glanced at his father.

The carter grinned. "Looks like you're the gay chap, old 'un," he told Clyde Goodliffe. "Ameriky, hey? There's a lot of talk about Ameriky now."

"It's the only place for a man as is a man," Clyde said.

"I'll hold my end up in England, for all of Ameriky," the carter said and spat over the side of the cart.

"Do," said Clyde. "Ameriky's on'y for them as wants room."

And yet not until they had climbed down from the cart and gone to the wharf did his sons feel that he was going. All the time it had seemed only another one of his big windy schemes. But on the coal-stained wharf it suddenly came true. There the ship lay that was to take him to Liverpool, a small freighter bobbing against its ropes. They went aboard and put down the bags on the deck, and then came the moment of good-by. They had never told him good-by before. For all his arguing and fuming, he had never left them. He became for the moment at once pitiable and heroic. He was going so far. There was the ocean and the unknown continent ahead of his solitary figure. How could he manage alone when he fuddled the least thing at home? And yet he was calm and full of courage.

"Good-by, lads," he said heartily. "Edward, I ask you not to let Millie take up your whole mind. Go to see your mother."

"I will, Father," Edward said solemnly.

"And, Jonathan," his father continued, "when I send for you all, help her to see it's right and for the best. She's that fond of you that if you want to come, she'll be more'n half ready to do it."

Jonathan felt still more softened. "Yes, Father," he said solemnly.

He grasped their hands and shook each of them hard.

"Now get along with you. I'll have no standin' about," he ended.

They obeyed him and walked slowly away from the ship. They turned once as by common accord. He was still there, and he motioned them sharply to go on—go on! They went on then until they reached the corner where Turner's chandlery stood, and here Edward stopped.

"Reckon I'll go in and finish my day's work," he said.

"I'll go on back, then," Jonathan answered.

They lingered a moment.

"Will you be home soon, Edward?" Jonathan asked.

"Yes, I will, and I plan to bring Millie as soon as it's announced," Edward said.

"That'll be nice for Mother," Jonathan replied.

They had nothing more to say to each other.

"Good-by, then, Jonnie," Edward said at last.

"Good-by, Ed," Jonathan replied.

They parted, each thinking of the solitary figure starting alone that night to cross the sea; and Jonathan, plodding home in the afternoon twilight, wondered at himself that he could feel so dreary because his father was gone.

Reckon there's something about him, after all, he thought. Ahead of him the severe horizon was black against a neutral sky.

❧ 3 ❧

HE MUST MAKE HIS MOTHER HAPPY. HE HAD ALWAYS FELT this necessity upon him, but now it became a passion. He alone could make her happy. Edward had Millie, but his mother had only him. He rose in the morning and lit the kitchen stove and had the porridge steaming before she came down. He stayed after breakfast to clear the table and rushed back at noon to help her with the children. And every Monday morning he got up at five o'clock to help her with the wash. That was the one thing his father had used to do. On Mondays his father got up and set the tubs for her and doused the clothes in them and wrung the sheets. He would not hang them on the line, but he carried the baskets out for her.

As long as Jonathan could remember, he knew Monday morning before he even came out of sleep, because of the soapy hot reek of soiled clothes rising from kitchen to roof. It filled his corner of the attic like a miasma, and he woke stifled, his nostrils acrid. The reek was the reek of poverty to him, dreary and sodden; and he got up weighted with the plight of his parents, who must work so hard. He felt apologetic for his existence when his father, blowing and blustering, sat down to breakfast. "Mind how you lads use your breeches and shirts, in God's name," he shouted. "I've about wore myself out on 'em today. If I had the doin' of it, I'd let you run naked, I would, and you'd wash your own skins when you dirtied 'em."

But now he liked being up early and alone with his mother. She had a routine—the white things first in the clean suds and

25

then the colored ones, and then the rinsings in the small tin tub
which they used for baths on Saturday nights. The smell of the
soap was sharp and clean when he plunged it into clean water.

"Let me wash my own shirt, now, Mother," he commanded.
"And them breeches with the mud on the knees I'll do."

"Those," she corrected him gently. "Take care, Jonathan,
how you speak. Grammar's sign and seal on a man. 'Tidn't his
clothes—he can put them on himself as fine as he likes, but
how his words come out of him tells you all he is."

She handed him his garments, and then she went on a little
diffidently, "If you'll copy your father's downright good heart
and speak after me, I'll be pleased."

"I'll take after you in everything if I have my way," he told
her.

"Mother's boy you always were," she said smoothly.

He felt a dear strong happiness warm in his belly as though
it were something hot he had drunk.

"I hope you're happy, Mother," he said dizzily. "I hope you
don't miss him too much."

He had never come out with it like that before. But he had
to know whether or not she was happy alone with him and the
children. Suppose his father never came back—would she be
happy?

"I do miss him," she said quietly. "But that has nothing to do
with you."

Her soft voice saying these words seemed to shut him out.
He felt his happiness throb and stop, wounded.

"Your bein' happy has a lot to do with me, Mother," he
replied hotly. "When you—aren't happy, I feel it so."

"How do you?" she asked. She looked at him curiously from
her tub.

"It's like cloud over sun," he answered.

She smiled ruefully. "I have to be gay whether my heart is or
not?"

"No, you don't," he answered, and then could not go on.
When he tried to tell her something he felt about her he was
always stopped by the tight thickness of his breast. He was
bound in by it. There was nothing to do until he had freed
himself by moving away from her. It was sweet and yet
intolerable to be so close to her. When she was gay he was
happiest, for then he felt she was all right, and it did not matter
whether he was there or not. When she was sorrowful he was

suffocated in her sorrow. He must make her happy so he could be free.

"I'm glad you like Millie so well, Mother," he said, to talk about something else. Edward had brought Millie yesterday afternoon.

"I do like her," his mother replied.

He tossed the wet, curled-up sheets to her as he finished them, and she rinsed them.

"She isn't a bit like you," he went on, making talk.

"That's nothing against her," she replied, smiling a little.

" 'Tis for me," he said stoutly. "When I marry, it'll only be when I find a girl like you, Mother."

"Oh, there're lots like me," she said. "You'll have a hard time pickin'."

"Likely I'll be a bacheldore," he returned politely.

She laughed, and he was pleased with himself and smiled and winked his eye at her.

"You're the girl for me," he repeated.

He thought of Millie Turner. She was a large, loosely built girl, big-boned and yet with a turn to fat. Her pale brown eyes, a little popped, under scattered brows, were anxiously kind, and her dark hair was scanty and straight. But she had tried very hard to do her share of getting tea, and not to seem a guest.

"Now let me cut the bread and butter it, do, Mother," she said, when Edward brought her to tea.

"It was 'Mother' here and 'Mother' there," Mary Goodliffe said to Jonathan when they were gone. Her eyes twinkled, and she laughed softly. "It makes me feel downright queer to have a great hulkin' woman callin' me 'Mother.' She's three years older than Edward and looks it. . . . Not but what the girl means well," she added, "and she'll be good in the chandlery and anxious to please her husband. That'll suit Edward." She had twinkled again. "Or any man—

"Go on, Jonathan Goodliffe," she retorted.

"As you say." He laughed and picked up the basket of wrung clothes and carried it out. His father would never hang them because the neighbors might laugh at a man doing such work, but he did not mind. He lifted the sheets and shook them out and felt their wetness flapping against him as he reached for the line.

She's happier than she ever was, he thought gladly. She's better with him away.

Very often during the day he thought she was happier. Together they planned the planting of the rented acres, and when he was able to get it plowed, she came out and seeded it to oats and corn and a little of the new maize that his father sent them in a tin box from America. Maize they had never planted before, but they had heard of it, and here were the big yellow grains. Part of it they had planted in furrows before the letter came, and then they found it must be put in hills, a few grains together.

"S'all we dig it all up again to do it right?" he asked his mother anxiously.

"No, indeed not," she replied stoutly. "They're planted in good English ground, and they'll come up however."

And so they did, big strong spears of bright green and of a shape they had never seen before.

"A savage, wild-lookin' grass, I'd say, if I didn't know," his mother said, staring at it. It grew faster than a reed as soon as summer came.

He had never worked so hard as he did that summer, and he found out once for all his life that he was no farmer. He hated the labor of the land, the back-break of weeding and the reluctance of proper growth.

Danged silly weak things, crops are, he thought, sweating in muggy July days. Now that school was out he attacked the land early and late. Weeds have all the strength. It's evil that's strong, after all.

He hated above all being dependent upon weather. To know that all his labor and thought brought to bear upon fruitage from seeds he had planted were nothing if there was no rain or if there was too much, forced him to desperation. And yet anxiety and revolt were useless. There the skies were, impervious as stone or turning suddenly to soft, endless rain.

It's the feeling that my brains are no use that I can't abide, he thought. A man may as well be a dolt as not if he's a farmer—thinkin' will do him no good.

But he was careful to hide this hatred from his mother. The land was precious to her.

Yet he was only sixteen, and he could not keep from shirking a little sometimes the endless routine of the land, nor from coaxing and bribing Jamie and sometimes sternly forcing him to help in cultivating. The maize when it was ripe they did not like. It tasted green, though they boiled it, as his father had written them to do, and when they dried it and ground it into meal it had a strange musty taste.

"It tastes like mice smells," Jamie said bluntly and, though they made it into porridge and poured milk on it and mixed sugar in it, none of them liked it. Even Maggie spat it out solemnly, aghast at its strangeness upon her tongue.

"There's a whole acre gone for nothing," Jonathan groaned. "And a million weeds hoed off it."

"We tried it, though," his mother said practically, "and we know we don't like it. That's something to know."

They did very well that autumn. They used almost none of the money his father sent now and again.

"Save it against your comin', if you don't spend it," he wrote them. So his mother saved it in a tin biscuit box she kept in her room.

The little shop did well, too. It was a good year in England. Crops were fair, and people had extra money to spend and gave their children pennies for sweeties.

"If I was sure your father was comin' back," his mother told Jonathan, "I'd put piece goods into the shop. But—" She shook her head.

"You still think we'll go, Mother?" he asked. He searched her face for all she might not say in answer.

"You wouldn't want me to leave my husband," she replied.

He turned away. None of his labor had any fruit if while he labored her mind was not there in her body.

He still dreaded the night. For then, when the younger children were in bed and only he and she sat there, he with a book and she sewing or knitting, the moment came when her eyes were far away, and he knew what she was thinking. In the summer when the twilight was long he could push the moment away. Sometimes, even, if they worked over her rose bed, the moment never came at all. Or it only came so much as this, that her face grew wistful and she said, "I just couldn't bear to leave this bit of a garden. I couldn't make a garden on other ground. Nought would grow for me when my heart wasn't there to make it grow."

Then he knew that England was working for him against his father. England was still holding her fast, and all that England was—the long reaches of soft green, the shallow hill where Dentwater lay, the old church and the trees stooped from the sea winds, and the cottage. When Mr. Hopkins came back to open school and asked, "Are ye going to America, Jonathan?" he answered with precious doubt, "It's far from sure, Mr. Hopkins."

"Good," Mr. Hopkins said. "Then you're still for Latin?"

"If you please, Mr. Hopkins," he answered gratefully.

"And your father?" Mr. Hopkins asked.

"He's workin' for a farmer there same as here," Jonathan answered with a grin.

And so indeed Clyde Goodliffe was, but always with the hope of land. Other chaps, he wrote, had come ahead of him. Kansas was not so open any more. He was not sure where they would stay when he got them there. He was not buying any land yet—only getting enough money together to bring them over. Then they would see. But still it was wonderful to have a country so big all around that, let a man look anywhere, he could know a thousand miles waited for him. His letters were like him—full of big things, all not done.

The letters were what Jonathan feared in the darkening autumn evenings that grew longer with the hurrying on of winter. For the first time a year was short to him. Until now in his life a month had been nearly endless, and a year eternity; but his father's letters cut time to pieces. Once a month they came, and it was too quick for peace.

For in the long dark evenings, when she had worked a while, his mother grew restless. First she would hear the wind, and then she would murmur, "Anyway, he's not on the sea. It's better to have him in America than a sailor."

Then she would put her work down and mend the fire and see if the cat were fed. And then she settled to nothing again. Sometimes she counted over their money, and sometimes she stirred up a batch of bread, or she went to the window and stared out. And Jonathan, his books spread on the kitchen table, waited until she went to the chest of drawers and pulled out the top one and found the letters. When she did this she was lost to him; for she sat down with them in her lap and read them over one by one, and pondered over them and over the last one the longest. And all he had of her were the bits she threw at him from her thoughts.

"For all he sayed, I can't see the place, can you, Jonathan?"

"No, Mother," he said miserably.

"All flat, as far as eye can see," she went on.

"Sounds terrible dull, Mother."

"I don't know—there's trees, he says, and the flowers growin' wild like nothin' we have here."

Clyde had put Kansas wildflowers into his letter, but their colors were gone when they reached England. Only their strange shapes were left, and even these soon crumbled to dust.

"'Rare colors,' he sayed," she repeated, looking at their dust.

Jonathan did not answer. He was beginning to learn that, out of the struggle within herself, if he agreed with her when she spoke against his father, she hastened to defense, either direct or by defending the country she had never seen.

And worst of all was the letter his father wrote when he had been ill. Malaria, he said, but none of them knew the word until he said chills and fever. Then she was nearly wild. She wrote him a long letter, sitting up half the night to do it, pleading with him to come home.

"What if your father should die out there alone among the savages?" she whispered to Jonathan. But her letter on the sea crossed his saying he was better again with the cold weather, and he told her about the colors on the autumn trees and how never had he seen such colors in England where the damp kept everything down to green and gray. A wonderful country, he said over and over, and violently beautiful. That letter reached them on a cold November day when the gray sea fog seeped up over Dentwater and shut them out of the world. The children had colds; and Maggie, staggering about, fell against the stove and burned her arm and shoulder. Jonathan saw tears come into his mother's eyes as she smeared lard over the screaming child. Neither he nor she had slept that night until nearly dawn because Maggie kept crying. Long after midnight Jonathan heard his mother murmur in her distress, "Dear God, can a lone woman stand this?" He wanted to cry out, "But I'm here, Mother!" and could not, being too humble for it. If she did not think of it herself, what good would it do him to remind her?

Even Edward's wedding, postponed until January, scarcely lifted the darkness of the damp winter. They all went to it, for Edward sent a wagon from Blackpool for them. They dressed in their best, and Jonathan yearned over his mother's sweet looks in her brown dress with its full skirt and cape and the little brown bonnet with pink ribbon quilted under the brim. She had the gift of putting her clothes on well and looking far better even than the vicar's wife, who was dressed always in black silk. His mother looked better than anyone at the wedding. Millie could not be pretty even as a bride. Her dress of heavy white satin only made her thicker, and her round red face never lost its anxiety for a moment under her veil of coarse lace. It was a solemn wedding until the eating and drinking began; and then, women with women and men with men, they began to talk, and Jonathan saw his mother always the center of a little cluster, listening to her tell of Clyde Goodliffe. She looked pretty and faintly important while she told them deprecatingly what he had written.

"A fearful country, so big and all, but the flowers wonderful and plenty of land and such a wide sky as you never see elsewhere unless in the middle of the ocean and big trees and plenty of black rich soil—deep as you can dig—"

"Has he bought land yet?" This was Millie's father, edging over to the woman, a thick man with a flat voice.

"Not until he's sure of the spot," his mother answered.

"You'll not be leavin' England, though, Mrs. Goodliffe?" Mrs. Turner, the bride's mother, said. She was a small wrinkled woman with a pursed mouth and a wide waist.

And then, though Jonathan strained to hear what his mother answered, he did not hear, for a fresh, sharp voice said beside him, "Are you Jonathan Goodliffe?"

He turned and saw a brown-faced girl beside him in a red woolen frock with a white lace collar. Her black hair was straight, and her eyes blue and strange-looking in her dark face.

"Yes, I am," he said. He was not exactly shy, because he was too self-reliant for that, but he had scarcely ever talked with a girl in his life.

"Constance Favor—Connie, I'm called—and in a manner we're related. At least now that my cousin Millie is married to your older brother, what does that make us?"

She spoke with a sort of laziness, her full, rather pale lips scarcely moving, and he felt at once that she must be older than he. But she was not quite as tall as he was, and he liked her clear blue eyes instantly.

"I don't know, but something surely," he said, and smiled.

"And are you goin' to America, or do you stay with your

brother?" she asked. Her hands, smoothing her collar, were as brown as her face.

"It depends on my mother," he said soberly. He turned his head back to his mother, but whatever she had said was said. He had missed it. She was talking now to Mr. Turner about Edward.

"You'll find him a bit stubborn at times, Mr. Turner—that's his father—but he's steady once he begins—that's me in him. And I don't believe your Millie will rue this day."

"Hope not," Mr. Turner replied.

Mrs. Goodliffe bristled a little under her pink quilted ribbon. "No, I hope not, too, and I hope Edward won't, either," she returned.

"Hope not," Mr. Turner said more mildly. "It's a little late for that after the knot's been tied." He paused and stroked his thick red moustache. "Anyways, as I see it, a marriage idn't just thinking of each other. It's the shop and gettin' on and the children and all that. Folks do best to remember that."

"Surely," Mary Goodliffe agreed.

The fresh clear voice was at Jonathan's ear again.

"If I were you, I'd go to America. It's stupid here. I'd go quick as a wink."

"Why?" Jonathan asked.

"Oh, I don't know," she answered.

"Connie—Connie!" Mrs. Turner called. "Come here, child!"

"Oh, dear!" the girl said. "Just when we was gettin' acquainted! Do you dance, Jonathan? There's to be dancin'!"

"I never did before," he answered.

"Then I'll show you," she said. "I'm a rare good dancer," she added, with a mischief in her eyes which suddenly lit her face.

Her going left him alone again in the crowd, and he sauntered over to his mother. She was sitting now with Maggie asleep on her lap and Arthur leaning against her, rubbing his eyes.

"Jonathan, help to put these children to nap," she told him. "They'll be underfoot, once they start dancin'."

He lifted the fat, inert child from his mother's lap, and they went into a dark bedroom, and he found a spot upon a bed where two children were already asleep and laid Maggie down. She did not stir.

"Lie here, my little lad, on this nice mat on the floor," his mother said to Arthur, and the little boy curled upon a wool mat by the bed, and she covered him. Music burst out in the other room.

"Where's Jamie and Ruth?" he whispered to his mother.

"Jamie's out in the chandlery," his mother replied, "watching the ships' sailors come and go. He asked if he could, and I said yes. And Ruth's gone to play with a little girl next door."

He was quite free, then. If Connie wanted to teach him to dance, there was no reason why he shouldn't learn, except that he was suddenly shy before his mother to be dancing with a girl.

"Mother," he said, "do you mind if I dance a bit?"

Her eyes were round. "I didn't know you could dance," she cried.

"Constance Favor said she'd teach me a bit," he said.

He felt his chest grow hot, and the heat spread upward into his cheeks. His mother looked at him with a mingled touch of doubt and surprise.

"Well, I reckon it won't matter," she said, and doubt grew uppermost in her face as he walked away from her.

They were already dancing when he came into the big room, a jiggy reel that made voices hum and sing as people danced. At the end of the line of dancers he saw the bride and groom, Edward more carefully casual than ever in his position as bridegroom, and Millie still anxious. She held up her skirts in both hands, her foot tapping and her head nodding, fearful lest she miss the movement. Even so, she lost it by a fraction. "Here, girl!" Edward cried.

"Oh, Ed!" she screamed.

But Edward swung out, and she rushed to meet him, while everyone laughed and clapped. And Jonathan, hesitating, felt his hand seized in Connie's firm grasp.

"Come along," she said. "I was looking for you. Now, mind you follow!"

There was no time to think about anything. He was swept into the dance and forced to take thought lest he disturb its pattern through his ignorance.

He thought sometimes that, if it had not been for that dance, all his life might have been different. But how could he know it then?

"A silly fool you looked," his mother said to him in sharp disgust, "leaning to hear all her gabble, and her dress so low you must have seen her stummick."

Here at home again in the kitchen he was drenched with shame.

"I didn't," he muttered. No, but he had seen a bosom, divided into its two full circles. He hadn't wanted to see anything, but he had looked again and again.

"I don't care for her nor any girl," he said angrily to his mother.

"It's a queer way to hate them, then," his mother retorted. On his shoulder Maggie began to whimper. The other children were already unlacing their shoes, silent, their faces white with the fatigue of pleasure. "Talkin' to her and dancin' with nobody else!"

"There was nobody else, Mother—except old women," he answered.

"She's too old for you, too, if that's what you mean," she cried. "One Turner's enough, I'll thank you to remember! Millie Turner's all right for Edward. She idn't bold like Connie. This girl's got foreign blood in her. Her father was a sailor, and he brought her home with him, a baby. The mother was dead—he said."

"Mother—Mother!" he begged her. "Don't talk so—as if I was thinkin' of marriage—when I've only seen her tonight!"

"She was thinkin' of it—the likes of her always is," his mother retorted. "Here, give that child to me. Anything in breeches, that sort always looks at. Oh, Jonathan, you're to be a teacher, remember, and go up in the world! Edward won't be a candle to you if you go on without gettin' mixed up."

"I won't get mixed up, Mother," he muttered.

He gave Maggie to her and bent and in blind confusion began to unbutton Arthur's little shirt.

"Sleep in your drawers tonight, eh, Artie?" he said. "It's so late and you're that tired."

He drew Arthur's thin little body into the curve of his shoulder and went upstairs with him and laid him in the bed and covered him. Jamie was already asleep in the same bed. He had gone to bed dressed, and Jonathan began carefully to untie his shoes and then slipped them off without waking him. There was comfort in taking care of these small and helpless creatures.

I didn't do anything, he thought sorely. 'Tidn't as if I went anywhere with the girl.

And then Ruth came stealing upstairs in her long flannel nightgown, and he tucked her into the cot in the same room.

"Kiss me good night, Jonnie," she begged him.

He bent and kissed her cheek and smelled the straw-sweet odor of her hair. She smelled different, even though she was only his sister Ruth, because she was a girl. Neither Jamie nor even Arthur would have begged him for a kiss or thrown arms about his neck when he gave it. Girls were different. He was a man. There was that in it which he did not understand. He went downstairs, feeling there was something between himself and his mother now that separated them until eternity. He would never be near her again. He did not know how to get near her any more. He had done nothing, and yet he had done everything.

He went miserably downstairs to find that she had apparently forgotten him. She was sitting by the fire still in her good brown dress. But she had put Maggie to bed and taken off her own bonnet and cape.

"I dunno," she said sadly. "I dunno but what we'll have to go to America, after all. He's not comin' back, Jonathan. I can tell it."

They looked at each other.

"Wait, Mother," he begged. Somehow now more than ever he did not want to leave England. "Wait till the spring comes."

His mother turned her head away from him. "Spring'll only make me want him more," she whispered. "I'm daft for him, Jonathan."

He could not answer. All that he did not know forced itself upon his consciousness. Night and his father and his mother, music and dancing with Connie's supple, plump body in his arms, and the circles of her bosom when he looked down and the smell of Ruth's hair and all the pull between human beings which he felt and could not understand. Millie and Edward on their wedding night! He thought of them and turned his mind away in self-disgust, and saw them still and loathed the sight.

"Whatever you say, Mother," he said in a low voice.

"You wouldn't mind, would you, Jonathan?" she said.

"Why should I be the one to say, Mother?" he replied.

"Lads usually like adventure and all," she said, beseeching him.

He thought of the sea with hatred. He had never liked the sea, even the bit of it he saw at Blackpool. And beyond it were thousands of acres of land. Twenty acres had been too much. Twenty acres of land had taught him he wanted to teach school.

"Everybody says I'm lucky to have so many sons to put on the land," his father had written. . . .

"It's likely to be fun for you," his mother said.

He looked away from her. He felt somehow that he had made her suddenly want to go, he and Connie, though he had done nothing.

"Maybe," he said bleakly.

There were in Dentwater countless small things he had not noticed until now that he must leave them, and each became precious. If he had been asked what he hated most to leave, he would have wavered between the hours he spent at his desk by a window in the schoolroom, and those in the kitchen of the cottage, especially the hours in the evenings when the curtains were drawn, or in the rare mornings when, because he could see the ships on the Irish Sea, he knew when he went downstairs the sun would be shining across the brick floor. From the window in the schoolroom there was very little view—a few old graves in a corner of the churchyard and then the gray wall of the church. But even this bit of view seemed dear when he knew that soon he would not see it again. He had never cared greatly for church because he did not like the vicar's wife. He knew his mother was shy because of this elderly woman and did not like to go to church when she had nothing to put in the collection box.

"Mrs. Clemony looks at me that sharp!" she said. "I daresay she thinks I ought to be a better manager. But I manage the best I can. 'Tidn't as if I had anything regular coming in like she does."

He had therefore a strong dislike for Mrs. Clemony, a tall skeleton of a woman always in black silk. Of the vicar he never thought unkindly and not much at all, because no one did. He was a vague sort of a man who never came out of the mists except to climb into his pulpit. Usually he mumbled over the sermons he wrote out on half-sheets of paper, but sometimes he was upset about something, and then he had no paper but preached out of his head, and then everybody listened to him, though no one could imagine why he was so excited. Why, for instance, should an old man whose white hair floated like a fog about his bald crown shout and wave his sticks of arms in the pulpit and groan that God would punish England because of what Englishmen were doing to the blacks in India? It was not as if anybody in Dentwater had anything to do with such things. Jonathan, hearing the talk after church, felt ashamed because he had been secretly moved by what the vicar had said.

"Suppose them blacks do feel things the same as us?" he had once asked his mother when he went home to dinner.

"Those," she corrected, and forgot to answer the rest of it.

On their last Sunday Mr. Clemony had come into the pulpit, and the moment he lifted his head after invocation they knew he was in one of his rare fits. But this time he began talking about the wildest thing he had ever talked about—"disarmament," he called it, everybody agreeing together not to make guns—and then he ended by praying for Lord Clarendon. Who was Lord Clarendon?

After church the men gathered in the churchyard in the weak sunshine of a mild day in late February to talk about it.

"Fair crazy, I calls it," Mr. Haynes, the butcher, said. He plucked a bit of dried grass from a forgotten grave and chewed it. ". . . when Proosia is thinkin' how to cut us up proper. If so be this Lord Clarendon's thinkin' like that, why, England's goin' to the dogs, I say." He spat and looked as gloomy as his round red face allowed.

Jonathan, hanging about with the older boys on the outskirts of the men, listened to this not so much for what it meant as for sorrow that on another Sunday he would not be here but on the sea. It was like thinking of how it would be if he were to die. Everything would go on exactly as it now did, only he would not be there.

At the dinner table he said out of his thoughts, "I'm glad the vicar had one of his days today, Mother. I like to remember him the way he was this mornin', his hair stickin' out and his eyes like lights."

"Queer how he looks two men," his mother agreed, "so shadowy when he doesn't care what he says and today like a lighted torch."

So now, though he did not mind never seeing Mrs. Clemony again, he did mind not seeing the old vicar any more. By the time he ever could come back to England, such a frail old gentleman would be gone, and he'd never hear him get excited and preach a real sermon again maybe.

It all became a melancholy death of many moments which Jonathan scarcely knew he had loved until now. Mr. Hopkins, who could be so sharp when he missed the ending of an irregular Latin verb, seemed now always to be gentle, and his furrowed, too-early-aging face less irritable than ever it had been. His very desk seemed impossible to leave behind, and the big inkstain upon it dear and familiar. Archie Bainter he had in his private heart considered a poor sort of chap, always talking of running away and never doing it; and yet in those days he became intimate even with him and found that Archie was a troubled soul who was afraid of himself because he had such dark thoughts of his father so that he wanted to kill him and was afraid he would. He confessed this to Jonathan, his pallid face twitching and his hands trembling.

"I've wanted to tell somebody this for a long time, Jonnie, and didn't dare. Do you think I'm the same as a murderer according to the Bible?"

"No," Jonathan said quickly, "no, I don't." He hesitated and then felt it dishonest to accept this confession from Archie and say nothing himself. "Fact is," he said in a low voice, "I reckon I've been glad all winter that my dad's in America."

"Ah, but he don't drink," Archie said.

"No, he don't do that," Jonathan admitted.

He wanted to go on and say what he felt about his father's rough ways and his big talk, and yet these seemed unimportant when he remembered Mrs. Bainter, sometimes with a black eye, sometimes with a bandaged head.

"He's wrenched her wrist now," Archie muttered.

"I wouldn't stand it!" Jonathan said angrily. What he saw was not that untidy, gawky Mrs. Bainter, but his own mother, pretty and fragile and always neat in her little print dresses, her head hanging limp. He could hear her voice, "Oh, Clyde, you hurt me!"

"Fact is," he said to Archie, swallowing as he spoke, "I'm agoin' to America just for my mother, to see that my dad is good to her. Else I'd stay behind and let 'em go."

And as soon as he said it he knew that this really was why he was going, although until now it had not been clear to him. Of course he must go to America, so that she would have someone to defend her and take care of her. Quietly, as he thought of it, this became his duty. He had not seen Constance Favor since the night of the wedding. Now he resolutely forgot her.

🦋 4 🦋

WHAT HIS MOTHER WOULD HAVE DONE HAD HE NOT SEEN his duty clear, he did not think of asking himself. No sea had ever been so vile as this one, and there was not time to think about anything except the next immediate demand upon him from the three who were ill—his mother, Ruth, and Arthur. This left him Maggie, who, once she became established to the change, wanted nothing except to be on her feet. She had learned to run anywhere before they left Dentwater and would now run, though the ship heaved and threw her against the long lines of trunks in the steerage. Then she fell and wept, her din mercifully lost in the crash of the rough seas and the creaking of timbers. Whenever he could, Jonathan held her, though against her will, to save her bruises and cuts. But there was not much time even for this, except when he fed her upon his knee while he himself ate at the rough board tables where twice a day they dipped into the tin bowls of soup or stew or porridge which the sailors put down for the steerage. The rest of the time, his eye upon Maggie, he went from one to the other of the ones ill, or he ran to mitigate some damage Jamie had done.

"Dang you, Jamie," he cried one day when a steward came to tell him that Jamie had been caught upstairs in the saloon. He was goaded by weariness and worn by the foolish, incessant motion of the ship and by Jamie's impudence, which sea air had only sharpened. "I wish you was good and sick like the others is! Can you not stay where you're told and not go peekin' and peerin' into the first class where you don't belong?"

"I'm as good as the folk there," Jamie said, his freckles lost in a red flush.

" 'Tidn't whether you're as good as them or not," Jonathan answered, "it's whether you can pay."

Jamie, his flush drenching away, flung out at his older brother, "You don't care what people think of us! You're just like a—a servant or somethin'—takin' things and never answerin'!"

"I don't take that from you, anyways!" Jonathan gave him a clip over the head, and then, at Jamie's hurt astonishment, hated himself. "There, give over, will you, Jamie? I don't want to be angered with you. On'y you do allays say the thing that makes me so."

"I wish I was with my father!" Jamie cried, and choked and bit his lip.

"There you go again," Jonathan said. "You want to be with him because he spoils you and leaves you to your own way."

This was interrupted by a weak cry from Artie. "Jonathan! Jonathan!"

"See to Maggie a minute, Jamie," Jonathan ordered the sulky boy. "She went around the bend there."

And he hastened to the berth where Arthur lay at one end and Ruth at the other. Ruth was sleeping, though it was mid-morning, but the little boy sat up, ghastly and white and retching. When he had vomited he lay back, trembling and spent.

"I be so sick," he whispered faintly.

"You'll be better sure," Jonathan answered heartily, though he was afraid to see the child's weakness. An hour ago he had persuaded him to eat, but since they came aboard he had been able to keep nothing down.

"Shall I die?" he whispered again, turning up his great pale blue eyes to see Jonathan's answer.

"Mercy on us, no!" Jonathan cried. He leaned over and took the small bone-thin boy in his arms.

"I don't want to be put in a box and thrown in the water," the child whispered, his eyes filling so that the tears overflowed them.

"Now, wherever did such notions come into your knowledge?" Jonathan cried angrily. He was so miserable that he wanted to weep, and his only refuge was anger.

"Jamie told me," Arthur answered.

"That Jamie!" Jonathan scolded. "Wait till I see him! I'll clip him harder nor I did a minute ago. Lie down, Artie. I must go and find Maggie. Lie still, or you'll wake Ruthie, and then she'll be sick, too. 'Tidn't but ten days more. Today noon we're half gone. Then every hour brings us nearer the good land."

"We don't have to go back no more, neither," Arthur said, faintly cheered.

"No, never," Jonathan agreed, against his heart. To himself he said steadily, "But I'll go back to England one day, when they're all growed up and Mother's safe somewhere. Maybe she'll go back with me—just her and me." He'd make her old age beautiful and full of peace if that happened. They wouldn't even go back to Dentwater. He'd find a good school, say in Devonshire, and a cottage nicer than the one they had left, although how dear it had seemed when they left it that morning, empty of them and all their life! It was so mad a thing to do—to walk out of a door he loved and lock it, knowing he would never enter it again! He peered into the upper berth where his mother lay. She was awake, the gray ship's blanket tucked under her chin.

"Is Maggie takin' her food?" she asked when her eyes met his.

"Like she was at home," he replied. "I don't give her the meat, though, Mother, even if she wants it."

"Give her a bit," she said apathetically. "She's a great one for meat—she'll eat it raw if you let her."

He longed to say something to comfort her and could think of nothing.

"Don't you worry," was all he could manage to say.

"I cannot," she replied simply. "I've not the strength for it."

Outside, the sea thundered and beat upon the sides of the ship so that it trembled in every joist and joint.

"Dear God!" his mother murmured and closed her eyes. Upon her forehead sweat broke out, and she pressed her lips together hard.

He had no time, and yet day and night were endless. There were many others in the crowded steerage who were going to America, but he had no time to talk with them or find out why they went. Most of them were families absorbed in themselves, but there were young men who were apparently alone. One of these slept in the berth next to Jonathan's, and that was the first face he saw every morning when he woke in the murky foul air. It was a blond English face, high-colored and big-nosed, handsome if one took it all into account as belonging to a huge man. They struck up a sidewise sort of friendship, the man amused at Jonathan's troubles, and Jonathan struggling to pretend he was not nurse to three sick and all but father to Jamie and mother to Maggie.

"Has your hands full, hasn't you, young chap?" the young man asked good-naturedly. "Here, give us the little tyke."

The "little tyke" was Maggie, at that moment howling for food. He carried her off with him to the breakfast table and did not bring her back for an hour.

"Eats anything, don't she?" he said admiringly when he brought her back, smiling and full of food. "Ate my porridge with me after she'd done her own, drank my coffee, and would ha' smoked my pipe if I'd let her. She's my sort, she is—hearty-like."

He came back every now and again to ask for her and carry her off, and when on the last day they stood watching the harbor of New York come into view, he handed Jonathan a bit of paper whereupon he had written in a large round writing, "George Tenney, Screw Falls, Arkansas."

"Got an uncle there, with a sheep farm," he said. "Write to me, will you, boy? I'd like to keep up with that red-headed little tyke. I'm fond of her. Makes me laugh, she does."

Jonathan folded the paper and put it in his breast pocket and went down with Maggie in his arms. Now nothing seemed of importance except getting all the children together and ready to put their feet on land. His mother and Ruth were dressed and lying in their berths, waiting, and he put Maggie beside his mother. Jamie he had sequestered in a spot between two life boats, on a strict promise that he stay there until he was fetched.

His mother was piteously thin, but she had been able to dress herself behind the blanket Jonathan had strung around their corner. And Ruth had grown well enough to eat a little the last two days and keep it down. But Arthur's delicate system could not right itself. He lay, his shrunken face anxious with fear lest he be forgotten.

"Jonnie, you wouldn't go away and leave me, would you?"

he begged in his little weak voice when Jonathan came to tell them New York lay on the edge of the sea.

"I shall hold you in my arms until we find Father," Jonathan promised, and he sat down on the berth beside the child.

He had told no one, but the great secret fear he had was that his father might not be there on the dock. They had had almost no money left after they paid for their tickets and cleared away the bits of bills they had at the butcher's and the baker's in Dentwater. The shop they had sold, good will and all, to a young couple just married in Dentwater, who were to come to live in the cottage after their honeymoon. Otherwise there would not have been enough for the bills.

He lifted Arthur up and wrapped him in a shawl and felt his heart thick with fear at the child's lightness and the looseness of his bones. Nothing seemed to hold them together.

"Put your arms about my neck, there's a good boy," he said, and felt Arthur's little arm creep about his neck and lie there as feebly as a shadow and scarcely more warm.

"Where's home, Jonnie?" Arthur inquired.

Jonathan stared down at him. "Danged if I know," he answered. "Anyways, somewhere in America."

If his father were not there to meet the ship, what would they do? I'll have to find work, he thought, as soon as ever I can.

He sat on the edge of the berth with the thin, clinging little boy in his arms. He was a grave youth of middle size and middling looks, neither dark nor fair, nor anything that one would remember. People were passing him quickly, hurrying to the deck to see the approaching city. Still he sat there, dreading to see the new shores of America, until at last even they must go upstairs and be ready to leave the ship.

But Clyde was in the crowd, straining his eyes like all the rest for a glimpse of them. Jamie saw him first.

"I can see my dad!" he screamed joyfully.

"Where?" Mary cried.

She had been watching the dock, her lips tight and her eyes narrowed. She would not for any cause have told her children how fearful this new shore looked to her, a bare terrain, with none of the soft, fulsome green of England. She knew Blackpool was not beautiful, but, receding from them, it had seemed beautiful, set and surrounded with the new green of spring. But there were no trees here, nothing to hide a flat city scattering itself to the water's edge. It looked, for all its houses, somehow still wild and unsettled, as though the buildings had been thrown up in haste, to endure no more than a day. And this, Clyde had told her, was the biggest city in America! Then all else must be wilderness indeed. Around her people were laughing and shrieking with excitement. But she felt only a huge mounting certainty within her.

I shall never see England again, she was thinking. And then she heard Jamie's scream and cried out and followed with her eyes the line of his small forefinger and saw Clyde.

The certainty turned less dark without leaving her. "Yes, that's him," she answered, and said nothing when Jamie tore himself loose from her hand and burrowed his way through the crowd like a mole underground and climbed the rail and, holding onto a post, screeched at his father, "Hello there, Dad! Dad—Dad!"

"Go and hold him by the legs, Ruthie," she said.

Now that she could see Clyde's face coming slowly clear, the certainty seemed less crushing by the moment. She lifted Maggie, clinging to her knees, and held her up, her arms still weak from her seasickness.

"See your daddy, Maggie!" she said.

She could see him now quite plainly. He wore the same suit in which he had left England. But it had been a good rough brown tweed, bought to last. His face was redder than it had been. That would be the sun and winds. He had spoken of the unending dry winds, but she could not imagine them. He was heavier than she remembered him, thicker and more solid. Maybe the hard work had done him good. She felt a shy, unwilling joy steal over her as she looked at him. A woman had to follow her man. She had done what was right. It would not have been well if she had refused to leave England, or had made him stay. He would have blamed her for every failure after. Now she was always in the stronger position, having done what he wanted her to do. It would not be her fault, whatever happened. She felt lightened and suddenly easier than she had felt in many months. That was the way a woman ought to feel when she could lean upon the man.

Then she was aware of something fastened upon her face, a heat and a pull, and she turned without will and found herself caught in the gaze of Jonathan's eyes, fixed upon her face. She could not understand this look, but instantly she was uncomfortable under it, and he felt her discomfort and looked away.

"Anyway, he's here!" she said defiantly, though why should she need to be defiant to her son about his father?

"Yes, he's here," Jonathan agreed, and voice and eyes and expression became as colorless as a mist. Behind that hiding mist he was not so much thinking as feeling, with a sick disgust that still was of heat and not of cold, that when these two who were his parents came together it would be the same thing all over again. His mother would always yield to his father. She had yielded even in being here. In his arms Arthur cried, astonished, "Why are you shakin', Jonnie?"

" 'Cause you're a mortal heavy load," Jonathan said gravely, and set him down abruptly.

Now that he had them all here, Clyde Goodliffe could not do enough for them. He was a different man; they all felt it at once and saw it in the look of his face, in the freedom of his movements. In England he had gone sullen and slouching, and when he spoke he was either reckless or surly. The recklessness had become a loud gaiety, and the surliness was gone. He had pushed his way onto the ship almost before the ropes were thrown out to hold her to the pier. He was there, and he lifted his wife off her feet and kissed her while she clung to him. Maggie was frightened and then angry and burst into weeping, and Arthur clung for a little moment to Jonathan because his father seemed a strange man. But Ruth and Jamie fell upon him and seized his legs, and then he was hugging them all, even Jonathan; and Jonathan, feeling the warm, strong clasp about his shoulders, let his doubts die a little. Maybe America had done his father good, and maybe they would all be happier.

"Dang me, if this idn't the happiest day of our lives, Mary!" Clyde shouted. "Better even than our wedding day for me! Everything is wunnerful, lass! Drought's broke out there. We've come just right. Wheat's headin' out, and it don't matter now if dryness does come back a while. We're sure. Hunnerds of acres, Mary, all stannin' even in wheat—hard red wheat like England never saw!"

"Thought you said it was corn, Clyde," she said.

"Corn's wheat here," he explained, "and maize is corn."

"Is it, now!" she cried, laughing. "Whatever made 'em get that mixed!"

They all laughed, and Maggie stopped crying.

"Now then, to the hotel," Clyde said. "I got two rooms for us there."

"But we're not stoppin' here, are we, Clyde?" Mary asked.

"To see the New York sights, we are," he replied. "We'll not be back East in a long time, Mary, and I've planned three days' good time before we take the train. Come, Magsie, to your dad."

He stooped to pick up Maggie, but she would not have him. Instead she clung to Jonathan's leg. They saw then the first glimpse of the old Clyde.

"Dang the brat!" he said with strong irritation. "She's not glad to see me!"

"She's wee, yet—that's all," his wife said quickly.

"Silly, I call it," he said carelessly, and turned away from her. "Come, Jamie," he said, "you and me against 'em all!"

The three of them went off, Jamie between his parents; and Maggie, seeing her mother go with this man, looked up at Jonathan and puckered her face and opened her mouth to cry.

"Don't cry," he said briefly. "I'll carry you." Stooping, he took her up in his arms and followed behind the family, Ruth clinging to one side of his coat and Arthur to her hand.

Long before three days were gone Maggie had forgotten that she was ever afraid of her father. They had all forgotten everything that had ever been unhappy, and they all believed in him. For the first time in his life Clyde Goodliffe felt himself head of his own family. Every day he decided what they would do and what they would see, and they followed him in a sort of joyful dream.

"Now you listen to me," he proclaimed. "I been plannin' this all winter long, how it'd be. I've it all fixed."

"But it oughtn't to cost too much, Clyde," his wife cried.

"Shut up, Mary!" he cried back at her, but with laughter. "It's me has made the money—it's my money from now on. There's more where this came from. Besides, just lookin' don't cost money, do it?"

In the three days it was the looking that she liked best. All of the children except Jamie were held back a little by her secret fear of cost, increased for them by Jonathan's silence when he felt her fear. Once this made Clyde angry. They had been walking the streets and had paused in front of a great hotel.

"Look at it!" he cried, as though he had made it. "Six stories high, it is, not counting the fresco around the top and chimneys!"

They stood in front of it, staring upward. Jamie began counting.

"One—two—three—four—five—yes, it's six, Father!"

"Carlton House." Mary Goodliffe read aloud the name over the door.

A man in a bright blue uniform with many brass buttons looked at them kindly.

"English, ain't you?" he asked through his nose.

"They're just from there," Clyde said, and added quickly, "but I'm from Kansas."

"I reckon you don't see anything like that out in Kansas, though," the man said, nodding at the building.

"Not yet," Clyde admitted, "but it'll come some day."

The man looked doubtful and changed the subject. "I reckon you've heard of Charles Dickens?" he inquired.

"We have," Mary replied. "It would be queer English folk not to know him."

The man kept an important silence, then spat before he spoke. "Once when I was a young feller just come to this job, he et here," he declared.

"No, never!" Jonathan exclaimed. He gazed up at the building.

"Such a crowd as we've never had since," the man said. "All the big fellows and their ladies. He was a little fellow himself, but he had big black eyes, and a way of lookin' as though he was ready to bust out laffin'!"

"Jonathan!" his mother breathed. "Think of that!"

"He come back two years ago," the man went on, enjoying the effect upon her. "But he was sick then. People said he was yellow and wrinkled and not the same man. Nobody saw him oncet."

Mary Goodliffe was not listening. She turned to Jonathan.

"It makes me feel we aren't so far from England," she said dreamily.

"It does," he agreed.

Time after time he had read aloud to her out of the paper pieces of stories Mr. Dickens had written. They were never able to buy them all so there were large parts they skipped. But Jonathan saved anything he found with them in, and Mr. Hopkins had sometimes given him papers he had bought.

"We s'all have dinner here ourselves, then," Clyde Goodliffe announced. "What does it cost, my chap?"

"Too much, with all them kids," the man said. "That is, if you're thinkin' of the big dinin' room where he et. The coffee shop, of course, wouldn't be so bad—"

"Oh, no, Clyde, please!" Mary begged. "Don't let's—we aren't fit to go in such a place."

"This ain't England," he retorted. "We're as good as anybody here."

"That's right," the man put in, grinning. "It's only if you can pay for it. That's all we ask."

"I can pay for it, right enough—" Clyde began.

But Mary interrupted him. "Clyde, you talk like a right-down fool. We're plain people, and you know it—and I know it. This idn't for us. If you want to eat there, go on and eat alone. The children and I'll find a public house or a little inn. Come, Jonathan—bring the little ones. Your father's out of his head."

And she marched down the street, her head up, one hand leading Maggie and the other Arthur, and Jamie and Ruth longing and uncertain.

For once Jonathan was sorry for his father. "Reckon we'll have to go," he said, apologizing for his mother.

But Clyde caught up with her in three strides and began his furious argument with her, an argument which began that day and was to go on to the day she died.

"You don't unnerstand how it is in Ameriky, Mary!"

"I understand what's right and fittin' to my station in life that I'm content with because I was born in it!"

"There ain't no high and low here!"

"Who's talkin' about high and low? It's folly and sense I'm talkin' about. And it'd be folly for us to push ourselves into that big fine place—us eatin' in there!"

"But we're as good as anybody!"

"Don't be a born fool, Clyde Goodliffe! My father was a shopkeeper and yours was a hired shepherd!"

"It don't matter here."

"It matters everywhere, so long as the world stands, and no shame to us or anybody."

"You're the same as you allays was—full of gloom and darkness and pullin' a man down where he was again when he gets himself up a little!"

"Wisest, if he gets where he don't belong!"

Even the sharp bright sunshine of New York, such sunshine as they had never seen before, was dimmed by the ferocity of this argument, until Mary Goodliffe, looking by chance at the shadowed young faces of her children, ceased it abruptly.

"Here's a place says beef stew for ten cents, and I could eat it fine," she announced.

And a moment later they were sitting around a clean, unpainted table in a room half underground, and a fat woman in a checked blue and white apron was saying kindly, "Sure, you can take one portion for the two little ones, and they kin have all the milk they want for nothin'. The boy looks pindlin'. You must eat plenty, little feller, and catch up with the rest of 'em."

She smiled at Arthur and planked thick white dishes upon the table.

"Here's where we belong," Mary said firmly, "and all of America won't make me believe different."

No one answered her, and so she relented, and in a few minutes it seemed all over, and she was feeding Maggie bread dipped in stew gravy.

Within herself she was thinking with inevitable remorse: I'm too hard on him—he meant to please me; and her eyes, soft with this remorse, looked at her husband.

"Would you like to treat us to a bit of that queer cold pudding?" she asked.

"Do you have ice cream?" Clyde asked the woman.

"Sure we do," she answered.

"Then ice cream for everybody," he ordered.

Then in showing off how he liked the frozen stuff which they ate so gingerly and with such astonishment, he forgot to be sullen any more, and when they came out and he hailed a passing horse car and they all climbed in, Mary held her peace and let him pay for everybody except for the two little ones. But even this she did in a whisper.

"You take Arthur, Jonathan, and I'll take Maggie. There's no use in payin' for them."

"Where are we going, Clyde?" she asked aloud when the car began its jolting way.

"To the Battery, to see the Aquarium," he said proudly.

"Well, if that's what you say," she agreed, and sat looking as peaceful and yielding as though she had never told her husband he could be wrong.

Jonathan, always watching her, caught her eye. She leaned over to him.

"We'll just let your father enjoy himself," she whispered.

Her eyes, looking into his, were bright with tender laughter. He felt drawn to her, close to her, moved by their secret mutual understanding of this huge child of a man who must be humored and circumvented without his knowing it. And in this partnership for the moment he was happy again.

❧ 5 ❧

THE TRAIN ROCKED AND JUMPED BENEATH THEM, SWERVING and bending and swaying. None of them had ever been on a train before.

"It does seem to me it doesn't need to go so mortal fast," Mary murmured. She was sitting upon the dust-filled, plush-covered seat, with Arthur's head in her lap. He was feverish, and his lips were black with parch.

"You'll find everything's fast in Ameriky," Clyde boasted. He was as restless as Jamie, who now was occupying himself by swinging up and down the car between the seats. The car was full of people—all, it seemed, with children, so none could mind another's child. "You sud be thankful you've a train to go on," he went on, folding and unfolding his legs. " 'Tidn't so many years since folks went West in covered wagons—do yet in some parts."

"No part I'd go to," Mary retorted.

" 'Tidn't too bad, Mary," he argued. "It's like a big picnic, the old folks say. They camp together every night and spread theirselves in a circle against the Indians, and inside they make a big fire and cook their food, and everybody is chummy-like."

Jamie, swinging past, caught the word "Indians."

"Shan't we never see Indians, Dad?" he inquired sadly.

"There's always talk of 'em," Clyde said. "But such few Indians as I see in Kansas don't look more excitable than ones that have been well beat. It's past me how folks was ever skeered of 'em."

He had told them they were going to a town called Median. It was a fine place, new and small as yet, but full of promise.

"You'd not be gettin' me there with all this family if they were still wild," his wife replied. She glanced at Jonathan. "Jonnie, fetch me a bit of water again, there's a dear good boy."

Jonathan rose from the seat where he sat beside his father and walked unsteadily down the aisle, thrown from side to side as he went. At the end was the water cooler, now nearly empty of its tepid supply. He filled the tin cup half-full, and then the slow stream ran dry. But it was late afternoon, and before sunset they would stop somewhere on this wild flat plain and draw water from a reservoir set like a sentinel tower in a desert. He guarded the cup, trying to catch the movement of the train and save its spilling.

"Here's all until we stop to fill up," he said to his mother.

"Then I'll dip a clean handkerchief in it and wet Artie's lips while he sleeps," she replied.

In the morning the bustle of people getting washed and fed and ready for the day made the car tolerable, but as evening came on and they were at the threshold of another night of discomfort, gloom fell upon them all.

"See what's left in the basket for Maggie, Jonathan," she said. "Best feed 'em all, maybe, before it's dark."

Jonathan opened the big wicker basket they had bought in New York and filled with bread and salt meat and cheese and fruit and preserved foods. Everything fresh was gone in these four days they had been on the train. But by now Maggie had proved her ability to digest anything. She took a wedge of bread and ham from Jonathan and sat down in the middle of the aisle to eat it, unconcerned by the procession of legs that stepped over and around her.

Jamie took his and gnawed it, his face pressed against the dirty windowpane. But when Jonathan gave some to Ruth, she shook her head. She was sitting quietly, her hand against her cheek.

"What's wrong?" he asked.

"Toothache," she whispered.

"Is that why you're so still, sittin' there with your back to us?" he exclaimed.

She nodded, and at his look and voice of sympathy, her eyes swam in tears.

"It's hurt me the day long," she said in the same whisper.

"And you didn't tell," he exclaimed.

"I didn't want to bother," she confessed. "Not when Artie's so fevered."

"But you could have told me," he reproached her. "It would have eased you, and maybe I could think of something."

Her lips trembled, and she wiped her eyes and did not answer.

"Wait a minute," he said.

He remembered that during the day he had several times seen a hard-faced man four seats away drink from a whisky bottle he took from his pocket. He had expected to see the man grow fuddled, but nothing of the sort had happened. He had gone on playing cards with three other men, hour after hour, in fierce concentration. He was still playing now as Jonathan drew near.

"I ask your pardon," he said sturdily. He hated talking to strangers, but he could do it if he had it to do. He touched the man on the arm, and for an instant the man looked up at him out of hard blue eyes.

"Whatcha want, boy?" he asked in a drawling nasal voice.

"My little sister has the toothache," Jonathan answered. "Could you let her have a drop of that whisky to hold in her mouth against it?"

"Sure it's your sister has the toothache?" the man inquired.

The other three men, bearded dirty fellows, laughed.

"It's her, right enough," Jonathan said calmly.

"I never refuse a lady," the man replied. He drew out his bottle and handed it to Jonathan and went back to his cards. And Jonathan, tipping Ruth's chin, poured a little of the hot raw stuff into her mouth. She gave a small scream of pain, but he encouraged her.

"Bear it, Ruthie—bear it a moment only and 'twill help.

I've done it myself. It's bad, but if you bear it, the ache grows numb, and then it's wunnerful easy for a while."

He corked the bottle and wiped her quivering face with her skirt and then carried the bottle back. The man paused one moment to glance at it.

"Looks like the truth," he said carelessly, and thrust it into his pocket again.

Now the smoky oil lamps were lit, and instantly darkness snatched the landscape away, and another night was upon them. One seat Clyde Goodliffe took for himself, his legs hanging into the aisle. Maggie slept on a rug put down on the floor between two seats. Mary sat immovable with the sick boy's head on her knees, and upon another seat Jamie lay against Ruth. The whisky had made her tooth numb, as Jonathan said it would, and she was sleepy with relief, and her head drooped against Jamie's. Jonathan sat opposite them, half-asleep, too, but waking every little while to look across at his mother.

So the hours dragged over them. Once he rose to go over to his mother.

"Shan't I take Artie on my lap so you can stretch out?" he asked.

But she shook her head, looking down at the little boy in her arms. "I don't like this long sleep," she said. "It's more as if he was unconscious-like."

Their eyes met in mutual anxiety.

"We'll get the doctor to him the minute we get to Median," Jonathan promised her.

"Aye, but is there a doctor?" she retorted.

"There must be in such a town," he said.

He lingered a moment and then went back to his place. People were sleeping everywhere in foolish helplessness. They looked like creatures in a nightmare, he thought. Once in Mr. Hopkins's room when he had stopped for tea he had seen a book of pictures of people in hell. They had looked like these people, sprawling in the convulsions of uncomforting sleep. He sat wide awake while the train bolted them all through darkness to their unknown end.

The train did not go to Median. They must get off at Fort Thomas, and drive from there all day in what Clyde called a hack.

"A wagon-like with a top," he explained to them.

The long journey was over, and they were sitting, as tidy as they could make themselves, ready to get off, all except Arthur, who lay in his lassitude, his head on his mother's lap. He was no better, and yet no worse. Today indeed, and now, he seemed even a little better. He had asked for an egg.

"There idn't an egg here, my love," his mother replied. "But surely there'll be one when we get there. Your dad'll find you one, won't he?"

"Surely will," Clyde replied heartily. "An' a few days of sun and wind'll cure 'im. Never was such a country for sun and wind."

"That I believe," his wife replied. All the days had been full of hard bright sunshine. Her head indeed ached with the light.

"The sky is surely bigger here than it was at home," she said now, gazing out the window.

" 'Tis only there's nothing between us and it," Clyde said.

No hill, no tree, no rise of any sort, indeed, cut off the sky from this earth. The earth lay flat and pressed down around its circular edge by the weight of the sky, heavy and metal-blue by day, and star-sprinkled steel by night. The sky was infinitely more important here than the earth. For the earth was unchanging. Nothing stopped the eye for mile upon mile of even green grass. The handful of houses that made a town were meaningless and passing. The sky was the pageant. The eye went to it again and again. Stars were of enormous size and shining color, and the moon by night was a spectacle. Sunrise and sunset were hidden by nothing and flung out their color like the flags of armies in the sky. There must be noise somehow to such color, Jonathan thought, staring half-fearfully night and morning at the skies. But when the train stopped, the silence was profound. At midday there was nothing between sky and earth. They shivered with cold in the night and morning, and at noon were at the mercy of the merciless sun; and women and children grew sick with heat. There had been no rain since they landed.

But now it was all over. As the time drew near for them to reach Fort Thomas, other passengers came up to bid them good-by. Half of them had already got off in one place or another, and as they left had given away what remained of food to those going farther. Now Mary also divided bread and meat among those who went still farther, keeping only what they might need before nightfall when they would have supper in Median.

It was early morning. Clyde Goodliffe pointed to a few dots ahead and to the right of them.

"It's there," he said. "That's the Fort."

"Why is it a fort, Dad?" Jamie asked.

"They had 'em against the Indians once," his father explained. "There's forts all the way to California—regular hand-over-fist string of 'em. 'Course they're not wanted now."

"It idn't much of a place," Jonathan said doubtfully.

The train was galloping along, and he could see a scattering of unpainted wooden shacks. If Median looked like this, what would he do? He realized that in his mind Median had come to be something like a new Dentwater, a neat little village with a church and a school and a post office, maybe, and the houses tidy-looking with their gardens held behind painted fences.

" 'Tidn't any reason why a fort should be big in these days," Clyde retorted. He picked Arthur up in his arms. The train was slowing down. "After me, now, all of you," he ordered.

Jonathan took Maggie on one arm and the big basket on the other, and all together they stood, holding their belongings. Kindly people helped them, and the man who had given the whisky for Ruth came up, hitching his pants over his hips.

"Toothache still gone, sister?" he shouted, and when she nodded, too shy to do more, he laughed. "Whisky's good for 'most anything in these parts," he said. He was on his way to Oregon. Kansas, he said, was too civilized for him. He had come lounging by to talk to them sometimes.

"Well, I'm plain glad to hear 'tis civilized," Mary Goodliffe said. "I don't desire to live in savagery."

"Kansas don't suit me, though, ma'am," he said. "Too many people."

He spat upon the floor a great blob of brown spittle, and she looked away and whispered fiercely to Jonathan, "Don't let the children step in it—oh, the dirty beast!" She pressed her lips together and gazed resolutely out of the window, and Jonathan could see she was determined not to be sick.

"Clyde Goodliffe," she said in a low fierce voice, "if you ever take to chewing that stuff, we'll not live in the same house longer!"

Clyde had burst out laughing. "I've tried it, though, lass.

But I don't like it, luckily, if to chew would make me a grass widower."

"Filthy, nasty, hateful!" she cried.

"Well—well," he said, pacifying her, "but good men do it, you'll find, Mary."

"I don't believe it," she retorted.

But the tall chap was very good to them now. He helped Ruth to the wooden platform and went back for their bundles and boxes until everything was piled around them, and swung himself on the train just in time, yelling to Jamie as the train carried him away, "When you're growed up, come West, boy!" A likable chap, Jonathan thought, though upon the platform he had left behind him his blobs of spittle, too, so that they had to heed them.

"Now wait here at the station till I see if Harvey Blake's got the hack ready," Clyde told them. "I ordered it before I went, but there's no tellin' what's happened between then and now."

"Give me Artie," Mary said. She sat down on a bundle and put out her arms for him.

Around the dusty platform had been standing six or seven men and three women. At every station there had been such people coming out of the unpainted wooden houses to stand in slack silence and stare at the train. They all looked the same, colored an even hue by weather, their flesh seasoned and dried by it. They were not Indians, and yet Jonathan was surprised when now one of the women came forward and said in a soft voice. "Is the little feller sick?" A foreign tongue would not have surprised him.

"Thank you kindly," his mother answered. "It was the sea upset him. He was that seasick he hasn't got over it."

"Where you goin'?" the woman asked again.

"To Median."

"Would it please you to come and lay the little feller on my bed? That's my shack there."

"No, thank you," Mary said, half-alarmed. "We must be getting on."

"Are you from around here?" the woman asked with a sort of gentle hunger in her voice as though it were pleasant to her merely to talk. She was looking at Mary's garments as she spoke.

"We're from England," Mary said primly.

Jonathan could feel her deciding against this woman with the withered, haggard face and sweet voice. After all, he could feel her thinking, this was a stranger. The woman felt it, too.

"Well, I'll be going," she said vaguely. "I'm real sorry about the little boy."

She drifted back toward one of the houses, and one by one the little group followed her until they were alone again.

"Are we home where we're going?" Arthur asked, and opened his eyes to inquire.

"Not yet, lovey," she answered.

She drew an edge of her shawl over his face to shield him from the sun. But mercifully at this moment great masses of billowing silver-edged cloud had come up and were floating between them and the sun, the first clouds they had seen for days. Between them the heat was dry and searing. They watched for the next cloud, and when its edge touched the sun it was like something cool and wet upon their flesh.

"I wish them huge big ones stuck there would come up," Jamie cried.

He pointed with his finger to the horizon, where a massy base of dark-gray cloud, silvery-white, piled up and up into rounded peaks and turrets. But they seemed immovable, so huge were they and so secure.

"They look stormy, or would in England," Mary said. "But the clouds have such space here I can't tell their meaning. They're merciful now, though."

They sat gratefully under the shade of a cloud as it passed across the sun, and then, before it was gone, Clyde was there with the hack. He was driving its two horses himself.

"There's a chap in Median wants to come back tomorrow," he explained. "So I'm to take it over, and he'll bring it back. Harvey don't want to take the time. Thinks a storm is brewin' and wants his hay in."

He paused and looked at the sky with strange anxiety. "If it wasn't for Artie, I'd say wait and see what the storm is," he said.

Mary Goodliffe looked up in surprise. "A summer storm won't kill us," she said.

"Storms here are bigger than what you're used to," he answered.

"I'll take the chance of storm rather than this child another night with no doctoring," she said decidedly.

"Well, I reckon it's best," Clyde admitted.

He got down and packed in their bundles and bags and the small trunk, and then they all got in and the horses began moving steadily across the flat green country—a green which the two dusty ruts that made the road scarcely broke, for between them the same grass grew.

The stillness was intense, except for the soft clip-clop of the horses' feet in the deep dust, a stillness felt and heard. It was more than absence of sound. It had weight and pressure, and nothing moved except them as they went across the endless green.

"There idn't a solitary tree," Jonathan said after a long while. And it was an effort to lift his voice against the silence.

No one spoke. He saw then that they were all half-asleep. Even his father, nodding, held the reins slack in his hands. But the horses seemed used to this and went steadily on. There was, indeed, no choice for them, since there was only the one road and no other crossed it. The pure air, the warmth, the slow rhythm of the wagon's movement had calmed them into sleep. But Jonathan had never felt farther from sleep. He felt oppressed and strange and half-afraid. Everything was too big here. In England one knew the sea held the land together, so there was an end to it. It was a fence around a field, and all within the fence belonged to you. But here the land went on and on. No one could possess it. Even if you cut off a piece of it, there would be all the rest.

He sat holding Maggie, now sleeping, and felt afraid to be the only one awake. For to his horror the great shining mass of cloud which had looked so immovable upon the horizon began now to swell and grow and spread out into brighter edges and higher peaks and more glittering towers. And the land which had lain so quiescent began to break into movement, or it seemed movement, though he knew it was only the quickly moving light and shade upon the green. But how could green look so dangerous and livid when there was no sun upon it? While he stared, the grass began to shiver and ripple as though the earth quaked beneath it. Was it the earth that rumbled? He heard a deep soft roar.

"Father!" he screamed. At the sound of his scream Maggie woke with loud crying and they were all awake.

"Hey!" Clyde shouted. He wiped his hand across his mouth. One of the horses tossed its head and whinnied.

"Father, look!" Jonathan cried. He pointed at the sky.

"Oh, it's goin' to come, after all," Clyde said, peering out. "Harvey said it would. I'd better get out the curtains and be ready."

They stopped, and from under a seat he brought out oilcloth curtains. "Help me, lads," he ordered.

Jonathan put Maggie, still crying, upon Ruth's knee, and he and Jamie fumbled at the curtains.

"Like this, butterfingers," Clyde commanded.

In a moment Jonathan had the way of it and was fastening them more quickly than his father did. He was compelled by terror. He had never in his life been so terrified. By seconds the sky had blackened, all except the horrible scarified edge of silver to the black clouds, all except such lightning as he had never seen in his life. The lightning in English skies was soft torchlight compared to the great furious rents which this lightning tore in the sky, and the thunder muffled drums compared to this crash heaped upon crash. He felt his sweat pouring down him, his tongue dry, his eyeballs tight in their sockets. Self-respect, pride, everything left him except terror. He wanted to run as fast as he could, anywhere. But his legs were lifeless, and he could not breathe. He felt his head swim. He barely heard his father's voice crying down the roar, "Now in with us all—here's the rain!"

He could barely crawl into the last curtain left open. His mother screamed at the sight of him.

"What's wrong with you, Jonathan?"

He could not answer. All his being was caught and held in a spasm.

"Clyde—Clyde—Jonathan's gone daft!"

He saw them turn to stare at him. But he could not speak, not while about him this crash and roar went on. And now here were the wind and the rain, a waterfall of rain, rain that dripped and ran through every crack. The horses were standing still, no more able to keep on their way.

He felt a sharp, strong slap on his cheek, and to his shame and agony, he burst into weeping. His father had struck him.

"Come to!" he ordered.

"Clyde Goodliffe!" Mary cried.

"Shut up, Mary," he said. "It's the thing to do—the lad's about to go out of himself with fright. He'll cry a minute and be himself."

But he was not himself. He kept shivering and crying, though he tried to hold himself back. Every time the lightning sprang at him and the thunder beat upon him, his being dissolved, and he lost himself. He could see even his mother only dimly. She was distressed for him and frightened herself, but he could do nothing for her because his being was dissolved. Only at last, when the thunder grew less and the rain went on like a dark wave, could he begin to gather himself together again.

They let him mercifully alone. He had frightened the children, and they sat staring at him. His father took off the curtains without speaking to him, and his mother found a towel and handed it to him.

"Wipe your face and head, Jonathan, love," she said tenderly. "You're wet with your sweat, and the air's cool. A terrible, terrible storm," she added kindly. "We were all scared of it."

He did not answer out of the depths of his shame. The horses, wet and shining, took up their way again, and the clouds retreated once more. He did not know what had happened to him. He sat, helpless in his exhaustion. After a long time his mother turned to him.

"Are you better?" she asked gently.

He nodded, and then he wanted to speak, but did not know how to explain anything.

"I was struck-like," he said.

"Not by lightning, or you'd not be able to say it," his father put in.

"No," Jonathan replied.

Then after a moment he admitted his enemy, a new enemy in this land.

"I reckon I was plain down scared," he said in a low voice.

"I reckon," his father said dryly.

"We must find a doctor for Artie at once, Clyde," Mary said an hour later. She swayed as she spoke, trying to take up in her own body the unevenness of the muddy road.

"Oh, he'll right himself in this air," Clyde said heartily.

"Wunnerful air it is. There's hardly no doctors can do business in it."

He did not want to tell her that there was not a doctor near Median. Time enough for everything, now that she was here. Besides, it was true that people were healthy. The lad would pick up now that he was off the sea. He turned his mind to his plans—big plans they were, and he was glad to see Jonathan had grown to be a man and could help him. It was queer, though, the scare he took in the storm. He glanced at his son as he sat beside him. A little on the small side, he thought. Jonathan would never be as big as his dad.

"Want to take the horses a bit?" he inquired.

"No, thanks, Father," Jonathan said. "I've not driven 'em like this before."

"Take 'em," Clyde said shortly and threw him the reins.

Jonathan bit his lip, but he took them; and the horses, seeming to feel the change in the grip, tossed their heads and tried to quicken their pace. It was impossible. The mud dragged at the wheels. But Jonathan, not yet knowing that mud, sat erect and silent, his heart beating against his father.

Clyde watched him. A pale dinky man Jonathan would make, he was thinking. Mary had put her smallness upon him. Edward was the better of the two.

"Did Edward say he'd be comin'?" he asked abruptly.

"Not a word," Jonathan replied, without turning his head.

"Edward's fixed well," Mary put in. "Some day maybe we'll be thankful there's one lad at home with a good shop."

"This is home now," Clyde retorted.

A strange wide place for a home, then, Jonathan thought. The heavy leather reins pulled at his hands. He threw a quick glance to the right and to the left. Ahead or aside, everything looked the same. The country was flat under the long waving grass. The road was two muddy ruts dividing north from south. Ahead of them the sun poured through a crack in the clouds a clear yellow light over the wet grass.

"Can't we see Median yet?" he asked.

"You can see it if you look at it," Clyde retorted. He nodded, and they all looked ahead. Against the yellow sky a low rectangular roof rose a few feet above the horizon, and another and another, until there were perhaps half a dozen.

"Them!" Jonathan said in a low voice.

"That's never Median!" his mother cried.

"Median it is," Clyde said half-sullenly. In the surrounding silence he defended himself. Let 'em think what they want, it's me has borne the brunt of it, he thought. He had worked a hard year with no home and no woman, and he had paid their way over the sea. Let 'em look at Median, because there's going to be time ahead when Median'll seem wunnerful and a place to remember, he thought.

"It's goin' to be a big place, Median is," he said aloud. "They're goin' to make it the county seat, and there'll be streets and houses and banks and a school, even."

"There's no school now, then," Jonathan said.

"There's no need for it," Clyde retorted.

"There'll be need for it when we get there," Jonathan said. But in this one moment he had given up all hope for his own learning. Who could teach him Latin here?

"Not for you," Clyde said.

"There're the little ones after him," Mary told him.

"Readin' and writin' and a little arithmetic is all a man needs here," Clyde answered. "It's one of the beauties of America," he said in a loud voice. "A man can get ahead with his hands and his own brains, and he don't need to sit with his nose in a book."

No one answered him. He lifted his eyes up and caught a look at that moment passing between Jonathan and his mother, and, leaning over, he seized the reins from Jonathan's hands and slapped the horses' backs.

"Get along, there!" he shouted at them. It was good to speak to beasts who could not jaw back at him.

But Jonathan, after the communication in that long look from his mother, took comfort. Ever since he had come to this country he had felt a wandering wretchedness in his mind. His mother had been so glad to see his father again that he felt he was no longer necessary to her. He had remembered mournfully the year in Dentwater when she had turned to him as the man in her house, a year full of a sweetness pathetic because now it was over. His father's presence had thrust him back to being young again and not much good. What he had done always for the younger children when his father was away was by his father's presence nothing but woman's work. And he had been made miserable by his mother's fondness for this man. In the New York streets she had hung upon his arm with both her hands, and he had looked away when he saw it.

Now in her long look she called him back to her. She needed him still, and in the warmth of this need he leaned over and took Maggie from where she sat half-asleep against Ruth.

"Give me the tiddlin' thing," he said gently. "She's all in a heap." He lifted the fat little lump in his arms and held her tenderly in the silent dusk.

≈ 6 ≈

MEDIAN WAS MUD. THEY LOOKED OVER THE SIDE OF THE wagon at the scarcely moving wheels and saw the black stuff clinging to the spokes and halfway to the hubs, a smooth, shining substance as thick as gum. The horses stopped and snorted.

"Dang 'em, I s'all have to get out and lead 'em," Clyde muttered.

"Can't you pull over to the side of the street and let's walk?" Mary asked.

"Walk where?" Clyde retorted. He crawled along a horse's back and leaped down and sank halfway to his knees. "Come on here, you beasties," he said, and seized the bit.

The wagon moved slowly again, a few inches at a time. They could hear the sucking sound of Clyde's boots as he forced his way. It was dark now, and the faint waves of light which the wagon lantern sent out showed them not even the side of the road, nothing but the thick surface of the mud, smooth until it curled heavily about moving feet and wheels.

"Is Kansas all mud, then, Clyde?" Mary called.

He did not hear her. He was pushing the reluctant horses along, urging them with the whip when they stopped. A quarter of a mile, and then they saw faint lights on either side of the wide mud. The wagon swerved and drew over and stopped.

"Here we be," Clyde panted. He threw the reins over the backs of the sweating horses and came to the side of the wagon and put out his arms to his wife. "I'll carry you both in," he said, and lifted her with Arthur in her arms. "Hi there, Drear!" he shouted.

A door opened, and in the light streaming out of the house stood a tall, thick figure.

"Hi there, yourself!" a deep voice roared.

Clyde staggered the four or five feet between wagon and door and set his wife upon the threshold.

"There's more to come," he cried. He went back. "Now you, Ruthie, and Jamie, the two of you." He lifted them, one on each arm, and stopped to look at Jonathan. But Jonathan was already taking off his shoes and socks.

"I'll roll up my trousers, Father," he said.

A moment later he slipped down into the dark mud. In the tidy, meager life of Dentwater he had not since he was a little boy felt his feet upon the ground. But this was nothing like the smooth wet cobblestones or the sandy soil of Dentwater. The mud sucked in his feet and his legs and dragged him down until he was afraid. He clung to the wagon and lowered himself by one hand, Maggie upon his right arm.

"Put your arms about my neck, Maggie," he told her. She did so, and he cautiously put down his other foot. He felt the mud bottomless until he was all but ready to pull himself up again. But it was more difficult to pull up than to sink down. He let himself go, desperately knowing the bottom must be there, and then felt it beneath him, the solid subsoil of the land. He walked upon it somehow, pushing himself through the mud until he stood at the inn door. He hesitated to step upon the floor, and then saw that he need not. Muddy feet had come and gone upon the rough planks until there was an inch of mud upon them like a carpet. His first thought was for his mother's skirt as she stood, still with Arthur in her arms, looking about her. She was dazed, he could see. And Maggie suddenly began to cry in a loud wail.

"Well, here we be, Drear," Clyde said. "A lot of us, when we're all together."

"We'll feed you," the man said heartily, "and bed you, if you don't mind where you sleep." He turned his head and bawled, "Wife!"

"What?" a shrill voice called back.

"Goodliffes is here!" he shouted.

"Well, I never!" she screamed.

But she came running in, a tall, broad woman of middle

age, with a sharp face and dry sandy hair combed into a braided knot on top of her head.

"Well, God save us," she said, staring at them. "I didn't expect you till tomorrow, but come on."

"I said maybe today," Clyde told her.

"Today's usually tomorrow with you," she retorted, though not unkindly.

But Mary, seeing another woman, came to herself. "Could I get a doctor for my little lad?" she asked. "He's very ill."

"A doctor!" the woman repeated, astonished. "Why, I haven't seen a doctor in these parts for nearly a year. There was one last summer goin' to the coast." She turned to her husband. "Henry, when did you hear tell of a doctor?"

He shook his head. "Don't know," he said. They both came over to look at the child. "Is he asleep?" the woman asked.

"He just lies so," Mary replied. Her lip quivered, and tears came into her eyes. "Clyde, if I'd ha' known there wouldn't be a doctor in Median, I wouldn't ha' come," she said fiercely.

"Oh, now, Mrs. Goodliffe!" the woman cried. "You're tired. Why, it's a wonderful country. He'll get well. I'll give him a little mush and milk. Lucky we've got a cow. Lay him in here on my bed." She moved to a doorway and put aside the blanket that was its curtain. Jonathan put Maggie down and, stepping forward, took Artie from his mother.

"I'll carry him," he said. He went into the room behind Mrs. Drear and laid the little boy down, while his mother followed. Beneath even Artie's lightness the straw of the mattress rustled. But it was a bed, covered with blankets and a woven counterpane of blue and white. Artie did not stir. Mrs. Drear leaned over him and felt his forehead.

"I've seen 'em come back from the very jaws of death," she said solemnly. "It's the air. I'll fetch some hot milk." She bustled away, and while Jonathan and his mother stood beside the bed his father came in.

"Drear's the right sort," Clyde said. "He says we can stay in this room for the night. Seems their other three rooms are full of a party going West. The rain's upset everything. They couldn't go on like they expected. Drear and Mrs. will sleep in the kitchen."

"But however—" Mary began, and stopped. Mrs. Drear came in again, a bowl and a spoon in her hand.

"Now then, folks," she commanded them, "Jennet—that's

my daughter—is ready to feed you. Get along and leave this little feller to me."

She sat down and began with a sort of clumsy gentleness to put the milk between Artie's lips. Without opening his eyes he swallowed.

"He's all right," Clyde exclaimed. "Come along."

"You all go," Mary said. "I shan't leave Artie."

"I'll come back quick then, Mother," Jonathan said.

He followed his father into the other room. Ruth was still standing in the middle of the muddy floor, holding Maggie's hand, and Jamie beside them, his hands in his pockets, staring at everything about him.

"Come along," Jonathan said and lifted Maggie up. They sat down beside a long unpainted table. A red-headed young girl with a dirty blue apron came in with a wooden bowl of mush and a jug of milk. She set them down and went away and came back with bread and slices of thick bacon. The rain had begun again in a long droning roar upon the roof.

"Lucky we made it," Clyde said. "Lucky I got the horses put away even."

Jonathan took Maggie on his lap and made ready to feed her, and as he did so a thin stream of water began to patter on the table from the roof. Drops flew into his face. He moved and the girl Jennet, seeing it, went out and brought in a pan and set it under the leak as though she were used to it. Jonathan watched her.

"Does the roof always leak like this?" he asked.

She looked at him with a sudden glint in her large greenish eyes. "No," she replied impudently, "only when it rains."

She went away in the midst of loud laughter from Clyde and Mr. Drear, her face straight but her eyes glittering with laughter she would not allow to escape.

Jonathan hated the laughter. There was nothing to laugh at that he could see. He hung his head and made an ado about feeding Maggie, refusing her bacon and insisting upon the mush and milk so sternly that she was unexpectedly cowed in this strange place and swallowed the spoonfuls that he ladled into her open mouth. He ate between whiles, loathing the food and yet too hungry to refuse it. His mother was a dainty cook, and he was accustomed to goodness in her simple dishes. But he ate, and when he was fed lifted Maggie and took her to bed in the other room. Mrs. Drear had gone, and his mother was alone.

"Where'll we all sleep?" she said when he came in. She was dazed, he could see, and dismayed.

"There'll be pallets," he said. "I'll just lay Maggie here by Artie."

Artie had not wakened. She watched him while he put Maggie down. She was so silent that he was startled and looked at her. Her eyes were full of fear.

"Your father's brought us to a terrible country," she said. He could not deny it. But he cried out to her what he had always cried.

"Don't you mind, Mother. I'll think of something!"

What he was thinking of was how to get her back to England. He would find work, and he would save and put together enough to take her back again. And even while he thought, his father came tramping cheerfully into the room, loosening his belt as he came.

"I'm full and sleepy, lass," he cried. "Mrs. Drear will put down the pallets for the young ones, and you and me'll sleep in the bed, eh, Mary?"

"Mother hasn't eaten yet," Jonathan said angrily. "Go on, Mother, and I'll sit here in your place."

"Go on yourself," Clyde said in good humor. "I'm going to take off my clothes as soon as Mrs. Drear's out."

She was coming in as he spoke, her arms full of quilts. "Don't stop for me," she shouted. "I've seen a plenty in my time. How many pallets, Mr. Goodliffe? Your young man—"

"I shan't sleep in here, if you please," Jonathan broke in.

"Oh, Godamercy," Mrs. Drear said laughing, "sleep in the other room then. Jennet takes a corner, but you needn't take the same!"

"Haw!" Clyde burst out, but Mary turned suddenly as lofty and cool as a lady. She put her hand on Jonathan's arm.

"We'll go out now. Do you see to Artie, Clyde," she said. Jonathan felt her small hand strong upon his arm, and as they went out, "A downright coarse woman—as if you'd look at a serving wench, Jonathan!" she murmured as he lifted the blanket curtain.

He could see in the morning the name of the tavern. A long, broad shingle was nailed across the door, and upon it

was painted in white the letters "American House." Above it
upon a square board was a stiff-looking gilt fowl meant to be
an eagle. The rain continued to fall. The house was full of
people, for at breakfast seven men came down a ladder from
the attic. To wash they held a tin basin under the streaming
eaves and brought it in. Jonathan, after a few questions which
always brought laughter, asked no more, but watched to see
what others did. Thus he waited, and in his turn caught rain
water and washed Maggie's face and hands and caught
again and took the basin in to his mother. She, he perceived
the moment he saw her, was in a mood of black despair.

Mary had spoken to Mrs. Drear about a house, and Mrs.
Drear had laughed.

"Lord love you, dear," she said. "Houses don't grow here—
they have to be made."

"You mean there isn't a house to be had in the town?"
Mary asked.

"There ain't but six houses besides ours," Mrs. Drear said.
"Some day we're goin' to be a big town, but everything's got
to begin, I guess."

Mary did not answer. She had got up early and had dressed
herself neatly and had seen to the children. Artie was a little
better. But she had gone into the kitchen for hot milk and
what she saw had sickened her. A tumbled dirty pallet was
still on the floor, and the girl Jennet was sauntering about her
business of breakfast, her face unwashed and her red hair
uncombed.

"I shan't eat until I'm in my own house," she told Clyde
when she was back.

He was sitting on the edge of the bed dressing himself.
"Don't be so choice, Mary," he said. "They've fed me when I
hadn't food."

"Clyde, how much money have you?" she demanded.

"None—or as good as none," he said frankly. "But I've got
the promise of work. Drear's puttin' up a chicken coop and
says I'm to do it."

"You!" she cried. "You never drew a saw in your life."

"I can try it," he retorted. "It don't take brains to draw a
saw. Besides, Jonathan s'all help me."

She did not answer. Jonathan must help indeed until they
were started.

"I must get a house," she said, half to herself. "But how?"

"We'll build one of sod," he replied.

"Sod!" she repeated.

"Sod," he said firmly.

It was at this moment that Jonathan came in, bringing the tin basin of rain water.

"Jonathan," she said, turning to him piteously, "there's only sod for houses here—"

He had not the least idea of what a sod house was, but he cried out with all his heart to comfort her.

"Never you mind, Mother! It'll be the best sod house there is!"

They lived eleven days and a half at American House. On the second day the rain cleared, but they were still imprisoned by mud. The door of the inn looked out upon an empty square, and from this square the grass was worn away by wagons and the feet of horses and oxen, so that now it was a field of thick dark mud. Once or twice, sometimes as much as four times a day, a wagon straggled up the road, painted with mud. The beasts that pulled it were caked to the eyes, and sometimes the man leading them had fallen and was an image of mud from which his eyes looked out whitely like a ghost's. The inn grew unbearably crowded. Quarreling and laughter and the crying of children crowded the air with noise. Jennet was silent with endless work until Jonathan took to carrying in the bowls of food for her and setting them down on the table. In a moment the food was gone. He could not see how it was that these men ate so quickly. The only silence of the day was while they ate, throwing bread into their mouths, gulping down great mugs of coffee, between dishes of meat and potatoes. They took the hunks of salt pork with their hands to chew off huge bites, and he was sick at the sight. Seeing Jamie imitating them, he cuffed him sharply over the left ear.

His father saw it. "What're you beatin' Jamie for?" he cried at Jonathan.

"I wasn't doin' anything," Jamie muttered sourly.

"You know what you were doin'," Jonathan said. "You know what Mother don't like!"

"And I say if there's beatin' to be done, I'll do it," his father retorted.

For answer Jonathan took his plate beside Ruth and ate slowly and fastidiously, cutting his meat before he ate and drinking his coffee quietly. He longed for a cup of tea, but there was none. Everybody drank mugs full of bitter black coffee sweetened with molasses. It made him gag unless he sipped it slowly.

In these few days he had completely forgotten school and books. He had first to find the means of living at all— somehow the shelter of a home and privacy and quiet. Artie was still in bed, a little better, or so he seemed. Ruth stayed with her mother, away from the roughness of men coming and going. But Jamie was excited and happy. He hung about the men listening to them and copied their swagger and their ways. And no one could stop Maggie from running about meddling everywhere. In these few days she had grown pert and willful because they all laughed at her and Jennet spoiled her with food and made her bold to disobey Jonathan so that one day when he told her to come and be cleaned she cried, "No—no!" and ran to Jennet, and Jennet laughed. He went glowering to find his mother.

"If we don't get away from here," he said, "Jamie and Maggie will be out of hand forever."

His mother sighed. "I wish I'd never come," she said.

"But if Dad was set on America?" Jonathan asked.

"I'd have let him have it without me," she replied. "Almost," she added, seeing his look.

By the seventh day the mud was drying and shrinking in cracks. Underneath the thick skin of its surface was still softness, but the skin held. By noon of that day the travelers were gone, and there were a few hours before night brought three more men, cattle drivers from Texas who had driven cattle up the trail to the Northeast.

In the afternoon's silence Jonathan sat down on a bench by a window in the big room and took a small book from his pocket. For the moment there was nothing to do, and in the emptiness he was aware of a yearning to read and to think. He had brought a few books with him, and this one was Virgil. He had not opened a book since he left Dentwater. He had scarcely opened this one when Jennet came in. She had taken off her kitchen apron and had brushed her red curly hair and washed her face. She sat down at the long trestle table, yawned, and laid her head upon her arms.

"I could sleep till my hair turns white," she said.

She had not spoken to him since the first night. He saw her

swinging pots on and off the stove, mopping the tables with sweeps of her long arm and a dirty rag in her hand.

"You have to work hard," Jonathan said politely.

"Dog hard," she agreed carelessly. Then she sat up. "Want to know what I'm goin' to do?"

"What?" Jonathan answered, seeing that she expected it.

"I want to go West, clear to Californy," she said. "Everybody's goin' West."

"But what would you do?" he inquired, astonished.

For answer she lifted her head and looked at him from under her drooped eyelids. Her pale eyes, as clear and pale a green as liquid shadows of trees upon water, gleamed out at him.

"You'd like to know, would you!" she said. "Well, I won't tell you!"

She got up and sauntered to the door and stood there leaning against the jamb, looking out. And he, bending his head over his book, wondered what she meant and did not dare to ask.

Mary, before dawn, urged Clyde in his bed, "It's a fair mornin', Clyde. Hadn't you better get up and have the start on the day?"

He was an incurably late sleeper, one of those who, slow to sleep at night, seem to find their midnight when others are rising for work.

"Let me be," he grunted without moving.

She lay a few moments longer until every muscle in her body ached to be up and at work. She could endure it no more, and she rose. The moment she stepped out of bed Ruth sat up, and Maggie rolled from the same pallet to the floor and picked herself up, and fell again, tangled in her long nightgown. Jamie was already up and outdoors somewhere. Arthur stirred and called out faintly, "S'all I have a drink, Mother?"

"You shall, this minute," Mary replied. He was better these last two days, but how weak! She longed to give him an egg, but there was not a fowl to be found in Median. She could not believe it, but so it was.

"I always aimed to get some hens," Mrs. Drear had said, "but I ain't got around to it."

Mary, hearing such a confession of shiftlessness, determined the moment she had her own roof to find a few hens somehow.

"Clyde!" she called sharply. The sun was streaming in the small window. "It'll be noon!"

Two days of full time, Clyde had said, and they could get up a sod house, that was, provided she did not have her notions. A sod house could be laid up rough or smooth, he said, sixteen feet wide and twenty feet long.

"I want it smooth," she said without waiting to find out what "smooth" was, "and there must be four rooms to it, Clyde, for decency."

This was what he called "notions." "Dang you, Mary," he said, "you can't be finer nor everybody else in America. It makes 'em mad. Why, nobody's got four rooms in a sod house in Median."

She had finally agreed that, for the present, if he would do it quickly, she would manage on the two rooms. Jonathan will help me, she thought privately.

She watched Clyde scramble out of bed and into his clothes. He could be so active and quick when he was awake, but half-asleep he moved as though he were drunk. She hurried out to see to his breakfast.

In the other room Jonathan was ready and dressed in his oldest clothes. "The horses are ready, Mother," he said. "Where's Dad? I've hitched 'em to the plow."

"He'll be along as quick as I can make him," she replied. "Where's Jamie? He's to help."

"So I told him," Jonathan said. She went on into the kitchen, and he let her go without telling her that half an hour earlier he had pulled Jamie out of a wagon going West. The boy had hidden under the big cover and had been found at the last minute by the owner, a tall New Englander. He had not let Jamie know himself discovered. Instead, grinning slightly, he had gone to find Jonathan.

"Reckon I've got some of your property by mistake," he said.

Jonathan, following him, saw Jamie crouching behind a small bureau among mattresses, pots, a clock, and bundles of clothes. He reached in and with an arm suddenly strong pulled the boy out and clapped him hard over the head.

"What are you in there for?" he asked severely.

"I don't want to stay here," Jamie said. His round face was red. "I want to go West to where the gold is."

"Gold!" Jonathan said scornfully. He held Jamie firmly by the collar and slid him back to the inn and sat him down on the doorstep.

"Think of our mother!" he said, and met Jamie's rebellious stare with a gaze so stern that Jamie's eyes fell.

"Get over to the barn," Jonathan went on, "and see if the horses are fed. Mr. Drear says we can borrow them and his plow today." He did not take his eyes from Jamie until he disappeared into the sod-house barn where the Drears had once lived. To think of Jamie, wanting to go West, like that girl Jennet! As if we wasn't at the ends of earth already, he thought, before his mother came back, and went outside to wait in the sunshine.

7

CLYDE, DRIVING THE HORSES, PUSHED THE PLOW DEEP INTO the sod and then looked behind him.

"Dang the beasts," he said to Jonathan. "They're cuttin' the furrows everyhow." He stopped and wiped his forehead.

"Give me a try," Jonathan said. He had hardly been able to endure the wavering of the furrows. Drear had told him the furrows must be even deep and even wide, or the house would be crazy. He handed his spade to his father and gave a sharp look to Jamie, who was piling the sod squares up on the float. In a little while there would be more help. Henry Drear had promised to come as soon as his chores were done, and three more men he could bring later in the day.

"I'll take spade, then," Clyde said. " 'Twill be easier to trust my own brains instead of beasties."

Jonathan took the reins and held them tightly, forcing the horses to slowness. They were young, and the morning air and sunshine made them gay, and there was grass green beneath their feet. He held them mercilessly to work.

His mother, when they left her at the door, had said to him quietly so only he could hear, "Keep them to work, son, else we'll never get the house done."

"I will, Mother," he had promised.

In his mind he understood the process of this building with the earth. He had talked it over with the Drears, asking a question now and then, and he had gone out to the old sod-house barn and studied it, and walked a mile down the quaking surface of the drying road to look at a sod house. A woman was hanging out clothes and stared at him.

"Do you mind if I look at the house?" he asked politely. "My dad's building, we're newcomers, and I want to see how they're done."

She was ready and eager for talk and led him in. He had been sickened with what he saw in the squalid windowless hole, but he said nothing. No reason why there shouldn't be windows in a sod house, he thought, nor why filth should lie on the floor. It's these folks.

Nevertheless, he determined as he took pains to drive his furrows deep and straight that they would have four windows somehow.

"Don't never build against the river hill," the woman had chattered. "The rattlesnakes come out. My ol' man built us a dugout on the river bank so's it would be handy to fetch water, and soon as we lit a fire the snakes came out. We moved quick, I kin tell you!" She laughed and showed her snaggy teeth.

"It's not to be by the river," he said briefly, and wondered if by a river she meant the sluggish little brook that crept south of Median under some small reedy trees.

The first day it did not rain his mother had stood looking over the endless grassy plain in which Median stood.

"Where are all the trees?" she had asked, bewildered by their lack.

"Why, there's the cottonwoods," Mrs. Drear had said, and made them sound like a forest.

"We'll plant trees, Mother," he had said.

"It's grass country, you'll find," Mrs. Drear replied.

But he was going to plant trees somehow about his mother's house.

"Does your floor always puddle?" he asked the slatternly woman.

"Only in spring thaws or so be it rains hard in a summer shower," she replied carelessly.

"Well, good-by," he said at last, and went away thinking he

had learned more from her what he did not want than what he did. And with his father he chose a site on Henry Drear's land, two acres whose rent was to be paid in such labor as Drear might ask. Clyde was very lordly about it.

"If I be horse tradin', as I s'all be come good weather," he said largely, "Jonathan'll fill the obligations."

The site was a little far from the road, but it stood high enough, though not a hill, to run off water and have no puddled floors. A little far, but Henry Drear said certainly, "Another year or two like Median's growing, and it'll be the middle of the town."

The sun beat down by nine o'clock, and Clyde sat down to rest, groaning and grunting.

"Seems a lively long time afore the men come," he said.

Jonathan did not answer. He had never loved the earth, and even in England plowing the small fields had been toil. Here a field stretched to the sky, and he liked a limit to everything. Yet to plow these furrows and cut them into squares and lift them in flat, solid mats of substance was good work. It was the air, perhaps. This air cleared the brain and fed the blood like food. It was clean and swept by the wind. He could even see the wind here. It began far away in a ripple of light on the long even grass and came rushing on like waves upon the sea, fresh and full of power, wave after wave.

"Is there always wind here, Dad?" he asked, watching it.

"Always," Clyde replied. "And wait till it ties itself into knots in a cyclone! A whirligig of a thing a cyclone is, grabbin' the earth and pullin' at the sky and movin' both." He took out his pipe as he talked. "A big large thing the wind is here," he said, "like everything else in America."

Jonathan did not answer. Across the grass he saw Henry Drear and three men coming, and he was ashamed to have them see his father sit smoking so early in the day's labor.

"Take the horses again, Dad," he said abruptly. "I'll lend a hand with Jamie."

But to his anger a few moments later Jamie was gone. He had taken the chance of the men's coming to slip away from Jonathan's eyes and run through the grass toward the town. Jonathan saw him and shouted, but Jamie did not pause.

"I'll go after him," he said firmly.

"No, you won't," Clyde said. "Leave him—he's too small for such work anyway."

The men were there. One of them was leading a team of mules, and Jonathan saw that which put everything else out of his mind. One of the men was black.

"Samuel Hasty, miller—come last year from Vermont," Harry Drear was saying, "and Lew Merridy, storekeeper and his mules, and this here's Stephen Parry."

"Pleased to meet you," Samuel Hasty said. He was a small man with a long nose on a long face.

"Glad to see you," Lew Merridy said heartily, putting out his hand to Clyde and then to Jonathan.

But the black man did not step forward or put out his hand. "Howdy, suh," he said in a soft bass voice and at once began to work, lifting the three-foot strips of sod to the float.

"Well, dang it, how the town grows!" Clyde said.

"Median grows," Henry Drear agreed. He spat into the grass. "She doubles her population every year or two. Ten years ago when I put up American House at the crossroads I was the only white man in a hundred miles, I reckon. Now they's a hundred people here, ain't there, Hasty?"

"A hundred and three," Samuel Hasty said.

"Twins was born last night in my house," Lew said shyly.

"A hundred and five, by God!" Drear roared. "Damn it, Lew, you're a good citizen!"

None of them were working except the black man, who said not a word; and Jonathan, feeling young and unnoticed, began to help him. He could not keep from looking at Stephen Parry. He had never been close to a black man before. When his father had written to them in England of Negroes and Indians, his mother had sighed, "The country's full of savages." But they had seen very few Negroes and as yet no Indians. Now he watched secretly the strangeness of black skin upon a human frame. But there was nothing savage in this man, he thought. His skin was not coal black, either. There was a light in it. He was the color of chocolate, and his head was handsome. His hands were most strange, so dark-fleshed, but the palms a pale, dead pink. Jonathan was shy of him and tried not to be.

"It's good of you to come and help us," he said stiffly.

"Folks has been kind to me, too," the man said in his soft deep voice. "Folks is mighty kind around hyeah."

"Have you been here long?" Jonathan asked.

The man hesitated, then answered, "The endurin' time of the big war I was hyeah." He hesitated again and saw the men were not listening to him, only this slight, gentle-faced young man. "I run away, suh, in de early days of de wah. I was a slave, suh."

Jonathan looked at him, revulsion in his bosom. A slave!

"I am glad you ran away," he said indignantly.

"We all free now," the man replied quietly.

"Float's full!" Henry Drear shouted, and Merridy began to hitch his horses to the sledlike frame. He smiled at Jonathan, a kind, comprehending smile.

"Want to come along and help unload?" he said.

"Certainly, sir," Jonathan replied.

He walked beside the float as it slid over the long grass.

"Think you're goin' to like the country?" Lew Merridy asked.

"I don't know," Jonathan replied.

Merridy looked surprised and then laughed. "Sure you will," he said. "It's a great country for a young fellow like you—greatest country in the world."

Jonathan did not answer. He was not used yet to the talkativeness of the Americans, nor to their shameless boasting. England was a great country, too, he told himself, but he would not say so. It makes things common-like to talk about 'em, he thought, and worked in steady silence until Lew Merridy gave up talk and whistled instead, a whistle as loud and clear as a wild bird's.

That night the house was drawn to its shape and guided by the North Star. They had worked all day plowing, cutting, and carrying the strips of sod to where the house was to be. Then, when the North Star appeared in the darkening sky, Henry Drear drew a line direct from its point and paced off twenty feet and drove in the stakes.

"There," he said, "the house sets right. It's straight to the Northern Star."

They went back to the inn, tired and hungry.

"Come in and have a drink," Clyde said at the door to the men who had helped him. "It's ill luck to a house not to drink when the foundation's decided."

Only Stephen Parry shook his head to refuse coming in.

"Thank you, suh, but I'll be gettin' along," he said. He touched his old straw hat to them all and went away.

"Good man, Steve," Henry Drear said as they entered the inn. "He's as good as anybody and he knows it, but he don't press it. Kansas is a free state and all that, but a nigger's got no business settin' down by a white man anywheres."

"Turns the stomach," Samuel Hasty agreed.

They sat down and from somewhere in his pockets Clyde brought out a coin. Drear shouted and Jennet came in, her hands white with flour.

"Rye," her father said without looking up.

"How can I git it in the middle of the bread?" she demanded.

"I'll get it for you," Jonathan said and rose.

"All right, then," she said.

He went after her and saw that her red hair, which he had never seen otherwise than tumbled upon her head, was brushed and braided in a long braid down her back to her knees.

"What wonderful long hair you have," he said, surprised. He had indeed never seen such long gleaming stuff. "It looks fine."

"I had time today to clean myself," she said shortly, but her face was not angry. She thrust out her chin at a low door. "In there," she said, "rye's in a keg. You can dip it out into a jug that stands on top."

She went back to her bread, and he went to the lean-to and dipped up the whisky. It smelled so strong it was fire in his nostrils, but when he took it to the tables, the men drank it like tea.

"Taste it," Clyde ordered him.

He poured out a glass, and Jonathan put it to his lips and felt his mouth go raw. He swallowed hastily, and his stomach curled. His eyes were full of tears, and he longed to rush for water, but they were laughing at him.

"What's the matter, boy?" his father roared.

"You'll have to learn to take rye down," Drear said, "else what'll you do when you get fever and snakebites?"

Samuel Hasty said nothing, but he laughed a silent mean laughter that was hateful. But Lew Merridy got up and fetched a dipperful of water and handed it to Jonathan.

"Drink it," he said, "and don't mind laughin'. Folks have to laugh at somethin' or other here."

Jonathan drank the water and cooled himself.

"Now take another," Clyde ordered him.

But Jonathan stood up. "No, I won't, thanks, Father," he said, and without waiting walked away into the other room to find his mother.

She was sitting by the bed where Arthur lay, and she was mending a torn garment. She looked up when he came in.

"How did it go?" she asked.

"Fair," he said. "Tomorrow we'll begin the walls." He frowned. "Did Jamie come back?" he asked.

"He did, and I let him go out with a man shooting hares," she said. "Jack rabbits, they call 'em here," she added.

"He gave me the slip," Jonathan said.

Mary smiled. "He's only a child," she replied.

"He's twelve," Jonathan said doggedly, "and at twelve I knew better."

"Oh, don't be so preaching," Mary said suddenly.

He was very tired, and he felt hurt to the core of his being. This was the one thing in her that he could never understand, that in the midst of his doing all for her, she could defend Jamie or his father for the very lack of what he was for her. It made him feel forever unsure of her and insecure in his being. He was angry now, but the fear made him mild. He was silent for a minute, then he searched for something to say to please her and found it.

"I'll tell you something pretty, Mother," he said. "It was dark and we set the house by the North Star."

She looked up, her face quickened and lightened with perception of poetry. "Oh, very pretty, Jonathan!" she cried warmly, and in her pleasure drew him near again.

By dawn they were working. Now the house was begun. The foundation was dug, not deep, for earth would join to earth by rain and snow. Into the foundation the first sod bricks were laid and others laid upon them three deep, except where the door was to face the south.

"Now put the cracks full of earth, and then two more layers of sod," Henry Drear ordered them. They all worked fast and hard today, and there was very little talk. Stephen

Parry stood at one corner and another, keeping them true, and shifting a sod if it did not perfectly break a joint.

"Three layers and then crosswise," Drear said sharply to Clyde, about to lay a fourth the wrong way. "Allow the window when you put up two more," he said.

Jonathan spoke. "There's to be four windows, please."

Every man stopped, astounded.

"Four windows!" Drear repeated, stupefied. "Why, boy, four windows will gather in the wind until the roof'll blow away."

Jonathan felt his face burn with shy blood. "My mother likes sun and light," he said stubbornly.

They looked at Clyde, and he spat on his hands. "It's folly," he declared. "I say build it as is best and let her lump it."

"She shan't, Father," Jonathan declared. "A sod house is bad enough, but it'll be a cave if there's not but one single solitary window."

"Why, a sod house is nothing wrong," Merridy said. "Cool in summer and warm in winter! I was born and raised in a sod house, and if you prop up the roof so it don't fall in with water and snow, it's a good house. But Drear's right about wind. Two windows is plenty—one to a room."

They made two windows and, building until night, had the house ready for its roof. Jonathan lingered by it after his father and the men were gone. The place looked solitary and without hope in the evening light. It would be hard to say whether it was new and had sheltered no one yet, or whether it was roofless from desertion. He walked about it sadly. It would have wooden window frames tomorrow, and there would be rafters to hold up the weight of the sod roof. Stephen Parry was to make the woodwork, and Samuel Hasty had lent the lumber, to be paid for half in cash when his father had it and half in labor at the busiest time at the mill. "And as soon as I have a penny of my own," Jonathan planned, "I'll put in a wooden floor."

The stone cottage in Dentwater had seemed poor enough when they were in it and knew themselves the poorest people in the village. But it was a rich man's house to this earthen heap, and yet here they would be as well off as most of Median, where only the inn, the store, and the mill were even of wood. But he was not yet an American. It gave him no cheer that most of them were like himself. Instead he felt it a doleful thing to think that this was true. It shut a door to somewhere better.

He went tramping back to the inn full of this dole. The ground was solid enough under his feet now, baked by the sun. He walked down the road, which was Median's only street, to where it ran around the empty barren square, which was the center of whatever Median was.

If I must stay here, he thought, I'll put trees there, too.

❧ 8 ❧

THE QUESTION OF WHETHER HE MUST STAY BECAME HIS inner being, but he never revealed it. Stay he must now because there was no way to go. There was no money to return to England, and of what use would it be to set out across the endless prairies? Median must be his life.

Somewhere in his mother he comprehended, by that delicate inexplicable communication which he had with her, that her own inner being was in despair as wild as his own. But if it was, she said not a word of it. She set herself to the house as soon as the roof was on and before glass was in the windows. Glass they would have as soon as Lew Merridy could get it fetched, but half of Median had no glass. Their windows were curtained with buffalo skins or old blankets.

"Leave the grass on the floor until we get wood," she told Clyde. "It'll be cleaner than mud."

Wood and glass she would have, and if she had to live in a sod house she would show everybody how to do it. The children would be brought up properly, too, and with their manners, and not rough the way Clyde had got to be. Jonathan'll help me, she thought.

Thus she made in a very few days a sort of home out of the earth. Mrs. Drear gave her an old bed from the inn, and one by one women she had not seen came over the quarter of a mile of grass and brought her a pot, a plate of food, a mended blanket, a wooden stool. From Merridy's General Store she had six wooden boxes. The store was the one place in Median where for an hour she could forget the limitless plains and sky which frightened her whenever she looked at them. She was

amazed at the store. Even in Dentwater there was not a
better collection of goods—all thrown together, it was true.

"If I could put my hands to it," she told Jonathan, "I could
make a place you could find something. People drive for
miles, Merridy says, to buy of him, and wagons stop for food
and clothing and blankets, and everybody has to wait till he
sorts out what they want."

"There's an idea, Mother," Jonathan said. "I'll hire myself
to him if he'll have me."

"You can't," Clyde said. "You're promised to Drear to pay
the rent of land and his horses to plow up a garden."

"I thought you were to work out for Drear," his wife
retorted.

"Me?" Clyde cried. "When the chicken coop's done I'm
workin' now, and it won't be but a matter of five days or six
for that, I s'all go and homestead somewheres. Land we must
get while it's free and before all the greedy ones has got it. It's
late now. Ten years earlier would have been better, and by
now I might ha' been a rich landowner with my cattle and my
horses. I s'all—"

"Oh, you!" Mary cried bitterly. "Shut up, do, Clyde!"

He went off in one of his sudden huffs, and Mary sewed
hard for a moment on a curtain she was making out of a flour
bag. Mrs. Drear had given her a heap, washed and bleached
and ready to use.

"Go to see Mr. Merridy tomorrow, son," she told Jonathan. He was putting up a shelf above the deep sod fireplace.
A ticklish job it was, too, for he had to drive two short, stout
blocks of wood into the thick sod wall to hold it. But he was
learning how to hold and use tools he had not needed in
England; and Stephen Parry, whose home was a dugout on
the side of the river bank below Median, had lent him a
hammer and saw and given him some nails. Thus he had
nailed together boxes to make a closet for their clothes and
upon boxes had nailed three boards for a table, and with a
broken scythe from Drear's barn he had smoothed the inner
walls of the house.

Labor was all he had to exchange for all else they needed,
and he worked until he fell upon his straw mattress at night.
Mindful of his need for a place of his own, his mother had
hung a blanket across a corner and put his mattress upon
boards behind it, and above it he had driven in wooden blocks

for a shelf for his books and some pegs to hold his clothes. It was almost as dark by day as it was by night, unless he lit a candle. Sometimes he remembered that he used to see from his window the Irish Sea and the sails of ships white in the sunshine.

But on that next day there was no doubt that he must hire himself wherever he could for best pay. It was halfway between morning and noon when Mary, hanging the curtains she had made, saw out of the window a wagon coming near. It was Henry Drear's wagon. She knew its red body, and in a moment she would see the yellow letters painted on its side, "American House." When it came near enough for that, she saw something else. It was Clyde, propped up on the seat and looking as if he were dead.

"Whatever now!" she muttered and put down her curtain and went hurrying out.

There he was, fainted sure enough, but not dead. Henry Drear was holding him up, and the horses stopped before the house.

"He's cut his leg," Henry Drear said impatiently. "A more orkward feller never was born, I told my wife yestiddy, watchin' him handle the ax."

"He's never chopped his own leg!" she cried, and knew he had, for his thick woolen trouser leg was soaked with blood, and blood was trickling out of his boot.

"Nigh off, I reckon," Drear said. "Is Jonathan about?"

"No, he's gone over to Merridy's this morning," Mary said; "and Jamie, of course, is never where he's wanted. Ruth!" she called.

Ruth came out. "What, Mother?" She clapped her hands to her mouth. "Dad!" she cried and stood still.

"Come here and help me, silly," Mary said. "Now, Mr. Drear, we'll hold him if you'll let him down."

Together she and Ruth took Clyde's dead weight until Drear could step down. Then he hoisted Clyde across his great shoulders.

"I'll carry him in," he said, "and I'd advise you to find Stephen Parry's wife. Some say she's a witch, but there's times you want a witch. Anyway, she sewed a man's head on again, they say, after he'd been to the gallows."

Clyde's blood was spurting, soaking into the drying grass on the floor, soaking into the straw of the mattress where Arthur lay, his blue eyes enormous. He had not said a word.

"Oh, that Jamie!" Mary cried in misery. "He's not here to send."

"I'll go for her myself," Drear said gravely. "Damn the man for a cussed baby, with an ax, but he don't look good. Tie his leg tight under the knee, Mrs. Goodliffe."

"Yes, yes," Mary moaned and tore off her apron and wrenched off the strings. "Help me, Ruth."

Henry Drear strode away, and Mary in terror wrapped the strings about Clyde's leg and cried to Ruth to hold the knot. Upon the threshold Maggie, wandering unheeded, saw a pool of bright red. She stooped carefully, being fat and unsteady, and dipped her finger in it, stared at her red finger, and then tasted it. It was not good, and she made a sickish face. But the color was irresistible, and now she dabbled in it.

Arthur called out faintly, "Mother, Maggie's playin' in Father's blood!"

"For shame, Maggie!" Mary screamed and flew to Maggie. "Wicked—wicked—wicked!" She shook the child with every word. "A wicked, unfeeling, naughty thing!" she cried and burst into angry sobs. Oh, Clyde would cut himself and maybe die and leave them helpless in the wilderness!

She sat down and for the first time since she had left England she cried aloud, and the children, seeing her, began to cry, too, Maggie loudly, Ruth in soft sobs, and Arthur in a sort of silent misery. But she paid no heed to them and cried on and on helplessly because, having once begun, she could not stop.

"Well, what's all dis to-do?" a soft voice said at the door. They looked up. Ruth stopped crying. It was the witch woman! Maggie, sitting on the floor, looked at her, astonished; but Mary saw only another woman.

"Oh, come in, if you please," she said, catching her breath. She was suddenly ashamed of herself for crying like a great baby. "My husband's cut his leg sorely, and Mr. Drear tells me you can mend anything."

"I can mend some things," Stephen Parry's wife said. She stepped in and around Maggie, smiled at her, and went to the bed and began unlacing Clyde's boot.

"Is the little feller sick, too?" she asked.

"I can't get him up," Mary said. "I don't know what's wrong with him."

The big brown woman did not answer. But Artie felt her glance upon him, warm, piercing him kindly so that he was not afraid. He stopped crying and lay still, waiting.

Steadily, quietly drawing off Clyde's boot and his woolen sock, she uncovered his wound. He had gashed himself to the bone, and the great lips of flesh hung quivering and raw. She shook her head.

"It'll be many a day befo' dis man walks," she said, "and it may be he'll never walk straight again, at dat."

She laid his leg down and took the kettle down from the fire and, opening a small package of brown paper, shook something into the tin basin which stood on a box, and poured water over it. Then, opening a closed cotton ball she had in her bundle, she took out the raw cotton and dipped it in the brew and washed the wound. Clyde muttered and groaned.

"Dang," he began, opened his eyes, and fainted again.

"I'd just as soon he didn't come to," the woman said. She took a needle and thread from a spool in her bundle and dipped them in the water; and then, as though she were sewing a rent in cloth, she drew together the lips of his wound.

They watched her silently, and then Ruth cried, "Is this how you sewed the man's head on, too?"

The woman smiled. "Honey, I didn't sew anybody's head on. They was a po' niggah down South once got slashed in the neck by some mad white folks, and he got away and hid in a swamp, and I fixed him up so he was whole again. Dat was befo' de wah."

"Oh," Ruth whispered. Her eyes were bright with questions, but she did not ask them. And when her sewing was done, the woman took some clean white strips out of her bundle and bound Clyde's leg carefully and tightly.

"Don' let him stir 'at leg," she told Mary. "He's just got to lie there. If he gets a fever, I'll come again. If he don't get a fever, he's all right." She tied up her bundle as she spoke and was ready to go.

"I do thank you, Mrs. Parry," Mary said, "and when I can, I will repay you."

"Nothin' to pay," the big woman said. "Nobody pays me for this kind of he'p. And nobody calls me Mrs. Parry. I'm just Sue." She gave them her slow, deep, peaceful smile and went away.

Jonathan walked across Median from Merridy's store and down the path toward the house. Some day this'll be a street, he thought. He felt in better spirits than he had since he left Dentwater. This morning, his shyness hidden under his usual sturdy stolidity, he had gone to Mr. Merridy and offered himself as a clerk. He came at a good moment for himself. Mr. Merridy was distracted by his wife's absence and by the prospect that for months to come the twins would take her time away from the store.

"I certainly do need somebody real bad," he said mournfully, looking about the disordered dusty room. It was being further disordered by farmers and their wives who had come in for Saturday buying and, impatient of being waited upon, were turning over garments and taking down goods from the shelves.

"Hi there, how much is them, Lew?" one after another shouted.

"Comin'!" he roared back and went on talking to Jonathan. "Even Katie—that's my oldest, and only thirteen—she's tied hand and foot to the babies till my wife gets around again. I tell you, you wouldn't realize the difference between twins and a solitary child. You ain't ready for it—it's a shock."

"Yes, sir," Jonathan said.

A thin, dark-haired little girl in a dress of faded red-and-green cotton plaid came to the inner door and said primly, "Papa, Mamma wants you."

"All right, Katie," Mr. Merridy said. He turned back to Jonathan. "There, that's the way it is. Kin you begin now?"

"Yes, sir," Jonathan said.

The little girl at the door waited. "Papa, are you coming?" she called. But she was looking at Jonathan from quiet, shrewd hazel eyes. She was not at all pretty, he thought, and forgot her.

"What can I do for you, sir?" he began at once to a stooped old man who stood without moving beside a barrel of crackers.

"Two pounds of them," he said, "and a side of salt pork and some beans and black molasses."

Between customers he tried to tidy the counters and sort the tumbled dry goods. It was noon before he knew it.

"You're welcome to a bite here," Merridy said.

"I'll just go back and tell my mother about the job, thanks," he replied. "I'll be back in an hour."

So he had struck over the path to the sod house which he could not yet call home. And yet, as he drew near, he imagined that he could see the touch of his mother even upon that rough earthen mass. Stephen Parry had put in the glass as soon as it came, and it shone in the two windows, and there was an edge of white curtain. From behind the house he caught the flutter of garments hanging on the line, and was surprised because his mother did not usually wash on Saturday. But he could not see what the garments were. She would never hang her wash near the road. "Family wash tells everything," she always said. "How many you have, how poor you are, and if you're good at your mending or not. I don't want strangers knowing all about us."

When he walked into the house she was on her hands and knees, chipping at the sod on the ground.

"Why, Mother!" he cried.

"Your father's bled all over," she said. "He's cut himself terrible, and there's nothing for it but to get rid of this grass."

"However did he cut himself?" Jonathan asked, stupefied.

"With the ax, chopping at Drear's, of course," his mother replied shortly. She kept on hacking at the sod.

"Don't, Mother," Jonathan said. He took the stump of a scythe away from her and down on his knees hacked out the stains of his father's blood.

On the bed he saw his father lying, but he did not speak to him at once. His father would cut himself and be past work, he thought bitterly. That was all he needed to do now when his work was all he had to give them.

"Well, Jonathan," Clyde said feebly, "there you be."

"Hello, Father," Jonathan said.

"I'm hurt terrible," Clyde said.

"Sorry for that, Father," Jonathan replied. He was ashamed of his coldness and went over to his father's side and stood looking down on him.

" 'Twas the ax," his father groaned. He looked sunken-eyed and white from loss of blood. "A long-handled, unhandy thing, flingin' itself everyway in your hands. I had just drove in a post for the corner, and the dang thing turned on me like a beast bitin', and first thing I know I was spoutin' blood. I couldn't no more'n get to Drear's door and stand there roarin', when I dropped."

"Too bad, Father," Jonathan said. He must not show disgust, for this was his father. But silence for once was hard. He leaned over and gathered Arthur's little body and lifted him.

"Come and sit on my knee a bit, Artie," he said. "Your wee bones must be tired layin'."

"Lying," Mary said abruptly from the stove.

"It don't matter here, I think, Mother," Jonathan said. "There's nobody to know the difference between right and wrong ways of talkin'."

"All the more reason to be right," she said sharply. Then she softened. "Jamie's getting clever at catching hares," she said. "Until I get fowl it's a help, too."

"Where is he?" Jonathan asked.

"He can't stay away from the wagons going West," she said. "Likely he's up there by the road, watchin' 'em. That's one thing about Median—he can't come to much evil."

Clyde interrupted them. "Jonathan, I reckon you'll have to finish the coop for me."

Jonathan cuddled Arthur in his arms. "I can't, Father, unless on Sundays. I have a job at Merridy's."

"No, Jonathan, never!" Mary turned a bright face toward him.

"Yes, steady, Mother. Wage we haven't talked yet, but I shall stick up for what's right and then do my best."

"Oh, good son, Jonathan!" his mother cried softly, and to his astonishment she came to him and kissed the top of his head as he sat. Then, because she was embarrassed, she bent and kissed Arthur and said, "Now, my own, you shall have something to make you better. Jonathan will bring it you."

And Maggie, seeing all this as she played on the sod, bawled out, "Kiss—kiss!"

"Oh, you," Mary said, laughing. "You must always have everything, too!" She lifted the heavy child and kissed her on the cheeks and set her down again and turned back to Jonathan. "Oh, Jonathan, it's a terrible helplessness for a woman to know nothing's to come in at the end of the week."

He could scarcely bear in these days his mother's dashes of

bravery and her moments of trembling. This was trembling, and something trembled in him, too. He said quickly, "We can take it in goods or cash as we need." And then, softened because he could do something for her, he said to his father, "I never made a fowl coop in my life, but I'll try, come Sunday, Dad; and this afternoon I'll tell Mr. Drear so. And now, Artie boy, I must eat and get back to work." He laid Arthur down tenderly beside his father and went to the table and sat down on a box that served for a chair.

Work was a good word to have upon the tongue, and he savored it with his food as he ate.

The store stood opposite the hotel and across the empty square. It was a frame building, made of planks nailed on a wooden skeleton and then covered outside with unpainted shingles and on the inside with thin lath and plaster, whitewashed. To Jonathan the shape of the building was like the dragon he had once seen in a picture of St. George and the Dragon at the vicarage in Dentwater. It had been a dragon with a great scaly ruff that stood up around the head but its body had been small. From the front the dragon had looked a terror, but behind it was nothing. He thought of this often with dry, secret amusement as he approached the store from the side each day. A great false front the store had, a high structure of painted boards, single thick, and across it painted in big letters "Merridy's General Store," and under that, in letters almost as big, "Median." From the front, with the two show windows for eyes and the door, always open, for a mouth, the store looked something stupendous. But behind this painted front was the boxlike building, an oblong for the store, cut off in the back to make three rooms for Lew Merridy's family. At almost any moment in the day customers could hear coming from those rooms a thin wailing duet. It prompted the kind to ask, "How's the twins, Lew?"

"Fine," he said. "Savin' their always wantin' more nourishment than their mother can give. What they need is a nanny goat."

From these rooms Katie came and went, a sharp, efficient child, quick to notice if Jonathan put a thing down where he had not taken it up. And yet he got on with her well enough in a curious meager way, with little speech and some dry joking. She was quick to see what he meant to do and to help him when she saw. The windows were his bane. Lew Merridy used them for dumps and leftovers, and this was an offense to Jonathan. He began on his fourth morning to carry out a plan he had been making in his mind from the first moment. It was midweek, and not many farmers came in, nor women; and he drew back the soiled gray half-curtains that separated the windows from the shop.

"What you at, Jonathan?" Mr. Merridy inquired. He sat on a keg of whisky reading a two-weeks-old newspaper that had reached him this morning by mail.

"Shall you mind, sir, if I clean a bit?" Jonathan answered.

"Naw," Merridy answered, his eyes on the paper, "though you'll find, Jonathan, it ain't no use to put time and stren'th in it. Kansas blows right thoo anything."

He forgot Jonathan and read the fine print, frowning. "Nigger population in Kansas is goin' up somethin' terrible," he said. "It's this talk of 'forty acres and a mule' is doin' it. Exodusters, they're called."

Jonathan, his head wreathed in dust, thought of Stephen Parry and his wife. I could do with more of them, he thought, and was about to say so when he sneezed violently, and when he came to himself Merridy had gone on. He began sorting everything into piles as neatly as he could—tobacco, lamp wicks, chipped dishes, candles, old copper, buttons, nails, yards of sheeting yellowed with rain from a leak, a heap of small mothy skins of rabbits and moles and badger brought in for barter. He whistled under his breath as he worked to keep himself from speaking out what he thought. All this refuse!

"They's a feller named Buffalo Bill," Mr. Merridy announced, "he's hired to shoot buffalo meat for the railroad out West, and he's killed four thousand and more buffalo—a regular David and Goliath!"

Jonathan looked up. "Shall we get a railroad in Median, Mr. Merridy?"

"Shore wish we would," Merridy replied. "I would git my stock in easy, and the town would boom. Why, some towns around hyere when the railroad skips 'em just pick up and move the whole shebang to where the railroad is, they're so anxious not to miss it—put the town on wheels and go—"

"Well, I never!" Jonathan said simply. He was sweeping the window floor, and now Mr. Merridy himself sneezed and looked stern.

"I swear it ain't healthy to stir up all that old dirt," he said.

"I'll sprinkle it," Jonathan said. He took up a pail and went to the pump outside. Katie was there pumping, her thin arms flailing up and down.

"Here, I'll do it," he said good-naturedly and pumped her pail full first. "Wouldn't have a bit of rag to scrub with, would you?" he asked.

"Scrub what?" she demanded.

"Windows," he replied.

"Ma was goin' to clean them windows," she said, "if she hadn't had twins."

"Those windows," Jonathan said gently. But she did not understand, and he laughed and went back. A queer sharp female thing, he thought, brown like a scrawny hen. But a moment later she came, a rag in her hand.

"It's hard to find a rag since the twins came," she said. "We've used everything up for diapers."

She stood, watching while he sprinkled the dusty boards and swept. Then she dipped the rag into the water. "I'll scrub it up," she said.

He watched her, amused by her body moving in little quick hops as she worked. Like a grasshopper, he thought.

"They's some talk here of Median bein' a county seat," Mr. Merridy said. "Well, why not? We got a river that don't go dry, and we're at a crossroads. We're bound to grow— growin' all the time. Why, we've trebled in the last two years! Drear was the first, then I built my store, and look at the way folks are beginnin' to pile up!"

Jonathan doused the windowpanes.

"I wouldn't bother about them panes," Mr. Merridy said. "The first little shower will dirty 'em again."

"I'll rub them again, then," Jonathan answered peaceably.

"Katie!" Mrs. Merridy's voice rose above an outburst of dual wailing.

Katie got up from her knees. "I'll have to go," she said quickly.

"Yes, sir," Mr. Merridy mused, "Median's goin' to be a great big town."

9

MEDIAN WAS THE SMALL HEART OF A VAST BODY. THERE were days when the heart scarcely beat, and then Median seemed to Jonathan as remote from all the other parts of the earth as though it were alone upon a star. On such days few customers came in. Jennet ran in from the inn to buy saleratus, or Mrs. Drear came in for dried apples to make a pie, and perhaps through the day a straggling one or two of the other women came in for spool thread or a package of needles or a pound of coffee. His mother could not leave the sod house so long as his father could hobble no farther than the door. His leg healed, but in a wealed scar so that, as long as Clyde lived, he would limp.

Jonathan welcomed all except Jennet, but her he disliked, or thought he disliked. But it was only when she was there that he disliked her. When she stood by the counter, her face, soft and bold together, somehow shocked him. She was not bad-looking, but he hated the green glass color of her eyes, and he distrusted the way in which she spoke to him, as though she had known him all her life when they had only talked a few times.

"Hello, Jonathan, boy!" she always said carelessly.

"How do you do, Miss Jennet," he always replied in his best clerkly manner. "What can I do for you today?"

"Well, say, you can stop talking like that," she said.

He waited stiffly. He would talk as he pleased.

"Oh, heck, what do I care how you talk?" she cried discontentedly. "Give me a yard and a half of red ribbon."

"Not for yourself, I hope," he said.

'Why not for myself?" she demanded.

"Not with that red hair," he said, without knowing why, for it was none of his business.

"It's my red hair," she retorted.

"There's enough of it without red ribbons," he said.

She snatched the ribbon from his hand and tied it about her hair and made a bow over her ear. "There," she said.

He would not say it was handsome, but it was, though everybody knows a red-haired woman should never wear red.

"Anything else?" he asked coolly.

"Red calico," she said, "for a red dress. That! Eight yards."

He measured off eight yards of striped red-and-white calico, folded it, and in intense silence handed it to her. Lucky she had queer pale skin and did not freckle as most redheads did! But he would not tell her so.

"I'll come and show you the dress when I've made it," she said insolently.

He did not reply. He disliked her presence, and yet when she was gone he could not forget her. She was one of those girls whose every movement one remembered. She made him think of Constance, who had taught him to dance. But Constance was fluttery, as though she knew all the time that perhaps she was not quite nice. Jennet would not even know what niceness was. He looked thoughtfully out of the windows he kept so clean, and his eyes wandered on and on over the prairies, and he put Jennet out of his mind. The skies changed but the prairies never, except when they borrowed light and shadow from the sky. One would say not a soul lived upon that flat, endless plain.

Yet the more he looked at the prairie, the more he perceived that it was not flat at all. It rose, smooth and even, on a long, slow, steady pull westward. Walking over it day by day, he felt the earth was flat under his feet; but if he could have made steps a mile long, he would have felt the earth swirl upward. Sometimes, if the sky was cloudless at the horizon, especially at the moment of clearest twilight between sunset and night, he saw the slant of the earth against the sky, and then Median was in the middle of it. That long, level, rising plain was Median's body, and the people who came out

of it were lifeblood flowing through Median. There were two
kinds of people: those who came only once on their way to the
West, and those who stayed and came again and again; and
Lew Merridy and Jonathan were never agreed as to who
should be served first if they came together.

For there were days when the store was full of clamoring,
impatient people, anxious to get their wagons stocked and on
the trail again, and others as anxious to get food and salt and
goods to take to their homes. There was rivalry and sometimes even dislike between the two kinds of people. Those
who were going on were sure that all who did not go with
them were stolid fools, losing all for the sake of supposed
prudence; and those who stayed and built sod houses and
cleared land for farms and grew cattle and pigs and fowl and
sowed crops and planted fruit trees scorned the great windy
dreams of those who were going West.

"Hey, Jonathan!" Mr. Merridy roared, "git them folks
waited on! They're goin' to Nebrasky and got to git started!"

"Just a minute," Jonathan called back, and went on filling
the careful order of a farmer who lived ten miles across the
long grass. "Two pounds of brown sugar—yes, sir—a small
keg of black molasses, and a pound of bacon, and some
nails—yes, sir—" This man would come again and again with
the same needs. "Nice day," Jonathan said as he added the
figures.

"A mite windy," the farmer replied. His eyebrows and hair
were full of dust, and dust lay in the wrinkles of his face.
"You don't get the wind here in town the way we do. Reckon
I'll take a stick of that there peppermint for my little fellow.
He's laid up today with a stone bruise and couldn't come."

Jonathan put in two sticks.

"Thanks," the farmer said. A look passed between the two,
and Jonathan smiled. This was the sort of man he liked, a
steady chap, working his bit of the prairie. He wrapped the
order carefully and cut the string extra long. String was handy
in a house. Then he went over to a huge hairy man with a big
hat who was waiting for him and pulling at his beard furiously.

"Damned if I wasn't about ready to pull out of here," the
man shouted. "I would have if the next store wasn't three
days away. Now you just hustle yourself, young feller, and get
me corn meal—a sack of it—and a side of bacon and plenty

of beans, dried apples, a keg of black molasses, and sugar and salt and coffee—a kettle, for we busted ours last night—"

Jonathan put things together in silence. This man would go on and never be seen again. At the end of the day in the quiet of closing Mr. Merridy would say gravely, "It's like this, Jonathan. The steadies will come again and again. You can let 'em wait. But you got to wait on the others quick and git what you can out of 'em."

"But the store is built on the steadies, Mr. Merridy," Jonathan said. "I should think it's them you ought to consider first."

"Well, not necessarily," Mr. Merridy said, "not at all necessarily so, Jonathan. Their money ain't so sure, when you let 'em run bills the way I have to do, and then again I git run over with the stuff they bring in instead of cash. But the others have got to pay cash, 'cause we won't see 'em again and can say so."

"In the long run—" Jonathan began.

"You don't need to think about the long run in a country like this," Mr. Merridy interrupted. "All you need to take care of is right here and now."

"I don't agree with you, Mr. Merridy," Jonathan replied.

Mr. Merridy stared at him over his pipe. "Well, don't then!" he said. "But you're kind of young to say so like that."

"Yes, sir," Jonathan said respectfully. But walking home across that long slant of land under Median, he thought stubbornly, I'm right, and Merridy's wrong, for all that. It's the steadies that come first, anywhere.

"Jonathan's got to go in my place."

Behind his blanket curtain he heard his father say this sullenly in the night. He had taught his ears to be dull once he slipped into his own corner of the sod house, but now they picked these words out of the darkness, and he heard them. He had been aware of a low conversation between his parents, just as in the evening when he came home earlier than usual he had been aware of controversy in the atmosphere. But his young manhood demanded some sort of privacy; and, since there was none except what he and his mother made, he ignored his father's restlessness and busied himself about an improvement.

"I don't need to sleep on the floor any more, Mother," he

said cheerfully. "Somebody told me something today, quite accidental-like. Seems folk make bedsteads just with slats driven into the walls and a post. I'm going to the river to cut cottonwood."

"Well, I never," Mary said without attention. Clyde must not say before Jonathan what he had been thinking and talking all day.

Jonathan took his father's ax and put it over his shoulder. Jamie, at home because he was hungry, started after him.

"Reckon I'll come and see if there's mushrats," he said.

"Muskrats it is, Jamie," Jonathan said kindly.

"Mushrats they call it here, though," Jamie retorted.

"You don't want to get talking like them, though," Jonathan said. "Most of them never had the chance for school."

It had not occurred to him for a long time to think about school. There had been no time since they had come to Median when anything could be thought of except shelter and food and the store.

"I don't need school here," Jamie said. "There's no books to read. And if I go with you, like Dad says I'm to, I'll never need school."

"What's Dad say?" Jonathan asked quickly.

"Him and Mother," Jamie replied. "They've been jawin' all day, every time I came in they were at it. Dad says you're to homestead for him over in the West. He says he can't make it this spring if he don't start, and he can't start with his sore leg, and so you're to go and me with you."

Plains and sky lengthened before Jonathan's eyes. "And who'll feed them while I'm gone?" he inquired bitterly. "That's like Father, saying what I'm to do and giving no thought to Mother and the little ones."

"He says he'll tend 'em," Jamie replied.

"And what did Mother say?" Jonathan asked.

"She says if you go, she goes," Jamie replied. He had been a step behind his brother, but he ran and caught up with him and cried, "And oh, Jon, don't say you won't go! Let's go! I hate this little bit of a place. Everybody says it's better out West."

Jonathan looked down into Jamie's pleading face. It looked suddenly strange to him, vivid and handsome as Jamie would look when he was a young man.

"You've got freckles," he said. "You didn't have them in England."

"There's more sun here than in England, that's why," Jamie said. "It idn't fog and rain all the time."

"Rained mud when we came," Jonathan said shortly.

"I know, but when it rains it rains, and then it's done with rain, and the sun comes out hot. It idn't betwixt rain and sun all the time like it was in Dentwater."

"You like it here?" Jonathan asked.

"Lots more than England," Jamie replied. "Do you?"

"No," Jonathan said.

They were at the river now. It flowed before them almost as straight as a ditch because there were no rocks to turn the current, and the dark soil was smooth and free from obstruction, and the cottonwoods grew in clumps near the muddy water. They slid down the side of the gully, and Jonathan began his search for a tree.

"You'll go, won't you, Jonathan?" Jamie clamored.

"It'll take thinkin' of," Jonathan replied sternly. But it did not. He would not go. He would not leave his mother and the children to his father. He would not leave the small certainty of his job. He wanted to build another room to the house. And what was the use of pulling up their new roots they had scarcely put down to go to another place? "Lucky there's the Pacific Ocean to stop folks," he said sarcastically, "else they'd be goin' round and round the globe like cats chasin' their own tails."

Jamie looked up from a hole he was prodding with a stick. "There's gold out West," he said.

"If you like digging," Jonathan retorted. He began to chop at a small strong tree until in a few strokes he had it down. Henry Drear had taught him the Sunday he had finished the fowl coop how to swing an ax clear of his legs. By this time the coop was finished, the ax felt comfortable in his hands. Now he stripped the branches off quickly and chopped off two lengths and a shorter one.

"I'm done," he said.

"I'll wait a little," Jamie said. "The feller's hidin' in here." He lay on his stomach peering into the hole and did not offer to help Jonathan pull the poles to the top of the gully, and Jonathan did not ask it.

Jamie's the only one of us like Dad, he thought, and struggled up alone and home again.

They were still quarreling. He knew because talk ceased so abruptly when he entered the house. But he would notice silence no more than talk, he had made up his mind by now. If his mother could win without putting her battle on him against his father, let her. Once he began that quarrel, there would be no end to it.

"Come and help me, Ruth," he commanded his sister. She was curling Maggie's hair.

"Wish I could help you, Jonathan," Arthur said. He was sitting by the fire in their only chair, a quilt folded behind him for a pillow.

"So you shall one of these days," Jonathan said. He went behind his curtain. "Now then, you see, Ruth, the post goes here, and then I jam one pole into this wall and the long pole the other way and notch 'em into the post. Now, what you're to do for me is to sew up those sacks I brought from the store, and we'll slip the poles through before I nail 'em firm, and I'll have myself a good bed off the floor."

"Oh, Jonathan, it's clever!" Ruth cried. "Whoever told you?"

"A chap told me at the store when he came in wantin' bags," Jonathan said.

His mother came to see, and Maggie trotted in and out while they worked; and to Jonathan the house seemed for the first time a home. The outdoor air was warm, but there was a fire in the sod fireplace for cooking their supper. They were more lucky than most, for Jonathan could bring home from the store boxes of wood too thin to use for planks, and these made the green cottonwood burn. There were still some women who used buffalo chips, but Mary hated the dung in the house. She had scraped the walls very smooth, and in the deep earthen window sills had set jars of prairie flowers. Since the flowers had bloomed she had been happier, though they were flowers strange to her and to everybody, so that most of them had no names. Jonathan had made two benches and stools, and had brought home red-and-white checked oilcloth for the table. Now when the oil lamp was lit the light upon white cotton curtains, the flowers, the fire, and the smell of cornbread baking made home.

Jamie came in late with three fish on a string.

"I'll clean 'em if you'll cook 'em, Ruth," he said.

And they sat down to their meal of cornbread and fish and a dish of beans, and dandelions that Ruth had picked and washed.

They ate, but Clyde was silent and Mary talked too much, as though she were trying to keep him silent. But Jonathan noticed a change in her. The last week her talk had been all of a garden if she could get the sod peeled off, and he had promised her now that the coop was done for Mr. Drear that he would chop out the sod tomorrow, which was his first Sunday, and she could scarcely wait. She had gathered seeds from here and there, but most from Stephen Parry's wife.

Tonight she said nothing of gardens. It was all of how glad she was to get his mattress off the ground and how good he was to think to hear about such a thing, and how Arthur had eaten well today with no coaxing, and how Maggie ran away twice and the second time came running back because there was what she called "a big long thing."

"A snake, of course," Mary said swiftly, "and I was in terror. It might have been a rattler or a copperhead, even. Naughty Maggie!"

"Naughty Maggie," Maggie repeated with pleasure. "Oh, oh, Maggie!"

Then, in the middle of the night in the unusual softness of his bed hung in sacking instead of spread upon the sod, he heard his father say, "Jonathan's got to go in my place," and knew what it meant.

He got up solemnly and put on his trousers and coat and went out into the space where the other children slept. His parents slept in the space beyond, and under the blanket hung in the doorway he saw a light. He went to it and called softly, "Mother!"

She was not in bed. But he saw when she came to put the curtain aside that she had been in bed and had got up, perhaps because she was angry, for she had her shawl wrapped about her. From under it her unbleached cotton nightgown flowed like a skirt.

"Mother, I couldn't help hearing," he said.

"Then come in," she replied. "You may as well hear everything."

He went in with her. A small oil lamp made out of a tin

can and a wick lit the dark walls in flickers of light and shadow. He sat down on a box.

"I heard what you said, Father," he repeated. "So I got up to see what it was all for."

Clyde sat up in bed. He had not shaved since he cut his leg, and his black beard shadowed his smooth, eternally youthful face. "I'm glad you did hear me," he said. "Your mother's been ahushin' me until I'm fit to bust. Wants to down me, she does, without your hearin' the yes and no of it. It's this way, Jonathan. Land's to be had cheap in the West, and 'tidn't goin' to last forever the way folks is goin'. Jamie says fourteen wagons come through yestiddy. Stands to reason it won't last, for the land is wunnerful. I herded sheep on it last summer for a chap. Grass is short but full of richness for stock. But I don't want to herd sheep. The land's too good for it. It's not black gummy stuff like this mud under our feet. It's sandy light, and wheat's the thing."

Mary broke in, her voice dry with scorn. "Seeing how you couldn't grow a bit of corn in England, I don't see how calling it wheat over here will teach you."

Clyde paid no heed. He was talking to his son now as man to man. "You can't do with a tiddlin' bit of land out there, neither. It ain't a matter of a horse and a cow and a couple of pigs and a little bit of this and that to harvest whenever it likes to grow ready. Out there a man must work in a big large way, and if he does, then he's rich."

Mary groaned, "Oh, I've heard everything big and large ever since the day I first saw you in Blackpool, lounging on a street corner, talking about how you'd caught a whale!"

"And you stopped to listen," Clyde said.

"Yes, and it was the devil I didn't see hanging on my skirts made me," Mary retorted, "for I was in good circumstances teaching school, and my pay like clockwork every week, and never was again after I married you."

Clyde laughed. "Wait till I get my section of land, Mary, and a big frame house built for you in the middle of it!"

"It'll have to have trees before I like it," Mary said moodily. "I'm sick of this naked country."

"Trees I s'all plant when the foundation's set," Clyde said largely.

"Oh, we're fools," Mary cried. "There's no house and no land, and we're talking about trees!"

"There'll be everything if you do as I say, Jonathan," Clyde said earnestly. "Here's the plan. You get a seat on a wagon and go out there and pick a place for us. Sooner the better, for maybe the best is gone a'ready. The law is you must put up a sign of habitation. Well, a bit of a sod house will do it, a shelter-like, and you can get help by tradin' your own help. That's easy. Then when my leg lets me—"

Jonathan sat watching his father's full red lips moving in his black beard.

Mary cried out, "I won't have Jonathan going there by himself. 'Tisn't fair, Clyde, the way you put your work on him."

"As if I weren't givin' him the better job!" Clyde roared. "Why, here I be, alayin' in a place as dull as a ditch, and everythin' waitin'!"

"Everywhere you are is always a ditch to you," she said, "and what's ahead is always everything. You've dragged us out of England here, and now it's not six months and this is a ditch—though I'm not against saying for once you're right."

The look Jonathan and his mother both knew came over Clyde's dark face. If he could have walked he would have walked out of the house. But he could not.

"Put up or shut up," he muttered.

And all the time they were quarreling Jonathan was making up his own mind. He was not deciding an answer so much as allowing his natural being to gather into a great negation.

"Father," he said, "I won't go."

"Now, Jonathan—" his father began.

"I don't mean to go," Jonathan said. "Why, I couldn't put in words, I didn't want to leave England, but I left it. Now I'm here, and I won't pull up again."

"Of all the danged silly talk for a young chap to make, that's the worst," Clyde shouted. "Where'd the world be if folk were like you, Jonathan? Why, the world wouldn't ha' been discovered at all, and we'd all be stayin' in the same little hole some'ere killin' each other and fightin' for the same bits of bread, and not knowin' that out beyond was plenty and richness."

"I'm not sayin' everybody ought to be like me, Father," Jonathan said mildly. "I'm only sayin' how I am. The way I look at it, there's two kinds of folk in the world, just like there's two kinds of life in a seed. Something sends one kind up to hunt its food in the light and air, and sends the other kind down into the earth to make the roots. Well, the root is me."

He was aware of his mother sitting on the side of the bed listening to all he said, her braid of yellow hair over her shoulder, her arms wrapped in her shawl; and he used his figure for her ears, though he spoke to his father, and his father answered in a snort.

" 'Tis only sense even in a root to find the best place."

"Root begins where seeds fall," Jonathan said calmly, "and here I stay."

"And I'll stay with you, son," Mary said.

Clyde flung out his arms and shut his eyes and ground his jaws together in a groan. Then he slid down into the bed and drew the patchwork quilt about him.

"Oh, dang the two of you together!" he muttered.

"All right, Father," Jonathan replied, and went back to his bed. To his mother he said nothing, but there passed between them a deep look, and it was enough.

The next morning when Jonathan came out his father was sitting at the table dipping cornbread into a cup of tea and biting it off. Jamie sat beside him.

"Well, Father," Jonathan said and sat down away from him. Ruth moved quickly and silently across from the stove and set tea before him. He nodded at her. "Where's Mother?" he asked.

"She's a headick, and I told her to stop abed and I'd do," Ruth said.

"Right," Jonathan replied. A good girl Ruth was getting to be, he thought, quiet and good. He must go in and see his mother before he left.

"You're up," he said to his father.

"Have to be," Clyde said bitterly. "My leg's no good to me yet, but I s'all have to do with it and Jamie—eh, Jamie?"

"Yes, Dad," Jamie said. He eyed Jonathan warily over a slab of cornbread spread with molasses.

"Jamie and me is goin' West," Clyde said loudly. "I'm goin' to get over to Drear's today and see to it."

This was why his mother had a headache, then! He was about to exclaim in answer to his father and saw that his father expected it, and so he did not. But would she let him go and take Jamie with him?

"Jamie s'all help his old dad," Clyde was saying in heavy self-pity. "Jamie's the only one in the family that feels like I do. We'll have a rare good time together, eh, Jamie? We'll see lots of sights. There's buffalo runnin' out there yet and wild horses, and you can snare quails and wild fowl, and at night we'll camp around a big fire. There's Indians, too, nice ones, not cruel, and they'll bring you maize with the husks off and show you how to catch fish by ticklin' them under their chins."

All the time his father talked to Jamie, Jonathan felt himself used as a channel through which to wound his mother. His father was striking at her. He tried by silence, by eating his food, by calling for Maggie to come and have a cup of tea, to close the channel, but Clyde kept talking.

"We'll ride over the mountains, and we'll find us a good place, Jamie and me together, and we'll build a fine house, and then when you all come we'll be stannin' at the front door sayin' we told 'em so, eh, Jamie?"

Jamie was disconcerted, feeling something beyond himself in all this. "All right, Father," he said.

"An' then we'll see about roots movin'," Clyde said in a loud voice.

Jonathan could bear no more. He rose. "Shall you be goin' today, Father?" he asked coldly. Maggie had his teacup tipped tight against her face, waiting for the molasses at the bottom of it to run into her mouth.

"As soon as I can find a wagon with a place empty," Clyde replied. "Happen today, happen tomorrow. I can't waste my time no more if I'm to get ahead of others."

"I'll hear news later, then," Jonathan said. And, holding his slender shoulders square, he went in to his mother. She was lying curled up very small on the spot where he had seen his father stretched last night.

"Are you feeling bad, Mother?" he asked.

"My head's fearful," she said faintly and did not open her eyes.

He stood there longing to comfort her, longing to say to her, "Don't mind him, Mother. Let him go. You and I'll manage." But his intuition told him that the balance of her soul at this moment was very delicate, and a little could change it away from him if he spoke against his father. So he put away what he longed to say and thought of something else.

"Mother, I'm going to Stephen Parry's this noon and ask him to lay the floor down. I can manage it now that I'm working Saturdays too."

She opened her eyes at this. "That'll be just fine, Jonathan," she said, and he saw the pleasure in her eyes.

"Good," he said and kissed her forehead, and as he stooped she put up her hand and touched his cheek, and he knew he had kept the balance of her soul.

Six days later Clyde left Median. The wound in his leg was not healed yet, but it was closing healthily from the bottom, and he was not as lame as he was to be later when the muscles made a knot under the scar. Still, his leg could not bear his weight, and he had a stick in one hand and with the other he leaned upon Jamie's shoulder.

Jonathan ran out of the store in midmorning to see the wagons start. What sort of a farewell there had been between his parents he had not been there to see, and he was glad of it. It was as well for his mother to have a few hours before he came in at noon.

"Good-by, Father," he said sedately.

Clyde did not hear him. He was full of joy, and his black eyes were snapping with laughter and light. Just now he chanced to look at Jennet, who came running out of the tavern door, her arms full of loaves of bread.

"Here—I baked 'em last night," she cried. A tall young man took them from her, and she did not hear Clyde calling her name. "I wish I was going," she said to the young man boldly.

"Come along," he replied as boldly. He was tall and blond, and he drawled as he spoke. "I'll take you," he said.

"But will I take you?" Jennet said, laughing.

"It's for you to say," the young man replied. He pulled his belt and knotted a red handkerchief around his neck and tilted a big straw hat he wore.

"Ask me again," Jennet said.

"When?" he asked.

"Oh, in a year or two," she said, pretending to be careless. But she did not move her green eyes from his face.

"Too long," he said. "You'll be too old. A month from today if a wagon comes along, hop on it, and ride till you come to a river that crosses the trail once and doubles on itself in a mile. Somewhere in that mile I'll be watching for you. What'll you be wearin', so I can see you far off?"

She caught sight of Jonathan. "A red dress," she said.

"That'll be topping," he said. He leaped up on the wagon beside Clyde.

"That's the kind of lass I admire," Clyde said heartily, "always ready."

The tall fair young man looked at him. "You old goat!" he said softly.

Jonathan went close to the wagon and touched his father's knee. "Good-by, Father," he said clearly.

Clyde jumped at the touch and looked down. "Good-by, Jonathan, I was lookin' for you."

"I was here all the time," Jonathan said dryly. "Good-by, Jamie, mind you take care of Father and don't run ahead of him."

"You needn't tell me," Jamie replied. His cheeks were red, and he sat squeezed against the side of the wagon beside his father, a bundle on his knees.

The wagon started, and the young man whipped his horses until they galloped away in whirls of black dust, in rushes of grinding wheels and squeaking axles. Jonathan watched them until the noise was lost in the distance and upon the wideness of the prairie the dust was no bigger than what a man might gather in his hand and let fall again.

Who, he wondered, was that tall young chap, and was he joking with Jennet or not? It was not easy always to know whether men on the prairie were joking or serious. They told of large happenings in cool, careless voices, and there was no line clear between truth and lying, either in their minds or out. He could only discover the truth of anything by chance and by his own common sense.

But when he turned his head Jennet had gone, and it was none of his business to follow her to find out what she meant. He had his work to do, and he went back to it. He went home at noon, dreading but dogged and determined to be usual. He was never sure of his mother's mood. If the farewell with his father had been hard, then she would find something to blame him for, and he prepared himself for this.

But he found her quiet and cheerful and full of some sort of relief that he could not understand. They had an hour at table that was gay as they had not been gay since they left Dentwater. He was so relieved that he could not but let her know. Alone with her a moment as she followed him out of the door, he said, "Mother, I was frightened to come home because you might be sorrowful."

"I am sorrowful," she said quickly. "A woman's always sorrowful when her man is away. Everything is tasteless, like salt left out."

He felt crestfallen, but did not speak because he saw she wanted to say more. It was something hard, for her smooth small face grew shell-pink.

"It's time I said something to you as a man, Jonathan," she said, "because some day you'll have a wife. I've asked your dad to speak to you and Edward, but he always dangs himself and won't, he says, for shame. But I think of your wife, and I thought of Millie, and on Edward's wedding day I screwed myself up and said to him, 'Let Millie have the say-so, between you.' That's been the one thing wrong 'twixt your father and me, Jonathan. He's always had the say-so, and however I was afraid of a child coming when I hadn't the strength for it, his was the say-so. I did cry when he went this morning because I do miss him sorely, and still I was glad to be shut of fear for a while. I don't want more children, Jonathan, though I love you all so dear."

She had grown more confident as she spoke and yet not less shy, and she spoke to him with a sort of tender, delicate dignity. As for him, he was repelled and drawn and a little sickened, too—not by her, but by the opening of a door he wanted closed between them. All other doors he wanted open, but not this one. For through it he saw her apart from him; he saw her not his mother, but a woman having secret problems in her womanhood which he could never understand, until perhaps he himself was married to a woman. He withdrew from the thought of this woman to come, wanting no confusion, indeed, no connection between her and this one now before him.

"I think I understand, Mother," he said, his mouth very dry. He looked out over the prairie, searching for something to see and mention. But there was nothing. The long grass waved for miles in the unfailing wind, and the sky was its

endless blue. He looked down to the earth at his feet, and
then he thought of something.

"I shall start your garden when I come home tonight,
Mother. Evenings are long now."

"Do, son," she said quietly and, in comprehension, they
parted.

❧ 10 ❧

As they had clung to the cottage in Dentwater after
Clyde left it, so now they clung to the sod house in Median.
But the cottage had not seemed so much an island as the sod
house. There had been a score of connections with life in
Dentwater, but here a line thrown out could never reach the
other side of anything. Median was a steppingstone, a wayside
stop. Even those who stayed had no life of their own. They
spent their days in serving those who were going on somewhere. The inn was made for these, and the store prospered
on travelers, and Stephen Parry put a blacksmith forge in his
carpenter shop that he might shoe horses that passed by.

He came to Jonathan one day with a smooth white pine
board. "Please, sir, Mr. Goodliffe," he said respectfully, "will
you write me some letters on this yere boa'd?"

"I will, of course," Jonathan said. He was a little startled at
being called Mr. Goodliffe. No one had ever given him that
name before. He was shy and pleased. "But what letters?"

"I don't know the name of any letter," Stephen Parry
confessed sadly.

"What do you want said?" Jonathan asked.

"I'd like my name put," the man answered, "and that I can
do carpenterin' and blacksmith's work and I don' cha'ge no
more'n fair."

Jonathan drew a sheet of paper toward him and printed,
"Stephen Parry, Carpenter and Blacksmith. Prices Moderate."

He looked up to see Parry's eyes full of wonder and
wistfulness upon his pencil.

"Sho' do wish I could read," he said. "A man's like in prison
when he don' read."

"Would you like me to teach you?" Jonathan asked.

Stephen Parry hesitated. "I'd shore like my children to learn," he said. "Wish they was a school for them." He looked at Jonathan with sudden earnestness. "Mr. Goodliffe, why don' you open a school?"

"No one has asked me," Jonathan said diffidently.

"Wish somebody would, then," Stephen Parry said.

"How many children have you?" Jonathan asked. He had seen small dark creatures coming out of the dugout in which Stephen lived.

"Six," the man replied, "but only four old enough to learn."

"Tell you what I'll do, Mr. Parry," Jonathan said. "If you'll lay a board floor in our house, I'll teach them Saturday afternoons and evenings."

"I'll do it gladly," Stephen Parry said. He stood turning his hat round and round. "I don' know if you noticed my son Beaumont, Mr. Goodliffe. My wife and me, we think he's real smart. We'd like him to have a chance, not jest because he's ours, but because we figger that now us colored folk got our freedom, next thing is to show what we can do with it. My wife and me, we figger we can't do much 'cept give our younguns a chance to do what we cain't. Beaumont's the one, or so we think."

"Beaumont," Jonathan repeated. "A queer name."

"My wife belonged to Beaumonts befo' we married," the man said. "I was always a Parry, though, and my father befo' me. Well, I'll be gettin', along, Mr. Goodliffe. It'll be good news to my fambly. And I'll git the lumber together right away for the floor." He walked away with his peculiar long, loping step. As a boy he had run beside his master's coach, and his muscles had grown to it.

Thus it came about that Jonathan taught his first school to four black children. They appeared early in the evening of that same day. Stephen Parry came with them.

"Here they are, suh," he said, when Jonathan came to the door from the supper table. "This yere's Beaumont. How old you, Beaumont?"

"Thirteen," the tall dark boy said quickly.

"He's the on'y one we had befo' de war," his father said. "The res' is all bohn fr.e. This yere's Melissa, and this one is Gemmie—name's Gem from that hymn about 'gems in His crown'—and this one's Paul. Kin I come in, suh, and take measure of the floor?"

"Come in," Jonathan said. He felt a little shy before the four children, all eager and very clean. But he pulled aside the buffalo skin that hung as a wind curtain against the door, and they came in, standing in a tight small circle. His mother looked up as she cleared the table of dishes and food.

"Sit down, children," she commanded them. They did give one a turn, she thought, looking at them, but God had made them, though why black it would be hard to tell. They sat down at once, the girls' starched dresses crackling. Mary laughed. "I haven't seen starch since I left England."

"Ma makes it out of 'taters," Melissa said in a small voice and coughed for shyness behind a dark little hand.

"I'll have to get the receipt," Mary said.

"She soaks 'em real good," Gem spoke up, not shy at all. "Somepin white comes out and lays in the bottom of de pan. It's starch."

They were all spellbound by the row of black children, lips so red, eyes so large and black and white. Now Maggie burst out of the spell with a loud bellow of fright, and Ruth caught her up and took her into the other room.

"For shame, Maggie!" Mary called, and to make amends cut four slices of bread and spread them with molasses. "Now eat before you begin to study," she said. "Reading is very hard. I know, for once I taught school myself in England."

Stephen Parry looked up from the ground he was measuring. "Did you, ma'am? That's how your son is so smart, I reckon."

"Jonathan's always been very hard-working," Mary said calmly.

And Jonathan, to rid himself of their talk about him, lifted Arthur to the chair at the end of the table. "This chap knows how to read as well as anybody," he said playfully. "You can help me, eh, Artie boy?"

He arranged the small boy carefully in a quilt and tucked it firmly about him to strengthen the bones that never seemed strong enough to uphold even the thin body.

Stephen watched him. "Ailin'?" he inquired gently.

"He's much better," Mary said.

"My wife mought be able to fix him some yarbs," he said.

"She's good on declines. She can tell in a look whether a body's goin' to get well or not."

"There's no doubt about Artie's gettin' well," Mary said quickly, and as quickly hurried on, "Now, Artie, lad, you shall tell the first letter. Draw it big, with chalk on the table."

She handed him the piece of crude chalk which Jonathan had brought home from the store, and carefully Arthur drew the two long triangular lines and the cross. Everyone watched. Mary watched the pale face. I don't want anybody looking at him to see death in him, she was thinking. The four black children leaned with passionate eagerness to watch.

"That's A," Arthur said, very gravely and clearly, looking up.

"A," all the black children said, loud and quick.

Jonathan felt something pull at him. He looked up involuntarily and saw Stephen Parry, staring at his children as though he had been struck. He raised his eyes to Jonathan, and suddenly they were full of tears that brimmed over his cheeks. He dabbed them away with his big black hand and laughed.

"Nobody in my fambly's ever been able to read a letter befo'," he said, "but I don' know why I have to cry about it now that they're gonna learn."

Two days later in the afternoon Jennet came into the store. He saw her as soon as she stood in the door. She was wearing her red dress and a small red bonnet that she had made of the same calico. Everyone in the store saw her. There were no women there. The rush of the day's business was over, and the seven or eight men were talking as they lingered over small purchases of snuff and a dipperful of whisky or a handful of sugar in a twist of brown paper.

The men around the cracker barrel drew aside to let her pass, and she went to Lew Merridy, who was dipping whisky out of a tub for an old man whose feet were tied up in rags.

"Any mail in today, Lew?" Her voice, carelessly clear, floated above their heads.

"No, the bag ain't come in yet today," Merridy replied. "You expectin' a letter?"

"Yes, I am," she said. She stood, her full red skirt swaying slightly. "What whisky is that?" she asked.

"Stuff I made myself outa corn," he replied. 'Wanta taste it?"

"Don't care if I do," she said, and put out her hand for the tin cup. She drank it as easily as water and tipped her head, and the eyes of every man were upon that white throat. She drank the last drop and handed the cup back.

"It's good," she said.

"Don't burn, eh?" Merridy replied.

"Nothin' burns me," she said. And then, her green eyes shining, she sauntered over to Jonathan, and he could smell her breath, sweet and strong.

"Folks tell me you're teachin' school, Jonathan," she said.

He looked at her and quickly looked away again. "Mr. Parry's making us a floor, and I'm teaching his children for pay," he said, and went on folding up calico that the morning's business had disarranged and piling it up.

"Don't know any Mr. Parry," she said. "I never heard of anybody but ol' Steve Parry. He's a nigger."

Jonathan did not answer. The men were recovering themselves now as they sat about the store. It was the quiet end of the day. No one was buying, only talking. He heard the bits of their talk, the news told and retold from mouth to mouth, the scraps of opinion, the forecasts, prophecies, reminiscences which were forming without his being aware of it a background of knowledge better than books or newspapers could have given.

"There's more'n twelve hundred miles of railroad in the state now, they say."

"Did ye hear that meat's bein' shipped clear to New York now, in them newfangled icebox cars? Looks like we all better take to cattle."

"Capital buildin's finished in Topeka—yep, I saw it last month myself. A mighty fine sight."

Thus he knew that telegraph lines ran across Kansas, that there were colleges begun, that railroads were taking out cattle by the thousand and bringing back money to be thrown away by wild cowboys in Abilene and Dodge City, that fortunes were to be made even out of buffalo bones picked up from the prairies and shipped east for fertilizer. But none of this had anything to do with Median nor with himself, when days for him were as evenly alike as though he had stayed in an ancient English village.

"Like my dress?" Jennet demanded.

"I haven't seen it," he said prudently from behind a pile of calico.

"Well, look at it," she retorted.

He waited a moment before he threw a glance at it.

"Very nice," he said, purposefully colorless. He was startled at heart to see how she wore red. The violent scarlet subdued her to real beauty. It dominated her red curls and made them gold and tawny, it deepened the whiteness of her skin. Only the green of her eyes remained sharpened for contrast. These eyes were now terrifying to him in their power. He knew as he knew his own name that he could love a girl and lose everything he was in loving her. He felt his body tremble and turned his back on her abruptly, pretending to search a shelf.

"I can wear red because I love it," she said. "A woman can always wear what she loves."

He tried to whistle softly as he ran his hands over the stuffs and could not because his lips were too dry.

Danged if I will love her, he thought, and suddenly felt sick enough to retch. He turned about to face her. "Time for me to go," he said.

"Time for school?" she teased him. "If I weren't older'n you, Jonathan, I'd come and be your pupil. As it is, what could you teach me?"

"Nothing, it's true," he said against his longing will. Too tight across the bosom her dress was, he thought, looking at it. He moved to the door and out into the square, and she followed him and caught up to his side. He was ashamed to have her there in her loud red dress, and, as conscious of all her beauty as though he had her in his arms, he walked sturdily on, not looking at her and enduring all the whirling of his blood.

She stopped him in the middle of the square. "Jonathan, I'm going away."

"Are you?" he said stupidly.

"Do you care?" She looked from under her red bonnet to his eyes, exactly level with hers.

"No," he said, and went white with the effort of the lie.

"You lie," she said.

He did not answer this, having no answer.

Then she asked him one more question. "Are you going to stay in this hole of a Median all your life, Jonathan?"

"Yes," he replied.

"Oh, well," she said, and parted from him abruptly, carelessly, moving through the clear summer light like fire springing along out of prairie grass. He looked away from her and went on. Fire, that was what she was. He could not play with her, for she would go on alive, but he would be ashes. Let her go into the West and burn it up if she would.

He heard the next day that she was gone. She had run away by the earliest wagon to leave the inn that morning. Who the man was that drove it no one could remember, once she was missed.

"It was that feller from Pennsylvania, that Dunkard or somethin' with a long beard," Henry Drear moaned.

"No, it wasn't," his wife snapped at him. She was shrill with anger. "It was one of them Rooshians from land knows where."

They thought by the end of the day it was neither of them, but an Englishman, the landless younger son of some nobleman, come to America to found an estate. He had come to Median two days earlier, very elegant in a waistcoat and high boots, his trousers tailored in London, and his blue coat tight across his shoulders. Jonathan had seen him and waited on him and had listened in silence to his frequent and impatient cry, "Good God, you don't have that, either?"

He had grown tired of it finally and had said quietly, "We carry all that the people here seem to want."

The young Englishman had been astonished at his impudence and looked stern for a moment.

"I say, you're never English!"

"I was," Jonathan said.

"Then you still are," the Englishman retorted.

"No, I'm not," Jonathan said firmly. He had not thought of such a controversy until this moment, and would not have dreamed of denying England until now. "I'm American," he said.

"The devil you are," the young man replied. "Well, certainly this isn't England," he added.

"No, it isn't," Jonathan said, and resisted and conquered the instinct to add "sir."

"A blasted proud feller if she's taken him," the opinion in the store said. "That sort of feller makes you glad we won the war in '76."

Jonathan at his post said nothing. If Jennet had gone with the Englishman, it would be for a purpose of her own. He thought of the directions the tall fair young man had given her three weeks ago, the day his father went away to homestead. Beyond the prairie, farther than the sight of his eyes would ever reach, a river doubled on itself and made a rich green valley. Somewhere in that valley she would stay, at least for a day, at least for a night. He felt a great wrench in his vitals and endured it and went on about his business.

That evening when he went home he stepped inside the door and felt beneath his feet a floor of clean white board. His mother hurried to meet him, and he saw her small face bright as it had not been since they left England.

"Oh, Jonathan, the floor's done!" she cried.

"Like it?" he asked. He pretended to test it, to examine it, as he walked about stamping on it here and there.

"It's just wonderful," she said; "it makes me feel at home again to have my feet on a floor."

"That's good, Mother," he said.

The wintry spring in which Clyde had gone gave way to a summer so different from any they had ever known that the very sun seemed another than the one which had shone upon England. Summer in Dentwater had been mornings of sunshot mists rolling away at noon over miles of soft green spreading to blue water in the distances. That green even on clear days was shadowy with trees and valleys; and under the trees, centuries old, cattle and men could lie at noon and always be cool.

But in Median there were no trees. The sun flattened the earth with light and heat which none could escape. Cattle went to the drying river and stood fetlock deep in the shallow water and moved as the thin/shadows of the cottonwoods moved and shrank and stretched again at evening. The store became a trap of heat, and if the windows were opened the dusty winds tore at every floating end of paper and scrap and string and rattled and cracked until the place was full of restless noise intolerable to hear.

Then the sod house seemed as quiet and cool as a cave. Jonathan left it reluctantly in the morning and at noon entered its dimness gladly. His mother kept the windows closed and the door shut and sprinkled water upon the walls, and the fresh smell of damp earth added to its coolness. She had continued somehow week by week to make a place of comfort out of what had begun as a hovel. The floor had been a cheerful thing to her, and after it was finished she braided rugs for it out of ends of goods Jonathan brought her. Remnants he had always. It was one of Merridy's complaints against women that they would not pay a penny more for a few inches which were useless to him. For the women of Median had not yet taken to making rugs and quilts and cushions and all those signs of staying that women have. They were not sure of Median yet, and if someday a man shouted, "We're moving on!" then all their work would become useless stuff in a wagon too small for necessities.

But Mary in Median had all the desperate certainty of one stranded upon an island in midocean, to which no ship sails. There was no hope of return for her, and she would go no farther; and so bit by bit she created about herself a little England. Thus, out of all the helter-skelter homes in Median, sod houses, dugouts, a few of frame, some of frame and earth together, only hers was like a home when one stepped into it. She had made a pair of chairs out of two barrels and cushioned them with brown-and-white calico, and they stood beside the fireplace. Her floor was clean, even though water was as dear as silver and had to be carried from the tavern well; and upon shelves made of boards resting on pegs driven in the wall her plates and tin cups were shining bright. When the spring flowers were gone she picked grasses and put them, merely for greenness, in the bottles and cans she had made into vases.

Until evening she did not stir beyond her door. The garden which Jonathan had planted rushed into fruitage, but now it was dying in the summer sun. There was too little water, and rain came in storm and deluge and in a few hours was gone.

"Everything in this country is crazed," she told Jonathan one Sunday while the sky above them sprang with light and roared and crackled and dropped down upon them in a fall of water. "Nothing is moderate and thoughtful-like." She was darting about as she spoke, putting pans and earthen crocks under familiar leaks. Now that the floor was done, the roof was their sorrow. Jonathan had talked with Stephen Parry about it.

"It'll have to be took off," Stephen had said, "and proper

rafters and a real roof put on. But it'll never be so cool no more."

"Wait until autumn, then," Jonathan had said. Let the roof shelter them from sun, at least. It was a queer-looking roof, for the sod had grown long grass, and the wild sunflowers had seeded in it, and it was like a garden. But it let the rain through in streams and grew sodden with the weight of water, until Jonathan, frightened at its sag, put posts and planks under it lest it fall upon them in their sleep and the sod house be their tomb.

"Crazy it is," Jonathan agreed with his mother.

He was glad it was Sunday when this storm came and that he was in this low earthen home that clung to the ground, instead of in the flimsy store building where the lightning seemed to dart through from window to window. He was ashamed to show fear after he had once seen Mrs. Merridy afraid. He scarcely ever saw her, for she seldom left the back rooms where she lived; but if the sky darkened to storm, she came into the store, a thin, nervous, silent woman, carrying on either arm a twin. She set them down in empty boxes and then, herself on a stool between them, she waited, her arms locked across her breast, until the storm was over. No cheerfulness could touch her. Between the cracks of thunder she said doleful things to her husband.

"It was a storm like this that struck Hasty's Mill last summer, Lew."

"Didn't do much hurt," Merridy said, twiddling his fingers at his baby sons sitting placidly in the packing boxes, sucking at hardtack.

"If they hadn't caught it, the whole place would have been burned up," she reminded him.

"Yep, but it wasn't," he said. "You never seem to remember that. Besides, couldn't nothing burn in a rain like this." The rain was pounding upon the tin roof.

Jonathan, working hard over books, trying not to see the flashes of greenish light, trying not to hear the falling of the heavens in thunder, felt the sweat under his clothes until he seemed to stand in water in his shoes. It occurred to him once to wonder where Katie was in storms. She darted in and out of the store daily to cry out, "Ma wants some crackers, Pop!" or "We're clear out of salt," or to bring the empty molasses jug. But in a storm he never saw her. He asked her once. "What do you do with yourself in a storm, Katie? I should think you'd come in where we are."

She threw her skimpy brown braid away from her shoulders.

"I ain't afeared like Ma is," she said, and after a moment went on, "Lightnin' only hits you if you're feared of it."

He thought of this saying of hers thereafter in any storm, and he thought of it now, under the dripping ceiling of the sod-house roof. If it were true, one day he would die by this prairie lightning.

But summer was made of storms and drought and dry blue sunshine. They were wrenched from one extreme to the other until they were physically weary of it, except Maggie, who thrived and grew. Against the violence of weather, each maintained himself as he was able. Ruth that summer began to study Latin. She begged it out of Jonathan at meals and while he hoed the garden in the morning, trying to coax dew into rain by his mulching. Arthur took to his bed again and lay long hours with his eyes closed, holding his life in him by silence and stillness. And Jonathan maintained himself by marking off the hours of his days into exact routine of one kind of work and another.

The one marvel which the days held was Beaumont, the black boy. For in this child of a strange race there was an intelligence the like of which Jonathan had never seen, and he knew humbly that it was far beyond his own. The other three children learned well enough, stammering through their primers by the end of summer; but Beaumont was reading not so much by letters and words in sentences as by the ideas he discovered. He was the tawniest of these dark children, in the brownness of his skin was a dark gold, and in the blackness of one of his eyes was a strange blue fleck. His hair, too, was thicker than that of the others and less like wool.

"What'll I do with you, lad?" Jonathan asked half in play, but in alarm, too. "My learning won't last like this."

"I don't know," Beaumont said simply, "and my mother, she don't know. She's always askin' me that."

They looked at each other in mutual wondering gravity. This boy, Jonathan told himself, must not be wasted; and yet was he not doomed to waste?

The summer ended sharply on a day that Clyde came home. Twice he had written, vague windy letters full of matters of which they could not discern whether they were plans or things already done. The land was filling fast, he wrote. It was lucky he had not delayed. People were coming in from all over the world, from England and Russia and Germany and Sweden. There was even an English duke's son, people said, with plenty of money. How would she like to be neighbors with a duke's son? But everybody was the same here and a duke's son no better than anybody else.

"Oh, the big zany!" Mary cried, when she had made this out of Clyde's wandering handwriting and fanciful spelling. "As if a duke's son could ever be a neighbor to us! Jonathan, you mark my words, some day there'll be trouble out of all this equality, for all of Clyde's talk don't make him equal to anybody if he isn't born so."

"That's sense, Mother," Jonathan agreed.

They put Clyde's letter away, both decently disturbed at the idea of a nobleman for a neighbor.

"What'll happen next?" Mary said severely.

On a September day, early and suddenly cool, Clyde came limping in, his leg healed but a stick still in his hand.

"Mary!" he shouted at the door. There was no one in sight, and they might have been dead if it were not that there were squashes yellow in the garden and the home so clean, and a painted green tin of autumn flowers on the table, which made him know that Mary was alive.

"Clyde!" she screamed and came running in from behind the curtain. "Oh, Clyde!"

She flung herself upon him, and he held her with one arm and laughed.

"You've wanted me!" he cried triumphantly. "You've missed me, eh, wife?"

"Terrible," she said, forgetting everything.

Nobody was in the house to hear her, except Arthur in bed—luckily Jonathan was not home yet and Ruth had gone out with Maggie to keep her safe from the snakes in the long grass.

"Oh, it's been sore without you," she sighed. "They do their best, the children, and Jonathan always a dear lad; but they're another generation from us, Clyde."

"Ah," he agreed. Now that he was sure of her, he suddenly felt hungry and tired. "Let me alone, dear heart, for a minute. My leg's hurtin'."

"Oh, is your leg still bad?" she cried. "Let me see, Clyde."

He sat down and stretched it out, and she pulled up his trouser leg and looked at the deep angry scar of twisted muscle in the side of his calf.

"It'll never be right," she mourned, touching it gently. His flesh was sweet to her again.

"I can manage," he replied. "I've managed wonderful."

"Where's Jamie?" she cried suddenly. "Why, I'm a wicked mother, forgetting my son. Where's the boy, Clyde?"

"I left him out there, Mary," Clyde said.

"Clyde!" she screamed. "Not alone in all that wild country!"

"There's neighbors in the next section hut," he said. "And you can't leave a foot of homesteadin' now, Mary. Somebody'll steal it while you're gone."

"Oh, but, Clyde, a little boy!"

"He's growed wonderful this summer," Clyde said. "And thirteen ain't a little boy. He was thirteen last month."

She was on her feet now, very angry. "All the same, you had no right to leave him, Clyde. But then, you never had proper feelings for a father. It's always what your children could do for you, never what's your duty to them."

"Of all the rambunctious silly notions!" Clyde cried. "If I hadn't begot 'em, where'd they be? I gave 'em life!"

"And dragged 'em here to live it!" she retorted. She sat down, sighing, and wrapped her arms together. "What's he living in?" she demanded. "Has the child a shelter?"

"Now, Mary," Clyde said. "Listen to me before you're all slathery and frettin'. He ain't goin' to be there long. I'm goin' back—with you and the children is my prayer, without you if so be I must. I've decided you're right about Jonathan. Seventeen is a man, and let him have his own mind. But I've a home and three hundred and twenty acres of the best land—"

"What kind of a house?" she interrupted him.

"Mary, I won't say it's anything but a good sod house, but frame's to come," he replied. "I'll promise you—"

Upon them at this moment Jonathan returned, for it was noon.

"Well, Father," he said.

"Well, lad," his father replied.

"Jonathan, your father's left Jamie behind," his mother cried.

"Only for a matter of a few weeks," Clyde said to him. "You wouldn't know Jamie. He's growed like a man—inches higher he is, and he rides a horse like a cowboy. There's wild horses out there, and he's corralled two of them and gentled one of them. Wonderful clever, he is, and born for the life. It's a big life and calls for big men."

Within himself, at that familiar loudness of his father's voice, Jonathan felt stubbornness solidify in his being.

"I daresay," he replied and, coming in, he poured a little water into the tin basin and washed himself before food. "Got to get back," he said. "Mr. Merridy's busy this afternoon with autumn stock." He threw his water carefully upon the squash plants outside the door.

His mother rose and began to set the table. In the distance over the rising slant of the land Ruth was following behind Maggie racing ahead of her.

"Median's growed, I see," Clyde said to his son.

"Twelve families," Jonathan replied.

"Too thick for me," Clyde remarked. "Now, out there you can look as far as eye can reach and see only your own land."

"And Jamie there without a living soul!" Mary cried. She could not forgive him.

"Oh, shut up, do!" Clyde shouted.

They're off again, Jonathan thought hopelessly. But somehow he felt himself no longer in the quarrel. He had no more to do with it. It lay deep between them, man and woman of whom now he was no longer a part.

He sat eating while they wrangled. When Maggie came in he lifted her to his knee and wiped the dusty sweat from her face and fed her from his plate. Then he left them still wrangling.

What might have been the end of that quarrel who could have known? It was ended by Arthur, that feeblest of all their house.

The quarrel had come to her saying over and over, "Anyhow, I will not take Artie so far, Clyde."

"You'll be no furder from doctors there nor here," he retorted. "And the air's better there—fine upland air it is, and it goes straight up till it hits the Rockies, folks say."

"We've kept him alive somehow by staying put," Mary said. "He'll never stand moving."

They discussed this, looking down at the pallid little boy upon the bed, and he looked up at them as though it were hard to draw his feeble breath between them.

"But would you come back, Mother?" he asked in his small weak voice.

"I'm not going, duckie," she replied.

"You could leave him with Jonathan until he grows stronger," Clyde said.

"I will not," Mary retorted. It was now taken for granted that Jonathan would not go. Neither of them saw the terror in the sick child's eyes.

Jonathan, that night, gathering up the little armful of bones to rest them, felt them feverish.

"You're hot, Artie," he said.

"Jonathan," the little skeleton whispered, "is my dad stronger than my mother?"

"He is, I reckon," Jonathan replied, "but what of it, my whippet?"

"Then I'm afraid of him," the child replied.

"Nonsense," Jonathan said cheerfully. "He's fond of you like all of us." He felt Arthur's forehead and was alarmed. "Mother!" he shouted. "This boy's burning!"

She came hurrying in and felt of Arthur's hands and head and feet. "He's cold and hot in different parts," she said. "Oh, Jonathan, put him down and go for that black woman!"

He ran through the autumn twilight for Stephen Parry's wife. But, with a strange slowness, she did not come at once. He left her promising to come, and they waited for her through a night of fitful sleeping wherein he sat for hours holding Arthur in his arms.

She came in the early morning when another clear autumn day poured out its sun, and in that strong light she looked carefully at the sick child, beside his thistledown so large and brown and strong that none of them doubted her for a moment. Then she went into the other room and stood among them.

"I kin bring him some yarbs," she said in her deep voice, "and I kin bring down his fever. But when it's brung down, he won't have nothin' strong enough to live in him. The fever'll draw his life all out when it goes." She looked at Mary. "I didn' wan' to tell you, ma'am, but the firs' time I saw him I knew his end."

She stood there as though she herself were beyond the life and death she seemed to understand so well. "I'm mighty sorry for you, ma'am," she said to Mary. "But not for him. It's a hard time to live now except for them that's strong. He'll be spared what would have been beyond his strength. You remember that."

She went away, and in the silence left behind her there was no more quarreling. Mary went to Clyde and crept into his arms, and he held her before them all, and Jonathan rose and went into the other room and, kneeling beside the bed where Arthur slept, he buried his face in the quilt and silently wept. In a moment he felt someone there and, looking up, saw it was Ruth. He need not be ashamed before her, but he rose and together they stood hand in hand, their eyes solemnly upon their brother.

Only Maggie knew nothing. She was outdoors, running after the big brown woman. But she could not keep up with that long, tireless stride, and after a few minutes she sat down in the middle of the road and happily sifted its dust in her hands.

The house was intolerable in the waiting hours. Strangely, it was Clyde whom they all comforted, for he was the one the least able to bear it. He sat with his stiff leg outstretched before him, blaming himself for everything until for sheer necessity of relief they comforted him.

"I'm the one that's killed him," he said again and again. "It's me that's wicked and wouldn't see how my poor little lad was."

"Hush. What could we have done?" Mary said.

"I could have took him back to the East," Clyde moaned. "I'd have took him to England afore this."

"He'd have died upon the sea, Father," Jonathan said.

"At least he'll be buried on proper land," Mary said. She had not wept nor for a moment left Arthur, except to come as she had now to fetch something for his need. Clyde rose to follow her, but she stopped him.

"Stay away from him, do," she said. "Let's let him sleep himself away in peace."

It was a heavy peace in which Arthur died. Stephen Parry, when his wife came home and told him that the child was set for death, had made a small coffin from green cottonwood.

"Shall I black it, Sue?" he asked her. "I got about enough lampblack to do it."

"He's so little," she replied. "Let's use whitewash."

He made the small casket as white as snow with lime inside and out and brought it on the day when it was needed, and lifted the little body in and laid it down.

Arthur was dressed in the suit he had worn when he left England. He had been proud of it that day because it had a tie, and Mary remembered. There was no cemetery in Median, but in an acre to the south of the town some lay buried, nearly all of them those who had been on their way westward and overtaken by age or illness had been delayed forever. Beside a newborn child whose mother had gone on, Arthur's grave was dug.

This day was the first in which Jonathan saw, all together, Median's people. They had come one by one to bring food and fuel and water and offers of help in those last days, but now they were all here. Samuel Hasty and his wife and two boys, Henry Drear and Mrs. Drear, and he remembered for a second Jennet and put her out of his mind again. He saw Stephen Parry and his family standing a little apart, and a man married to an Indian squaw and his five half-breed children, all whom he knew well or less well. They made a blur of people, poorly dressed, sunburned and windblown. They were strangers until Lew Merridy, because there was no minister among them, began to read aloud a psalm.

"For the days of our life are as grass that perishes," he read.

Around them the long prairie grass waved in the autumn sunlight. But in the midst of it stood this handful of people gathered about something of their own now to be buried here. Jonathan saw their faces kind and full of sorrow. Some, to whom this hour brought memory, were weeping, and suddenly he felt them friends.

That night in the house that seemed empty because something out of its life was gone, he was not surprised when his mother said, "Jonathan, I'm going with your father, after all."

"I know, Mother," he answered.

"There's Jamie to think of," she said.

"I know," he said again.

Once she had set her mind, she could not quickly enough do

what she had decided, and Clyde hurried her because he said they must not waste the autumn weather. Winter would fall soon that year, everybody said. The prairie beasts were already digging deeper holes, and the grass was dying early.

In sad haste to be gone, Mary packed into a wagon that Clyde had bought the things that she must have—a mattress, quilts and her English blankets, their winter clothing and other heavier clothing from Merridy's store, dried food and seeds of all kinds, and she sliced the best of her squashes into strips as the Indian woman who lived in Median had showed her how to do and dried them in the sun and wind.

But all she truly valued she left behind with Jonathan. There was the family Bible which she had brought from England, into which at her bidding he now wrote in his most careful hand, "Arthur John Goodliffe, born in Dentwater, England, November 10, 1862. Died September 3, 1871, in Median, Kansas, in the United States of America." There were the pictures of her mother and father and of herself and Clyde on their wedding day. There were her few linen sheets and her two pair of pillowcases edged with crocheted lace she had made, and her half-dozen china plates and teacups, and a silver necklace with an agate set in a locket, and a brooch with her mother's hair, and the picture of Edward and Millie on their wedding day, and the picture, only newly come, of their first child, a boy, Tim, named after Millie's father.

And with all she put into the wagon she took care to leave the house looking as it had for Jonathan's sake. In the midst of her daze of sorrow and unwillingness she had her moments of thinking of how he would manage and even of whether she ought not to leave Ruth to take care of the house for him.

"Though how to do with that Maggie without Ruth I don't know," she sighed. "Sometimes it seems as if Maggie took all after Clyde. She's on the run from dawn till dark, and what with the deathly snakes and holes in the ground and now out there wolves maybe and Indians and I don't know what, I haven't the strength for her. Jamie was the same, only it's worse when a girl's like that."

"You keep Ruth, Mother," he said. "I'll manage."

And to Ruth he said privately, "Mind you think and spare her all you can, and some day I'll make it up to you and give you whatever it is you want most."

"Oh, I will without that," she said.

He noticed her shadowy sweet eyes when she spoke, and thought to himself that somehow none of them noticed Ruth enough. She was one of those easily forgotten, whatever they do. It would have been pleasant to have her here, but he could let his mother go more easily if Ruth went with her.

"Do you think you could manage a letter to me sometimes to tell me how Mother is?" he asked.

"I never wrote a letter, as you know, Jonathan," she said seriously, "but I can try, and the words I don't know I can ask Mother."

"It's you I should have been helping instead of those black children," he said in quick remorse. "But it's too late now."

"I had always to get Maggie to sleep and see to things at night," she said patiently.

They left in seven days from the day it was decided, and Jonathan stayed away from work that morning to help them off. There was agitation and excitement, and Clyde kept shouting things forgotten and promises of what was ahead. He hustled them into the wagon at the door of the sod house. Two mules he had not paid for pulled it, but Jonathan had signed the note that promised payment if his father failed to do it.

"Get in, get in, woman!" he shouted to his wife. "A late start is bad luck all the way."

But he delayed them after all. They were in the wagon, and the wheels all but turning when Mary said, "Have you the homestead papers, Clyde?"

"Of course, of all things," he retorted. But he felt in his pockets, and the papers were not there. Then began the tumbling of goods and the searching and Clyde's cursing and swearing, until Ruth, looking up at the family Bible on the shelf, saw papers sticking out and pulled at them, and there they were. Clyde had put them there.

"Dang it, the Bible's the place for safekeeping things, and I never dreamed you wouldn't put it in," he cried to Mary.

"The Bible's to stay here with Jonathan," she said.

"What, and we have no Bible?" he roared.

"I want it with Jonathan," she said stubbornly. "Then I'll know it's safe."

He yielded at last, and they were off in such confusion that there was only a moment left to Jonathan in which to say good-by to anyone. He gave it all to his mother.

"Oh, Jonathan," she cried, weeping, "take care of everything."

"You take care of yourself, Mother," he said. He held her in his arms, and for the first time knew how big he had grown because she felt so small to him. "Good-by, my dearest dear," he muttered, and let her go.

Part Two

and comforted their poor tired bodies, and the wind, weird singing

❧ II ❧

WHETHER HE HAD STOOD LOOKING AFTER THEM OR WHETHER he had turned blindly back into the house, he never knew. He saw their faces, each stark clear for an instant—his father's full of haste and absorption, Ruth's frightened, Maggie's round with wonder, and then his mother's, yearning and weeping as she looked at him. Her gaze reached for him. He felt a tangle of pain in his breast, and his eyes smarted. He must have rushed back into the house, because when he was clear again he was working in a fury at the dishes to be washed and floors to be swept.

"I hate to leave such a mess for you, Jonathan," his mother had said in her last look about the rooms.

"I'll clean up in a jiffy," he had answered.

But it was not a jiffy. He lingered over everything, exhausted now that there was no more need for him to be strong. And now that his mother was gone, there seemed no reason why he should not have gone with her. The house and the garden, which had been impossible to leave when she was in it, was nothing when she had left it; and his job, that had been an anchor when it brought into the house the only sure sum of money each week, seemed worthless. He did not like shopkeeping, he thought moodily to himself as he went about the house. Shopkeeping ancestry and his mother's belief in the soundness of trade made him good enough at it, but it did not satisfy his own hungers.

He had had no time in these months to think of his

hungers, but now they rose up in him. He paid them heed as he worked through the afternoon. His mother had said, "When we're gone, Jonathan, make the house comfortable for yourself. Take the inside room for sleeping, and then you can live in this one with the fireplace, and it'll be more convenient."

He had asked Merridy for the day free and had been given it, and he moved his belongings and took down the curtains from his corner. The sod house seemed big and full of room now when only he was in it; and, as the hours moved on, the quiet and the space enlarged, and with them his loneliness and his unsatisfied longings. He felt himself grown and a man. But a man's life must have more substance than he had in Median. In Dentwater there had been sources to which he could go—Mr. Hopkins and school and colleges and books and learning; the vicar and those good days when he had tinder in him; the sea and the ships at Blackpool and Edward's business in the chandlery, which, buying and selling only common things, yet touched every port in the world. He thought of his own room in the stone cottage when upon a fair day he could see white sails upon the Irish Sea, and he went to the door of the sod house and stood looking out. He saw nothing except the long, unchanging slope of the prairie. There were no sources for him here.

But as he watched he saw coming across that space, so nearly level, four small black figures. They were his pupils, Stephen Parry's children. He wished that he had told them not to come because he was tired and because he wanted to go on with his mood of dreaming melancholy. He had forgotten to tell them anything, and so they were here as usual.

He watched them drawing nearer. The two youngest loitered behind, and Gem walked quietly along alone. But Beaumont, when he saw Jonathan, broke into a loping run and reached him far ahead of the others.

"Hullo, Mr. Goodliffe," he panted.

"Hullo, Beaumont," Jonathan replied. The boy's dark face was in an ecstasy. "What's happened?" he asked.

"Say, Mr. Goodliffe, I finished that whole book you gave me yesterday. I couldn't stop—I kept on reading, and my father let me have the candle last night until I was finished."

The book was *Robinson Crusoe*. Jonathan had won it once as a school prize in Dentwater. What he saw was himself, now in Beaumont, mustering his courage once, long ago, to walk bravely to Mr. Hopkins and to say to him, out of deep excitement, "I finished the whole of that book, sir—I couldn't put it down."

His book had been a translation of the *Odyssey*, but that did not matter. What mattered was the eagerness and even the adoration with which he had looked upon the schoolmaster as the source in which he could find knowledge and wisdom. Now he saw in this boy's eyes the same adoration and the same eagerness, and it was he who was the source.

"Good," he said shortly.

He was too touched and too alarmed to say anything more. But at the head of the table he taught twice his usual length of time and with a new and stern exactness.

The next morning he rose early and made and ate his breakfast. Then he crossed the square to the store. The door was open and he went in, but nobody was there except Mr. Merridy, picking his teeth and looking at the last newspaper to reach Median.

"Good morning, Mr. Merridy," Jonathan said.

"Hello there," Lew replied without looking up.

"Mr. Merridy, I want to give you my resignation. I hope you won't mind," Jonathan said.

"What's the matter?" Merridy demanded.

"I'm going to start a school," Jonathan replied.

Mr. Merridy put down his paper and looked up. "We don't need a school here, Jonathan," he said. "There ain't enough children to support it."

"There's sixteen children that I know, sir," Jonathan replied.

"No, there ain't," Mr. Merridy replied. "Hasty's have only two young boys, and that fambly down in that dugout on top of the river bank has four. That's only six. And the newcomers ain't settled yet whether they're stayin' or not. Median's a town that's bound to grow, but there'll be a lot of comin' and goin' before the final shakedown, and folks that's on the move can't bother with schools."

"There're four Parry children," Jonathan said gently, "and Bill White has six."

"You ain't goin' to have a school for niggers and half-breed Indians!" Mr. Merridy cried. "Why, it'll ruin 'em if we begin educatin' them. Besides, what'll we do with them when they're educated? They'll be fit for nothin', I tell you, Jonathan. I been meanin' to speak to you a long time about your teachin' those children. You're doin' them no real good, nor the town."

"Beaumont's a very bright boy," Jonathan said. "He's much brighter than I am, Mr. Merridy, and I know it."

"Then there's all the more reason why he shouldn't be educated, for the day he knows it will be a sad day for you and for all of us," Mr. Merridy said. His voice grew severe. "I tell you, Jonathan, it was a terrible thing to bring black slaves to this white man's country, but it was more terrible to set 'em free. No man knows what'll come of it for any of us. And when you teach 'em to read and write and figger, you're puttin' the white man's weapons into their hands, and they'll use 'em on you and on me."

They looked at each other steadily.

"I can take that risk better than I can the risk of saying I won't teach Beaumont," Jonathan said, and after a moment he said again, "Not to free the mind after you've freed the body doesn't seem to me fair."

Lew Merridy grunted, picked up the paper, shook it, and pretended to read.

"Besides," Jonathan went on, "there's Katie, sir. I should think you'd want her to go to school."

"No, I don't," Merridy replied. "I don't believe in educatin' females. She's learned to read from her mother, and I've taught her how to count up figgers to help me. I can't see any mortal use for her to know more."

He rattled the paper, looked grim, smoothed his uncut moustaches and coughed.

"Will you take my resignation, sir?" Jonathan inquired.

Mr. Merridy threw down the paper once more. "Why, you son-of-a-gun, are you still resignin'?" he shouted.

"Yes, sir."

"Well, go on and git out of here!"

"I will," Jonathan replied, and he put on his hat and walked out, his knees trembling. Merridy owed him nothing. He had drawn the last of his wages to give to his mother two days before. And he had nothing except the small stores of food in the sod house. If he was to have a school, he must have it at once—that he might live as well as work.

But there was only himself to feed. For the first time he saw good in his loneliness. If they had not gone away and left him, he would not have dared to do what he was doing. He would not have recognized himself in Beaumont's eyes or waked in the night to discover that what he wanted to do was to teach school and not to stand behind a counter.

He suddenly ceased to miss even his mother. The front room he would make into the schoolroom, and the fireplace would heat it in winter. The other would be all he needed for himself. If each pupil brought his own stool, he could put up long planks on posts for desks, two rows of them with an aisle between. He had only his own few books, but there was the big Bible, and in every house which he entered he would ask for books. A blackboard he could make easily enough, and there were lumps of chalk in the store. He had enough wherewith to do his work.

It was a fine day, he now noticed, a fine day for his family moving somewhere over the edges of that horizon between earth and sky. But it was a fine day for him, too. The autumn sky was blue, there were no clouds, and the long grass was turning a deep red-brown. It moved in the ceaseless waves of the wind, but the wind was no enemy today. It blew the clean air across the prairies, and he breathed it in and was strengthened and excited. This was a good country, and maybe all the better because there was everything to do in it. In England he would have been struggling to get a job ahead of hundreds of other chaps wanting schools. Here he was the only one between east and west, north and south, as far as his eyes could see, who wanted to teach a school; and suddenly in loneliness he recognized adventure.

Ah, here was the biggest adventure under the sky right here in Median! Why did folk go traipsing West? Tramping along he began to whistle loudly an old song his mother sang, "Oh, you'll tak' the high road, and I'll tak' the low road, and I'll be in Scotland afore ye!" and, still whistling, he knocked on the door of an old, usually empty sod house. A new family was stopping there for a few days. He knew their name was Cobb, and that they were moving on. But they might not go on if there was to be a school in Median. He had seen boys and girls running about.

A small plain-looking woman came to the door. "What do you want?" she asked.

"How do you do, ma'am?" Jonathan said gently, taking off his cap. "I'm about to start a school here, and wanted to know if you'd be interested."

"Come in," she replied. "Come right in."

He stooped as he went in, for the door was too low even for his medium height.

"Sit down," she commanded him. "Now then, tell me about the school. What's your own abilities, young man?"

Her sharp gray eyes picked out of him what she liked, and he submitted to them.

"I've been taught in England," he said. "I was to have gone up for the college exams if I'd stayed. My mother was a teacher, too."

"Why ain't you goin' West like everybody else?" she demanded.

He did not want to open his soul to her. "This seems far enough to me," he replied.

"So 'tis," she agreed. "More'n far enough for me, too. Ohio was what we started for, but as long as there's any West left, my husband seems bound to get at it. I tell him he'll keep on till he hits the Pacific and then go on wadin' until he's drowned. It's a disease, that's what it is."

A boy and a girl of nine and twelve came in softly on their bare feet and stood behind her, staring at Jonathan.

"If we could get some kind of a job to tide us along, maybe I could persuade Adam to spend the winter here and give 'em six months of school, anyways," she said.

"He could ask for my job at the store," Jonathan said. "I've just quit it."

"Say," she cried, "that's an idea!"

She jumped up, a dry little figure of energy. "I'm goin' to put it through—what's your name, young fellow?"

"Jonathan Goodliffe."

"That's a mouthful," she said, laughing. "Well, Mr. Goodliffe, this is Martha and this is Matthew, and they'll be there—if we can pay the tuition, that is."

"The fee'll depend on how many I can get," Jonathan replied. He had only this moment thought of it. "Maybe a dollar a month apiece wouldn't be too much?"

"If we get the job, we can manage somehow," she said. "The oxen we won't need if we stay, and we can maybe sell 'em. Yes, sir, put down Martha and Matthew Cobb."

"Oh, Maw!" Matthew wailed. "Ain't we goin' West?"

"Not this winter if I have the say-so," she said firmly. "It'll be your last chance at books."

"But you always have the say-so!" he cried.

"So I do," she agreed.

"Well, good-by, Mrs. Cobb," Jonathan said. Matthew and Martha—he gave them a quick look. Martha had said not a word. She stood motionless, a sandy-haired, drab girl in a sacklike dress of buff calico.

"Good-by," he said, putting out his hand to her.

She was still speechless, but he felt her rough little hand in his.

"Good-by, Matthew," he said. "I think you'll like school, maybe."

"No, I won't," the boy said. "I don't see any use in books."

"I'll remember that," Jonathan replied with mildness. This was a queer grim-looking lad, his mouth narrow and tight and his eyes already sharp.

He went away and walked across the square and down the road a quarter of a mile to the mill on the edge of the river. He knew it very well, because he had taken grain there which farmers brought to the store to exchange for goods, and now he went to the mill door instead of to the house. Samuel Hasty was there in the midst of a dimness as white as mist with flour.

"Hello, Mr. Hasty!" Jonathan shouted above the racket of wooden machinery.

The little miller saw him and came out, as white as a moth, from behind a bin. "Hello," he said. "What you want, Jonathan?"

"I'm going to start a school, Mr. Hasty."

He went on, and the miller, chewing tobacco steadily, listened. That black hole of a mouth was startling in the dusty whiteness which covered him from head to foot, so that even his pale blue eyes were lost in it. He spat a blob of black saliva that rolled into a ball in the floury dust at his feet.

"I dunno," he said. "Schools are awful dear, and boys get such notions at 'em. I don't know about the whole idea. Afore we know it we'll be havin' an aristocracy in this country with all this education."

"But I plan to have everybody send their children," Jonathan said. "Stephen Parry and Bill White—"

"I dunno's I want my sons goin' to school with truck like that, though," the miller objected.

Jonathan did not answer for a moment. Then he began gently, "A school's a civilizing thing, Mr. Hasty. We can scarcely call this country equal to England if we don't build schools."

Mr. Hasty looked away. "I can't pay your costs," he said.

"Pay me what you like," Jonathan replied, "in meal or in flour or in hay bundles. Fuel will be my problem. I won't have time to gather grass."

"Well, it'll take thinkin'," the miller said.

"Think about it, then, sir, and send me Jim and Sam if you think well of it," Jonathan replied.

He tipped his hat and went on. By the end of the day out of Median's thirteen houses and out of four farmhouses within walking distance he had the promise of seventeen pupils. And then in the late afternoon, being well content, he turned toward Stephen Parry's carpentry and forge.

It was empty when he stepped into it, but there was a fragrance of cooked and seasoned meat and of corn pone. He grew ravenously hungry as he smelled it and, picking up a horseshoe, he struck a slab of iron which stood against the wall. Beaumont came running out, a piece of pone in his hand. He put it behind him when he saw Jonathan.

"Pa'll come right out," he said.

"No, I'll come in, Beau," Jonathan said gaily. "I'm hungry, and you can give me a bite, maybe."

He did not see Beaumont's look because he was already across the room, and then because he clapped the boy's shoulder and walked along beside him through the door.

The family were at supper, but everyone sprang up.

"Don't get up!" Jonathan cried. "I just thought maybe you'd give me a bite, Mrs. Parry. I want to talk to your husband about school desks. I'm going to have a school. Will you give me a bite?"

"Yes, suh," Sue Parry said in her soft big voice. "I'll set you a place in the shop, Mr. Jonathan."

"No, you won't," Jonathan said. "I'll sit right here between Beau and Gem. Then we can talk."

He was already sitting down when Stephen stopped him. None of them had sat down.

"Mr. Goodliffe, suh, we take it as an honoh. But it won't do you no good, suh. They's goin' to be trouble enough without it, anyways. It's hyere a'ready, suh."

"What trouble?" Jonathan demanded. He stood up, compelled by their refusal to sit down with him.

"The town's split clean in two just today already," Stephen Parry said. "Right on your trail Mr. Sam'l Hasty has been follerin', and it looks like I oughtn't to send my children at all, on account of the trouble it'll make, suh. I got my livin' to make."

This, Jonathan perceived, was what Hasty had meant by "thinking." "You mean you're not going to send your children to me?"

Stephen looked down. "Ain't no use educatin' 'em if I cain't feed 'em," he said simply.

"Mrs. Parry," Jonathan began, but she stopped him.

"Mr. Goodliffe, you're newcomer, suh, of co'se, and I know that you means kindness. But it would be better if you jes' said Steve and Sue, like everybody does. We's black and we knows it."

"Beaumont," Jonathan began again but she took it away from him.

"Beaumont is black, too," she said firmly.

"Why, there was a war about this!" Jonathan said.

"War ain't changed no feelin's," Sue said.

She was so large, so sure, so wise, so sad, and all of them were so silent, that he felt overpowered. Then he saw Beaumont. All his life he had hated his father's petulant profanity, and out of this hatred he had never once used it. Now suddenly he needed it, and it burst out of him.

"Of all the dangety-dang, dod-blasted, goddamned injustice!" he shouted. "I won't give in to it!"

"Beau ain't my son," Stephen said quietly, and Jonathan stopped as suddenly as though a sword had been put to his neck.

"His father's a Beaumont," Stephen said, "young Pierre Beaumont."

"I hadn't no choice," Sue said, sadly, "I wasn't but fifteen when he was bawn, and I belonged to the Beaumonts."

"When ol' Mrs. Beaumont found out," Stephen went on, "she wanted to marry Sue away, and I heard about it, and I had seen her, and so ol' Mr. Stephen Parry, mah massa, spoke for me. Beaumont knows how it all happened, don't you, son?"

"Yes," Beaumont said, "I know."

That purely shaped golden-brown face did not quiver, but Jonathan looked away from it.

"I shan't give up," he said stubbornly.

All of his blood was troubled and sickened and stirred by what Stephen had said, but he was determined in spite of it. Somehow in the end he would have them all sitting together in his school.

"You're mighty kind," Stephen Parry said.

"No, I'm not," Jonathan said. He frowned. "What I really came for, Mr. Parry, was to see if you would make some long desks—planks set on posts will do."

"Yes, suh, I'll be glad to," Stephen said.

"All right." Jonathan hesitated. They were all looking at him except Sue. She stood with her head drooped and her hands hanging by her sides. Upon her soft, full face there was a look as still and as curtaining as a cloud.

"Well, good night, Mrs. Parry," he said sharply.

"Good night, suh," she replied, without lifting her eyes.

He went out, walking very quickly and loudly, and turned toward the sod house. He was not hungry any more, but when he got there he would boil some milk and stir a little corn meal into it and feed himself.

This he did, and all the time angry and confused and torn between caution and impetuous wish to go out and demand justice from everyone for the black children. Why had Stephen told him that story? He could make nothing out of it for a reason. It was not white blood that had put any genius into that dark body. Plenty of white blood was stuff as dull as skim milk. No, it was Beaumont seed in Sue Parry's fertile flesh.

He felt an excitement so strong that he was abashed by it, and he got up and began to pull at the furniture he wanted to arrange. Yet it was not an excitement of the flesh, nor had it anything to do with anyone he had ever seen, nor even with himself. It was as vague and as powerful as the pull of the earth beneath his feet and as the light of the moon and the stars now above his head, and its excitement lay in the mind. For suddenly his mind perceived that, when two bodies lay together, male and female, anything might come of it, and it all depended on the two. For the first time he thought definitely of his own marriage and of the sort of woman he wanted and would have.

No middling sort, he thought, but someone big and glorious, like what I've never seen. Except, maybe, a little like Jennet outside, if inside she could be like his mother. He meditated upon this magic until his head was swirling and his face was hot, and the floor scrubbed so clean that he could not bear to step on it himself.

The school opened on the first day of October, and he was tolerably content because before that day he went to every house and argued out, whenever it was necessary, the matter of the Parry children. To some it meant nothing. Bill White, drowsing in the autumn sunshine, woke up to laugh.

"Hell, I don't care," he said. "Some likes 'em black, some likes 'em white. Myself, I like 'em brown. My squaw satisfies me. It don't worry me none when she has a papoose what it'll be. I figure in a country like this, give 'em time, we'll all be mixed anyway. There's yeller men from China over at the Gold Coast, they tell me. Hey, there!" he yelled at the Indian woman who was cutting pumpkins into long strips, "you don't care what color your ol' man is, do ye?"

She shook her head and laughed and showed big white teeth.

"Naw, she don't care," he grunted.

So three half-Indian children sat in school as erect as statues and stared at Jonathan as he wrote the alphabet upon the blackboard. For days they would say nothing, and never was he to know how much was silence and how much ignorance. But they were the ones who brought him prairie fruits he had never eaten before, wild plums and grapes and hazelnuts and pecans and black walnuts of trees so distant he did not know they existed. They brought strings of diced dried pumpkin and dried blackberries and raspberries and rhubarb and pickled buffalo peas and, before frost came, sheep sorrel that Katie stayed after school one day to make into a pie, still sourish even though she poured in molasses. And they brought him freshly killed rabbit and quail and prairie chickens. He had half his living from the Indian children, and never a dollar in cash.

But not all were so easy. Lew Merridy held out against the school until Katie herself settled it. "Sure I'm coming to your school, Jonathan," she said. She had come into the store one day when she heard his voice.

"Oh, you are, hey?" Merridy said. "And how about your ma and the twins?"

"Ma's got 'em about weaned now," Katie said in her practical little voice.

Merridy stared at her, scratched his head, and laughed. "Well, if she says she's goin', she's goin'," he said. "But it don't alter anything I said, Jonathan. I don't believe in educatin' colored people, Indians, and females. They don't need it, and it only makes trouble for the rest of us."

A farmer and his wife came to the door, and Mr. Merridy shouted at his new clerk.

"Hi there, Cobb!"

A long-legged man unfolded himself from behind the counter and Merridy watched him.

"Says he's goin' on in the spring," he turned his head to tell Jonathan, "but I ain't so sure. Looks like the missus wears the pants there, however long his be!"

"Wouldn't it be better to educate females, then?" Jonathan asked, smiling.

But Merridy shook his head. "Naw! Naw, sir! They'd all be wearin' pants then!"

So out of the bustling little handful of individuals that made up Median, Jonathan gathered together the children and started his school.

In late autumn he had his first letter from his mother. He read it over and over again, trying to lift the curtain of the stiffness which fell upon her whenever she took up a pen. But the years in school had shaped her beyond change. He had seen her when she wrote, her preparations, her gravity, her solemn summoning of pious phrases.

"My dear son Jonathan!"

He could see her small pursed mouth and straight figure, and the pen held elegantly upon her little third finger.

"I take my pen in hand to say that we have with God's help reached our destination and, while our circumstances are not the best, we can endure them for the winter. Your father plans in the spring to stake out still another claim in the hope and expectation that by large-scale farming of cattle . . ."

"Oh, my little soul, but how are you?" Jonathan muttered.

There was no finding out. If he had not had his school, he would have set forth to find her. But he had these children, for another family of his spirit, and he could not leave them. To teach them satisfied him in ways he could not himself understand or indeed perceive. He only knew that he was happier than he had ever been, even in Dentwater; and, though he often missed his mother sorely and in other ways missed Ruth and even the lively mischievous presence of Maggie, he had other things. He had that profound fulfillment of putting into hungry minds something which fed them. Not that all minds were hungry! Even in these children of all ages and several bloods, there were as many minds as he could imagine. But he learned to know them one by one—which wanted food and which must be fed even against its will; and which, like Katie, knew positively what it wanted and would have no more.

He laughed at Katie a good deal. She had suddenly begun to grow, and her spare little body took on the curves of a meager adolescence. This seemed ridiculous to him. The first time he observed the slight swelling of her new breasts under an outgrown cotton dress, he thought them as absurd as pinfeathers on a bristling pullet. When she began to put on grown-up airs he teased her and pretended to defer to her. But she was always equal to him.

"Jonathan, you should lay up hay bundles for winter, else you'll get caught by the snows," she told him one day after school.

"If I must I will," he said good-humoredly.

"And you must ask one of the big boys to tend fire for you," she said. "Better ask the biggest Indian. And the water bucket isn't filled often enough, and I saw that biggest Cobb boy pour back the water out of his dipper today."

"I'll attend to everything, Madame," he said.

She was such an ugly little thing, he thought, looking at her out of laughter; so completely commonplace except for that aggressiveness of her nature which burst out of her stiff pigtails and her sharp hazel eyes and out of every movement of her quick, thin little body. He could not imagine her growing up into a real woman.

"Jonathan, there's a preacher coming through on Sunday," she said.

"A preacher!" he repeated. "Well, I never, Katie! There's never been a preacher in Median before, has there?"

"Yes, sometimes he comes once a year or maybe twice," she said. "And I want you should go to the meeting, Jonathan."

"Why?" he asked, amused.

" 'Cause folks say you ain't hardly religious enough to be the teacher of a school," she said. "They say you don't read the Bible and pray before school like you ought."

"Oh, that's what they say now, is it?" Jonathan retorted.

He thought about this a moment. He did not doubt for a moment that it was true. Katie brought him everything she heard said in the store.

"Well, it won't hurt me to go to church once a year," he said. Then to tease her he added, "Will you be there, Katie?"

"Of course," she replied solemnly. "I'm a baptized Christian."

For some reason he could not understand, he went into loud laughter, and when she plainly thought him mad, only laughed the more.

"Oh, dear," he cried at last. "Oh, Katie!"

"Are you laughing at me?" she inquired.

He nodded and began to laugh again.

"Don't you like me?" she inquired again, and he saw she was hurt.

"Of course I do," he said and stopped at once, and on an impulse reached over and took her little claw of a hand and patted it. Then to his horror he saw her thin child's face change and turn crimson.

"I like you—something terrible," she whispered.

"That's nice," he stammered, and dropped her hand as though it burned him.

12

JUDY SPENDER, WAITING FOR HER FATHER TO ANNOUNCE THE hymn, sat holding upon her knees the big old accordion she had played for him ever since her mother died. He was at least six minutes away from the hymn, and so she looked idly upon the faces of the people gathered in the main room of the tavern this Sunday morning to worship God. She knew American House very well. Off and on they had come here, she and her mother and father, almost as long as she could remember clearly, which, since she was seventeen, was now almost a dozen years. At first there was only the tavern at the crossroads, east and west, north and south, and people drove to it for meetings. Then year after year a few houses began to collect in this place called Median, until now it was a prairie town like so many she knew. Her mother used to think that her father would be a great preacher some day, maybe in a city church, and then they would settle down. But long before she died she had stopped talking about it, and they all knew this hard traveling from one small town to another was what had been and would be, as long as Joel Spender lived. "A bearer of good tidings," Joel called himself.

"What's to become of you, Judy?" her mother had fretted. Her fretting kept her alive long after she wanted to die. "I could go in peace if I knew what was going to happen to Judy," she moaned to her husband.

"The Lord'll look after His own," Joel said positively.

"There's never been any sign of Judy's being the Lord's," Mrs. Spender retorted with a faint revival of old rebellion.

"Well, she can come along with me, and certainly I am the Lord's," Joel said.

His wife groaned. But there was nothing she could do about anything; and one day, when Judy was not quite twelve, Mrs. Spender gave up to the tumor that had enlarged her thin figure into obscene shapes. Years before she had wanted an operation for this tumor, in the days when it was still manageable; but Joel would not hear of it.

"I would hold it to be a lack of faith," he said. "You know I'm a faith healer, Mitty, and I'm not goin' to yield to temptation."

He prayed faithfully at certain hours every day that God would heal his wife and believed each day that she was better, and then, as the tumor grew in size and power, he lengthened his hours of prayer and increased the strength of his pleas.

"O God!" They could hear his voice booming heavenward through thin boardinghouse walls in towns and under trees beside inns and out of the shadeless prairies. "Hear Thy servant and heal Thy servant's wife! Thy servant don't ask for anything beyond Thy will, O God, but I do ask that it is Thy will to heal Mitty!"

When she spoke again of operation, he was sterner than ever. "No, Mitty, there ain't goin' to be any operations. This here's come to a tussle between me and God, and I'm goin' to win."

Mrs. Spender said no more. She had hoped in God for a good many years, but now it became plain to her that the trouble all along had been that there was no way of discovering what God's will was until it was too late to do anything about it. And it began to be clear to her before long that in her case God would triumph over Joel. She did not tell him so, but she made her own preparations. One of these was to talk as plainly as she could to Judy, who was the only child she had left out of seven. The other six had died young, and sometimes when she lay helplessly supporting the parasite that fed upon her, she remembered them, and she wished she had not given them Bible names. Only Judy had not died, and Judy she had named after a woman on a boat who had helped her when the child was born. "Judy" the woman had been named, and that was all Mrs. Spender knew about her. Later she had found the name Judith in the Bible, and then she told Judy, "Your name is just Judy, not short for anything else."

Or maybe the child had lived because she was born on the Missouri. People said it was good luck to be born on water. Anyway, she had always been a strong, healthy little creature with red cheeks and bright dark eyes and yellow curls. Joel was dark, too, but he had never been healthy because of his weak digestion, nor ever smart enough to account for Judy's forwardness. It was terrible to die when Judy was just beginning to need her mother's care. But God's will was the one unchangeable thing in the world, and there was no use in asking for mercy if God had made up His mind. She called Judy to her one day and said, "Judy, I'm going to die."

Judy opened her brown eyes enormously. "How do you know, Mama?"

"It's God's will, so there is no use in talking about it. What I want to talk about is you, and what you're to do after I'm gone. You listen to me now, Judy."

"Yes, Mama," Judy replied. Her mother was so matter-of-fact that it was like being left behind at a boardinghouse the time she had whooping cough.

"You go on with your father and play the accordion for him like I do, and lead the hymns real good and loud. And don't ever let a man put his hands on you—never! Not for nothing! But if a plain hard-working man with a job in a steady place asks you to marry him, you leave the work right away and let your father fend for himself, and stay with your husband as long as you live."

"All right, Mama," Judy said.

"That's all, but don't you forget it."

"No, Mama."

At the bottom of her heart she never had forgotten it. She kept it there as a secret with her mother from her father. When her mother was alive they had often had secrets together, such as the keeping back of pennies from the collection to save for a dress for Judy.

"It's all right to have secrets from Father, if God knows," her mother said.

"Did you tell God?" she once asked her mother.

"God knows everything anyway," her mother had answered.

If God knew about this secret, He gave no sign of it, though sometimes she was sure He did know and purposely kept anybody with a steady job from asking her to marry him. Now in the tavern at Median she yawned, and remembered that her mother had told her to put up her hand whenever she did. Then in the middle of her yawn she caught a pair of blue eyes looking at her with secret laughter, and she closed her mouth abruptly. The eyes belonged to a young man of medium height whom she had never seen before. He did not look like anybody else in the room. He wore a neat suit of brownish cloth and a stock and collar, and his brown hair was smoothly brushed. His face, she noticed in the quick, all-seeing glance she gave him, was pale, a little thin, and, while it was neither ugly nor handsome, it was pleasant.

Her attention was snatched by her father.

"Judy!" he said sternly. "I've called the hymn—it's 'Beulah Land.' "

She started into the tune and pumped her accordion back and forth as hard as she could. Then she lifted her voice, loud and clear.

Watching her, Jonathan thought to himself that he had
never looked at so pretty a girl. He had seen her almost at
once when he entered the room. Coming out of the brilliant
sunshine of late autumn, for a moment everyone had looked
pallid to him and shadowy, everybody except a fair-haired,
brown-eyed girl in a dark red dress who sat with an old
accordion across her knee. She did not see him, for her eyes
kept wandering, but he watched her while the people gathered
to sit on stools and benches and on kegs and boxes set in
ragged rows in front of the bar. The shelves behind it were
decently draped with Indian blankets to hide the bottles, and
the bar was made into a pulpit with a white sheet. Mrs. Drear
had put a salt jar full of goldenrod on it, and behind it a tall
dark man stood to preach and pray.

Jonathan, his ears too sensitive, could not listen to him. The
preacher's fervor was poured into sentences every one of
which had words pronounced awry and mistaken in grammar.
So he kept looking instead at the young girl, a beautiful,
pouting thing, sitting so carelessly beside the pulpit that, if one
brown hand had not held the accordion firmly, it would have
slid from her knees. She had sat smiling and brooding and
certainly not listening and then suddenly lifted her head for a
great yawn, and in the middle of it she had seen him laughing
at her.

He was a little alarmed by the suddenness with which she
shut her jaw and by the look she gave him. Then he decided
doggedly not to be afraid of her, and to give her look for
look. He kept on looking at her when the preacher called to
her, and she began to play furiously with all her strength upon
the accordion. When she sang in a clear loud voice he found
himself singing, too, although he hated singing in church. The
vicar in Dentwater had not encouraged the congregation to
sing, and it seemed indecent so to expose oneself.

But he excused it now because here was, after all, only the
tavern, which was always full of noise and roistering, and he
could not believe this ranting evangelist was a minister like
the vicar, and this was no proper hymn tune, either. The girl
was playing it like a dance, swaying as she played it, exagger-
ating its rhythm and letting her voice soar—a glorious voice,
but not for hymns. In Dentwater he would have been shocked
by it, but here it made him want to sing too.

"A pleasant true voice, our Jonathan has, but not good

enough for the church choir," was what his mother had said once long ago. He cleared his throat and let his voice out a little louder.

And after the meeting was over he went up, not to the preacher, but to her. He had always to forget his own shyness, and he fought it now.

"I am Jonathan Goodliffe," he said. "Excuse me if I introduce myself."

She put out her brown hand, and he felt it soft and plump. "I am Judy Spender," she said.

"The minister's daughter?"

"Yes."

He could not restrain himself. "Then you'll be going on, won't you?" he asked.

"It depends," she said. "Sometimes we stay, if folks want a protracted meeting."

"Then I hope they will," he said earnestly; "in fact— That is, I'm very sure they will."

She laughed with a hearty parting of the reddest lips he had ever seen. "I hope so," she said. "I'd like to stay somewhere for a few days, anyway, just to get a chance to wash our clothes."

"You must stay," he said. Under his calm face his heart echoed, "You must—you must," and then he felt her hand pulling softly out of his and realized, to his horror, that he had been holding it all this while.

He went away so confused that he did not think of anything else until the middle of the Sunday dinner which he was eating with the Merridys. How it had come about that this was his weekly habit he could not have said himself, but so it had become. Katie had begun it by demanding one day what he had to eat in the house because, she declared, he was looking thin, and then had answered herself by looking into his crocks and opening all the boxes and bags. The next day she said firmly, "Maw says you're to have Sunday dinner with us reg'lar, and if you're too proud you can take it off my tuition."

That was at least the beginning of his going each week into the three rooms back of the store and playing with the twins while Katie and her mother worked. Mrs. Merridy, thin and pallid and corded with stringy muscles, was a born cook. Her rabbit pies, her saleratus biscuits, her corn dodgers with pork cracklings, her spoon breads and sour-cream cakes, her greens and pickles and preserves and corn-meal puddings were concocted for strength and delight; and in spite of himself once a week Jonathan ate to the full and spent Sunday afternoon in a pleasant stupor with the family. He was aware at such times of a great deal of comfort in these three rooms. With the resources of the store at her command, Mrs. Merridy had muslin curtains looped back from the windows, braided rag rugs on her wooden floors, a big circular stove in winter, and rocking chairs and cushions padded with cotton. She had somehow found plants to pot for her windows, red geraniums and swollen begonias and a hearty Boston fern. Upon the walls were texts and mottos worked in wool, and two large crayon portraits of her parents framed in gilded wood.

In the midst of all this comfort Jonathan was aware, without noticing it, of Katie's narrow, bustling figure, arranging and rearranging, setting the table, lifting the cat out of a chair, keeping the twins quiet with sharp little slaps and sudden scoldings, and insisting upon some whim of her own for his greater comfort. She darted at him from time to time. "Jonathan, don't sit there. The brown rocker's better . . . Jonathan, put your feet on this stool."

He always submitted to the pushing and pulling of her determined little hands, because it was easier to submit to her than not. She was capable of endless argument until she had her way.

Today in the midst of dinner she said sharply, "Jonathan, you ain't eatin' a mite."

"Yes, I am, Katie." He was embarrassed by her notice, for it was true he had no appetite. He could neither eat nor think because of Judy.

"Leave him be, Katie," Mrs. Merridy said dolefully. "I know how it is when you've been to meetin'. It takes your appetite sure enough to get thinkin' again on eternal things, and then it don't hardly seem worth while to feed the body. I declare, Mr. Merridy, I think we ought to ask Brother Spender to hold a week's meetin' before the winter sets in. 'Twould give us somethin' to think about in the long evenin's, and maybe save some souls from goin' to hell if anybody should die, as they're bound to do."

Lew gave a grunting chuckle and swallowed a great mouth-

ful of roast pork. A farmer had brought him a side of freshly
killed pig in payment of the season's bill, and he loved it.

"Well, you know what I always say, Lula—they's more
souls made than saved at these here protracted meetin's."

"And I always say for shame, Lew Merridy, for such talk,
especially before young folks, to put such notions into words."

"Godamighty, Lula, Jonathan's a grown man—"

"Well, you'd oughta begin to think about your own daughter," Mrs. Merridy said.

Mr. Merridy gasped. "Why, Katie—she ain't but a little
girl."

"I'm almost fifteen, Paw," Katie said severely.

He looked at her, pretending to be astonished. "Why, so
you are, you little pullet!"

"And I know what you mean," Katie said virtuously, "and I
don't think you ought to talk about it."

Lew, about to pick up his great mug of coffee, set it down
again and burst into big laughter and clapped Jonathan on the
back.

"You and me'll have to go eat in the kitchen, Jonathan," he
bellowed. "We ain't decent."

Jonathan smiled and glanced at Katie with a faint disgust
he did not understand, except to know that he did not like to
think that her mind comprehended such things as—as the
making of souls. But, though he did not know it, this disgust,
too, was because of Judy. Ever since he came walking in a
daze and a glory into these rooms he had been thinking of
Judy and of how to go about getting a protracted meeting. He
was too honest to pretend to a religious need. Such vague
need as he had was satisfied by the chapter of the Bible he
read occasionally at night before he slept, and by the prayers
he said night and morning, simple ritual prayers that his
mother had taught each of her children when they began to
talk. Such variations as he had privately added to them had
never come to anything. When he had prayed the last one it
had been that his brother Arthur might not die, and when
Arthur died, his first thought had been. "I'll never ask God for
anything again." There was no rebellion in this decision, but
the simple giving up of hope that his destiny could be altered
by any plea of his. God's mind, whatever it was, was always
made up beforehand, and it seemed more dignified in a man
not to go whining and begging with his own prayers. He could

not honorably persuade his neighbors to have a week's meetings of prayer and preaching when he himself considered such prayers futile and wanted only to see a beautiful young girl every day for as long as he could.

He listened when Mrs. Merridy began scolding, "Now, Lew, stop acting like a behemoth and give me some help. There's a lot of unconverted people come into Median over the summer, and if we could get 'em converted we'd all have a better winter. You know you say yourself meetin's do a lot of good—folks pay their bills and men buy things for their families."

"Oh, I ain't objectin'," Lew said. "Howsomever, it's a little late for folks to sit outside, and I don't believe Drear could let 'em have the tavern every day right now when folks are humpin' through to get West before winter."

An inspiration fell upon Jonathan. He lifted his head and said quickly, "They could use my schoolroom, if the parents were willing for school to let out a week."

Lew was struck. "So they could," he said. "That's a real idee, Jonathan, and parents won't mind. They're always glad to get their children converted young—it saves a lot of switchin' sometimes. I ain't switched you since you was babtized, have I, Katie?"

"No, Paw," Katie replied.

"Don't know but what it's a good idee all round," Merridy said. "Folks can drive in and get their winter stores and get some soul food, too. You gotta have religion in a community, or folks get to killin' each other, especially in the winter when they're all shut up together. Don't know but what I'll mosey around myself this afternoon and see Brother Spender and the Median folks. I'm a religious man at bottom, Jonathan." He laughed somewhere down in his belly. "That is, if you can find bottom!"

Jonathan pushed his plate away. Food dried and swelled in his mouth, and he could not swallow.

"I don't feel quite well, after all," he said. "Please excuse me, Mrs. Merridy." He leaped to his feet and went out of the room. He was so excited that he could not sit still nor listen nor speak. He must get away by himself to think and to try if he could to see what to do with himself. He was going to fall into love with Judy Spender!

In those days of the protracted meeting, because of a peculiar inarticulate honesty, he gave up his own private prayers. His house was full of praying, but he felt embarrassed to pray his little childish prayer. He rose early every morning and swept out the rooms and wiped off the benches and tables and the blackboard, and went outdoors and picked purple autumn flowers and put them on his table that was Joel Spender's pulpit. Then he ate his breakfast and waited. But he had only to wait a little while. For Joel came early to have him write upon the blackboard his text for the day, and with him came Judy. In his neat, square, very clear script Jonathan wrote great violent thundering curses, while Joel stood roaring them out.

"Thou shalt be brought down to Hell, to the sides of the Pit. They that see thee shall look upon thee saying, 'Is this the man that made the Earth to tremble, that did shake Kingdoms?' . . . Thou art cast out of thy Grave, as a carcass trodden under foot, for the End of Evildoers shall never be renowned."

"Howl, O gate! Cry, O city!"

"The cry is gone round about the borders of Moab, the howling thereof unto Eglaim, for the waters of Dimon shall be full of blood."

"Father's practicin' on you, Jonathan," Judy said mischievously. She stood by the door, pulling whispers of fragmentary music out of her accordion, beginnings of tunes she did not finish, the catch of a gospel chorus, the lilt of a tune she had heard in a river boat somewhere, a deep chord or two unfulfilled. She looked sometimes at Jonathan, but more often out of the door at the sky and the prairie.

"I ain't," Joel said. But he could not go on rolling out his words. He was pricked and angered. "You're a real thorn in the flesh, Judy, like your ma was to me," he said indignantly. "I prayed God like Paul for years to pluck it out, and when your ma died, I thought He had. But He shore left a stinger behind in you."

She did not answer, and Jonathan, turning his head quickly, saw her profile, smiling, and he turned away again, frightened at the vehemence of his first love.

Then, that men and women and even children might be quickened to hear God's word, there came over the prairies that week such long golden days as he had never seen. People from Median came walking in the quiet sunshine and along the path the school children's feet had beaten every day to the sod-house door, and through the long grass a few wagons came in, bringing men and women and children. They looked alike, their garments faded to drab, and their skins burned red and brown. But when they talked they changed, and their eyes kindled differently, blue eyes though most of them were. They lingered outside to talk, starved for talk, and Joel had to call to Judy to start music before one by one they came into the shadowy room.

"My squaw says it's the Indians' summer," Bill White said. He sat in the sun, drowsing upon a bench at the door from which he could look away from Joel's dark face out to the smooth tawny red of the grass, quiet for once under a windless sky. When he looked long enough for peace he would listen to Joel's demands. "I will confess before men that God is good," he drawled.

"Are you saved, Brother White?" Joel yelled.

"I been saved a long time," Bill White said.

"Anybody else been saved? Anybody else want to be saved?" Joel cried and raked them with his red-hot eyes.

If nobody answered, he shouted at Judy, "Play something, girl! Play something to waken 'em outen their death-sleep!"

And Judy, her beautiful face unmoved, played "Just As I Am Without One Plea" with such passion, such pleading that they stirred upon their seats, and a few rose miserable and sweating to mumble out their sins. But Jonathan could not move. He was not for one instant deceived. When Judy played he knew he thought, not about God, but about her.

As day went into another day, his thinking ceased to be thought and became mere longing; until one afternoon, unable to endure, he rose and went into his bedroom and sat there upon a stool waiting for them all to be gone. When they were gone she came in, pushing back her hair from her face.

"Oh, I'm tired," she sighed and, seeming to belong here as she belonged anywhere, she threw herself upon his bed.

He was shocked and yet he trembled and looked at her and saw every turn of her bosom and her thigh. And she opened her eyes which she had closed and saw him.

"Come here, Jonathan," she said.

He rose, unwilling and yet compelled, and went over to her and sat upon the very edge of the bed.

"Is this your home, Jonathan?"

"Yes," he said.

"And shall you live here always?" she asked.

"I daresay."

"Oh!" She sighed and flung out her arms. "Think of waking up in the same place every day!"

He did not answer this, being too busy with his own feelings. "Oh, my lovely," he was crying to her inside himself. "Oh, my lovely, lovely dear!"

"Jonathan, lie beside me!" she said suddenly.

"No," he said grimly.

She opened her eyes at him. "Didn't you ever hear of bundling?" she demanded.

"No," he said.

"Well, it's nothing wicked," she said, and laughed at him. "Why, you just lie down together, all dressed, like this, and talk, an' that's all."

"How could it be all?" he muttered. And, terrified because he was rushing headlong down into the pit he saw ahead of him, he leaped to his feet and strode into the other room. It was empty. Even Joel had gone, forgetting Judy, as he often did. And when Jonathan saw the emptiness, he went straight out of the door and on to Median.

I'm terrible wicked, he thought. Wicked he was if it meant what he wanted to do and would have done if he had stayed a moment more beside her. He went into the tavern. Henry Drear was behind the bar.

"Give me a mug of whisky," he ordered.

"Never knew you to want that," Drear said, grinning. He dipped up the liquor from a tubful that stood on the floor behind the counter.

"Never wanted it before," Jonathan replied. He stood drinking the hot stuff morosely and waiting the subsidence of another heat in himself.

"Guess it's religion," Henry Drear said affably. "A lot more folks stop in here for a drink when meetin's are goin' on."

"They do, eh?" Jonathan said.

He hung about the tavern silently all evening while men came and went. Once he went into the kitchen where Mrs. Drear was cooking over the red-hot iron range.

"I sure do miss Jennet," Mrs. Drear said, mourning. "I wish I could get a letter from her. But I reckon she can't find nobody to write it, and she never would learn her letters to write herself."

He had not thought of Jennet in weeks, but it seemed to him now that Jennet had begun the love of Judy in him. He went home at last and listened half-fearfully as he lit the candle. If Judy were here, he was lost. But she was gone. He lifted the curtain between the two rooms and saw his bed tumbled where she had lain on it, perhaps to sleep. He went and stood looking at that impress, and love came creeping into him again. She was innocent, an innocent untaught child. Was she not innocent? His heart cried out that she was; and then his mind, remembering her flung upon his bed, put forth its cold little doubt. Could she be innocent?

The strange heat of delaying summer steeped the prairies in warmth and in silence. Day after day of the seven days even the wind was still, and in the sod house Joel Spender changed the manner of his preaching. He left the prophets and turned to the Song of Solomon. He showed them a God no longer angry, but pleading and longing to win their hearts by love. He stood before them in his old black suit, a shabby man until one forgot him in the dark fire of his eyes and in the power of his sonorous, pliant voice. If this was the voice of God, then these were the words of love, and hearts of flesh were moved to answer love with vague love. They stood up, ashamed, shy, muttering something of what they felt without understanding what it was, their faces red or pale, but always disturbed and always ashamed as though they were miserable. Only Beaumont was joyful and without shame in his confession.

"I do praise Gawd!" he cried gladly, and leaped to his feet.

"Praise Gawd!" Sue murmured from the corner where they sat apart.

But they forgot their shame when Judy played her accordion in great surges of sound. They were at her mercy when she played, and she played as she willed, and they followed her. Sometimes she made them gay, and once the little black children even began to clap to her rhythm.

She played more quickly, and suddenly Sue's high voice seized the melody and led it along to ecstasy, and they were all singing:

> "Jesus! Thy very name I love,
> Thy sweetness fills my breast."

Jonathan, his eyes upon Judy, felt his heart smolder in his bosom. For she, drawing her accordion to and fro, swaying to its measure, turned to him and looked at him directly as he sat in his corner far from the door. They had not spoken together again, and tomorrow would be the last day. He had not prayed, nor had he risen when Joel had cried out for them to speak and to declare what God had done for them. He had sat through all exhortations, disliking them and feeling shamed by them. Yet he was converted and he was changed, though not, he knew, by God.

Lew Merridy, sitting next to him, nudged him suddenly. "The devil's goin' to make the most of this, Jonathan!" he whispered. "You cain't take the lid off folks without somethin' happens!"

Jonathan did not answer. He must speak once more to Judy. What he would say he did not know, for he did not know what he wanted of her. But he could not let her go without tying between them some sort of bond. Not a promise, for he was not ready to promise and too prudent to do it unless he was ready. Only he must know at least that she was coming back.

At the end of that day when the people, weary with exhortation, were straggling across the ragged square into their homes, into the tavern, some of them harnessing horses to wagons to go to their farms, Judy delayed at his door. Joel had gone ahead and did not look back to see whether or not she followed him.

"Well," she said, "it's almost over."

"Yes, it is," he agreed. He spoke with the mild preciseness that was natural to him and that hid so completely his turmoil.

"Has it been like you thought it would be?" she asked.

"You mean—the meetings?" he asked.

"I mean—any of it."

"I don't think I thought how it would be," he replied.

How would he ask her anything when he did not know what he wanted to ask her? How seek an assurance when he did not know what he wanted assured?

"I hope we'll meet again," he said.

"I reckon I'll be back in the spring," she said carelessly. She was looking away over the prairies as she spoke; she was always looking over the prairies. "We usually come to Median about twice a year, and I don't see any change ahead. We're heading south now because Father can't preach up here in winter. Folks don't get out once the blizzards begin."

She seemed so careless, as though it did not matter to her where they went, that he was terrified. He wanted to pull her gaze back to himself.

"I hope you'll come back in the spring," he said earnestly. "If you do, I'll look forward to it all winter."

"You want me to promise?"

Her black-lashed eyes flashed to him, and their gaze upon him was so warm that he was moved out of all prudence.

"Yes, I do," he said.

"All right, I promise," she said. She smiled, then suddenly she put out her hand and touched him on the cheek with the palm of her hand, a touch too light for a caress, and immediately she went away into the twilight.

And he stood there, by the touch upon his cheek her slave, and she knew it. From what wisdom she had known that this young man would be repelled by passion shown too soon she had not stopped to think. But instinctively she had chosen the one right spell to put upon him, a touch of flesh to flesh, sweet, fleeting, and not to be repeated, because she was going away. She liked this young man, so different in all ways from her father, whom she half-despised, and different, too, from the unshaven rough men she saw every day.

He looks clean, as if he bathed every day, she thought. She knew he did not, of course, bathe every day. Nobody could do that on the prairie where water was more precious than whisky. Something about Jonathan made her think of her mother. If he asks me to marry him next spring, I maybe will, she thought and, thus thinking, entered the tavern, gave a peculiarly brilliant smile to three strange men standing at the bar, and went into the kitchen.

"Shan't I help peel potatoes?" she inquired of Mrs. Drear.

" 'Twould be a mighty help," Mrs. Drear said fervently. Judy tied an apron about her waist and peeled in long nimble curls of skin.

"Your paw satisfied enough to come back in the spring?" Mrs. Drear asked. She was mixing corn meal furiously with milk.

"I reckon," Judy said dreamily.

His cheek had been as smooth as her own, she thought. She

could feel it still on the palm of her hand. There was no reason why a man's cheek should not be smooth.

And yet the next day they did not once speak to each other, not so much avoiding each other as knowing there was no more to be said. Winter must come before spring.

Jonathan's school was restored, and once more he began to teach. But it had become a task. The taste for it had gone out of his mouth. He looked at the children with deep doubt. A dirty ragged lot, he thought gloomily. The Brewitt children from the river dugout wore sacks with holes cut out for sleeves. What they had on besides was little, and already they shivered. All of the children were barefoot, but then so was most of Median. But hair was not combed and faces were not clean. Among them only Martha and Matthew Cobb looked tended and washed.

"Everybody with a dirty face can take time off to wash," he ordered suddenly. "That's all of you Whites, and Sam and Abram Hasty and all of Brewitts and Mary Anson and Jim Anson—the lot of you except the two Cobbs. Cobbs and Parrys are clean."

He watched their astonishment with some shame. He had never lost his temper before with any of them, and it was not their fault if they were dirty.

"Reckon we'll have to git water then from Drear's well," Sam Hasty said.

"I ain't goin' to wash," Abram said. He was a tall strong boy with black hair to his shoulders. At fourteen he was unwillingly beginning his letters.

"You will, Abram," Jonathan said. He wished that he had let them be dirty, for after all it had nothing to do with their brains, and he had seen their dirt to mind it so much only because he was full of his own gloom. Judy was gone. He had not told her good-by. He had simply let her walk away on the last night without a word.

"Eight dollars," Joel had said sadly after he had counted collection. "I reckon we'll have to preach our way south, Judy. God didn't prosper me much in Median, Mr. Goodliffe."

She had spoken for him quickly. "It depends on whether you're countin' souls or dollars, Mr. Goodliffe will be thinkin', Pa."

"That's a cruel sharp thought of your own, Judy," Joel retorted. "The Lord knows He's responsible for feedin' His own. Who's goin' to feed me if He don't?"

She did not answer this, but she went away and as she went she gave Jonathan a look, full of pleading for his mercy. And he gave her mercy quick with comprehension. It was their only good-by.

She's not like her father, he thought. She's good and delicate—she *is* innocent!

He had watched her walk away, her head bare and her bonnet in her hand, and now winter stretched between them, an eternity.

"Sam, you and Abram take the two buckets and fill them," he said sharply.

Sam got on his feet and hesitated, glancing at his older brother.

"Sam ain't goin'," Abram said, and Sam sat down.

"Yes, he is," Jonathan said, "inside of three minutes."

What he would do in three minutes with this great boy he did not know, and he had only three minutes. He had never been a fighter, nor had he ever struck a pupil. He had been criticized for this. "No learnin' without the rod," Mrs. Cobb had said to him one day.

"Folks say you're too mild to be a teacher, Jonathan," Lew Merridy said to him at a Sunday dinner table.

"Everybody's feared of Jonathan's light-colored eyes, though," Katie had said.

"Afraid of my eyes!" Jonathan had repeated.

"They say you've got a queer eye," she said.

"Why?"

"I dunno," she answered. "It's the way you drill into a body when you look at 'em."

He remembered this now, and he rose and slowly and steadily went toward the big boy. Abram watched him sullenly out of his hair, like an angry dog, until he stood near him.

"Abram," Jonathan said, "I could fight you, but I won't because I can do something else that'll be easier for me. You're going to fetch that water." He paused, then slowly began to recite the opening lines of Virgil, which he had once learned by heart because of their music.

"Arma virumque cano—"

He chanted them slowly and clearly, his eyes never moving from that dark face, until suddenly Abram howled and jumped up and leaped for the door, and Sam after him. They snatched the two buckets as they went, and Jonathan walked to the blackboard and put down twenty words.

"Study these until they come back," he said sternly. There was no sound of stir or whisper in the room. He waited a moment and then sat down by his table and opened the big Bible. It fell by magic to that Song of Solomon, and he read it, his heart aching for love.

"Let thy breasts be as clusters of the vine
    And the smell of thy breath like apples,
    And thy mouth like the best wine
    That goeth down smoothly for my beloved,
    Gliding through the lips of those that are asleep."

God, speaking to His blessed bride, the Church, Joel had said when he read aloud those words. But Jonathan knew better. They were the words of a man to a woman. He shut the book.

13

THE END OF THE AUTUMN WAS COME. THE GRASS WAS RED and then brown. The wind stayed, and there was no cloud large enough to hold in it the hope of rain. Day went into day until the tenth day after Judy had gone. It was night, and Beaumont was there. He stored up in himself questions and thoughts and wonders which he poured upon Jonathan at night; and Jonathan, struggling to keep his wits clear in the swirl of Beaumont's mind, was stimulated and strengthened and always at last exhausted because he knew he was not enough for this boy.

Beaumont had grown fast in the last few months. He was taller than Jonathan and much heavier, though without fat. He carried his weight in the size of his skeleton, and yet his bones were well shaped and even graceful.

"I wish you could go away to school," Jonathan said. "In England you'd be thinking of going up to a university."

"Would they let me, in England?" Beaumont, suddenly alert, lifted his head.

"I reckon," Jonathan said. "At least I never heard them say there they let a man's skin decide his brains."

They went outdoors as they talked. Whatever Beaumont would have said next was not said. His head up, he sniffed the darkness.

"I smell something," Beaumont said.

They stood still together, smelling the darkness.

"I can only smell the dusty dry grass," Jonathan said after a moment.

But Beaumont's nostrils quivered in and out like a dog's. "I smell fire," he said.

And yet there was no fire to be seen. If it were over the horizon, there would be a glow against the sky. But there was no glow. The sky was close down upon them, deep and soft and black.

"Nothing," said Jonathan.

"Fire," Beaumont repeated.

Then, while they waited, there was a quiver of wind out of the west. It was scarcely more than a night breeze rearing out of the grass, except that it carried the mild faint fragrance of smoke. It was no breeze, but the first thrust of a very distant wind.

"Smoke!" Jonathan exclaimed.

The moment he said "smoke," it seemed to him he could smell it. He had heard of fire upon the prairies; men talked of fire as they talked of the wind and lightning and snow and all those forces which were their enemies. He had listened to their stories when he clerked in the store. Men sat upon barrels and leaned against the counters, spat and rubbed their noses and scratched their heads, and laughed ruefully.

"We-ll, I declare, when I saw them flames r'arin' round me I knowed that I had to run like the gophers and the coyotes, and I loped along, kickin' 'em outa my way. On'y thing that kep' ahead of me was the wild horses, but soon I was areachin' for their tails—"

He had listened, not knowing how much was truth and how much the enormous lying which the prairies taught men to do. But there had been the storm and the wind, larger than even they were able to lie; and he knew inevitably that sometime he would have to fight fire, too—the fire that began no one knew how and ended none knew where.

"Gotta tell folks," Beaumont said. He began to run with long leaping steps toward the tavern. Jonathan moved to run after him and then halted. All he had was here in the sod house. It was his home and the one refuge he had for his mother and the children. He thought a moment, remembering what men had said they did against fire. The river people were safe. But the sod house stood a mile away from the river. He had no beast to help him haul water, and no water here except what he carried for his own use from Drear's well or collected in a barrel when it rained. But it had not rained for many days. Once, they said, a woman had poured upon her roof the milk she had saved to churn butter. But he had not even tasted milk for months. All he had wherewith to fight fire was more fire, and even as he thought of what men had said about this he saw other fires lighting out of the darkness about the scattered houses of Median. Men were setting the prairie on fire, and he went in and brought a stick of fire out of the fireplace. The wind was growing moment by moment, and he stood a second to catch its direction, that it might carry the flames away from the house. And as he stood he saw his garden full of yellow pumpkins. He had left them to ripen continually one day after another, daring frost. In the corner of the sod house he had piled those already ripe.

"Send I get ours dried, I'll dry them for you, Jonathan," Katie had once said. "And I'll make them Indians help."

"Those," Jonathan had said gently, but she had paid no attention to him.

While the grass burned he would gather the rest of the pumpkins and throw them inside the door. He stooped and, sheltering his face with his hands, lit a blade of grass. It caught instantly, as dry as any dust, and then blade lit blade as the wind hurried it. He stepped back, full of solemn fear. It was a grave thing he had done—to set fire to the prairie. He looked across Median for courage and saw the other fires already. They were blazing in circles about homes. Men were beating them back when they came too close. He ran and lit one blaze after another in a huge circle about the sod house, and then ran to his pumpkins and snatched them from the vines and rolled them into the door. His patch of corn he had plucked a week before, and there was nothing but the stalks left, and yet he bitterly regretted them because they were to have been part of his winter fuel. But he must let them go, for the fire he had started farthest from the house was already too close. He rushed at it to stamp it out and flail it out with an old broom. In a few minutes it was beyond him, and he was terrified. Better to have let the wild fire burn him than the fire he had set with his own hands, he thought. He leaped from one quickening flame to another, but the fire seemed turned into a liquid to creep along under the grass, red as blood until it burst out into flames, small but eluding him everywhere. He began to sweat with heat and with fright, and then suddenly he heard his name roared at him.

"Jonathan!"

It was Henry Drear, carrying two great pails of water and around his neck some old buffalo hides.

"Jonathan, wet these and hang 'em over the windows and doors. Then give over fighting this bit of fire. It can't damage the sod house. We got to get out and do some burnin'. Real fire's comin'—look at that sky!"

Drear was already dipping the robes and packing them into the window frames. "Got no time to waste, Jonathan," he said. "Any minute we'll see fire blazin' there at the edge of the sky."

Jonathan hung a long dripping hide into the open crack of the door and closed it hard. Then he followed Drear, running with him toward the west. Far out from Median fires were beginning to blaze. Everybody was out lighting a huge circle of fire. He could see men on foot, on horseback, bright for a moment against the blaze.

"Git as far as we can," Drear panted. "The wind's blowin' against us."

They ran toward the burning sky until they saw the black horizon line break into points of flame.

"All right!" Drear shouted. "We dassent go furder!"

They stooped and lighted the grass and with handfuls of blazing grass for torches lit other grass, parting and running in opposite directions until in the broken darkness and light Jonathan was lost. But he went on blindly lighting fire after fire until suddenly he was in the midst of a roar of flames, and choked with smoke. He stood up, and a jack rabbit ran between his legs and nearly knocked him down. He caught himself and then he saw the big fire was upon him, and he turned and ran from it. He ran for the only shelter he knew, the sod house. The sky was as bright as though a bloody sun were lighting it, and in that hideous light he saw he was only one of many animals. He did not stop, but he saw beside him a deer and a fox; and ahead of him a small squat animal he did not know humped itself along upon its short legs; and prairie chickens half-ran, half-flew upon the blackening grass; and birds rushed through the smoky air. But he stopped for none of them. He was a fair runner, steady though not swift, and his wind was good. He had need of good wind, for the air was hot with smoke, and by the time he reached the sod house and jerked the door open and closed it again he was gasping.

The air in the sod house was still good and cool, and he flung himself on the floor to breathe for a moment. But not for more. In a very little while the fire would be around him, and he must save the air he had. He leaped to his feet again and looked for rugs, for paper, for anything to stuff in the crevices of the windows and doors. All he had was not enough, and he seized upon a few sheets of paper he had given the children. Paper was precious, and only when a composition was perfect could he allow them to have a sheet of paper to write it upon. Now he snatched them up, crumpled them in his hand, and then saw that one of them was Beaumont's. The boy had written the story of a pet he had kept in a cage and had freed at last because it became torture to him to hold it in a cage. It was a strange little tale, half-childish and half-passionate. He stopped and took out this paper from the others and put it back upon the table.

Then for half the night he sat waiting for the fire to end. At first he could not sit. He was compelled to move, to walk about, to do anything except sit and wait. He had to fight continually a stupid compelling desire to open the door and run. But he controlled this by cold reason. Run—with all the animals? The river was too shallow to hide him. Even if it were not, would he drown or burn? No, the walls of the sod house were thick, and earth could withstand fire, so he made himself calm. He lay down upon his bed and thought how well it was that his mother was not here nor the children, and how doomed by terror they would have been. And Judy—he was glad now that she was gone. He thought of her as he had seen her most, in the long hours when Joel was preaching. She

never listened, so upon what did she brood in that deep
musing out of which she roused herself only to play the
throbbing rhythms she put into hymns?

He was afraid even to think of her, lest he never see her
again. He sat up, stifled with heat, and lit the candle on the
box beside his bed which served as a table, and took up his
Virgil and began to read. Yet all the time he read with only a
part of his mind. If he lived would he ever be able to cope
with this huge willful country? Was it not too vast for a man
such as he, who loved his world small and clear and sure? If
he lived to walk out of this house, should he not turn away
from it forever and go back to England and, by hook or
crook, work his way to what he knew?

He felt the air of the room grow hotter and heavier with
smoke. A huge deep roar was growing about him, a dry
crackling growl that was the voice of fire. He got up, not able
to breathe, and dipped a towel into his pail of drinking water
and bound it about his face and breathed through it. But his
lungs were stretched tight and ached. He stripped off his shirt
and sat half-naked, and the sweat streamed down his flesh,
black with smoke. He would die, he thought grimly. This
would be his end, the sod house about him like an oven.

When he was at the point of fainting with the heat and the
smoke was forcing its way into the house, suddenly he felt the
fire pass over his head and sweep on. He waited a few
minutes. The air grew cooler. The hideous growling roar was
quieting. He made himself wait. When he could wait no more
and it seemed sure he would die without air, carefully he
opened the door. There was no light. He looked out into a pit
of blackness. Sky and earth were black. But the air was cooler
and the silence was good. He stood breathing. Only to breathe
was enough. It was acrid air full of ash, but it was air, and
cool, and he took it into himself like drink and grew strong.
When he went back into the candlelight he was black. His
hands and his face were covered with grass soot. But he did
not care. He left the door open and threw himself upon his
bed and slept.

None came to wake him in the morning. Median slept—
men, women, and children—unwashed, unfed, but safe.

When it was late afternoon he waked and sat up in his bed.
Everything in the house was black. Bed, table, chairs, floor
were covered with ash. Upon the walls, upon every slight

ledge, were layers of black ash. But the air was clear and cold, and his lungs felt clean and sound again. He leaped up and went to the door. The sky was blue, and the unshadowed sunshine poured down upon a strange blackened land. As far as his eyes could reach there was not a sign of life in all the dark desert. The sod house, upon the roof of which grass and weeds had grown, stood as black as an oven; and Median was a few scattered black lumps. Over the tavern door the sign had been burned away, and it hung down, a charred board or two. The wooden ell to the store was gone. He saw no signs of any human being. Yet if he was alive there would be others.

He had planned to go to the tavern first, but as he came to the store, there at the door was Katie, her head in a cloth and her face a smudge. She was sweeping furiously.

"Jonathan!" she screamed and waved her broom.

He stopped and she cried, "Soon as I finish here, I'll come and clean you up, Jonathan!"

"What are you cleaning with?" he asked.

She was sweeping out piles of blackness.

"Dirt," she said cheerfully. "Dirt cures dirt. Water's no good against this soot. You want to sprinkle everything good with dry dirt so's nothing can fly and sweep it all out together."

She looked so cheerful that he laughed.

"What's the matter?" she inquired. She never saw any cause for laughter.

"Oh, you," he replied.

"Why, what's the matter with me?"

"Nothing," he said.

She was so ugly, and so careless of her ugliness, that he felt an affection for her and, reaching for her ear, he pulled it.

"You're a good girl," he said and went on to the tavern, marveling that the world could contain two female creatures so different as Katie and Judy.

Katie was bawling something after him and he stopped to hear her.

"It'll be winter now," she was saying. "That fire burned up the fall!"

❧ 14 ❧

THE WICKEDNESS OF THE FIRE WAS THAT IT HAD TAKEN ALL
the fuel for winter. There was nothing more to burn upon the
prairies.

In the schoolroom the children sat bundled in all their own
garments and old coats and skirts of their parents. The Indian
children were the most comfortable, for they were wrapped in
blankets; and the Negro children were the most miserable,
and they looked gray with cold.

The winter grew deep. It became the occupation of Jonathan's life to find fuel for his school. On days when there was
no school he borrowed Henry Drear's wagon and horses and
drove for miles beyond the barrenness the fire had left. When
he found long grass again, he pulled it up and pressed it into
the wagon. He walked along the river and caught at branches
and roots which the water had torn out of soft banks. In the
evenings when he sat alone he took the grass he had cut in the
daytime and twisted it into cats and stacked them against the
end walls. In the tavern there was a hay-burning stove; and,
after seeing it, Jonathan bought a tin washtub at the store and
took it to Stephen Parry.

"Cut me a top to this, if you please, Mr. Parry, and set in a
stovepipe at the side."

"You fixin' a hay burner?" Stephen inquired.

"That's so," Jonathan replied.

Stephen Parry brought it the next day and set it up in one

side of the big sod fireplace. When it was full of the hay cats, it could burn for an hour.

But before Christmas Jonathan saw that there must be help if he were to keep the children warm. He spent a Sunday going from house to house to tell the parents.

"I can't teach and keep them warm together," he said over and over again. "It takes a man's time to fetch fuel and keep the fire going. Since the school's a public concern, in a way, I thought you might help."

"Surely we will," one man said and another.

Before Christmas Day, Jonathan had half his bedroom stacked with fuel, with hay cats and cornstalks and bundled weeds and sunflower stalks, carted from beyond the fire area. He even accepted the cow chips which the Indians brought by the basketload.

"Sun and wind has cleaned 'em good," Bill White said.

"I'm glad even for dung," Jonathan said.

He thought of his mother when he spoke and, as he always did, suffered for an instant a pinch of dulled pain. Since winter had begun and the movement West was stopped, he felt as cut off from her as though by an ocean. But if she were alive, she would send him something for Christmas.

And he did not need her as much as he once had. Other lesser securities were growing up in him. Thus the store of fuel in his room was a small security, not merely for its own sake, but because the people of Median had come to his help and put it there. He felt them united about him in a friendliness—not intimate, yet solid. Lying in his bed sometimes in the straight, still way which was his, he thought of them, one by one. Cottonwood was from the Bentleys' down in the river dugout, and Cobbs brought hay cats, and from somewhere Parrys had brought cornstalks. Stephen must have traded them for labor somehow. And Hastys had brought straw twists from the mill refuse. Poor Abram Hasty would never get beyond the second reader, however long he stayed, and perhaps it was only fair to tell his father. Then he remembered something. Last night Beaumont had said he wanted to be a surgeon.

"A surgeon!" Jonathan had exclaimed. He looked at Beaumont's hands, olive-skinned, the fingers long and square at the tips. "I never thought of you wanting to be that," he said. "Where did you ever hear of surgeons?"

"My grandfather Beaumont's a surgeon," the boy answered, and in the proud look he gave Jonathan he was suddenly as alien to Sue as though her blood had forsaken him. For the moment all his white blood took command.

"That gives me a notion," Jonathan said, thinking. "You say your grandfather's living?"

"He's a very old man," Beaumont replied. "But I know he's alive. My mother has ways of knowing. If he was to die she says she would know."

"Where does he live?" Jonathan asked.

"In New Orleans," Beaumont said. "Pierre Beaumont's his name, and Pierre is my first name, too. I took it for myself, when I found out who I was."

Excitement sounded in his voice and shone in his eyes, and Jonathan, feeling it, retreated to prudence. The boy was always too eager.

"Well, I don't know," he said. "I'll have to think a while."

"Yes, sir." Beaumont's face shadowed quickly. He was hurt, and yet what could Jonathan promise? The boy was sensitively ready to hope at a straw, and as quick to retreat if the hope were delayed an instant. Without another word he went off into the winter twilight.

Thinking it over now slowly and carefully, Jonathan came to a determination to write to Pierre Beaumont in New Orleans without saying anything to Sue or Stephen Parry. Something must be done with this glorious boy, and what was there in Median?

This morning was the Sunday before Christmas, and when Jonathan had washed himself and eaten, he put on his stock and coat and sat down close by a small fire to write the letter to Pierre Beaumont.

"Honored Sir," he wrote in his clear colorless handwriting, "I take up my pen to address you upon a matter Personal to yourself. I am a Schoolmaster, and in my School I have as a pupil a youth whose name is Pierre Beaumont."

He wrote carefully and baldly in the literal plain way that was natural to him and made his request.

"It seems to me, therefore, Sir, that the Instincts of Nature and Virtue will move you to educate this unusual Youth in whose Veins is your own Blood and who bears your Name."

He signed his name and after it wrote "Schoolmaster." Folding the sheet, he sealed it with wax and superscribed it

"Doctor Pierre Beaumont, New Orleans, State of Louisiana, in the United States of America"; and took the letter with him to Lew Merridy's when he went to dinner. The mail went once a week from the store, on Monday or Tuesday, except in storm.

On this day, as he walked across the black, frozen ground, he felt a new and vicious bitterness in the wind. Lew came to open the door for him.

"Takes a man to hold the door against this wind," Lew said. "Come in, Jonathan. I don't know as you'll get back today. It's fixin' to come a blizzard."

They walked together across the store, unheated because it was Sunday. "It's early for blizzards," Lew said. "Mostly we get 'em after Christmas."

The wind forcing itself under the door caught at their ankles. But when they went into the back rooms they were full of comfort. Lew had old boxes and kegs to burn, and sometimes farmers brought him hay cats and corncobs instead of cash for goods. Katie was throwing cobs into the stove now, and the room was roaring warm.

"Well, Jonathan," she said. She never called him by his name in school, but outside of school hours she maintained an equality with him. "Sit here," she commanded him, "and put up your feet to the fire." She pulled a stool to a chair.

He sat down obediently. Now that he was in the warmth, he knew he had been very cold in the sod house. But it seemed not right to use for himself the fuel parents had brought for their children. He drew out his letter from his breast pocket.

"See that this letter gets stamped when the mail comes by, will you, Katie?" he asked.

She took it and spelled out the name. "Who's this Pierre Beaumont?" she demanded.

"Oh, I'll tell you one of these days," he said to tease her, knowing he would never tell her. "Mind you mail it, Katie."

"Katie'll mail it," Lew said, spitting carefully into a tin can full of ashes near the stove. "She tends mail now reg'lar and takes a hand in the store Satidays. She's gettin' so she earns her salt."

"Store work's easy," Katie said. She threw a look at Jonathan as she spoke, and he smiled, aware of her longing for praise and touched by it. He smiled at her, and then he thought of Judy and looked away from her.

By midafternoon, when they had finished dinner and the dishes were washed, it was evident that the blizzard was come.

"You'll stay with us, Jonathan," Lew said.

"But there's school tomorrow," Jonathan demurred.

"There'll be no school this side of Christmas, with a wind like this," Lew said.

In an hour he saw that Lew was right again. The wind had risen, and the house shook in its blasts, and the sky was already dark with snow. By three o'clock Jonathan, peering out of a window, saw only his own face staring back at him into the lamplight. He ought to be at home, he thought.

"Reckon I ought to get back, though," he told Lew.

"Why?" Lew retorted. "You ain't got a beast or a human there waitin' for you."

It was true, he had not. There was no reason why he should go back to the sod house, except that in some vague way it had become home, since he had no other, and he wanted to be at home.

"You'd never find your way there, Jonathan," Lew said. "Why, in a blizzard a man can get lost and froze to death between his house and his barn. Stay here with us. We'd admire to have you."

"Reckon I must then, thanks," Jonathan said after a moment, still unwillingly—though, when he thought of it, he could not tell why he should be unwilling. There was indeed no living creature waiting for him anywhere. He was struck with sudden loneliness, and he turned away from the window to the warm room and the light and fire and to the sight of Katie, tying bibs around the necks of two small boys sitting in little high chairs Lew had built out of barrels.

"Stop your racket, you two," she said loudly, and then kissed them. She looked practical, sure of herself, sound in all her habits. He said, "You're a rare good girl, Katie."

She looked up at him with a shyness so strange upon her sallow plain features that he was moved by it.

"I mean it," he said.

For once she had nothing to say. She hesitated a moment, her cheeks reddening, and then suddenly she turned and ran out of the room.

In the roar of the storm that night he and Lew sat alone by the stove. Mrs. Merridy had gone to bed early.

"I might as well sleep if you're settin' up, Lew," she said. "You can let me know if the house blows away."

"I'll tell ye," he replied dryly.

Then Katie got up.

"You goin' too?" Lew inquired.

She nodded.

"You're mighty quiet," he said. "Ain't sick, be you?"

"No, Pa," she replied.

"Never knowed you to be quiet before," he said.

"A body can be quiet sometimes," she said.

"Oh, shore, if it's natural," he said, staring at her with doubt.

And then in the stillness of the warm room, in the midst of the shrieking wind, he lit his pipe and smoked. "A man takes thought out in these here prairies, Jonathan, when he's settin' in the middle of a storm," he said after a while.

"Ah, he does," Jonathan agreed.

"He takes thought for them as he's brought into the world," Lew said mournfully.

Jonathan did not answer, having no idea of what was in Lew's mind. But it was his habit to wait.

"A man," Lew said, raising his voice, "says to himself, how will he pervide for his children, especially the females? A female has a sorry chance in this life, Jonathan. Bound to be dependent on some man or other, and it's all luck what she gets. She has to take her pick of what's before her at best, and a girl like Katie has to take her pick of what wants her."

Still Jonathan did not see what was behind Lew's graying moustache and bushy eyebrows. But he became aware of embarrassment in Lew's look.

"I daresay," he said wondering.

"Katie'll make a wonderful wife," Lew said, "but it'll have to be for a man wise enough to see behind her face."

Jonathan did not speak. Prudence began to stir in him.

"Hell," Lew said suddenly and smacked his knee, "it'd be a Godamighty relief to me, Jonathan, if you was that wise man."

Jonathan felt his body grow stiff as he sat. He could not have spoken if he had known how to speak what he knew. He was fond of this big slatternly man, fond, too, of Mrs. Merridy with all her acid, and fond of this home where he was always welcomed. But he knew he could not marry Katie.

"She's like a good fierce faithful bitch dog," Lew said. He did not look at Jonathan. He filled his pipe, picked a coal out of the ashes under the stove and lit it. "She'll stick to a man as fierce and faithful, and she'll have younguns and keep 'em clean, and teach 'em to fight fair and tell no lies, and she's a good cook and savin'. A man'll be lucky if he can see what Katie is."

Jonathan cleared his throat. "I'm sure that's all true, Mr. Merridy," he said. His voice sounded thin. The roar of the blood in his ears was stronger than the wind wrenching at the windows. Lew waited, but Jonathan could not say more, and this penetrated into Lew's mind at last. He drew a few long breaths of smoke and then knocked the ash from his pipe.

"Don't you mind my sayin' it, Jonathan," he said.

"I do mind, though," Jonathan replied. "I mind it terrible, for I'm—I'm fond of you, sir—"

"Call me Lew, like anybody else," Lew broke in.

"Yes, sir," Jonathan said sweating. "I will, thank you—and I'm fond of Katie, but I am not free—in a manner, that is—" He stopped.

"Why, I never see you lookin' at nobody!" Lew exclaimed.

"But I'm—in love," Jonathan confessed.

Lew stared at him, and his blue eyes grew solemn.

"Then I'm sorry I spoke," he said. "I shouldn't have spoke if I'd dreamed it. But I didn't. And Katie's fond of you. She's terrible fond of you. It's seein' that put it in my mind to speak. She can't coax and tease and drawr a man like some girls can. She can't p'int to herself—somebuddy has to do it for her, and since you and me is good friends, why, I says to myself, I can speak for my own child. It's goin' to be hard on her."

"Does she know you were going to speak?" Jonathan asked.

"No, but I gotta tell her, Jonathan, that she mustn't think about you."

Jonathan's head began to hum. "She's just a child," he murmured.

"Fifteen ain't a child for a girl here," Lew said. "A girl hereabouts marries any time after she's sixteen."

He got up and took the lamp and went to the window. In

the light the furious snow seemed stabbing at them with darts.

"I feel I oughtn't to stay here," Jonathan said miserably. "I feel I ought to get right out of your house."

"You can't," Lew said. "Besides, I wouldn't let you. What I've said is to be fergot. I'll be downright mad with you if you don't fergit it. Now let's go to bed. Think you can sleep on that sofy?"

"Yes, of course," Jonathan said. He stood up involuntarily as Lew went to the door.

"Well, so long till mornin', and we have to dig ourselves out," Lew said over his shoulder. "You'll fix the fire?"

"I will," Jonathan replied.

Alone, he tended the fire and banked it with ash, and then he lay down on the narrow sofa and drew a buffalo hide over him. Katie had brought it in and left it there for him. He lay under it warm and comfortable if he did not turn, but he could not sleep. He was thinking of Katie while all his being steadily refused her.

I couldn't have spoken other than I did, he thought solemnly, with sorrow for his own ingratitude. How willful was love that it denied itself to one who deserved it and poured itself out upon another who did nothing except to look as Judy looked, to walk and smile and talk as she did! He was sorry that it was so, but there was no cure for it. And in the same mood of destiny and fate he thought, I've engaged myself to Judy tonight, though she doesn't know it. I'm promised to her.

He lay awake and trembling in the midst of the clatter of the storm and did not notice it, until long after midnight he perceived it had ended. He rose and lit the lamp and saw that the silence was because the snow was deeper than the windows, and so the wind was no longer to be heard. He was buried in this house.

15

IN THE SMALL DUGOUT WHICH CLYDE HAD MADE AGAINST A hill in the middle of his acres, Mary, lying back upon her pillow wrapped in a bit of old gray blanket, looked at her child just born. Then she looked at Ruth, who stood hesitating beside the bed. It was indecent that Ruth, her own daughter and still a child herself, had had to help her. But the baby had come too soon. Clyde was away, and there had been no one else. She was only grateful that Jamie was hired to a man for herding sheep on the foothills. She looked at Ruth with miserable and apologetic eyes.

"I'm sorry to the heart," she said weakly. "I've done you a wrong, Ruthie."

"Oh, no, Mother," Ruth said quickly. But she would never forget, never; and Mary saw it in her sick averted eyes.

"Don't let it turn you," she said pleadingly. "After all, it's natural—a thing women must endure in one way or another; only not you, pray God, like this."

Ruth did not answer. She could not, for she was ashamed that her mother had seen what she was thinking.

"Shan't I fetch you some tea, Mother?" she asked.

"I'd be grateful," her mother said faintly. The tiny creature on her arm was barely alive. She looked again at its little curled shape. "Oh, my poor wee!" she muttered, and closed her eyes.

But Ruth said nothing. When she had brought in the cup of tea and had lifted her mother's head with her hand so that she could sip it, she went out to loose the rope with which she had tied Maggie to a scrub tree to keep her from running away while she tended her mother. Maggie had cried in great roars and then wailed herself to sleep. She lay now in the short brown upland grass, her face muddy and her sunburned red hair full of bits of grass and earth.

Ruth stooped and lifted her, but the stout child was heavy for her in her sleep, and so she sat down on the ground and cradled her head on her knees. It was too cold to stay long, though the day was Indian summer.

She shook Maggie gently. "Maggie, wake up!" she said. "It's gettin' cold." She rose and dragged the little girl to her feet, and they went into the house.

"Ruth!" Her mother's voice from the bed was suddenly alert.

"Yes, Mother?"

"Don't tell Jonathan anything. Have you written him?"

"Not yet."

"Then leave it to me to tell. He'll be disgusted-like with your father."

"All right, Mother."

She went on cleaning Maggie and picking the bits out of her hair, and then she fed her with corn-meal mush and put her to bed.

But Mary did not write to Jonathan even when she got up. She could not. How could a middle-aged woman explain to a young man, sensitive and fastidious and her son, why she went on bearing children against her will? So she told herself she was too tired.

She scarcely put the little thing out of her arms. Everything else was neglected. She let Ruth manage as she could, and day and night she lay upon the bed or sat up against a pillow holding the scrap of a child to her body to keep it warm. Clyde grew impatient.

"You act like it was all you had," he grumbled.

She did not answer. She ignored him unless at night she felt him press against her. Then she whispered fiercely, "You keep to yourself, Clyde! I've enough on my conscience with this wee sorrowful child."

"Oh, you're always thinkin' of one dinged thing when I come around," he retorted. "And it's the last thing I want of you when you're like this."

"Stay away, then," she said. "Children are wickedness in a hole like this."

She kept her voice to a whisper because of the indecency of all their life having to go on in this one room.

They were living like beasts in a den. She had no furniture. Her bed was a mattress on posts driven into the ground and crossed with slats. The children slept on pallets spread on dried grass. And the last beastliness was to give birth to a child in this hole—she, a decent Englishwoman! She remembered the cottage in Dentwater and how nice her kitchen had been and how shining were her bits of copper and brass and what a good window it had for a plant or two.

I don't have anything good to write to Jonathan, so I'll not write, she thought.

Her strength did not come back, and at last she did not rise from the bed. The child grew weaker with her weakness, and on Christmas Day it died in her arms. Upon the bed she turned to Ruth.

"The little thing's gone," she said. She had told herself ever since its birth that it would be better if this little creature did not live, and yet she had thought of nothing except how to make it live. Scarcely mine it seemed all the time it was livin', she thought. But now it's dead, I know it was mine.

"Oh, Mother, and we didn't even name it!" Ruth cried and burst into weeping.

"We'll call her after me," Mary said.

She covered her dead child and waited until evening when Maggie was asleep, and then with Ruth's help she washed it carefully and put on the little christening robe she had saved and brought with her from Dentwater because all the children had worn it. And then, because there would be nothing better, she told Ruth to bring one of the good boxes they used for stools, and she laid the gray blanket in it and then the child. All the time Ruth wept silently.

"Don't weep, my dear," her mother said sadly. "How could we want her back into this place? But I wish she could have been christened, somehow. It's like the animals, else."

"Oh, Mother, don't!" Ruth wailed.

She flung herself upon the bed, and Clyde came in and found them so.

"What's the to-do?" he began, and then saw the little figure in the box like a doll in its long white dress, and he stood still, and his face altered. "Why, when did it happen like this?" he said.

"This afternoon," Mary answered. Her face quivered. "Oh, Clyde, it was bound to come!"

"I reckon it was," he said slowly.

He stood a moment, then asked, timidly, humbly, "What'll I do, Mary?"

"Take it over to that little hollow, Clyde—you know, the one I always called the Fold. And, oh, Clyde, put a stone on top—against the coyotes."

"Sure—I would have—" he said.

He searched and found some planks and was about to nail them down when he paused.

"What is it?" Mary whispered.

"This bit of gray blanket, Mary—she don't need it and we will."

Mary's eyes burned at him. "Clyde, you leave that on her!"

"But, Mary—"

"It's all she has—that miserable bit of stuff—no proper coffin, no burial—"

"All right, Mary! Godamighty, I just was thinkin' of the livin' instead of the dead!"

"I know—" She began to cry, and he came over to her and sat down beside her.

"Mary, my dear—"

She could not stop crying, and after a while he sighed and gave her up and went to the door, the box under his arm. Then she called to him and he stopped. "What is it, Mary?"

"Clyde, don't put her away without saying something."

"I'll say the Lord's Prayer," he said in a low voice.

When he was gone, she lay quiet on the bed. At last she could rest, if this feeling of weakness and loss could be rest. She had no strength. The child's birth had taken what she had left. An unwanted birth was a deadly thing for a woman to endure. It tore the strength out of body and will. She lay, too tired to weep, now that Clyde was gone.

And then in the stillness, with only Ruth sobbing softly, she thought of Jonathan. She had not written and she would not write. There was no use in telling him anything at all. 'Twould only be to his distress. At least I can be spared that, she thought.

Thus Christmas had brought no letter from Jonathan's mother or Ruth. For three days Jonathan had stayed in Lew's house. Lew had taken advantage of a moment alone with Jonathan to say, "I ain't goin' to hint nothin' to Katie till you kin go home."

"I feel that badly I don't know how to express myself," Jonathan said sorrowfully.

"You needn't," Lew said. "You cain't help it. I know how 'tis. I picked my own wife without knowin' why. Lotsa prettier girls, lotsa girls more fun; but I had to have only her. Craziest thing! I sit an' think about it sometimes."

On Christmas Eve they tunneled through to the main road and there found a great patch of bare black ground. The blizzard had freakishly heaped up snow in drifts twenty feet deep, but to do it the wind had scooped an acre bare. Over barren ground Jonathan walked to wallow again through shallow drifts and dig through deep ones until he stood once more in the sod house. Everything was as he had left it. The air was damp and icy cold, but he was glad to be there. He was home again. He was even glad he had refused Lew's invitation to stay to Christmas dinner. He had brought food along, crackers and corn meal and dried peaches, and he would rather eat here alone. In Lew's home he had felt ashamed even to think of Judy. Here he could summon her as he would, sit at his table and remember her, lie on his bed and dream of her, read his few books and see her in every line of poetry and every picturing word. He had written to her three times, but she had not answered. He suspected, half-tenderly, that she could not write, and she would be too delicate to give another her thoughts of him. Ah, well, I'm a master at waiting, he thought.

But he was not alone on Christmas Day after all. Henry Drear came roaring through the snow to the sod-house door and beat upon it so hard that the top of the tunnel caved in upon him. When Jonathan opened the door, in fell man and snow until it seemed the room was half-full of both.

"Of all the darned ways to treat a man on Christmas morning!" Henry shouted. "And me come to ask you to drink my hot buttered rum!"

Jonathan grinned. "You've made a fair mess here," he said in his calm voice and reached for the shovel and began to ladle out the snow.

"It's your snow," Henry returned, "and all I did was to bring it in with me. Well, Jonathan, come along at noon or so and drink with Median folks at American House."

"Thanks, I will," Jonathan replied, "though I'm no great drinker, as you know."

"Oh, well, you're schoolmaster and folks'll want you there."

"And I want it, too," Jonathan said.

"Good," Henry shouted. To shout was his only voice, and everything he said was a bellow. He clapped Jonathan's shoulder. "Come along out and help clear the roads—we're all at it."

"I will," Jonathan said.

He spent Christmas morning shoveling snow as dry and crystalline as salt. But he enjoyed it. He saw men he had not seen since Joel's meeting, and in the brilliant sunshine they stopped to talk and compare this blizzard with blizzards of other years. It was easy, neighborly talk, and full of the boasting to which he was now used, though he could never take part in it.

"This-here blizzard," Bill White said, spitting a great stain upon the snow, "ain't nothing like the blizzards we used to have when I first come to the prairie. Them was blizzards! First the snow would all come down. Then the wind would toss it all up and stir it round until it made you dizzy did you look out of the window. And if you opened the door you never got it shut again. I've knowed folks whose doors busted open and they froze solid in their beds and was excavated in the spring!"

"This is enough of a blizzard for me, though, Mr. White," Jonathan said mildly.

"You have to get used to big things out here," Bill said.

They spent Christmas afternoon at the tavern. Everybody in Median was there except the Parrys. Now that he saw them all merrymaking, it occurred to him how youthful Median was. There were few white heads. Mrs. Cobb's mother was there and an old man he had not seen before, but most of Median was young. There was singing and dancing, and he saw Katie dancing again and again. There were no other young girls in Median since Jennet went away, and Katie shone in a solitary glory which, if it could not be splendid because of her plain face and dun-colored hair, was nevertheless real. She was young, less than a woman but more than a child, and men danced with her half-teasingly, half-provocatively, and she went from one to the other with a sedate industrious energy. She did not once look at Jonathan.

Ah, she knows! he thought and was at once relieved and foolishly hurt. He was fond of Katie. Sometime when he could he must tell her how a chap could be fond of one girl even when he was in love with another. But he did not go near her. He danced a little with Mrs. Drear, who told him she had heard from Jennet. She was in San Francisco and hoping to be married to a rich man. There were plenty of rich men there.

"Have you heard from your folks?" she asked.

"No, but I'll hear as soon as the roads open," he replied.

"Sure you will," she said and laughed. "There, Jonathan, leave me be. I'm breathless and too old for a young feller."

He let her go and stood watching the crowd. Tired of dancing, they had suddenly begun to sing, and when they sang they were most themselves. Each dropped unaware into what he was. And Jonathan, who had only once yielded to one of Joel's hymns, was suddenly moved, and he lifted his voice shyly and began to sing, too. But he would never be able to sing himself out in Henry Drear's rollicking roar, and he could only sip his hot buttered rum instead of swallowing it down in big gulps. The scum of butter was too rich for him, and after a moment he put his mug down.

Yet all was good, and he liked being there. They liked him, and he felt this. He was deeply pleased when Mrs. Cobb came up to him and said in her plain way, "I want to tell you, Mr. Goodliffe, that it's been real worth while stoppin' in Median. The children both read wonderful."

"I'm glad of that, Mrs. Cobb," he said earnestly.

"And I'm just as pleased that Martha's a mite smarter than Matthew," she said. "I tell her, too. I aim to have my girls hold their heads as high as any man."

"Why not?" he agreed, though privately he did not. A woman ought not to be quite as smart as a man. Even with all his feelings against his father, he would have loved his mother less if she had not been subject to him. "Though I have a very high opinion of Matthew," he said. "He is very able in mathematics."

Mrs. Cobb looked proud. "So he ought to be, for he has the skinflintest grandfather in the state of Massachusetts. Old Mr. Cobb's a real rich man, but it don't do anybody any good, because he hoards it all. That's why we left the store and come West."

"Is it now!" Jonathan said politely.

What touched him most that Christmas Day was to go home at dusk and find upon his table a small bundle tied in newspaper dyed red with something and secured with string made of woven grass. "Merry Christmas from Parrys" was written upon a piece of paper in Beaumont's best hand, and a branch of berries was thrust under the string. Inside the package were molasses candy and dried wild raspberries and some black walnut meats in a little wooden box made very light and thin and polished until it was like porcelain to his touch.

He lit a small fire and sat near it and ate some of the candy and nuts and thought of his mother and the children and Judy. Then, to his own amazement, he thought a little of

Katie. He discovered that he was hurt because she had let this day go by without a mention of something he knew she had long been making for him. He suspected it was a shirt because more than a month before this she had brought a piece of string to school and measured his arm and the breadth of his shoulder and chest.

"Don't you ast me nothin', Jonathan," she had said importantly. "You'll know sometime—Christmas, maybe."

But this was the end of Christmas, and she had not spoken to him. He felt foolishly irritated with himself that he cared. I'm an unreasonable chap, he thought, after some pondering, and was much surprised at himself.

❧ 16 ❧

ON THE RAGGED NORTHERN FRINGE OF THE CITY OF NEW Orleans, Judy stood in a crowd and watched its behavior. It was a crowd mostly of men, but this did not trouble her. Crowds were usually made up of men because most women stayed at home. If she had a home, maybe she would stay in it. When she thought of this she thought vaguely of Jonathan without deciding anything. Her wandering life had made her able to live only in the moment.

Around the jail between two and three hundred men stood stolidly waiting for something. She knew what it was, because she had asked. She had come out of the boardinghouse where she and Joel had rooms, and with a basket on her arm she was going to the market to buy food. Across the street down which she went every day, she found the dense mass of men, and she paused.

"What are you here for?" she asked a young man in a drab brown suit and a tall hat.

"Lem Beaumont's to be taken from jail to court today," he replied.

When she heard that, she gave up the marketing. She could do that any time, but she could not see any time this big Negro who had killed old Pierre Beaumont's son, Pierre. She had heard all about it because everybody was talking about it. Nobody cared whether young Pierre died or not. He was the worthless son of a good father. But he was a white man, and Lem was the son of a black mother, a mulatto who had once been a Beaumont slave. People said young Pierre was his father, but Lem's real sin was not patricide. It was that a black man had killed a white man—and, more than that, a white man to whom he would have belonged legally if the war had not turned the wrong way.

The crowd was quiet. Had they been noisy she would not have been afraid of them. She was used to men in excitement, and it did not matter much what the excitement was. But these men were perfectly still, their faces turned attentively to the door of the jail. A man spat, another tore a bite from a plug of tobacco and put the plug back into his pocket. But these slight movements scarcely broke the rigidity of the mass.

A fat elderly man in a dirty linen suit stared at Judy. When she looked up, her eyes drawn unconsciously by his, he said, "You'd better go on where you were goin'. What's about to happen is for us men to see—"

"I don't mind," Judy replied. She gave him a look from her eyes, so purposely pure and fearless that he was disconcerted and moved away from her.

Under the quietness something waited. It stirred when the door opened and the sheriff came out. He was a tall, lazy-looking man, and he surveyed the crowd with tolerant eyes. When he spoke it was with a sort of slow and genial power.

"Lookahyeah, you-all oughtn't to act like this. The co'se of justice is proceedin'. They ain't a mite of doubt Lem's gonna be hung. I'm willin' to give my pehsonal wuhd of honah."

The men stared back at him in silence and stillness. He spat and, taking off his broad-brimmed hat, scratched his head.

"Well, I ain't responsible," he muttered, and he turned and went back into the jail.

Now little movements were to be felt rather than seen. Men shuffled their feet in the dust, men tightened their belts, men drew their hands across their mouths and pulled down their hats over their eyes and waited.

The door opened, and the sheriff came out again. Behind him were two guards and between the guards was a big Negro with mud-colored wool and slaty eyes.

The crowd, like an animal long crouched and waiting, leaped forward. Judy, behind them, saw them spring, fasten

upon their prey, and move away with him. The silence was
broken with moans and mutterings, and then suddenly with
the Negro's yelps. She stood motionless, watching them go.
Across the emptiness between her and the doorway to the jail
she saw the sheriff and the guards. They did not look at her,
but she heard their voices clearly through the sunshine.

"Reckon old Doc Beaumont'll be mighty mad with me," the
sheriff said.

"He shorely will," a guard agreed.

"Seems like they just couldn't stand it when they heard old
Doc didn't want the State to prosecute. It made 'em mad."

"It shore ain't healthy in this here town not to prosecute a
niggra to the full extent of his crime," the guard agreed.

The sheriff turned to spit and, seeing Judy, paused to smile;
and she, at the familiar sight of that sort of smile on a man's
lazy, handsome face, recalled her errand and went on her way
thoughtfully.

Beaumont! There was a handsome boy in Jonathan's school
called Beaumont. When spring came, if they went back to
Median, if it happened that she and Jonathan met again, she
would tell him about this morning. She felt sobered by what
must now be happening to that gray-skinned Negro with his
wrong-colored eyes, but she was not shocked. Such things had
to happen. Even the sheriff could not stop them. There was
something like the will of God in them. Everything was God's
will, and there was nothing to do about it. If she got back to
Median, if she married Jonathan and obeyed her mother, that
would be God's will. But if she did not, that would be God's
will, too.

She bought beans and corn and some greens and a piece of
cow's meat and stared at some bright red fruit.

"What's those?" she asked the slatternly white woman who
served her.

"Them's love apples," the woman said.

"Are they good to eat?" Judy asked.

"Some folks say they're pison, and some folks eats 'em," the
woman replied. "I dunno, I've always stayed on the safe side,
myself."

"I'll take two," Judy said.

On the way home she paused under a magnolia tree and,
putting her hand into her basket, picked up one of the
brilliant fruits and bit into it. It was full of juice, and the red

juice ran down her chin. It had a strange bland taste at first, but after she had eaten it her mouth was acid. She wiped her chin and went on, waiting for anything.

If it's poison, it'll be God's will, she thought, and if it isn't poison, that's God's will, too.

She walked on, meditating, and reached the shabby boardinghouse and went into the two rooms on the ground floor where she and her father were stopping. He was not there, and she put away her vegetables, all except the love apple, which she put on the mantelpiece above the iron grate.

I feel perfectly all right, she thought calmly, looking at it. And then it seemed to her that she had discovered the only way to know God's will. It was to do as she liked and wait for God to do something to her—or nothing, if He did not mind. She laughed, yawned, and threw herself on her bed. She could sleep at any time of day, and now, after a moment, she fell into sleep, her head turned a little to one side, her red lips closed and smiling.

In his library old Dr. Pierre Beaumont sat motionless while he listened to the sheriff.

"Sit down, Harry," he said suddenly.

"No, suh, I'd rawtha stand," the sheriff replied. "Anyway, I've said all I kin say, jes' as I did all I could. They was plumb determined, Doc. Nothin' I could say, nothin' I could do, would hold 'em back. Seems like they was druv by somethin' inside 'em."

Dr. Beaumont did not answer. The room was dark with the shadows of vines from the windows, vine shadows upon oak panels. But he would not have anything in the garden cut because years ago his young wife Lavinia had planned that garden. "My garden," she had called it.

She had died under the knife when their son Pierre was not quite four years old. She had had a strange internal inflammation, and in a few hours was in such fever and agony that he had insisted upon an operation. Young Mallory Bain had done it, a brilliant surgeon, and he had stood by. Thousands of times he had recalled that hour and examined it second by second. He could not have operated. To have cut into that sweet romantic flesh would have been beyond his power. His hand would have trembled. Love could not take up a knife even to save. It needed Bain's cold youth. There was nothing he could say was done wrong. And yet if he had forced himself to operate, with all his experience, could he not have saved the few minutes too much for her heart? And yet, if she had died under his hand, could he have lived for Pierre? Much of his life had been spent in this pondering. He pondered it more and more as Pierre grew up into a worthless youth, and then into an idle and worthless man.

Eleven days ago when he was killed by a slate-colored Negro boy, the son of one of the Beaumont slaves, the question was answered finally. He ought to have operated and tried to save Lavinia because the boy was not worth saving.

"I reckon you did do all you could, Harry," he said now. He was a very old man, eighty-one his next birthday. He felt tired and wanted the room to himself, and this big, sweat-smelling man filled it and used up the air. "I reckon if the boy was doomed to die, it was just as well to get it over with. But I hate to have my family mixed up in lynching. I believe in a fair trial for a nigger, even if he has killed my only son."

"Yes, suh," the sheriff replied. "Ev'ybody knows how you love justice, Doc."

"Yes," said the old man slowly. "I love justice."

He was reminded by this of the letter he had received from a young man in Kansas which he had not answered. It was in regard to a lad named Beaumont—Pierre Beaumont. A false claim, he could have said, except that there was the name Sue. He remembered Sue very well, a beautiful mulatto child that had belonged to Lavinia's Bettina. Bettina had come with Lavinia and had brought with her a six-months-old baby. He had asked Lavinia once about it, and Lavinia had shaken her head.

"Don't ask me, Pierre. We don't know. Bettina's half-white, and the baby is more than that. I've never asked Bettina. We don't want to know. Anyway, the white blood doesn't count—the black blood decides." Lavinia, so soft and exquisite a creature, could sometimes be crystal hard.

"Good-by, Harry," he said faintly.

"Good-by, Doc. Sho' do regret it happened like it did."

He backed away out of the door, and outside in the hall came upon an old Negro man, straightening up from the keyhole.

"Hey, you," he said. "What you doin', Joe?"

"Nuthin'," Joe answered.

The sheriff stared at him. "Don't look like nothin'," he remarked. "It looks doggone funny when a man bends hisself over to look in a keyhole."

"I wa'n't lookin', I was listenin'," Joe said. "I wanted to know somepin'."

"What?" the sheriff asked.

"Did I unastan' you to say, suh, 'at dey got Lem?"

"They did," the sheriff replied.

Joe's wrinkled face quivered. " 'At's all I wanted to know, suh," he said.

"What's it to you?" the sheriff demanded.

"Lem was my boy," the old Negro replied. "Least, he was my wife's boy. She guv 'im birth eighteen years ago when she was chambermaid hyeah and Doc Beaumont tol' me to mah'y her, because somebody oughta do it quick. I did it to oblige him, and then Lem was bawn. But she was all right. She was a good wife 'cept she always loved Lem bes' of all de chillen. Reckon I gotta go tell her Lem is daid."

He shambled away. The sheriff stared after him, shrugged, and put on his wide hat.

Everythin's all mixed up, he thought. How you goin' to get justice that-a-way? He let himself out of the house and ran down the marble steps to the lawn.

In the library old Dr. Beaumont sighed and stirred himself. Justice must be done, he thought wearily. He found his quill pen and sharpened it, and with long pains and many small waverings and unnecessary movements he sat down at his big table of English oak to answer Jonathan Goodliffe's letter.

DEAR SIR:

In view of your letter of the twenty-first December I beg to say that if the Young Man in question has Merit and Ability I shall be pleased to extend to him the Sum of Five Hundred Dollars a Year until his medical Education is completed, provided it is understood he makes no Claim upon me otherwise.

I remain, sir, yours faithfully,
PIERRE DUBOIS BEAUMONT, M.D.

Then he sat down again and watched the long hanging shadows upon the dark oak. . . . How could a little blond boy with Lavinia's eyes grow up to be a tall laughing stranger, an idler, a wastrel? When had the change begun, and how had he not seen it until it was finished and too late? He had failed in everything—a brilliant surgeon, but not able to save his own wife; a father, but not able to save his own son. Justice! It was a great cold word, but it was all that remained to a solitary old man.

I must put it in my will, he thought.

⚜ 17 ⚜

WINTER ENDED AND SPRING WAS COME, AND MEDIAN WAS beleaguered in mud. Each year Jonathan forgot the mud, and it was worse each spring. To be snowbound was one thing, but to be mudbound was another. A blizzard, a roaring tigerish wind, snow banked to the roof—these could be large noble enemies. Men boasted of them and compared their labors against them. But mud was a disgusting slime, ensnaring the feet. It was enraging to look into a sky as softly blue as a field of English forget-me-nots, with clouds as innocent and white as lambs upon it, and to have the feet held and made filthy in a spreading of mire.

"There'll be no wagons until the worst of this is over," Henry Drear said dolefully in his empty inn.

Jonathan gave up cleaning his floor because the children came muddied to the knees. He was a harder teacher than he had ever been because he was so impatient with the mud. There was no good in spring as long as there was this mud. Judy would not be coming, for he suspected Joel's comfort and the will of God would be closely allied. It was misery to sit at his desk with the door open and feel the sweet warm air and know that if he stepped beyond the threshold he would sink into black mud. He loathed it with a personal fury because he hated to be unclean. He could not go about all day as the rest of Median did with a casing of mud upon his legs, halfway to his thighs. It put him into a fret.

"I'll begin roads," he said one day in the store where he had gone for food.

"You'll be beginnin' somethin' if you do," Lew said dryly.

"Where'll they begin and where'll they go to in a country like this that spreads itself out over everything?"

"They'll begin at Median," Jonathan said firmly, "and they'll go as far as Median folk need to go."

He did indeed begin his work on roads that spring by himself digging from the sod house toward the square the path of a straight narrow walk.

"What you goin' to put in it?" Bill White asked, having heard of it. "There ain't a stone in a hundred miles."

"I'm going to put in posts and boards," Jonathan replied.

"It'll be like layin' a floor to the square," Bill said, astonished.

"It'll do until someday we'll have roads like a Christian country," Jonathan retorted.

That was the beginning of boardwalks in Median. When Jonathan could walk out of the sod house and around a side of the square to the store in eleven minutes Lew said, "Reckon I can add on as far as Drear's, and Drear can finish out to the corner if he feels good."

Drear did, after great objections. And then Jonathan, looking into the drying mud of the square, thought of something else.

" 'Twould be pretty to plant trees and grass there," he said, " 'twould improve the town wonderfully. Why shouldn't the school do it?"

He impressed his pupils, though it was against the will of some. Abram Hasty saw no good in it, but Beaumont was ardent to help and, to Jonathan's surprise, so was Matthew Cobb.

"Where we come from in Massachusetts there was trees and grass along the streets," Matthew said.

"When are you folks going West?" Jonathan asked.

"Don't look hardly like we're goin'," Matthew said despondently. "Maw's made up her mind she won't go no farther now that Paw's got a good store job. She likes it here."

"And you don't, I take it, from your looks," Jonathan said.

"There's nothin' to do in Median," Matthew said.

"Nothing to do!" Jonathan said.

"Well, anyways, no Indians to fight or gold to dig out of the ground, and no cowboys."

"We won't hold school tomorrow," Jonathan said. "We'll plant trees instead."

He saw Katie, tying her books with a string, look severe at this. "I can't get my feet wet," she said.

"You don't have to get your feet wet," Jonathan retorted. Katie had come regularly to school since Christmas, but now she never stayed to sweep up or straighten as once she had. She came and did her lessons moderately and went home with the others. And he had broken abruptly his habit of Sunday dinner by saying frankly to Lew, "I'll feel better not to come Sundays, Lew, if you'll forgive me."

"Sure," Lew said casually.

Now he glanced at Katie with private disgust. He perceived her meaning. She looked important and remote and her bristling little pigtails she had tied up in loops around her head. He felt suddenly angry with her for growing up into a woman.

The next morning he took the boys to the river. They found small cottonwoods and dried them and put them into a mud sledge and, with a team loaned by a boy's father who was a farmer near Median, they dragged them to the square and planted them. Katie did not appear, and he was glad of it. With the others he worked hard, and by the end of the third day they had planted fifty young cottonwoods. People stopped to look at them with curiosity and pleasure.

"Don't know why nobody thought of plantin' trees before," Henry Drear said.

"Makes a body feel the town's here to stay," Jim Cobb said from the door of the store.

"It's a good job," Jonathan said heartily to the muddy children. "School on Monday'll be more fun after it. And you, Abram"—he turned to the great gawky boy—"you were good at it. I saw you heaving the trees."

Abram was abashed and spat before he spoke. " 'Twa'n't nothin' to me," he said.

"It goes to show books aren't everything for some jobs," Jonathan said pleasantly.

Abram, dazed by this perception in his teacher, could look only confused.

"Good night, all, until Monday," Jonathan said tranquilly.

Sundays were his good days. He portioned them out carefully into what he had to do. First there was his shaving and washing, then he ate breakfast, and then he cleaned house. That took most of his morning.

He was in the midst of this the next day when, looking up from sweeping the floor, he saw Sue upon the threshold. She carried a live chicken in her hand by the legs.

"Come in, Mrs. Parry," he said surprised. He saw Stephen often, but not Sue.

"I'll only take a minute, Mr. Goodliffe," she said.

"Sit down," Jonathan said, putting down his broom.

But she could not sit easily in his presence. She sat on the corner of a chair, and the chicken began to flutter and squawk.

"I brought this-hyeah fowl," she said, "thinkin' you might like to start chickens. She's full of eggs and will set, I'm sure."

"Thank you, I'll be glad of it," he said.

She stooped and tore a bit of the hem from her petticoat and tied the bird's legs and took it outside. Then she came back and sat down edgewise again and looked at him out of sad and solemnly dark eyes.

"Mr. Goodliffe, did you evah git an answer to dat letter Beaumont tol' me you wrote for him?"

"I never did," Jonathan said. "I was about to write another as soon as the mud clears. The mail's delayed by mud."

"I been waitin'," Sue said, " 'cause I know somepin'."

"What?" Jonathan asked.

"A Beaumont is daid," she replied gravely.

"Have you had a letter?" he asked. There was something strange about her.

"No," she replied. She wore round gold earrings in her ears set with small grayish pearls. "But I know. I began to know a while back. But I wa'n't sure. Now I am."

"How?" he asked. He wanted to be amused and somehow was not.

She turned her strong profile to him, first one side and then the other. "See, Mr. Goodliffe? Them earrings was soldered on my ears by my Beaumont master. He said I wasn't never to take 'em off until he died. He said they was full of spell, and as long as he was alive the pearls would shine. But when they turned dark I could know he was daid. Then I could take 'em off."

He saw them gray against her fine dark skin.

"I can't believe that, Mrs. Parry," he said firmly. "I believe he said it, of course, but not that it can be true."

"No, suh, I wouldn't expect you to believe it," she said quietly. "But of co'se I knows what I knows, suh. All I wanted to know was if you heard anything."

"No, I haven't," he said. "But I'll let you know if I do, and if I don't I'll write again."

She went away, and he went on sweeping. He did not believe in that sort of thing.

But the first mail brought him a letter folded and sealed with wax, and when he opened it he found it was from a lawyer's firm. Old Dr. Pierre Beaumont, the letter said, was dead. His last act, apparently, for he died alone in his library, was to write a letter granting five hundred dollars a year to a young man named Pierre Beaumont. Could information be sent concerning this individual?

Jonathan was so astonished that he forgot that five minutes before he had been sore with disappointment because this was his only letter, and that still there was no word from Judy or his mother. He took the letter at once to Sue Parry. She was washing clothes outdoors under a cottonwood tree, and Jonathan hastened to her.

"You were right," he said. "A Beaumont is dead. And it looks as though he had left enough money to your boy to make him free."

She lifted her dark hands out of the suds and raised them upward. "Thank You, God," she said to the sky. Her hands dropped and she cried out for Beaumont. He came running barefoot out of the house. "Boy, you is free," she said solemnly.

Beaumont's red lips parted. He looked at Jonathan, speechless, and Jonathan said quickly, "I think it's all right—I'm going to write back to the lawyers and tell them who you are."

He gave the letter to Beaumont. The boy took it and read it carefully, and handed it back.

"Thank you, Mr. Goodliffe," he said, and stood still for an instant and then raced away over the plains, and Jonathan and Sue looked at each other and smiled.

The mud dried, and the caravans of spring came upon Median. Jonathan, happening one day to be at the tavern to fetch his loaf of bread, found the house lively with people he had never seen before.

"Folks are on the move," Henry roared at him. "Two wagonloads today, and looks like there was another comin'."

Jonathan turned involuntarily to the door. Over the soft, deepening green of the new grass he could indeed see not one wagon but three, hurrying, doubtless, to make the haven of American House by night.

"When I see the first wagon, I know winter's over," Henry said. A young woman came out of the kitchen with a bowl of mush and disappeared into the inner room. Henry watched her, then he spat into the tin spittoon inside the bar. "Awful nice folks," he said. "Seems like every spring we get nicer folks. Don't know what the East'll do with all the up-and-comin' ones gone. She's from around Philadelphy, she and her husband and two little boys. Little feller's got a upset stomach, so they're layin' over a day. Then they're goin' straight on West."

"Why do they all want to keep going West?" he asked curiously.

A tall, long-faced young man came in. "Howdy," he said and passed by them into the inner room.

"That's her husband—name's Blume," Henry said. "Hell, I don't know," he went on. "It's maybe because the world whirls that way. 'Least, that's how I figger it. We don't know we feel it, but somehow'r other, we do feel it aturnin' and th'owin' us west. Look at Columbus—what made him come this-a-way? And I bet you the Pacific Ocean won't stop us, neither. Come the land is full up to the shore line, we'll just keep goin' on across to Chiny."

"It's senseless," Jonathan said. "At that rate, we'll just keep goin' forever, round and round." He got up and went into the kitchen and took from a board table one of the freshly baked loaves there. Mrs. Drear, her face purple with the heat of the hot range, looked up at him.

"Jennet's not goin' to marry that feller after all," she said abruptly.

"No?" Jonathan said. "Why not?"

"She don't say why," Mrs. Drear said irritably. She wiped sweat from her eye with her thick hand. "It's a curse to have a pretty girl in these-hyere parts, Jonathan. There's too many men to pick and choose from. A girl tosses 'em up like dice to see which one'll give her most. I wish Jennet'd come home, but she won't. Now she's talkin' about Oregon. What's a troupe, Jonathan?"

"Why, it's actresses," he said, astonished.

"She's in a troupe," Mrs. Drear said gloomily and clattered the oven door.

Jonathan went out. The wagons were driving up now, and he could see the faces of people in the brightness of the late afternoon. But he went on toward home. Under his arm the loaf of bread smelled deliciously fresh, and he pulled off a bit of crust and ate it. . . . Why should people go on and on restlessly when all they needed for happiness was in four walls under a roof upon a bit of ground? If wagons were coming, Judy was coming.

By the door Beaumont was spading up his garden. Jonathan, remembering his own first hungers, had told the boy he would give him a dollar if he would do the first spading, and with the dollar buy him some writing paper and a pen of his own or, if he preferred, a book.

"I'll wait to decide till I feel the money in my hand," Beaumont said. "Whichever makes it feel lightest, I'll spend it for that."

When he saw Jonathan come, he straightened and leaned on his spade.

"Did you hyeah from them lawyers in N'Orleans yet, Mr. Goodliffe?"

"No, I haven't, Beau," Jonathan replied. "If I don't hear soon, I'm going to write again."

"And if you don't hyeah again, suh?"

"Maybe I'll have to go and see them," Jonathan said. "But I don't want to go just now."

"No, suh," Beaumont said.

Jonathan went into the house. He did not want to leave here just now when Judy might be coming any day.

Beaumont's handsome head thrust itself in at the door.

"Mr. Goodliffe, did you tell 'em I wasn't white?"

"No, I didn't," Jonathan said sharply. "It wasn't their business, I considered. But I think I ought to tell them you were a natural son. That's their legal right to know. Want some bread and treacle, Beau?"

"I do indeed, suh, thank you. I'm hongry all the time." Beaumont smiled, shamefaced. "Last night we trapped somepin' like a groundhog, only it wasn't exactly, Paw said, and Maw made a stew an' I kep' on eatin' after evybody was full, but today I'm empty again. It's real discouragin'."

He put out a big delicately shaped earth-soiled hand. Jonathan looked at it as he always did. He knew Beaumont's hand better than his own. There was nothing of any interest to him in his own, indeed, with its broad palm and rather short fingers. He did not like his own hand better for being like his father's.

He cut two slices of the loaf, gently because it was so fresh, and spread it with molasses, and they stood at the door eating it. Then Jonathan put his hand in his pocket and took out a silver dollar.

"Here's your money, Beau," he said. "What's its weight?"

Beaumont, smiling, held it a moment. "It weighs lightest when I think of a book," he said.

"What book?" Jonathan asked.

"An anatomy book, please, suh," Beaumont said. "I'm mighty curious about people's insides."

"Very well, Beau," Jonathan said. He had long ago cut from newspapers the advertisements of bookshops in the East and had bought, during the course of the year, four books, though always with a sense of guilt because his mother might suddenly need all the money he could muster. He had at times a serious sense of disaster overwhelming her, because still she did not write.

"Thank you, Mr. Goodliffe," Beaumont said. "I'll be goin' home, then."

"Good night, Beau," Jonathan answered.

He stood a moment, as he often did now, looking out over the smooth green prairie, so joyful after the sodden black of the burned ground. If he did not look toward Median he could imagine that no human being was upon the earth and under the sky except himself. Then, against the afterglow in the eastern sky, he saw the cocked black shape of a wagon top. There was still another wagon coming. If he did not get some word from his mother, soon he would have to get a seat in one of them and go to see how she was, he thought; and then remembered that he might have to go to New Orleans. He would have to go if there was any trouble about the legacy for Beaumont.

At the barest thought of going anywhere, this foothold of

his upon the prairie was suddenly precious. I shan't go before Judy comes, he thought. Upon this great prairie two people, after waiting all winter, might miss each other in the spring, if one did not stay steadily where he was.

❦ 18 ❦

HE WOULD HAVE SAID THAT THE DAY OF JUDY'S COMING must be different from any other, or at least that he would wake with a sense of her approach. Every day now brought more wagons, and Median was full of restlessness. In the store Lew was so busy that Katie stopped coming to school. Jonathan saw her one afternoon cleaning her bit of the shelf underneath the long table at which they all sat. He paid no heed to her because she often cleaned and rearranged her small belongings. Today she tied everything together with string, and he saw this and knew what was about to happen. But he said nothing. He seldom said anything to her nowadays. It was she who spoke to him.

"Jonathan, I'm not coming to school any more. Pop needs me in the store."

"Well, Katie!" he said. She stood before him, an angular young girl, slight but without any grace except goodness. But because she was so good, his heart pricked him.

"Good-by," she said.

"Why do you say good-by?" he answered. "I'll see you whenever I come to the store, and maybe you'll be coming this way sometimes to tell me how badly I keep house, and maybe even clean a bit for me—eh, Katie? Like old times, eh?"

He had the impulse to put out his hand and did not yield to it, knowing that he did not really want to touch her hand. She was watching him closely.

"I'm goin' to be busy," she said sullenly.

But he understood that sullenness of hers and forgave it.

"Then I'll come sometimes and help you," he said. "Good-by then, Katie."

He went back to his work of setting a lesson on the board for the next day, and so he let her go, though somehow he felt, even though his back was turned to her, a faint pull of the heart, or perhaps only of the conscience, as she went. But he let her go and did not turn his head until he knew she was gone, and then she was trudging along the boardwalk. And what he saw then was that her long feet turned out too much as she walked.

Nevertheless, this faint regret, this compunction or whatever it was, clouded his being slightly. Otherwise how was it that he did not perceive Judy's coming the next day?

It was a Saturday and a holiday. But his school tasks were shortened now anyway because the older boys had work to do on farms. Only the Hasty boys were still able to stay because the mill would have little work to do until a harvest came. And Jonathan, some weeks before, turning over in his mind ways of earning something more, had found that on Saturdays and Sundays he could work at the tavern for Henry Drear for his food and half a dollar a day. Thus it happened that in the midst of Saturday morning's stir he saw a wagon come in, and out of it unfolded Joel's long stiff shape, and then he saw Judy, poised with her skirts in her hands, waiting an instant before she jumped to the ground. He saw her from the tavern door, a beautiful girl in a full green dress and a green bonnet, her golden-brown curls on either side of her rosy face. He saw her great black eyes glancing everywhere and thought with a lift of the heart that they searched for him. He went out, wanting to run; but, compelled by the habit of his shyness, he walked sedately toward her.

"Hello, Judy," he said in so offhand a voice that he was disgusted with himself. But he could not speak differently or make his voice warmer, because his heart beat so strongly that he had to hide it. Then he perceived that people were looking at her, men and women, as they came and went from store to tavern from their wagons, and he hated her to stand there before them.

"I'll help you down," he said.

"I can get down myself," she said quickly and jumped before he could help her. He felt her fall against him for a second and he put out his arm. But she righted herself.

"How are you, Jonathan?" she asked.

"I'm well enough," he replied. "And you?"

"I'm well," she said.

This was stupid talk and like nothing he had planned. He

was angry with it, and yet he could do nothing. Whenever he had dreamed of their meeting, it was always alone.

Joel came hurrying up, full of his business. "Good day, Goodliffe." He put out his long, thin, always-dirty hand. "Nice to see you. Judy, we aren't stopping. There's a wagon pulling out this afternoon for California. It is against my principles, of course, to travel on the Lord's Day, but I've just prayed and God tells me to go ahead, since it's hard to find a wagon that can take two people straight to California without stop. But God has prepared this way. The brother's wife died and one of the older girls, and so there's plenty of room. Well, Mr. Goodliffe, I've long felt the call to California, and now it looks like I'm goin' to get there, a land flowing with milk and honey. So, Judy, just get out and rest a little, and after we've eaten we'll start. Excuse me, Mr. Goodliffe. I have some details to attend to."

He nodded, his dark eyes glittering, the wind under his broad hat lifting his long, straight black hair from his shoulders, and hurried off. But what he had said drove away Jonathan's shyness.

"Oh, Judy," he gasped, "you can't go—not when we've had no chance—Judy, you didn't even write to me!"

"I was going to write," she said in that slow, pleasant, rich voice of hers, "but somehow the time just escaped me."

She could write, then! He was suddenly very angry.

"Judy, you knew how I'd be hoping and hoping—and all my letters to you!"

"I kept them, Jonathan," she said.

He was comforted a little and grew gentler. "Judy, that's sweet. But think of me, without a letter from you to keep!"

"I surely ought to have written," she said sadly, turning her big eyes to him. When she looked at him full he saw again how extraordinary were her eyes. The irises were unusually large, the whites so clear, and the lashes long and thick.

"Oh, Judy," he muttered, "where shall we go?"

"Let's go to your house," she said.

His head swam, and he struggled for reason. "You oughtn't maybe to come to a bachelor's home alone," he said. "We're not children any more, Judy." Certainly no child could feel as he did, he thought solemnly.

She laughed. "Well, you go along yourself, and then I'll just walk that way," she said.

He caught at her words and smiled back at her, and, feeling more reckless than he ever had in his life, he strode to the sod house.

Judy, looking after him and seeing everything, seemed to have forgotten him. She tugged at a small cherrywood box in the back of the wagon. Two men from different directions who were apparently in great haste on their own business stopped.

"Let me help you," the elder one said.

But the younger one was there first. "Let me," he said, and lifted down the small box.

"Oh, thank you," she said to them both, with her lovely smile for each.

"Where shall I take it, Miss—?" the young man asked and hesitated, hopefully, for her name.

But she did not give it. She took the box from him gently. "I can take it now, thank you," she said and let him for reward just touch her fingers. She understood men so well and allowed them these small harmless rewards. She took the box and went into the tavern, pausing at the kitchen door to speak to Mrs. Drear.

"Well, mercy me," Mrs. Drear said, "are you and Joel here, too, Judy? Every room's full, my dear. Seems like the whole East is movin' at once this spring."

"We're not stopping, thank you, Mrs. Drear," Judy said. "May I just brush my hair in your bedroom?"

"Do, child," Mrs. Drear said in absent distraction. How to feed thirty people at once was a puzzle, she thought. And Judy, perceiving she was forgotten, smiled and sauntered toward the bedroom. It was in morning confusion, the bed still not made and Henry's clothes on the floor. Not from any compulsion but merely out of half-lazy kindness, she made the bed and hung up the clothes on a nail on the wall. Then she poured water from a pitcher into a china basin on the washstand and washed her face and hands. Opening the cherrywood box, she took out a small round mirror and her comb and brush and brushed her hair into ringlets and brushed her eyebrows with a feather, and powdered her nose from a little bag of cornstarch. She put on her hat and closed the box. Looking as fresh as though she had not been weeks traveling, she went quietly down the walk toward the sod house, avoiding her father without seeming to do so. He was arguing with Lew Merridy outside the door of the general store. Lew, she noticed calmly, was sweating, and that meant her father had God on his side.

As for herself, she had not the least idea what God's will was going to be for her in the next hour.

"Jonathan?" she called softly but very clearly at the door of the sod house. He came out instantly from his bedroom. She saw that he had changed his shirt and smoothed his brown hair, and she smiled at him.

"Judy, come in—sit down. I made some tea, without even knowing if you like tea, but my mother always wants a cup of tea. Sit down here in this chair. Oh, Judy!"

She sat down, and he stood looking at her.

"Judy," he said solemnly, "I've seen you here again and again—all through this long winter."

She smiled, quite understanding how he felt. "Where's your mother?" she asked.

"She's out in the West with my father and the children. Judy, let's not talk except about you and me—Judy, did you think of me?"

He longed to kneel beside her and was too shy to do it, at least until she gave him a sign. She was taking off her hat and smoothing her curls, and he watched every movement of her white hands in that bright hair.

"I did think of you, Jonathan, often."

How, she was wondering, would she know God's will? Maybe if she could make up her own mind it would be easier.

"Did you, dear?" he cried. "And did you long to see me as I longed to see you?" Now he could kneel and he did and was surprised to find that he was scarcely shy at all.

"I did want to see you," she said gravely. Her eyes upon his face were so honest and pure that he could not put out his arms. He was awed before this lovely goodness.

"Oh, Judy, you can't go, when you've just come!" he cried. "I can't bear it. We haven't met for so long, we love each other—don't we, dearest?—but we scarcely know each other. Can't you persuade your father to let you stay behind?"

"Where would I stay?" she asked innocently.

He longed with all his heart to cry out, "Stay with me— marry me—" But his native prudence forbade it. A man ought not to marry a woman he did not know, even if he loved her. It was not prudent, and in his heart he knew that he was compelled above all else by love of wisdom.

And she, waiting, thought, If he asks me to marry him, maybe I'll let that be God's will.

"You could stay with Mrs. Drear until—until we know each other better," he faltered and cursed himself, and then thought irrelevantly of his father and how if he had been his father's son he would have Judy in his arms and be telling her quickly all he longed to tell her. But he was not thus his father's son.

Judy's voice broke, sweet and troubled. "Suppose you didn't like me so well when you knew me, Jonathan, and then I'd be all alone here."

This at least he could deny. "Oh, my dearie dear," he cried, "I'd only love you more."

She looked at him, her eyes very large and full of question.

"What is it, Judy?" he urged her.

"Nothing, Jonathan," she said in a small voice. But what she was thinking was that if he would only love her more, then why did he not ask her now to marry him and so let God's will be done? She would have said this except it was not fair, perhaps, to force God's hand.

"Judy, it's something—I can tell by your eyes."

"No, it isn't," she insisted, and then, to deny this, she allowed two large clear tears to well up in her eyes as she gazed at him. Jonathan was distracted. He put out his arms without knowing that he did, and she came into them gracefully, with a little sob, and put her head upon his shoulder, and he felt her sweet weight.

"Oh," he groaned, and held her to him breast to breast, cheek to cheek. The breath went out of his body. She was so clinging, her flesh so yielding and warm. Only once had he ever held a girl in his arms, and that had been when he danced with Constance Favor in Dentwater. But her body, stiff with stays, had been nothing like Judy's here in his arms. Beneath her gown he felt her sweet, unrestrained shape, slender and soft. He moved his hand to hold her more closely and touched under her bodice her lovely breast. He was stupefied with the wonder of this, and then he drew his hand away again quickly, knowing by instinct that he must stay master of himself, for she could not help him.

"Oh, my little dear," he said tenderly, and smoothed her hair from her face so that he could see her closed eyes.

This, she thought, is just the same as if he asked me to marry him. We'll be engaged now, and if I like being engaged to him, we'll be married.

And he was thinking, in the core of the whirling of blood and brain, that when he told his mother she'd be asking him a hundred questions about Judy that he could not answer. Was she a clever girl and did she like books, to match him, and could she sew and cook and make a sod house into a home, and did she like children and was she brave to stay alone with little children when the man must be away, and did she lie abed late in the morning, and was she saving and sweet-tempered in poverty and wise in riches—only he'd never be rich!—in this beautiful body had she wisdom—had she wisdom—

Judy lifted her head suddenly. "I couldn't just stay behind and give my father no excuse," she said.

He stared at her. "No, you couldn't," he agreed. He felt a strange little pushing force come from her to him, as though she were compelling him to a point he was not able quite to reach himself.

She waited, and after a moment said in her gentlest voice, "So I reckon I had better go on, Jonathan."

"But you'll come back!" he whispered. "You will come back, Judy? See, dear, we'll write letters—we'll get to know each other very well in letters, and then we'll know what we ought to do."

She did not move her eyes from his face. He felt their warm, unmoving gaze flicker once to his lips and then back to his eyes again.

"Judy, you do love me?" he demanded.

The beautiful clear eyes did not fall. "How do I know, Jonathan?" Judy said. "I don't know you well enough."

That night after she was gone, in the midst of the most acute suffering he had ever had, he discovered this speech of hers hurt like a small dagger thrust secretly into the tenderest part of his being. She had risen soon after the thrust, saying so amiably that he was wholly deceived, "I must go back now, Jonathan—it'll be time to go."

"But you will write, dearest?"

"Every week, Jonathan, if you will."

"I will—I promise, without one fail!"

"Good-by, Jonathan." She lifted her face and kissed him on the cheek so sweetly that his knees trembled.

"Oh, Judy, I can't—" he gasped.

But she moved away from him with a gentle quickness toward the door, paused to smile and give him a look. He made to run after her and then stayed himself. He could never hide from that teasing, hearty, eager crowd what he was feeling. If he stood there to see her go, all his habits of restraint would burst and leave him what he was, a wretched suffering man, in love with a woman and yet determined to keep his own soul.

He let her go and spent the hours after she was gone working fiercely upon his garden. Work, work— But the sun went down and he was hungry and must eat and then it was night and he lay down to sleep, and then he discovered the dagger she had left in him. Somehow or other she had taken his wise and right decision and twisted it and sharpened it and thrust it back into him. How did she know she loved him, she had inquired of him calmly, when she did not know him well enough?

This was only his own wisdom. He recognized it, thus returned to him, and then the wound bled. He could have had her; she would have stayed.

"But I know I was right," he said doggedly. "I was right, and she'll have to love me that way or I'll have to go without—"

But the wound bled steadily on, for all that, and for him the spring was over.

🐉 19 🐉

"WHAT GOOD'S LAND TO A MAN WHO'LL NEVER KNOW HOW to farm it?" Mary said bitterly. In the hot summer wind that blew endlessly across the short, stiff grass, she put back a lock of her dry hair. She was talking to Clyde, but they all heard her, because they were at the table. She knew she was violating her deepest instinct of decency when thus she accused Clyde before his children; for if a woman destroyed a man in the eyes of his children, the center of the home was gone. All through the years she had insisted that the children respect their father. Even from Jonathan she had refused to hear complaint against him. But now she could no longer hold back her own bitterness.

"If you couldn't make harvest from a rich bit of earth in England, how can you do it here in this wild place, full of savages?"

"It ain't full of savages, Mother," Jamie said. He was home for a Sunday, a tall, brown-faced, blue-eyed boy with curly black hair burned by the sun. He was in the swiftest of his growth, and he ate corn and beans and the fish he himself had caught, and many of the scones Mary had made for a treat spread with black molasses. "Just because an Indian stopped by yesterday and scared you doesn't mean the country's full of savages!"

"I don't like them and I'll never like them," Mary said bitterly. She was not less bitter because she could not tell them the real fear that still darkened her. In usual circumstances she could have let it pass that she was frightened badly by an Indian, though she had never seen one close before. She had not even thought of them, knowing that they had been taken away from Kansas and put into a reservation to the south. And then yesterday, in the middle of the afternoon when she was alone in the house, with Clyde away buying sheep and Ruth out in the fields with Maggie to guard her from snakes, an Indian had come straight into the house.

"Without knocking or so much as a cry to know if anybody was in, or a by your leave," Mary had said angrily, telling them about it over and over in the evening. "I was standing there mixing my dough for bread, and I felt a hard hand on my shoulder, and I looked up and there was a big ragged Indian, his wicked dark face right by mine. I dropped the crock and screamed and dough all over to clean up, and then he pointed into his mouth. He was hungry, if you please! And I had to go and fetch him bread and good meat before he would go."

She told none of them, not even Clyde, the reason for her remaining terror. It was that, at the moment of her fright, when she looked up into that wild face, she felt the first quickening of the child in her womb. What good could come of a child thus awakened to life? She kept brooding over this, and because she was afraid she could bear nothing.

"Besides, Mother," Jamie said, "sheep's the thing here, and sheep're easy. Mr. Banks says he'll easy clear three thousand on the herds, and that's not to count the cattle, neither."

"If your father gets sheep, they'll all die of something or other," she said.

"Give over, Mary, do, there's a good girl," Clyde said, restraining himself. She was angry, he thought sullenly, because she was going to have another child. Women were danged creatures at best. They wanted husbands, and when they'd got them they were everlastingly complaining because they were men. And Mary, he thought resentfully, would be the first to be angry if he looked sidewise and cross cuts at any other woman. He'd found that out when he was only ordinary to Jennet Drear. It had not been in his mind to think about Jennet Drear that time she came West in the same lot of wagons as theirs, except to mind how nice it was to see a girl laugh again. Women turned solemn so soon. And then Mary had said to him, "I'm coming all this way to see you go hanging your tongue out at a loud young girl, Clyde Goodliffe."

"Oh, you be danged!" he had shouted.

"You just remember," she had said so gravely that he was roaring mad and had flung away. Still, he had remembered, and he had turned his back when Jennet laughed, next time. He had enough trouble with the homestead and his family on his hands without Mary angry at him. She was so small and at times so amiable that only fearful experience had taught him what she could be when she was angry with him.

"There's no luck in you, Clyde, and there never will be," Mary said sadly. But she did give over, not because of Clyde or Jamie, who always defended his father, but because she saw Ruth's eyes suddenly fill with tears that she turned to hide as she cut Maggie's meat. Ruth was adolescent and so filled with sensitive feeling that everything hurt her, and most of all quarreling in the house.

"I want more meat," Maggie said loudly.

"Here 'tis, poppet," Clyde said at once. He laughed at the child's hearty red face. "Pity she's a girl, eh, Mary? She'd have made a rare boy an' we could do with another boy. A man can't have too many boys on a homestead."

"That's easy to say, seeing a man don't have to bear them," Mary said.

Clyde gave up. He pushed back his chair furiously. "Reckon I'll get along," he said furiously. "It's pleasanter anywhere than here."

"I'm sure it is," Mary cried after him, "yet here is where I've got to stay!"

"Oh, Mother, don't!" Ruth pleaded.

Mary sighed and wiped her face. "You're right," she said, "for what's the good? Nothing'll change a man from the moment he's born."

"You're at him so, Mother," Jamie said. "It makes my teeth on edge, too."

Mary looked from one to the other of her children. "Take his side, do," she said sharply. "It's always that way—a mother has to bear the children and teach 'em decency and how to behave, and a man pays 'em no heed, and so they love him best after all."

"No, we don't, Mother," Ruth began, her eyes filling again. "We love you best, but it isn't that—what Jamie means—"

Mary gathered the scattered bits of her dignity together and rose to her feet. Everything about her she loathed—the earth-dark walls of the dugout, the earth floor, the table made of boards, the few miserable dishes, the old ragged clothes they wore, the food that she could not make worth eating. The garden she had begun in the spring had come to nothing. She had longed for the taste of fresh green in her mouth and had nagged at Clyde until he had plowed up a patch of the tough, short grass. But one plowing had not been enough to kill those tenacious roots. They had come to life again, crowding down her tender seedlings, and then had come the dry summer winds and long weeks with no rain, and there was no shade anywhere, and she had given up the garden, and the prairie had seized it. She could scarcely tell that the grass had ever been disturbed.

And now with all her being she rebelled against her pregnancy. Yet what was one to do when she had to live with a man who turned sullen and tempestuous if she refused him her body? It seemed incredible to her now that once Clyde's kiss had been magic and his flesh her deepest excitement. Something was wrong between men and women forever if usage could so dim a glory. But she knew of nothing to do to save it, though its loss had become the tragic atmosphere of her being in a way that she could not understand and only dimly felt. Sometimes she longed to recall the old glory and yet when she let Clyde see her longing in some slight look or appealing word it had always the same end in this which had somehow become meaningless except as a thing to fear.

"I'm going to lie down a bit," she said. And then her quick heart was touched by these three, her children—Ruth so troubled and Jamie sullen, and even Maggie not knowing what to say. "Don't heed me," she said. "Poor things, you'll never remember me as I really am—not a tired, cross old woman—"

In their silence she went away and saw through the open door the distant road. It was only a trail across the grass, the beginning of which was far to the east and the end at the edge of the Pacific Ocean. She could see tiny moving spots in the heat shimmering above the summer-burned grass, spots shining white in the sun. They were wagons.

"Go on," she muttered, "keep on going, as if there was any sense to it!"

Jonathan wrote to his mother: "Now that the summer season is full, I will not be idle. I have my plans in my head and even transcribed in part upon paper for the improvement of Median. The town is well located as to water and crossroads, but it is being allowed to grow up haphazardly and presents a careless appearance. When you return, it will present a very different face, I hope."

The letter lengthened into the fullness of his plans, and upon the back of the sheet he drew like a map what he hoped Median might become. It was a picture as neat as a draughtsman could have made it of streets crossing each other evenly. He had taken the present few houses of Median and the square and had drawn them into the plan so skillfully that one would have said they had been placed purposely as they were instead of anyhow and by chance.

No one in Median knew of this plan. He would have been abashed to show it to anyone because he well knew it was presumptuous for a young man and a newcomer to plan the town. Yet only to himself was Jonathan a newcomer. He was used to the long life of father and son and grandsons in a place such as Dentwater. But to the people in Median Jonathan seemed, in spite of his youth, one of the settled citizens, because upon the prairie to stay a day was usual and men delayed longer in a place only if there were illness or an impediment of some sort, and beyond that only if it was a destination. And for most of them there seemed no cause to make Median a destination. It was not better than any other little village in the middle of the prairie, and there was no reason to stay in it when the uplands lay covered with rich grass for cattle, and beyond were mountains where gold could be washed from the sands of the streams. Median was a place only to pause for a night.

But to Jonathan it was a place as good as any other. He had come here by chance, like a seed dropped by winds or a flying bird; and, like the seed, having found here earth and sky and water, he could put down his roots and send up his leaf.

For it was not in him to dream the big dreams of his father and to imagine the best always beyond, so it was not in him either to mope and sit idle where he was. He was more restless after Judy went than he had ever been in his life. Food was tasteless in his mouth and the school a drudgery until it was over in the summer. Nothing he started could be finished, and ill luck seemed to follow him in small ways. Thus his garden, like all others that year, grew lushly in June but in July was set upon by grasshoppers. There were not many, not more indeed than could be caught by careful picking two or three times a day; but Jonathan hated the feel in his hands of their soft bodies and crackling dry wings as he picked them off into a bucket with a few inches of coal oil in the bottom to catch them.

He heard nothing from the lawyers concerning Beaumont's legacy, and when he had begged his mother to write to him she wrote one of her stiff, short letters beginning, "I take my pen in hand—" He read it many times, unable to tell anything from it. "The weather is very fine," he read. "But are you, Mother?" he muttered, striving to see behind the neat writing. "The wind blows tiresome, but I try not to complain." —Ah, but did she have something much to complain of? "Your father has bought two hundred head of sheep to be paid for when he sells. Jamie is fretting to go West to hunt gold. He is not fond of farming. But he must help his father. Ruth is my comfort, but Maggie is a trial, so willful and naughty and her voice very loud, and I have little time to teach her manners.

Dear Son, I long to see you and pray God we will meet somehow. Your loving Mother."

She did not complain, and yet, breathing through the bare words, he felt the atmosphere of a secret despair. But it might only be his imagination, always too quick to feel trouble in her. When he was even a little boy he used sometimes to go to her when he saw her grave and say sorrowfully, "Mother, why don't you smile?" And sometimes she kissed him, but sometimes she was impatient and said, "A body can't be always laughing, Jonathan. There's serious things, too, and one has to think of them."

So now, to comfort himself, he wrote of what he was planning and drew the map of Median for her with the streets all neatly locked together and where a church would stand some day and a bank and a schoolhouse and a post office and a town hall such as Blackpool had and where new shops would go—stores, they would call them—and maybe some day a little factory for spinning wool from the sheep that men in the western parts raised. But he told her nothing at all of Judy, and his letters to Judy were not about Median. They were about himself and her.

And Judy, in California, found the letters waiting for her at the post office in San Francisco, where he had told her he would write. She had written him almost every week, but not letters like his. She had not written of herself because she spent little time thinking of herself or of what was ahead. She had learned to let what was about her be her life. Thus she wrote to Jonathan that on such a day they had made twenty-six miles, and at a certain town they had come to a railroad and for a day had ridden on the train, which was very filthy with dust and had frightened them all because it went so fast, and the road was so rough they could scarcely keep their seats and the bell on the engine rang continuously because of the jar, and once the conductor's gun went off by accident. Nobody was hurt, but they were all frightened, thinking that Indians had attacked. And at another place when they came down from the train they had to wait a week before they could find a wagon to cross the mountains.

As he read these gently flowing letters over and over alone in his house, Jonathan felt that he had her and yet that she escaped him, that telling him everything she yet told him nothing.

"Write me what you think and feel, my dearest dear," he wrote her, "though I want to know everything else, too, and it's sweet to read everything that happens to you, but I want most of all to know what you are thinking and feeling about everything, but most about you and me."

Judy sat in a small, gray-walled shabby bedroom in a cheap hotel in San Francisco, his letters in her lap, looking down into the vivid, ugly street below. She tried to think and to feel so that she could write to Jonathan, but she could not keep her mind on it. The street was a wonderful sight. It was full of ragged gold miners from the hills and well-to-do farmers and their wives in wagons full of vegetables and fruits and ladies driving in carriages and gentlemen in tall hats and bright waistcoats and carrying canes. It looked mixed and gay and as though everybody was friendly, except she noticed shrewdly that the ladies and gentlemen only spoke to each other. But there were quite a lot of them and some of them were very handsome. She wondered if the ladies bought their dresses here and if indeed such dresses could be bought in San Francisco.

She had honestly planned when she had read all of Jonathan's letters to write him a long letter full of her thoughts and feelings. Instead, after a while she got up in her slow, graceful fashion and laid the letters away in a drawer; and, putting on her best straw bonnet that she had herself lined with rows and rows of narrow ruffled lace, she went out into the sunny street.

I can think and feel while Papa is preaching and I'll write him afterward, she thought. And to a tall young gentleman who happened then to be passing she said, her eyes upturned with their purest, most innocent look, "Excuse me, sir, but will you tell me how to find the best shops for ladies? I am a stranger in this city."

He lifted his high silk hat. "I shall be charmed," he said, and his voice was delightful.

🐝 20 🐝

On that day Jonathan was actually farther away from Judy than he had planned. He sat in the law offices of Bartlatt and Bayne, in the city of New Orleans. He had come here so unexpectedly that he could scarcely believe he was here. He had been at work one morning upon whitewashing the inner earth walls of the sod house. It had occurred to him thus to lighten the schoolroom for the new session. He was to have seven new pupils this year, and he was hard put to it to find the space. He had been thinking of the new schoolhouse he had put down in his plan for Median and wished he might have it now. It was put opposite the church on the square. At any moment, night or day, he could see that schoolhouse clearly in his mind. It was to have two rooms and many windows. While he was whitewashing the sod house, Beaumont had come in.

"I've brought you a letter, suh," he said. "I was in the sto' and Mr. Merridy said mail had just come in and I said I'd take yours to you. It's from N'Orleans, suh."

At the word "letter" Jonathan's heart had turned over, because there was always the possibility of a letter from Judy. Then it ordered itself again and he put out his hand.

"Let me see, Beau."

It was from New Orleans, a curt legal letter from the firm of lawyers in whose offices he now sat. The letter asked for proofs of the alleged Pierre Beaumont's birth, and it desired to know whether or not the alleged son was born of a white mother.

"In case the mother was not white," the letter concluded, "the whole case must be reconsidered."

"I'll have to go and talk to them," Jonathan said when he had read the last sentence.

But first he had gone that night to the Parrys' dugout home and had stayed for hours probing Sue gently. They sat out in the moonlight under a cottonwood tree, out of hearing of the children in bed. Beaumont had slipped away into the darkness, knowing that his mother could speak more freely if he were not there, and they let him go.

"Anything you can tell me will be of use, Mrs. Parry," Jonathan said gravely.

"Maybe I better go, too," Stephen said.

"No!" Sue cried. "What for need you go, Stephen? I've tol' you ev'ything, many a time."

But still he sat apart from her a little, upon a stump and in the shadow of the tree. In the river not far away the frogs croaked. Beneath their feet the grassless bit of earth was as hard and dry as a floor. Stephen worked under this tree by day, and the family ate here, and here the children played.

And then after a silence Sue began.

"What'll I say? I wasn't a fiel' hand, Mr. Jonathan. My motheh was Bettina, and own maid to Miss Lavinia, who was Pierre's motheh. I'm more'n half-white—my fawtheh was Miss Lavinia's brotheh, suh. My motheh grew up in a great house just like I did. We hadn't anything to do with otheh niggras, even hardly in the house, 'ceptin' to eat with 'em. But my motheh didn' even eat with 'em. We just pieced along wherever we were, so's we needn't."

"Then Beaumont is nearly white," Jonathan said.

"It's the black bit that counts, though," Sue said bitterly. "Don't mattah that his brains is white or that his skin is light and his hair brown. Why, Beaumont could pass for white if he went away fum us."

"He must go away with this money," Jonathan said.

Stephen's voice came deep and melancholy out of the darkness under the tree. "Honey, don't let him try to pass. It's like a man gets out of jail. Some'eres dey'll fin' him and put him back again, and then he cain't stan' it sho'."

"What was the wah for?" Sue asked.

There was silence and the soft full throatiness of the frogs, and the moonlight as white as a mild sunshine; and then Jonathan said, trying to be natural, "If you could tell me the circumstances of—of your relationship with Beaumont's father, it might help me later. That is—if force was used—if you were cruelly treated—"

"No, suh," Sue said sadly. "There wasn't any force, I guess—unless you could say a slave would always feel sort of forced by her young master if he tol' her to—to—let him come into her room."

In the shadows the darkness that was Stephen stirred a little, but he did not speak.

"My motheh brung me up wrong," Sue said suddenly. "She used to tell me, 'Ef a white man wants you, you go to him. Any kind of a white man is bettah than a niggra. A bad white man is bettah than a good niggra,' she said. 'Don' eveh let a niggra touch you, you hyeah, Sue? But when a white man wants you, you say, "I'm comin'."' "

"You nevah tole me dat, Sue," Stephen moaned out of the shadow.

"I know it," she said. "I didn't tell you 'cause it ain't so, that's why. I know it ain't so. Any kin' of a niggra is bettah than a white man that wants a niggra girl. That's what I found out for myse'f. My motheh was wrong. She said, 'The on'y way we can git out of bein' niggras, is by changin' our blood. Ev'y niggra woman with a white man's chile in her is steppin' up and up and gettin' away to freedom.' But that was befo' the wah showed us different. It showed us that liberty don't make us free. We're always put back where we was— black blood to black blood."

"Oh, Lawd God!" Stephen moaned out of the shadows.

Sue said, "I thought Pierre loved me—he tol' me he loved me. Once he said he'd even maybe marry me and go no'th, and we could say I was Spanish. And I was sixteen and believed him ev'y word he tol' me. He was eighteen—maybe he believed himself—I don't know. But when Beaumont was bawn Pierre was th'oo with me just like that." In the moonlight Sue's hand was raised and her thumb and finger snapped and her hand fell again. "And Ol' Marster come and said to my motheh that she must marry me off to a good niggra, and he gave her money and two new dresses, and when she tol' me I said, 'I want the blackest niggra man in God's worl'.' "

"That's me," Stephen moaned.

"That's you, I thank the Lawd," Sue said. She got up and went over to him and stood by him and he clasped his arms about her strong waist.

Jonathan turned away delicately. "Now I know. Good night, and I thank you both."

And so he had gone away from them, leaving them there together in the shadows.

Now in this office he sat and waited. He would have said he could wait easily enough for anything if needful, but this waiting made him angry. Twice he had come here in the last two days, only to be put off until today, and he had during the days seen a good deal that he did not like. This city was beautiful and ugly. The Negroes and poverty made the ugliness, and white gentlemen and ladies and their luxury made the beauty. Negroes stood in the presence of the white, and they stepped quickly aside out of a white man's path. An old man had so stepped out of his own way yesterday and when he said, as he would to anyone, "I ask your pardon," the aged black man had only looked frightened, as though he had been spoken to by a lunatic. A beautiful city with mansions and gardens and flowers growing among moss-hung trees, but he smelled the air foul as he sat stiffly in the office, dressed in his best brown suit, waiting, though the room was empty.

At last a young Negro manservant came in, his hands full of letters.

"Mr. Bayne's ready for you now, suh," he said, holding the door open.

Jonathan rose quickly and went into an office where everything, it seemed to him, was covered with a snowdrift of open letters, documents, and newspapers. At the table sat a tall, black-haired young man with his coat off and his feet on the table. He was so handsome that Jonathan's anger changed instantly into shyness.

"Morning," the young man said in a gay voice, but without getting up. "Come in. I hope you don't mind seeing the junior partner. I'm Evan Bayne. Mr. Bartlatt's pleading a case."

"I'm glad to see anyone," Jonathan said.

The young man laughed as if he would laugh at any possible excuse. "Lawyers always keep clients waiting," he said. "We're taught that in law school."

The impudence of this made Jonathan speechless. He sat

down and for a moment looked stern. Evan Bayne did not notice it. He was lighting a long thin brown cigar.

"Have one?" he asked.

Jonathan shook his head. "I don't smoke," he said, "and if you please, Mr. Bayne, I should like to proceed to my business. I am a schoolmaster and my duties begin on a date which compels my early return."

Evan Bayne brought his long legs down from the table nimbly.

"Sorry, sir," he said and with quickly moving, supple hands found by some miracle a letter upon which Jonathan saw his own handwriting. Evan Bayne studied it, his dark straight eyebrows drawn down. He looked serious for a moment. Then his mobile face changed. His black eyes sparkled, and his right eyebrow flew up.

"You're from Kansas! I've always thought I'd like to go there. Say, what's it like?"

"I only know what Median's like," Jonathan said carefully.

"Well, what's Median like?" Evan Bayne demanded.

He put his feet on the desk again, and Jonathan felt his gaze like a warm light upon him.

"It's not much now," he said. "In fact, it's not a town you'd pick to go to. I'm there because my father brought us all over from England. They've all gone to the West, but I'm the staying sort. It doesn't seem any good to me just to keep on going somewhere."

"You'd find it hard to get many people to believe that," Evan Bayne laughed at him.

"Median's not too bad," Jonathan said. "It's at a crossroads north and south, east and west, and there's a river—small, but it never dries up. The wagons all come through."

"They do?" Evan Bayne took his feet from the desk again and sat up.

"I've made a sort of plan in my mind for Median," Jonathan went on, "not that it's anything of my business, but I like planning for something to grow, and Median can grow, I think."

"Does the railroad go there?" Evan asked. His eyes were brilliant, warm, sharp, and shining.

"Not yet," Jonathan said.

"Any reason why it shouldn't?" Evan demanded. "There's

another road projected through to the coast, south of the Union Pacific to Denver."

"No, reckon not," Jonathan said slowly.

They had both forgotten altogether why he was here.

"Go on," Evan Bayne said. "What's your plan?"

Jonathan pulled his chair to the table and drew a pencil and envelope out of his pocket. In the envelope was Judy's last letter, but he did not notice this. He turned it over and began to draw.

"See, here's the square," he said, "a fair big square, and my pupils planted it full of trees this year. Over here's the general store, and here's the inn. There's empty land to the west and east. Down here toward the south is my house—schoolhouse, too—and here's four or five other houses. Down here's Parry's, carpenter he is, and whatnot—and over here near the river is the mill."

"Farmers come in from a long way?" Bayne asked.

"Thirty and forty miles, and sometimes more," Jonathan said. "Now this spring we put in boardwalk around the square—mud's fearful in the spring. That'll come out one day and macadam go down, if macadam's as good as I hear on Kansas bottom. The square we'll keep as a park, but put the town hall in the middle, and the post office here, and the new schoolhouse here. Then off from the square will run the streets, like this—"

He drew a Median he felt he knew as well as the one that stood there now, and Evan Bayne watched him.

"Say," he demanded, "how do you know all this is going to happen?"

Jonathan, looking up to meet doubt, felt a flare of defense for his town. "There's enough folks there now to make it happen," he said. "The land around is rich, and there's no town for miles for farmers to go to for spending their money; and, besides, there's the wagons. Why, all spring and summer there's been a dozen and two dozen wagons a day around the inn."

"Any lawyer there?" Bayne asked.

"No lawyer, no doctor, no church," Jonathan said, "and need for all."

Bayne laughed. "You're persuading me," he said.

"No, I'm not," Jonathan said quickly. "If I am, it's not meant. I know very well how Median looks to a stranger.

When I first saw it it seemed to me a mudhole in the prairie and the prairie nothing but a green desert."

"But you don't feel so now?" Bayne said.

"And I can't tell you why I don't," Jonathan said frankly, "for it was as muddy as ever this spring, and winter was long and bitter, and a fire swept away the autumn grass so fuel was scarce and dearer than gold, and for five months nobody came near the place. But the prairie doesn't seem a desert any more. I've grown to like plenty of sky overhead. And though I live in nothing but a sod house, I teach school in it, and there's no other school in two hundred miles for those children to go to. I keep thinking there's no reason why Median shouldn't grow."

"I am persuaded," Evan Bayne said with gaiety.

"Never say I persuaded you," Jonathan retorted.

"No, I won't. The truth is, I was three-fourths persuaded before you came. I'm sick of this office. It was my father's. He's dead but his old partner isn't, and I have to jog along with him. I want to get out on my own. But I can't do it here—too many old family associations."

They sat for a moment in silence and in that silence Jonathan found to his surprise that he liked this young man exceedingly. He had never seen a man in his life that he liked so quickly and so well. There was something about him that was frank and open, tempestuous, humorous and unaffected and swift. It occurred to Jonathan that he had not a single man near his own age with whom he could be friends. It would enrich Median for him to have such a young man as this there, a man educated and able to argue with him about everything and able to be his companion as no one in Median was able.

"I daresay Median would grow faster if you were in it," he said with a glint of a smile.

Evan Bayne burst into his loud musical laugh. "It would grow or bust," he cried. He leaped to his feet and put out his hand. "I'm coming," he declared. "At least, I think I'm coming. When are you going back?"

"As soon as my business is done," Jonathan said, smiling now very broadly.

Up shot that fluent right eyebrow on the handsome face before him. "God, that's right—what was it? Never mind, consider it done!"

"No, not until you know at least what it is," Jonathan said, and by his gravity compelled the young man to his seat again. Then he told Bayne all that Sue had told him and what Beaumont was and how he had written to old Dr. Beaumont, and what the letter from Bartlatt had said.

Evan Bayne sat turning a quill pen over and over in his hands, his eyes downward, listening. "Everybody knows that young Pierre Beaumont was rotten," he said. "I call him young but he wasn't young. He was forty when he was killed last winter, but he'd never done anything but live off the old man. The old gentleman was good—a wealthy man who needn't have done a day's work, but he was a great surgeon because he wanted to be. The son was nothing."

"Killed?" Jonathan inquired.

"Murdered," Bayne said shortly, "by a niggra. It was patricide."

"No!" Jonathan cried.

"Yes," Bayne repeated, and then told him how Lem had died. "I heard that the crowd was gathering at the prison-house gate, and I went to see the sheriff. Old Dr. Beaumont was our client. Bartlatt always had him, but I knew all about the case, of course. Dr. Beaumont wouldn't prosecute. He had a long talk with Lem in jail, and when he came out he looked sick. 'My son's dead,' he said, 'but I make no charge.'

"Well, the state had to prosecute, of course. But the people took things in their own hands. I was there in the crowd, and I saw it was going to begin. The crowd was too quiet. If they sing and yell you can hope to do something with a crowd, but not when they're quiet. They hanged Lem."

"But why—if the state was prosecuting?" Jonathan demanded.

"A black man can't kill a white man here and be sure of living to be tried," Evan Bayne said simply.

"I shall never tell Beaumont," Jonathan said in a low voice, "no, nor his mother either."

He rose and stood looking down at this man he liked. "You see how it is—this lad of mine's three-fourths white. He's no darker than a Spaniard—nothing so dark as an Indian. And his lips are thin and his hair barely curly. And there's genius in him. If we could get him somewhere to a place where in a crowd he could mingle—if I could get him to England, say—he'd grow to be a great man. You can feel it. If I could get him to England I'd write a man there I know—my old teacher, he is—and he'd see to him and get him on."

"But he'll always be a niggra if he comes back here," Evan Bayne reminded him.

"Maybe by the time he's ready to come back, things'll be different here, too," Jonathan said.

"Don't build on that hope," Bayne returned. "Black will be black, and so will black and white be black, as long as memory lasts in this country."

"I will hope, nevertheless," Jonathan replied steadfastly. "And if I am wrong, then he can stay abroad. There are other countries."

They looked at each other, doubt meeting hope until doubt gave in. Bayne smiled.

"I like you," he said without shyness. "I've never liked anybody as much at first meeting—who wasn't a woman, that is," he added mischievously.

And Jonathan, though he felt himself blushing and knew his face was so crimson he was ashamed of it, forced himself against his shyness and answered, "I like you in the same way."

"My name's Evan."

"And mine's Jonathan."

"I'm coming to Kansas with you."

"I'm glad of that."

They clasped hands warmly and firmly and Evan stood up. "When are you going?" he asked.

"As soon as my business is done," said Jonathan, twinkling at him.

"Oh, God, again!" Evan cried.

They laughed together, and Evan said, "See here, I'll manage it for you. I'll tell old Bartlatt he has to give in—not a legal leg to stand on. I'll tell him the boy's pure white."

"No, that you must not," Jonathan said instantly. "You must tell him the truth."

Bayne was laughing again. "What—and I a lawyer?"

Then he had Jonathan in confusion and not knowing how to put aside this joke. So he gave over.

"I won't tell that particular lie," he said. "Now go on and be content. I won't tell you how I'll do it, but I'll do it for you. When do you start?"

"Tomorrow?" Jonathan asked.

"Day after," Evan said. "I have to make it right with my mother and my sisters."

"Very well," said Jonathan.

"And dine with us tonight, so they can see you and trust me in your company," said Evan, with that quick laughter brimming up again. He scrawled a name and a place on a bit of paper as he spoke.

"I will, thanks," Jonathan said, taking it.

They shook hands again and parted, each content with the other and secretly astonished at the speed of their friendship.

At half past six Jonathan stood before a big cream-painted door in an old brick house and struck the brass knocker. He had walked from his small hotel through streets of shops into streets of houses, and at last into this quiet wide street where large old houses of brick or painted white wood stood, set in vine-draped, moss-hung trees. Every home had its flower garden, and he walked along a path lined with flowers to this door. It was opened by a black manservant who said gently, "Come in, suh, if you please," and took his hat.

The door opened into a hall out of which a wide staircase swept up. And then Evan came hurrying out of an open door, looking very handsome in fresh garments. He should have changed his own clothing, Jonathan thought ruefully, but he had only these, and he had put on his last clean shirt this morning.

"Come in, come in!" Evan cried. "I knew you'd be on time, so I was, too. I could see you'd be the sort of fellow who was always where he said he'd be at the time he said he'd be." He clapped Jonathan on the back and whispered, "Your business is done!"

"How did you—" Jonathan began.

"Hush!" Evan said. "Didn't I tell you not to ask? Come in—my mother's here and the girls are all titivated at the idea of a new young man. You're English, now remember, Jonathan—not a Yankee. You'd never get in this house if you were a Yankee!"

This he poured out upon Jonathan in his bantering musical voice, his eyes mischievous and his mouth playful and the right eyebrow dancing. One hand had Jonathan's coat lapel and the other was punching him gently in the ribs.

"Evan!" a clear voice called.

"Coming, Mother!" he cried.

His arm through Jonathan's, Evan marched into a big oval drawing room where a small red-haired lady sat on a green tapestried chair, her feet crossed on a stool before her. Behind her was a tall pretty girl who looked like Evan, and a smaller younger girl, not yet out of her childhood, who looked like her mother.

"This is Mr. Jonathan Goodliffe, Mother," Evan said.

Mrs. Bayne put out a little hand so abruptly that it seemed a thrust. "You're welcome, Mr. Goodliffe. This is my elder daughter Laura, and this is Louisa."

The two girls bowed, the tall one gently and the small one slightly. Mrs. Bayne withdrew her hand as quickly as she had put it out. For the moment it had touched Jonathan's it had lain in his palm like a dried leaf.

"Sit down," she said. "My son tells me you are English. Do you live in London? I know London very well. My husband's father was a famous barrister there, and I went to visit in his house as a bride on our honeymoon."

Her voice, so clear and all the consonants soft and the vowels lengthened, was nevertheless imperious, just as her tiny feet in black satin slippers, though crossed upon the stool, seemed not resting there but merely waiting to run.

"I don't know London, ma'am," Jonathan said, seating himself on a gray satin sofa. "My home was in a village near Blackpool, a small village it was, and we came here to better my father's conditions."

"I hope they are bettered for being in Kansas, but I doubt it," Mrs. Bayne said with soft sharpness.

Evan laughed. "That's for me, Jonathan. She thinks me a fool."

"I don't, because you're my son," Mrs. Bayne retorted. "But I think going to Kansas is silly, no matter who does it."

Evan laughed at her and bent to kiss her, but she pushed him away with her hand.

"No, you're not to kiss me. You think you can do as you like and then come and kiss me, and I'll forgive you. But I won't forgive you!"

She spoke playfully, and yet there was something in her that was not playful, and Jonathan felt it. But if the girls felt it they said nothing, and if Evan felt it he was still gay.

"Let's say I'm only going on a visit, Mother, or a trip or

whatever it is that young men do when they finish their education."

"If your father hadn't died, you'd have taken the grand tour like a gentleman," she said.

"Being an excellent and patriotic American, I'll go West instead," he replied.

"It's not the same," she retorted.

All during this gay battle that was not altogether gay, the two girls stood, Louisa smiling a little and Laura not smiling at all. She was, indeed, looking at her mother furiously, and at last her mother seemed to feel this look and she turned her head.

"Laura, go and tell Jeems to have dinner," she commanded.

"I'll go." Evan sprang to his feet.

"No, I!" Laura said eagerly.

They met at the door behind their mother's chair, and Jonathan saw that meeting, merry enough, but meaningful, for Laura put her arms about her brother's waist and gave him a great squeeze and Evan pulled one of her short red curls. And Louisa, behind her mother's chair, smiled at them.

"Sit down, Louisa—you make me nervous standing behind me like that," Mrs. Bayne said, and Louisa sat down on a seat by the window.

All through the evening Jonathan felt those three pulling at Evan, each in her own way. Talk was gentle, there was plenty of laughter, and Evan was constantly teasing one and the other of the three; but underneath there was the pull of love too sharp and diverse for ease. Jonathan, saying little and listening much, saw how Evan, without knowing he did it, continually watched the three women. When one was silent, he turned to her, and somehow one after the other and together he seemed to be talking to each and to all. It made Jonathan think of a juggler he had once seen on the green in Blackpool on a holiday, who kept three plates whirling in the air at once so skillfully that none struck another and none fell to the ground. And yet throughout the meal, anyone would have said here was a home of plenty and ease where all was well with the people in it. The light fell softly from a chandelier above the table, and long windows were open from ceiling to floor, and a small night wind cooled the air. The food was well served and more delicious than he had ever eaten in his life—a turtle soup, very thick and smooth, young chicken fried brown with a creamy gravy, biscuits, and new peas and a lettuce salad and an orange pudding. And yet with everything there was the underplay of love pulling this way and that between the three against one, though it was strongest between Louisa and her mother, and Laura took the smallest part in it. So it went on until Mrs. Bayne rose and the girls followed her and left him and Evan together, and the black manservant put wine and nuts on the table. Then the strain went away with them, and Evan sat silent for a moment and he looked tired.

"I miss my father," he said.

"It is inevitable," Jonathan replied, merely to make an answer.

"I never knew how we all leaned on him until he died," Evan said. And then he looked at Jonathan with all his gaiety gone. "Do you think I should stay with my mother and my sisters?"

Jonathan was taken back. "How can I tell?" he replied. "Is there another man in the family anywhere, and do they need your support in money?"

"Louisa is engaged," Evan said, "and will be married in June to an old friend of mine, and live next door, almost. And we have two uncles here and their families—hundreds of cousins, more or less. And my mother doesn't need money. And my God, but I need—freedom!"

He whispered the word. Jonathan nodded.

"I know how it is," he said soberly. "I love my own mother and grieved when she went away, and yet I'm happier. There's not something deep inside pulling at a man all the time if he's alone."

"Exactly," Evan said. He poured out wine for them both. He lifted his glass. "Here's to you and me and Kansas," he said, and drank. Gaiety came back again, and Jonathan drank and knew that another part of his life was begun.

❧ 21 ❧

THE JOURNEY BACK WAS MORE OF A JAUNT FOR JONATHAN than anything he had ever had. Evan made it so by his very presence. To have a young man only two years older than himself his companion, and such a companion, so seeing and full of talk about all he saw, so amiable in his quick eagerness to share every good, so courteous even in the narrowness of their cabin upon the river steamer in which much of their journey was made, was to make every moment pleasurable.

Whatever Evan's parting with his mother and sisters had been, he told Jonathan nothing of it. They met at the quay, Jonathan there early with his one carpetbag, and Evan leaping out of his carriage at the last moment with two Negro boys carrying four bags and two boxes of books and a carryall.

Evan glanced about in mock fear. "I won't be easy until I'm sure old Bartlatt's not here to grab me," he said. "I never knew I was so indispensable to the firm! I thought I was an office boy, dirt under the old fellow's spats, or a nurse, a niggra, anything but an indispensable junior partner. But I was wrong."

He took off his tall hat and wiped his forehead with a white handkerchief. The boat whistled and a mulatto roustabout rattled the gangway. Jonathan had been standing with his hand on the rope watching for Evan.

"Cast off there!" a loud voice shouted.

They hurried aboard, the two Negroes pushing and pulling

Evan's bags and boxes. " 'By, Marse Evan—'by, suh! We sho' hopes you don' like Kansas!"

Evan flung some money to them. "Goddamn you, Pete and Solon, of course I'm goin' to like Kansas! Get along home and mind you take good care of things!"

"Yas, suh!"

They ran off. The gangway was lifted and that good journey began—good, because every day the two young men liked each other better and talked more freely of all their lives. Jonathan listened more than he talked, while Evan told him of the travels he had made, the girls he had loved, always gaily and lightly and never very long. And yet there was a sweetness in this young man which drew out of Jonathan, too, his own story. But he did not speak once of Judy. He kept her for himself.

As they came to the end of the journey and Median was only two days away, Jonathan found himself uneasy lest he had made Median better than the truth. It was hard for him not to see Median as in thought it would be some day. When they left the train and began the drive across the prairie he found himself still more anxious. Evan was staring across the prairie.

"My God," he said, "does it simply go on and on like this?"

"It does," Jonathan said.

"Not a hill nor a rock," Evan said.

"Never," Jonathan answered, "at least not until you go far westward. The land slopes upward, but you don't see it unless you see the long horizon of it."

"Good land, though, if it grows this grass," Evan said.

"It's said to be," Jonathan said cautiously.

Evan glanced at his profile. "You don't care whether I like it or not," he said.

"I do care," Jonathan replied, "but I will not persuade. You see what it is for yourself."

So at last they came to Median. The sky was gold in the west, and even the east was lit with that western light. Median was so set that, coming into the town from the east, they saw between the few houses across the empty square to the west; and, since there were not yet any houses except north and south of the square, Median was like a gate to the west at sunset.

It looked well tonight. Mrs. Drear had washed the flag that

flew from a pole on American House, and it fluttered, red and white and blue, and the store had new cloth in the windows, and Katie had picked a great bunch of grasses and put them in the middle in a big green bottle. Around the doorways of the dozen or so houses late sunflowers grew, and Mrs. Cobb had asters from seed she had brought from her home in New England. There had been recent rain, for the young trees in the square were green and so was the grass growing under them.

Evan pulled at the reins in Jonathan's hands. "Stop," he said, "let me look at it." He gazed ahead. "Not much of a town," he said. "But what a West beyond!"

"Ah," Jonathan said, "you're like all the rest."

He picked up the reins and drove across the grass to the sod house. He was depressed by the thought that Evan might not want to stay in Median after all, but he determined not to show it. Let him stay or go, he would manage for himself, and in Median.

In the twilight the sod house looked as small as a hut, and the garden in front less than nothing in the long wild grass all around. Jonathan opened the door in silence, remembering the house from which Evan had come.

"It will seem a poor place to you," he said. "But here is where I live and work."

They stood together a moment, and while Evan looked about Jonathan looked at Evan.

"It looks comfortable," Evan said.

"I've found it so," Jonathan replied.

He lit the oil lamp. It was one of his luxuries, because it had enabled him to read at night with more ease than he would have had with a flickering candle. In the yellow light he seemed to see for the first time how his home, grown as familiar to him as his mother's face, might look to a stranger. He saw small things he had not noticed—the scars his pupils had made on the unpainted table, Abram Hasty's initials cut there in one end, the unevenness of the board floor, the leaks from the roof which had washed streaks in the whitewash, holes burned about the fireplace, the meagerness of his chairs and his garments hung upon pegs on the wall.

"I shall have to go to the store for some food," he said. "Will you come or stay?"

"Stay and wash off some of this dust," Evan replied.

"I'll have to fetch water first," Jonathan said.

"Then I'll help," Evan replied. Still in his long brown frock coat and tall hat, he took up one of two buckets and Jonathan the other, and they went to Drear's well.

In the door of the store Katie stood with the two little boys and watched them.

"How are you, Katie?" Jonathan called.

"Fine," Katie replied, still staring.

"That's one of my former pupils," Jonathan said, pulling the windlass rope.

"I trust she's no fair sample of Median girls," Evan replied in a low voice.

"There aren't any girls here," Jonathan said.

"Now that you should have told me," Evan said teasingly. "That's important."

"You should—" Jonathan began, and stopped. What he was about to say was "You should see Judy," and he changed his mind. There was no reason why Evan should see Judy.

Two and the school was too much for the sod house, Evan said. Seven days had passed, and each day Jonathan felt Evan as uncertain in Median as a bird in passage. He himself had spent the rarest week of his life until now, and he knew it. Not even Judy had given him what Evan gave him—the constant gay resourceful companionship of a mind more varied than his own. If Evan felt lack of ease and comfort, he never spoke of it or indeed seemed to notice it. He ate salt meat and river fish and boiled potatoes and corn meal in bread and mush as though it were what he would have chosen to eat, and when Jonathan picked fresh beans from the garden Evan made them a treat.

In the week Evan had come to know all of Median, always gay and seemingly careless and always able at night to talk shrewdly with Jonathan about each one he had met.

"Drear's a man to tie to," he said, "and so is Merridy. Hasty is an ignorant low fellow, and Cobb is from stock run thin. He's left New England too late. But his wife's different stuff, and she's put good strong blood into the children, though the weak will come out sometime or other."

But what won Jonathan was that Evan joined altogether in what he thought of Beaumont. Beaumont came to see him the first morning, diffident and yet hot with eagerness to know

what his fate was. He arrived at the door when the two young men were eating breakfast and waited. Jonathan saw him there when he came out for water to wash dishes.

"Come in, Beaumont," he said. "I have good news."

And to Evan he said, "This is Pierre Beaumont."

The boy bowed, and Evan, his hands full of dishes, did not need to greet him except by a nod and a smile. "Hello," he said.

"Good morning, suh," Beaumont replied.

"This gentleman, Beau," Jonathan said, looking with affection at Evan, "is the one you must thank. He is the one who, in some way or other which he will not tell me, settled your case for you."

"I thank you, suh," Beaumont said. He was light enough to flush, Evan saw. In France he could pass as a Frenchman.

"You must go to Paris, you know," he said lightly. "I can see you there, growing very French, and all that—not England, Jonnie, after all, but Paris!"

"I don't know anybody in Paris," Jonathan said with doubt.

"You're not the only man in the world," Evan retorted. "Let me remind you of myself. I happen to know some Beaumonts in Paris—second cousins of the old gentleman. He had me look them up once when I was there with Mother after my father died. We took her abroad."

"I've never heard of any solid folk in Paris," Jonathan said.

"They run a nation, somehow," Evan replied, laughing.

"I've never seen a Frenchman, though. How do I know what Beau might grow into there? Besides, they might not be good to him."

"They'd love him," Evan declared. "A bar sinister is their joy."

Thus they argued until Jonathan saw the boy's dark eyes look afraid. Then he stopped it.

"Oh, well, we can decide later," he said. "The thing is, you've your legacy, Beau, and Mr. Bayne got it for you, and you're going to be a surgeon."

Beaumont listened and took this into his mind, opened his mouth, closed it again, and shook his head.

"I thank both you gentlemen," he gasped and rushed out of the room. They went to the door and saw him running and leaping through the grass, not homeward, but out toward the open prairie.

Evan laughed aloud. "Precious little niggra there, certainly."

But Jonathan did not laugh. He perfectly understood that Beaumont was crying as he ran. He would run crying until he was exhausted, and then he would curl down into the grass and sleep. And after he had slept he would come back, and then they could plan.

"Paris is right, you know, Jon," Evan said, looking after that leaping, flying figure.

"Perhaps," Jonathan said. At this moment he too could not imagine Beaumont in London. "Well, we'll see what we must," he added reluctantly.

"Paris is a good town, you know, Jon," Evan said, smiling.

"Is it?" Jonathan retorted without believing him.

Evan burst out laughing. "Oh, Jon, I swear I love you! Do you mind my calling you Jon?"

Jonathan felt himself red from head to foot and answered therefore with utmost calm, "You can call me that," he said, "though until now I've never let anyone call me out of my name."

Once, dreaming of Judy, he had thought she might want to call him Jon, later, when they were married, perhaps. But let Evan have the name if he wanted it. In a day or two Evan had made it seem more natural than any other. Jon—when he heard it Jonathan felt quickened and brightened, a gayer fellow and more able to put down his conscience.

So now when Evan said, "Two and a school is too much for a sod house," Jonathan was frightened.

"You're leaving Median," he said slowly. "I knew you would—it's not big enough for you."

"I'm not leaving," Evan replied. "I'm only deciding to build myself an office. It'll be an office, but I'll live in it, too, and you and I'll see what we can do. Why shouldn't Median be the county seat? Drear says they're going to split this county into two. A county seat, and then we'll get the railroad to come this way, and no reason why Median shouldn't grow to be a city as big as Chicago some day. I believe in planning big."

"Ah," Jonathan said, "that makes you sound like my dad. But you've got more wisdom than him. He's always talking bigness, but he never does anything to bring it about. But I don't know as I want Median to be like Chicago."

"You won't be able to stop it once I get started," Evan said.

He began it by moving into American House on the day that Jonathan opened school. Next door to the inn he bought a square piece of land from Henry Drear and contracted with Stephen Parry to put up a two-story frame building, one room on top of the other, the one below to be his office and the one above his home, the whole to be finished in two months.

Meanwhile, he paid Henry Drear ten dollars a month for his storeroom cleaned out except for a table and two chairs, and under the new eagle which Drear had put up after the fire had burned the old sign, Evan nailed a neat block he had drawn and painted himself, "Evan Bayne, Lawyer."

To this sign, as sinners approaching heaven, came all those who were discontented with their neighbors, and those who had been cheated in land claims and mortgages and by cattle thieves, and many so troubled. But Evan seemed never to be busy with what he did. All day long he sat in his office, his feet on the table, listening, laughing, shouting to someone passing the always-open door.

Everyone in Median liked him. If Jonathan had been able to be jealous, he might have been now, for everyone went to Evan and claimed him for a friend. But Jonathan could not be jealous. Besides, sooner or later each night Evan would stroll down the boardwalk to the sod house and come in and help Jonathan at whatever he was doing. Sometimes it was midnight before he went away again.

Those were good hours. In them they planned for Beaumont, and they sent him away one day, dressed in Evan's own suit of drab broadcloth. It was a little tight on Beaumont's broader frame, but their height was equal enough, and Beaumont, with his hair cut close, looked a gentleman.

"Never say you are a niggra," Evan told him. "From now on, forget anything except that you are returning to the land of your ancestors. And learn French until it is your mind's language."

The boy took everything into his heart and went away, his purse full of money and his few clothes in Evan's best bag. No one else in Median except Stephen and his mother knew where he was going, or indeed that he was gone. To have said "Paris" as a destination would have seemed madness, and Evan and Jonathan agreed not to let it be said.

These two young men, sitting in the moonlit darkness of the door open to the prairie through the mild evenings of early autumn and by the fire when autumn deepened, shaped their world to their imagination. They were made to work together, Jonathan often thought.

"Now what we need—" Evan would begin, and Jonathan listened.

When his turn came he would begin, "The first step we must take is—"

And in argument and argument and argument again before they parted, Jonathan forgot for hours together what distressed him when he was alone—that Judy did not keep her promise to write him every week. If Evan thought of his mother and his two sisters, he never spoke of them to Jonathan.

Stephen Parry, working overtime on Evan Bayne's house, had most of it to do himself, for labor was hard to find. No one wanted to stop to lend a hand at a house on the prairie when land was to be had farther west, and the eastern markets were opening for all the cattle the West could muster. He had a week's help from a Pennsylvanian whose wife gave birth to a child at American House before they went on. Mrs. Drear took time to be midwife and start another lusty boy westward. "That's the ninety-sixth," she said proudly. Stephen had a few more days from a man who had lost his wife in childbirth; then they, too, went on. The Hasty boys did crude labor when their father could spare them, but the best help was from Matthew Cobb. Matthew was growing into a tall thin boy whose squeaking, broken voice made a joke of him, but he was able to put his brains to what he did and fit a joint and nail a beam as well as a real carpenter. For the first time he found something to make him content with Median.

"I like wood," he told Stephen. "It's clean and dry, and there's no muck when you work in it." Even after the sod-house school began, Matthew spent his other hours at carpentering for Stephen. It was now accepted that the Cobb family was to be a part of Median. Mrs. Cobb was planning the making of a new house near the store.

Judy had only once written to Jonathan every week for three weeks together. Of his letters she had one for every week and one other which he wrote in the overflow of his heart at Thanksgiving. After he had taken a great deal of thought, he put down what the year had brought him for which he thanked God. These two gifts, he told Judy, would be always the two best parts of his life whatever else was to come. The first was Judy herself—"My dear, my love," Jonathan wrote, "whose least little look I have as my treasure, and every touch of your hand my precious memory." After Judy came Evan, "my friend," he wrote Judy, "a clever, honorable, gay man. In him are the best qualities a man can have, such gaiety as my own father has, but not in Evan joined to rashness and heedlessness; such honor that he will do anything for a friend, as indeed he has for me; clever, because he has come to Median and in a few weeks he has won a name that makes anyone whom he takes sure of winning the case. His office, only newly opened in his new house, is already full, and he talks of enlarging it. He can persuade anyone to anything."

Jonathan sat alone as he wrote, for Evan was giving a great dance at American House that Thanksgiving night. Jonathan was only waiting until the hour to go to it; and, feeling thankful and buoyant and full of sure hope for the future, he put down in words the warmth of his heart. Evan had made him less prudent than it was his nature to be, and he had come twice as quickly to writing these words as he would have had he never met Evan.

"My dear darling," he wrote to Judy when he had written the two causes for his deepest Thanksgiving, "now I am ready to ask you, will you be my own wife? I have missed you so fearfully these months. Darling Judy, I do not reproach you for writing me such a few letters that in all these weeks I have only eleven. When Sunday comes and there is no new letter from you, I sit down and read the old ones again. But we must have it so that we are always together and then there need be no blame if letters are not written."

When he had written this he stayed for a while feeling very solemn. Much must be done if Judy was to come into this house as bride and wife. The school, for one thing, must be moved. He would talk it over with Evan and see if by issuing bonds there could be collected enough money to put up the schoolhouse he had planned on the side of the square nearest the church that was not yet there.

He rose and walked back and forth once or twice; and then, happening to glance at the face of the school clock hanging on the wall above the fireplace, he saw that if he did not make haste he would be late for what Evan had called his "shindig." He hastened across the moonlit square to the tavern. It was bright at every window. Though the night promised frost, the door was open, and from it came the sound of voices and laughter and dancing feet. He went to the door and stood looking in. Everyone was there who could drive a farm wagon to come. Small children not yet asleep ran about or clung to their mothers' skirts. When sleep overcame them they would be laid on a mattress somewhere. Every face was gay. A childlike lovable folk, Jonathan thought, and loved them. Yet he wondered, curious at himself, that he could not ever cast prudence aside and be as childlike. Was it only the childlike, perhaps, who left hearth and home somewhere as these had and went westward without knowing where they went?

Evan swung past him in the dancing. He was dancing with Katie, and he saw Jonathan and paused for a moment, his arm still about her. "Well, Jon! I was about to send somebody for you!" he shouted.

He was so handsome, his dark eyes so clear, that Jonathan took fresh pride in him. Even Katie, in the effulgence of Evan's beauty, height, and health, was nearly pretty. She wore a pink dress he had never seen before. Her shoulders were bare, and the skirt ruffled to the floor.

"Why, Katie!" he said.

"Isn't she fine?" Evan cried.

"Change your partners!" Bill White's voice rang out. Bill White, long ago too fat to dance, played a banjo and called the dances.

Evan made a large gesture. "Here, Jon—I've been keeping her for you, the youngest and prettiest girl in Median!"

He bowed deeply and handed Katie to Jonathan and went away. Jonathan saw him a few minutes later not dancing but leaning over the bar talking to a strange man; a cattleman, he guessed, by the man's leather trousers and open collar. There was an increasing number of cattlemen now coming through Median, rough noisy men who drank too much and swaggered about the store and the tavern.

Then he looked down at Katie. She was dancing sedately to

the new tune Bill was plucking, her thin little face quite grave. In his hand Jonathan felt hers lying passive and without pressure.

"I don't dance as well as Evan, I fear," he said ruefully. Evan had taken away with him the small glow she had seemed to have.

"You dance all right, though," she replied quickly. But she did not look at him nor smile, and though he knew she had no coquetry in her, it occurred to him that perhaps Lew had been wrong. Perhaps she had never cared for him. They were too much alike, two somewhat grave young people, too ready to think of work instead of play. What more right than that she should rather love Evan when it came time? He examined her face just beneath his own—a plain, regular little face, each feature well enough, but the combination somehow lacking the magic for beauty. He thought of Judy with sudden and enormous desire and knew that, for him, she alone was beauty and there could be none other.

The music stopped, and he and Katie stood for a moment uncertain. "Thank you, Katie," he said and let her go.

He and Evan returned to the sod house when the night was near to dawn. Houses were darkening as they walked back and wagons rumbling out of the town homeward, sleepy children crying. Again and again Evan had shouted, "Good night—good night all! Mighty glad you came, mighty glad!" Each time, Jonathan thought, listening, his voice was as joyous to one as to another.

"Grand folks," Evan said, sitting down at last in Jonathan's most comfortable chair. "Mend your fire, boy—your house is as cold as a cave. I shall be staying the night with you, Jon. I'm as full of talk as an egg of meat. Don't hope for sleep, for you shan't get it."

"Well, tomorrow's a holiday, luckily," Jonathan replied. He reached for the bellows as he spoke and blew the embers red and built corn cobs above them skillfully and the flame burst out. Evan sat sprawling in the chair, his feet to the blaze and his hands locked behind his head.

"Jon," he said suddenly, "I'm going to make Median a cattle town."

Jonathan, on his knees, held the bellows. "Evan, you didn't tell that chap—I mistrusted he was a Texas rancher!"

"I did," Evan said. "Why not? Why shouldn't Median have

their money? American House would profit, the store would profit, it would bring all sorts of business in."

"But the trail's end is too far north," Jonathan said slowly.

"Median would bring it two days nearer the railroad—we're going to have a railroad, Jon."

Jonathan put three pieces of wood on the fire, sparely and so that the fire would catch them all. Then he rose, dusted himself, and sat down on a wooden stool.

"And where would Median be?" he demanded.

"What do you mean?" Evan retorted. "There'd be more Median than ever!"

"There'd be lunch wagons and dance halls, and American House would be a saloon, and there'd be brothels and fightings and killings—there wouldn't be any room for Median."

"Why, you son of a gun," Evan said, laughing. "Median would boom! There'd be thousands of men paid off here if this was the shipping point, and the men would leave their money here."

"Yes, and what else? Tick fever for every cow around and bad diseases for our own folk, and sicknesses worse than that for us all. No, Evan!"

Evan brought his chair down with a crash and his hands from behind his head. "Jonathan, you're not serious!"

"I am," Jonathan said.

"Why, it's the law of growth, man! You can't stop the sources and expect Median to grow!"

"Maybe you and I don't see Median the same," Jonathan said.

"Maybe we don't," Evan said. "Maybe you don't see Median a prosperous city, bigger every year, drawing money into her banks, business into her stores, sending goods out all over the West, an exchange between the two halves of the country. No reason why not, when we are geographically almost the exact center of the nation! And you and I, Jon, could be anything we liked—governor, senator—anyway, rich men."

"I don't want to be rich," Jonathan said shortly.

"You certainly don't want to live in a sod house all your life, Jonathan! You don't want to live miles from a railroad and use candles and oil lamps all your life and draw water out of a well like—like Abraham did!"

"I want a good town," Jonathan said stubbornly. "I want a

town with a schoolhouse in it and a proper church. Business, of course, but not the brawling, cursing, fighting sort of business cattlemen bring in."

"What's going to bring in business, though, Jonathan? You can't just sit and expect it to come! You must hold out some promise!"

"Median's in the middle of a lot of good land," Jonathan said soberly. "Stands to reason solid farm folk have to buy and sell somewhere and put their children in school and have fairs and meetings. They'll move to town, when they've done well enough on the land and get old, and they have money to spend, too, as well as cattlemen, and better money."

"But we'll be gray-headed before Median gets anywhere!" Evan cried.

"It'll be solid when she gets there and good going the whole way," Jonathan declared. "The sort of town a man would want to settle in and bring up his family," he added.

The two young men looked at each other, their faces clear in the firelight. Evan laughed.

"You're in love, Jonathan!" he said, not suspecting he had hit truth.

"Yes, I am, I own it," Jonathan said simply, "and I speak out of all my thoughts about what's most valuable to me."

"Why, who could it be, Jon? There's nobody here—it's not little Katie Merridy!"

"No, it isn't," Jonathan said, growing red. "It's nobody you know, Evan, though I've been going to tell you a long time. It's a young lady I've known a year now and fell in love with as soon as I saw her. Her father's an evangelist and she's in California, and I wrote her today asking her to marry me and posted the letter tonight."

"And have you reason to hope she will have you?" Evan asked, his eyes merry and full of affection at the same time. How impossible not to love this Jonathan, he thought with tenderness and impatience!

"Yes, I have reason to hope," Jonathan replied.

He sat there with his hands on his knees, looking so innocent in his determination that Evan grew quizzical.

"And so all of Median is to be shaped to you, is it?"

"Not to me," Jonathan replied, "but to the thing that's best."

"And suppose I don't agree?" Evan asked.

"Then I reckon we'll have to see who of us can win," Jonathan said calmly.

"Well, I'm damned," Evan said.

❧ 22 ❧

IN A TALL NARROW HOUSE IN PARIS, BEAUMONT WAS FEELING his way. He was like a blind man. Nothing he had seen before helped him here, beyond the ordinary objects in a room. That is, a chair was to sit upon, a bed was to sleep in, the stairs were to climb up and down from the room he shared with Georges, his second cousin. He had not yet dared to call Georges cousin, though Georges introduced him proudly at school as "my cousin, Pierre, from America." Once in an excess of honesty when the two of them lay awake in their cots after Marie the maid had put out the lamp, Beaumont said, "I ought to tell you, I reckon, Georges. My mother— was a slave."

What he had wanted to say was, "My mother is a Negro." But he could not. It was easier to say "slave."

To this Georges answered in surprise. "But what is it? All slaves are now freed in America. My father says it is so."

Pierre did not reply at once. Then he said, his temples beating, "She is—not white, you know, Georges."

"And what of it?" Georges asked. "I once saw a black man in a great carriage on the Champs Élysées. There were ten carriages following him, and he was dressed in red and gold, and he wore on his head a gold turban with a white cockade with diamonds as big as apricots. He was an African prince, and he was also French." Georges yawned. "Pierre," he said with sudden interest, "did you see that fat boy who pushed me today purposely as we came from gymnastics? Tomorrow I shall push him twice as hard, and with all my strength. He is a German sausage, that boy!" Georges, two years younger than Beaumont, ground his teeth together in the dark.

Beaumont laughed and then fell silent. Between Georges and him were years never to be shared. He could never share entirely with anyone what it was to come here where no one cared what his race was. At first he felt Georges' parents must be pretending when they said he was to call them uncle and aunt. "Though we are only your cousins, dear Pierre," Georges' mother said kindly, "it is more suitable, since we are so much older, that you say *'mon oncle'* and *'ma tante.'* It is fortunate, dear Pierre, that you have come to us, since we have only our Georges, and sometimes he is lonely with only elderly parents. We married too late, and now it only remains that you learn to speak our language quickly, so that we may be a happy family. English we cannot."

He was learning to speak French very quickly. He was glad to change even his language. He wanted to change everything. Perhaps his very skin was changed now that people did not call him a Negro. But he was not sure of his complete change until nearly a year later when he met Michelle DuBois. This meeting was stiffly polite, in the narrow gold and white drawing room. Madame DuBois was Georges' aunt on his mother's side, a widow who lived in the DuBois house in the country. Once a year, at New Year's, she came, with Michelle, to spend the holiday in the city with her sister. Georges had talked, a little and carelessly, of Michelle, as a brother might speak of a sister.

"She's a nice girl—rather pretty, but a girl!"

But Beaumont, coming forward to bow as Madame Beaumont had taught him, saw a young angel, whose fair curling hair, cut in bangs over a white forehead, was a cloud of gold about the heaven blue of her eyes. When he touched her hand his heart spilled out of his bosom and lay at her feet.

Two days later they had declared their love secretly to each other.

"But I am so dark, Michelle!"

"But you are so handsome, mon Beau!"

From that day on he was Beau to his beloved.

Across the mountains in San Francisco Judy read Jonathan's love letter, put it down on the bureau, and went on brushing her long, softly waving bright hair. She sat before the bureau in her full white petticoat and camisole and watched herself thoughtfully in the splotched mirror. The room in which she had been living for several months was neat and even pretty, because she always succeeded in making her rooms so. Thus, over the blistery top of the bureau she had spread a clean hand towel and upon the bed a crocheted spread of her own making. Joel's room next door, with exactly the same rough furniture, had none of the same air.

When she had brushed her hair to a flying mass of electric life, she subdued it with her comb and curled it about her fingers. Then she pinned the curls carefully to the back of her head in a waterfall and, rising, slipped under the full skirt of her gown hanging from a hook on the door. A smooth slide, a graceful undulation of her body, and her head came through the low neck, the curls undamaged. The gown was a yellow muslin, a fall of ruffles from her bosom to the floor, with a ribbon sash at the waist. She had made it herself, hemming the ruffles with fine stitches. It had been the work of her whole summer, but she considered it worth all the hours she had spent upon it. She dampened a scrap of turkey-red cotton cloth in the jug on the washstand and touched it to her cheeks and lips, and then she dusted her face and neck and arms with cornstarch. The gown had a small reticule of muslin. Into it she put her cornstarch bag, her handkerchief, and then Jonathan's letter.

Thus frocked, she tidied her bureau, touched her ears and bosom with perfume, and knocked on her father's door.

"Come in!" Joel shouted.

She went in and found him at the window frowning out over the bay.

"I'm ready now, Father," she said. "Capt'n Lusty will be coming for me any minute."

"You made up your mind?" Joel asked sharply.

"No, I haven't," she replied quietly.

Behind him his room was in its usual disorder. Almost as though she were unaware of what she did, she began to straighten it.

"The truth is, Father," she said, hanging up Joel's snuff-brown coat tidily, "the Capt'n hasn't spoke of marriage."

"He will," Joel declared. "If you manage right, Judy, so he'll know he ain't goin' to get what he wants by any sinful means and he'll be compelled to righteousness. That's the way God works."

"Yes, Father," Judy replied. She was sorting Joel's shirts, clean from soiled. "And what'll you do, Father, if he doesn't give in to God?"

"It'll be kind of hard to know," Joel replied. He sat down

and put the fingers of his long, thin, never-clean hands together. "I reckon I'll just have to search the Scriptures."

There was a loud thump on the door, and a boy's voice shouted, "Capt'n Lusty's downstairs!"

"Good-by, Father," she said, as nearly in haste as she ever spoke.

"Good-by," Joel said, without looking at her or without changing his frown.

Judy, moving smoothly down the narrow corridor of the rooming house, went down the stairs with the same gliding steps, holding up her skirts on either side. She knew how she looked to the tall man waiting for her in the hall below and was content without caring enough to be vain.

"Well, my beautiful," he said in a hearty voice when she had reached the last step.

"Good evening, Capt'n Lusty," she said, putting out her right hand. Her middle finger was rough with stitching, and he felt it as he put her hand to his lips.

"Why, what's this?" he asked, examining it.

"I always stitch my finger when I hem ruffles," she said, and smiled so innocently that he felt a swirl in his head. There was no one else in the hall, and he slipped his hand around her shoulders. His fingers were in the soft warm pit under her left arm. They sent shattering messages to his brain, and he was lost.

"I'm going to kiss you," he muttered.

She did not speak, but she swayed to him gently and closed her eyes. Upon her full warm mouth she felt his kiss without returning it. It was, she reflected, pleasant enough—too moist, perhaps, but men's kisses were usually so. She allowed him to continue it for a second more and then opened her black eyes wide. The sight of those eyes, so close to his and so direct in their gaze, spoiled the kiss for Captain Lusty. He was not able to go on, and he straightened himself and laughed unsteadily, still conscious of his fingers in their warm nest.

"You've about got me," he remarked.

She moved a little without any appearance of repulse, and he found his arms empty.

"Shan't we go?" she asked.

"You want to go?" he countered.

"Well, I want to see the ship," she said. "I've never been on a real sea ship. They're not like river boats, are they?"

"They are not," he retorted scornfully.

She put her hand on his arm and by an imperceptible pressure guided him to the door.

"I know," she said with a fresh, urging eagerness. "That's what I say—I want to see how a real ship is, and how folks live on it."

Outside the door a cab waited. Captain Lusty handed her into it, leaped in, and then thrust his head out of the window.

"Ahoy there!" he shouted to the driver. "Get along back to the docks where I picked you up and stop alongside the *Virgin Queen*."

The cabman grunted and they set off. Captain Lusty sat back. While he dressed himself for the evening in his cabin he had thought persistently of the possibilities of this half-hour, alone in the cab with a beautiful, childishly innocent girl. But now he was aware only of her dark eyes and of how queer they had looked just under his—eyes too big and too black. She was chattering along, sitting gracefully erect as the cab lurched over the rough street.

"Oh, I'd admire to see the Sandwich Islands," she was saying earnestly. "Seems as if I never hear enough when you talk about them!"

Captain Lusty took her hand and fondled it. "You'll come with me maybe, eh, lady, some day?"

She let him have her hand, she even smiled. But when she spoke it was with simple gravity. "If it's God's will, Capt'n Lusty," she said.

He put her hand down. "You've a real discomforting way of talkin', sometimes," he said.

"Do I?" Judy asked, surprised. "But I couldn't do what wasn't God's will—you wouldn't want me to, would you, Capt'n Lusty?"

Captain Lusty swore to himself in a mutter.

"What's that, Capt'n Lusty?" Judy asked.

"I said, Goddamn," he replied.

She laughed, and in the flickering street lights he saw her lovely face suddenly quiver and grow warm with amusement. She was laughing at him! All these months when he had been wanting her she had perhaps been laughing at him. Plying back and forth between Honolulu and California, he had thought of nothing but her ever since one day on the street she had asked him where to find a store. He had gone with her that day, thinking her easy in her virtue. He still thought her easy. When he was away from her he was sure of it. And yet, though she had allowed him to kiss her sometimes, she had allowed no more—not, he felt wrathfully, from refusal so much as lack of interest in love-making. And yet he could not be mistaken in a woman who had mouth and eyes like hers.

He sat up, full of sudden dignity, and made no effort to touch her. After all, he was the captain of a good vessel, and a well-to-do and successful man, and what was she but the daughter of a crazy traveling preacher? He had said carelessly, "Come and preach in Honolulu, man—there's lots of sin there," and Joel had lit as though a fire had been kindled in him.

"Maybe that's what God means, always leading me westward," he had exclaimed. . . .

"Here's my ship," Captain Lusty said suddenly.

There she was, her well-known lines trim and sharp against the still-bright sky. The cab stopped. He got out and paid the fare, then, taking Judy's hand with ceremony, he led her to the gangway. A sailor standing on the deck saluted and stared at her.

"All well?" the captain inquired.

"All's well, sir," the sailor replied, "and the others are waiting."

There were others, for Judy had refused to come alone, and he had been compelled to invite his mate and bid him bring his wife. "But clear out, you hear," he had said carelessly. "Aye, sir," the mate had replied, thinking of the gold piece that was his when he obeyed his captain.

And Judy, following the captain and caring nothing for the stares to which she was so accustomed, was full of pure pleasure at everything she saw. In the saloon she dimpled sweetly when she bowed to a gray-haired woman with a hearty red face and a man whom the captain introduced as "my mate, Mr. Briggs, and Mrs. Briggs—my thanks to you, Mrs. Briggs," he added.

"My pleasure, Capt'n," Mrs. Briggs said demurely, without looking at Judy.

It was all pleasant, Judy thought. The dinner was delicious—guinea hen, which she had never eaten before, and wine, which she tasted and did not drink. They laughed and the others told stories at which she laughed and it was all delight until suddenly the Briggses were sent for because their little boy was taken ill.

They went so quickly that she scarcely knew them gone, and then she was alone with Captain Lusty. And yet not really alone, she told herself, for there were the sailors and the steward.

"Take the coffee and dessert to the cabin," Captain Lusty ordered the steward, and he rose and put Judy's hand on his arm.

"We won't part for dessert, since there's only the two of us," he said, and she went with him doubtfully, and yet saying to herself that she must go in if only to discover what God's will was. Besides, there was so much she had not yet seen about the ship.

The moment she entered the cabin she knew it was wrong. The devil, not God, had led her here. Behind her the Captain shut the door. His handsome face was red, and his hand trembled as he took up the coffeepot. Judy's eyes, flying about the small luxurious room, fell upon a photograph standing on a shelf below the mirror. It was the picture of a woman, a delicate fair face, with sad eyes and a small sad mouth.

"Who is that?" she asked.

"That's my wife," Captain Lusty replied.

And then she knew that indeed she should not be here.

"You never told me you were a married man," she said.

"You never asked me," he retorted. He put down the pot he was holding and turned on her. "You never asked me anything, my dear."

"Because I took you for an honorable good man with right intentions," she said in a whisper of horror. It occurred to her how narrow was the path to salvation for her—only, indeed, that bit of a plank between her and the shore.

"Dear God, save me," she said aloud in simplest tones.

"It's a little late for God," the Captain replied, smiling. He went up to her and put his hands on her warm bare shoulders. "A little late," he repeated, and slowly moved his hands down her arms and back again and into the two pits under her shoulders, and then he lifted her sharply.

And she, in solid horror, hung limp as a doll. She felt herself go cold, and she suffered without an answering movement his kiss.

And he in the midst of that hot kiss saw those great wide

black eyes that had so disconcerted him before. They stared into his eyes so blank, so empty of all feeling, that to save himself he drew back. Was the girl crazy like her father? He shook her. It was like shaking a sack.

"What's ailing you?" he shouted.

"None of this is God's will," Judy whispered. "None of it, I say!"

"You're mad," he said, and let her go.

She sank down upon the seat, and panted, and felt in her little yellow muslin bag, Yes, there was Jonathan's letter.

"I'm engaged," she said. "I'm engaged to a solid good young man that's asked me to marry him, and I never dreamed you were so wicked."

"You don't act innocent, so you must be a fool," was all he said. He rang a bell and when the steward came he said, "See that this lady gets safe ashore, Tom."

"Aye, aye, sir," the steward said. He was astonished, but he did not show it. He waited while Judy rose and passed through the door and then led her to the gangway. It was there safely leading to the shore, and she trod it as joyfully as any sinner ever looked toward heaven.

But her face was as innocent again when she entered Joel's room.

"I came to say good night, Father," she said.

Joel turned on her with eyes of solemn fire.

"Judy, I've been on my knees since you went. God has bade me go westward to the islands of the sea."

She looked at him without moving. "Has He, Father? Then you and I must part."

"But J-Judy——" Joel's astonishment broke against the calmness of her eyes.

"I'm going to marry Jonathan Goodliffe," she said.

23

IN THE SOD HOUSE JONATHAN READ THE WORDS AGAIN AND again.

"For my mind is set, dear Jonathan, and it is to marry you."

Judy's letter was short. Why should she write much when she was starting at once for Median? The roads would soon be closed for winter, and if she delayed it must be for months. And there was nothing more to delay her. Captain Lusty she had swept from her mind as a woman sweeps dust from a room before she closes the door upon it, clean and empty. Judy had the gift for finality which was finality itself, so that she saw no irony in Joel's sailing for Hawaii in the *Virgin Queen*. None of it now had anything to do with her. She had set about her own journey with composure, and with growing pleasure.

I shall have something to call mine, anyway, she had thought after she had written the letter, as she folded ruffled skirts carefully into a small round-backed trunk. The trunk had been her mother's, and of her mother she now thought with pensiveness as she made quick, exact movements that in so short a time left the room in which she had lived for months emptied of her presence.

I must go and see Mrs. Drear, Jonathan thought. Judy'll have to stay there a bit. His pale face reddened as he thought of Judy. She would be here before Christmas. They would be married at once. What could he do with his school? He pondered the possibility of persuading Henry Drear to let him hold it in American House. It was impossible to have it here if he and Judy were married. He wanted the house to himself, alone with her. And Evan—Evan must be told, first of all. He leaped to his feet. Lucky it was a Saturday, he thought, so he was not tied to his work. If he had everything ready, he could wait better for her coming.

He found Evan, as he was always to be found these days, in his office and surrounded by men. In the midst of them Evan sat smoking his pipe, his feet on the desk, listening, laughing. It was hard to know whether the men had business or were only there to talk. To Evan everything was business. A man who came to talk might stay to tell him a grievance against a neighbor that would develop into a lawsuit. Evan's dark, warm eyes, his easy laughter, his endless patience for listening, drew men to him. Lew complained of it openly, with grumbling good nature.

"Doggone you, Evan, you're takin' away my trade. Fellers used to come into my store to talk—then they'd buy somepin' to take home to their younguns. Now they stop at your door before they ever get here, and when you're through with them they can't afford to buy a salt cracker offen me."

"Then I'll bring them," Evan said. He did bring them, sometimes a dozen at once, to buy a dipperful of Lew's home-made whisky. Just often enough to keep Henry Drear content, he took them to the bar at American House, though there he went most often with one or two men, not farmers, but men from railroads and in the cattle business in other states. Together they talked long in low voices, sitting at the corner end of the table.

But to Jonathan Evan was always the same. He said now as Jonathan entered, "It's only fair to tell you, Jon, that we stand a mighty good chance of being a cattle town!" He smiled his beautiful lazy smile at the men sitting about his office, where there were always plenty of chairs and spittoons.

Jonathan did not reply. Judy's name was not to be mentioned here. He came in and sat down. Evan introduced him casually. "This is my best friend and warmest enemy, fellows. He agrees with me on everything except how to make Median a big town."

"Hell, nothin'll do it quicker'n cattle," the man cried.

"That's what I tell him," Evan said. His brown eyes upon Jonathan were full of affection. "But he's a stubborn son of an Englishman. He doesn't want you here, fellows," he said. "I do. Want to bet on which of us is goin' to win?"

"Bet on you, Evan," a man shouted. "Yeah, ten to one," another growled, and spat his brown juice to the far side of the nearest spittoon. Evan, who did not chew, had covered his floor with sawdust. Once a week Sue Parry swept it all out and Stephen put it down new.

"These fellows are from 'way down in Texas," Evan said amiably to Jonathan. "The railroad's certainly going to run south, Jon—I had their promise for that when I was in Topeka last week. It'll come through Median if plans go right. It'll sure come through if we make Median a big cattle center. Sit down, Jon."

"English, hey?" a man said to him, wondering. "Say, what's it like over there?"

"It's another country," Jonathan said dryly.

"Goin' back?" another asked idly.

"No," Jonathan replied.

He caught out of the air in the room, out of the slightly excited triumph he could perceive in Evan, a feeling of immediacy. Before he did anything else he must measure the speed of whatever Evan was about, and to do that he must wait here and listen. But Evan was quick to discern him as well. Between these two was something so close that neither could hide himself wholly from the other. It made Evan want now to be away from Jonathan's eyes. He was not ready yet to tell Jonathan everything. When he had finished what he was determined to do and had made it irretrievable, he would tell him. He rose from his chair.

"Come on over to Lew's, you fellows," he said lazily after a moment. "I'll buy you a drink."

He let them all pass through the door and then he turned to Jonathan. "Anything you want of me, Jon?"

"Only to tell you I'm to be married," Jonathan said. His voice was quiet but weighted with his feeling, and to his own astonishment tears came into his eyes. "I couldn't speak before strangers," he added.

And suddenly Evan was all he wanted him to be. He came back into the room and threw his arm about Jonathan's shoulder and hugged him, and his joyfulness was real.

"Jon! Is it Judy?" he cried.

"It could be no other," Jonathan said solemnly.

"Oh, Jupiter, but I'm glad!" Evan was squeezing him and patting him and now with his right hand he seized Jonathan's hand. "Now I'll see her and I shall tell her if she doesn't make you a good wife, it's I who'll take a hickory switch to her. You'd never beat your wife, Jon—you're so softhearted! But she's got to make you happy—I swear she's got to!"

There was an edge of breaking in Evan's voice. He laughed to avoid it. "Gosh, I—I—love you, too, you know!" he said.

Jonathan, dreading the edge, grew calm. "Thanks, Evan—and it's only fair to warn you, I s'll do all I can against Median's being a cattle town, now more than ever."

"What? Oh, all right!" Evan laughed. He clapped Jonathan's shoulder. "Go on, man. Don't forget the odds are ten to one against you, though!" He ran out of the door and after the men now sauntering down the boardwalk toward the general store.

And Jonathan, looking after him, thought to himself that his work lay ahead of him. He must see every man in Median before Evan could reach him and tell him what it would mean if Median were a cattle town. Henry Drear would be for it, because American House would prosper. But Drear had no sons, and Jennet was gone. He would not waste time on Drear. He would begin with family men like Cobb and White and the Irvings, who had just come from Illinois, and the Bennetts from New York State. They all had big families. He went out into the cool sunlit noon and turned his steps toward White's house. Judy would have to wait while he made a home for her.

Evan said, "We'll put it to the town."

There was not the smallest seeming difference in his manner toward Jonathan. The last few days might have been, for all he showed otherwise, a game between them. A grim game, though, Jonathan thought as he looked at Evan with his quiet blue eyes. It had come to be a race between them as day went into day, to see who was to be first at the scattered farms. A few times they had arrived together at a lonely dugout or sod house. Then each had been scrupulously fair. Turn and turn about each had stood to let the other one go in first. Neither inquired of the other what had been said. But Jonathan came to know fairly well which would be Evan's men and which his. What he called "solid folk" were on his side, men who came determined to farm and to stay, who wanted to send their children to school. Jonathan found that to these it was best indeed to begin by talking about the school. If Median were to be the proper town he wanted it to be, the sooner he got a schoolhouse built, the better it would be. Bonds were the thing for it, he thought. He had first thought of bonds from hearing Evan talk about issuing railroad bonds. If men paid for railroads in such ways, why not a schoolhouse?

Thereafter when he went into a farmhouse he put the matter first of all thus: "I'm the schoolteacher in Median. I see you have school-age children here. Would you want to send them to school?"

It was more often the woman than the man who spoke, "Sure we want 'em to git schoolin'."

"I dunno," the man said. "I can't get along 'thout the boys' help."

"You can get along as good as I can 'thout the girls," the

woman cried, "Anyway, we can manage. How much would it cost, mister?"

"Well, it depends," Jonathan said in his slow, plain manner which always made what he said seem the voice of truth. "A dollar a month is the regular, but I'm thinking of a schoolhouse. We need it. My little sod house can hardly hold another pupil. Anyway, Median ought to have a schoolhouse. Would you feel to put something in it? I'd be willing to take half my price and put the rest into the building, if so be you could add to it."

"I ain't got cash," the man would say more often than not, "but I could put in labor." Or he might say corn cobs or hay cats for fuel, or a team for hauling, or rarely, if he lived along a stream, a few trees for wood. Most often of all were notes on next year's harvest. "If it's a fair harvest, I could let you have maybe fifty or even a hundred dollars." After that it was easy to talk about the sort of town Median ought to be. Jonathan at the end of two weeks and a day had his pockets full of such promises, written upon pieces of paper.

"I'm willing to put it to the town," he said to Evan. "That's fair enough. And I'll tell them about the schoolhouse at the same time."

"Will you want your school in a cattle town?" Evan's mischievous eyebrows flew up at Jonathan.

"It isn't going to be a cattle town," Jonathan said calmly, and smiled when Evan laughed.

The first town meeting of Median was held in American House. Evan had been quick to say, "Your schoolroom is too small."

"So's your office," Jonathan had replied.

Each refusing the other the advantage of his own ground, they had agreed upon the big room in the tavern. Drear, all for Evan in the matter, was hearty and willing.

"I'll stand to treat everybody twice around free," he declared. "Though if I'd known what a crowd there'd be," he declared the day of the meeting, "I'd have thunk twice."

Jonathan himself was secretly surprised to see the number of people who came in to Median that cool December day. It was a day such as early winter may give on the prairies, a day mild and without wind at morning and evening. At night anything might happen. The wind might rise and bring winter in by the next day, or a sodden rain set in and turn the earth to its old bottomless mud, and this would freeze until spring. As though they knew it might be their last fair day, every family within horse distance and return came in, their food in baskets, and women with babies in their arms.

Evan and Jonathan had discussed together how they should begin.

"We must have an order of talk," Jonathan said. "There ought to be some sort of head to the meeting."

They had looked at each other.

"You'd be better than me, and I know it," Jonathan said. "But all the same, I shan't yield you the advantage unless I can see reason."

"Don't blame you," Evan had said carelessly. "How about lots?"

Jonathan stooped and picked two leaves from a scrubby bush and put them in his hat.

"Red leaf'll begin, yellow leaf'll wait," he said. "Fair?"

"Fair," Evan agreed.

He turned his head away and put his hand into Jonathan's hat and drew the red leaf.

"Fair?" he had asked Jonathan.

"Fair enough," Jonathan had said steadily.

When the people gathered in the tavern on this day long before noon, Evan stood up first and Jonathan sat waiting and watchful.

"Ladies and gentlemen," Evan began, "friends all—" He went on. The natural friendliness of his brown eyes grew warm. Faces turned toward him, and he let his eyes grow warmer. "Jonathan Goodliffe and I have taken a mighty big responsibility on ourselves in asking you to come, some of you a mighty long way. But he and I have two propositions to put before you, and since it concerns everybody the only fair thing seems to be to put it to all of you folks and let you decide. We drew by lots who should talk first, and that's why I'm doing it."

He let his eyes pass from face to face, lingering upon each long enough to catch response. Then he went on.

"We each of us maybe see Median in a different way. Jonathan, here, sees one kind of a town. I see another. Folks, here's my town. It's more than a town—it's a growing, busy, prosperous city. It's a railroad city—trains come here from

the East, taking cattle and grain from all over the Southwest.
These trains will come back again to bring us manufactured
goods of all kinds. There won't be sod houses and dugouts in
my town. There'll be fine houses and schools and churches,
and big stores and hotels. We'll be a great center, we can be,
because we're on a thoroughfare east and west, north and
south. We're the center of the great country west of the
Mississippi. Now, folks, a city doesn't just come because you
whistle for it. You've got to make it come this way. Money
must be spent here, business attracted. And our great chance
is the cattle business. All the cattle regions can head up here.
That means thousands upon thousands of dollars spent here in
Median. Men will get paid off here, they'll have money to
spend."

Jonathan, watching the faces before him, saw hard, fearless
eyes, firm mouths, hands rough and misshapen with work.
There was scarcely a soft face even among the women.

"What about saloons?" a white-haired woman spoke from
the end of a bench. She had refused the drink Henry Drear
had offered her. Evan turned to her at once, his face full of
sympathy.

"Madam, I know what you mean, but we can do what we
want to do about that," he said. "Nobody can make us do
what we don't want to do, not in this free country. We can
put the cattle concession away off at the end of the town, if
we like, far enough off so that the cattlemen will disturb
nobody." Evan's face grew solemn. "Madam, we can do more
than that. We can make Median an ideal cattle town, a place
where men will grow better rather than worse. We can refuse
to license—"

Henry Drear broke in. "Hell, Evan, if you won't sell
licenses, where's your money goin' to come from?"

"That's right, Henry," Samuel Hasty's high voice cackled.

A dozen voices began at once. Evan let them talk and stood
at ease, listening to one, catching a few words from another,
somehow making each feel he was heard. From the confusion
his ear sorted any aid to himself. When he found it he raised
his voice.

"Here's a man with a good idea. Stand up, mister, and tell
everybody—"

A man would shout out, "What I say is, why should we let
some other place get the business? What I say is, get the

business, and then let's talk about how to run it when we've got it—it's too good a chance to miss!"

After an hour Jonathan could endure no more of it. He and Evan had agreed to talk an hour each. Evan had talked less, but by the skillfullest trickery—"for trickery it is," Jonathan said to himself wrathfully—Evan was repeating what he wished to repeat from what was being said among voices shouting and crying down each other. He was making it seem that what they wanted was the cattle business. Upon some faces dismay was growing. Men and women cried out, "We don't want 'em!" but others were talking, and Evan did not hear them. In the confusion of the room Henry Drear had long since forgotten that he was treating only two drinks to a person.

Jonathan rose. His was never a conspicuous figure, and nobody now saw the neat young man of middle height as he stood in the back of the tavern. Jonathan waited a moment to catch Evan's eye; and then, since it was not to be caught, he walked across the room toward the bar against which Evan leaned as he stood, smiling, listening, talking.

"Your hour is up, Evan," Jonathan said clearly.

Evan looked surprised and took his gold watch from his pocket.

"So it is," he said. "I thought it only about half gone. But, Jon, you won't hold me to it? I thought it only fair to let people speak for themselves. I haven't half said—"

"I shall stick by our bargain," Jonathan said.

"A pound of flesh, eh, Shylock?" Evan's eyes, still smiling, sparkled too brightly.

"If you like," Jonathan said doggedly, meeting those eyes full.

They looked at each other, and in the moment the room fell silent. Everyone was staring at these two young men. Evan gave up gracefully.

"Oh, all right, Jon," he said. "Folks, this is my friend the schoolmaster. He's on the other side of the debate and wants to keep Median the way it is!"

A roar of laughter provided for Evan the opportunity to bow and stand aside. He did not sit down. Jonathan waited, but still he did not sit down. He continued to stand gracefully aside, his face humorous, his eyes affectionate.

"Go on, Jon," he said cheerfully.

He was going to stand there, as a guide to people's opinion. They would look at him and see him taller than Jonathan, far handsomer, quick to laugh, to look tolerant and scornful, as a man of business looks at a schoolmaster.

This Jonathan perceived. Then he put it aside. He stood without leaning, and with his hands in his pockets he began to speak in the quiet rather colorless voice of his usual conversation. He addressed them by no name, but he looked from one face to the other as he spoke. Some he knew, some he did not.

" 'Tisn't that I want to keep Median as it is," he said. "In fact, I don't, as Evan very well knows if he stops joking. It's just that I see Median a different kind of a town from a cattleman's town. That's natural, because I think of my pupils—and all of them are your children, too. It's no use hiding from ourselves or each other what the money's spent on in a cattleman's town. Those men spend their cash on drink, gambling, and women. They eat as little as they can, and they need little in garments. If we want their money, we've got to let brothels come in and saloons and gambling halls. The choice is a plain good town with a library and school and a church and homes and shops, or a cattleman's town. Theirs'll be the town—it always is. Our boys'll grow up thinking it's wonderful to ride horses and gallop up and down drunk and shooting off their guns, and our girls'll have to stay indoors. And what's the use of money to us if we have to live in that way to get it?"

Jonathan's quiet passionless voice in the heated room was like cool water.

"Amen!" a woman's voice cried.

"Amen—amen—" women's voices echoed.

"The ladies commend you, Jon," Evan said, his voice full of laughter.

Behind his bar Henry Drear looked alarmed. "See here, fellows," he cried, "this hyere's a man's country!"

Lew rose lumberingly to his feet. But upon the tails of his coat two women laid their hands. One was his wife, but the other was Katie, and Jonathan's quick eye saw it.

"What do you say, Lew?" he inquired.

But the two hands held Lew fast. He stood for a moment stubborn, and then the eyes of everyone were fastened upon him in his predicament. He was a florid man at all times, burned crimson with prairie wind and sun. Now his face grew purple as he saw the faces about him grinning at him.

"Nothin'," he muttered and sat down abruptly.

Around him the room bellowed with laughter. And on the surge of this laughter Jonathan won his town.

"I hope you don't let it come between us, Evan," he said apologetically. He had asked Evan home with him to eat bacon and mush. Evan had hesitated, struggling against a wish not to go. Then he had yielded and come. Now they were walking side by side along the boardwalk to Jonathan's house.

"Of course I don't," he said quickly. His dark eyes glinted. "What really hurts me, Jon, is that it was the women who helped you win against me. I had the men easy enough. There isn't a man who won't groan in his heart this night at the good chance lost. But the women were for you, and I'm hurt. I always thought I could win a woman, Jon!"

Jonathan smiled. This was the sort of banter he never could answer or share in, but it showed him Evan was unchanged. He felt his admiration of Evan quicken. A big man, Evan was, and beyond any little grudging envy. He could lose without loss of his own good nature.

"I never was so successful like that before," Jonathan said, trying to answer Evan in kind.

"I don't know why you say that," Evan retorted. "On your own word you're engaged to the prettiest girl you've ever seen. Of course I haven't seen her, but—"

"You'll say so too when you see her," Jonathan said with gravity. "Not that beauty's the best of Judy, as you'll find, Evan. She's a solid good girl, too—a minister's daughter."

"Oh, I'm sure you're right," Evan said teasingly. "But my point is, how do you win them all, Jon? You're a nice-looking fellow, but—"

"Give over, do," Jonathan said. He was always miserable under such teasing. "You're ten times as much as me for looks, Evan, and well you know it and so do I."

"Not ten," Evan said with mock judicial accuracy, "but maybe two times—yes, I'll go that far with you."

Then he saw he was tormenting Jonathan and gave it up with a great laugh and a nudge of his elbow in Jonathan's ribs. "Oh, Jonnie," he cried, "I wouldn't trade you off for all the girls in Kansas! If your Judy takes you away from me, I'll hate her. Promise me a wife won't come between us!"

"Judy'll like you as well as I do, Evan—I know that," Jonathan promised him. In his grave young heart he made his promise deeper. Never as long as he lived would he forget that Evan was his friend.

Near the end of a gray day Judy stepped down from a wagon. The cold had only deepened her pallor. Even the tip of her straight small nose was not red. She accepted pleasantly the help the two men in the wagon gave her with her bag and box, not seeming to notice that the other woman struggled alone with her goods. The wagon held no family but only the few persons who at this time of year had wanted to come eastward. Judy had tried to talk to the hard-faced elderly woman, but had given it up. It was always easier to converse with men, she thought.

American House stood solid and welcoming as she stepped down the dry bare earth of the roadway and up a step to the boardwalk. Jonathan's trees in the square were beginning to look big. She saw everything sharply because now everything in Median would be a part of her life. Then she stepped into the tavern.

Mrs. Drear, bustling out of the kitchen, embraced her with floury arms.

"Goodness gracious, it's Judy!" she cried. "Now I must send someone straight off and tell Jonathan."

There were men at the tavern bar, as there always were, and one of them came forward instantly.

"Let me go, Mrs. Drear," he said.

In the quick habit of her eye, Judy saw a handsome man, tall and young, whose eyes were dark.

"I'd admire to be the one to go, Miss Judy, I'm Jon's best friend—Evan Bayne. He's expecting you."

He put out his hand, and she put hers in it an instant. Then she withdrew it.

"Wait just a bit of a while," she begged him. "I'm hungry and tired and real cold."

"Sure," Mrs. Drear chuckled, "she wants her young man to see her at her prettiest. Wait till she's fed, Evan, I've got supper ready. Will you have it in the kitchen, Judy, or right here?"

"Right here," Judy sighed.

Without seeming to see anyone she sank to the bench beside the table and drew off her gloves and took off her brown felt hat with velvet bows. Warmth brought back to her cheeks their usual soft color, and her lips were growing red again.

"Had a hard trip, Judy?" Henry Drear called from behind the bar.

"The cars were dirty, and then the wind was cold, that's all," she replied.

"Want a nip?" he inquired.

"A little hard cider, please," she said. She smiled up at him as he set a small tin cup before her.

He inquired, "Where's your paw?"

"He's had a call to be a missionary in the Sandwich Isles," she said.

Henry grinned. "Still goin' west?"

She nodded, her cup at her lips.

"He'll be comin' in here from the east one of these days if he keeps on goin'," Henry chuckled, and Judy smiled again.

She sat sipping her cider, seeming to see none of them, her head bent, her eyelids demure; but they were all watching her, helpless not to watch her. Even Mrs. Drear stood in the kitchen door watching her, though she was thinking of Jennet. She had not heard from Jennet in many months. The girl had become lost in that West which changed and grew so fast that in that growth it threw human beings from one chance to another.

"You didn't hear tell of Jennet anywhere out there, did you, Judy?"

Judy lifted her great innocent eyes. "No, I didn't, Mrs. Drear, and I'm sorry."

Mrs. Drear sighed. "Well, I didn't expect it—it would be a needle in a haystack if you did." She went back to her kitchen.

Evan did not move as he watched her. He would wait, he thought, filled with fury, until this girl had finished her supper to the last mouthful before he went to find Jonathan. He hated her already, a selfish, cold woman, thinking of herself instead of Jonathan. He thought of Jonathan with a passion of protection. Jonathan had been engrossed in this business of getting the school out of his house so that this woman might have a home. It was folly, and everybody told him so, to get the schoolhouse built before winter. Ice froze already except in the middle hours of the day, and at any moment there might be a blizzard. The winter winds made work on a house beyond endurance of frozen hands and cheeks. But for Jonathan's sake Stephen Parry was trying to do it.

"Your only hope is a temporary sod house, Jon," Evan had said.

But Jonathan had shaken his head. "I shan't put the bit of money I have into something to be torn down in the spring. It's not fair to the people who've given it."

What does this girl care? Evan thought gloomily, staring at Judy's beautiful face. She doesn't even hurry herself over her food.

It was true. Judy, always dainty at table, was daintier tonight than ever. It was her only response to the eyes upon her. Evan made a deep bow when at last she put down her spoon.

"Now, Madam, may I go and tell my friend that his fiancée has arrived?"

His voice was weighted with sarcasm, but Judy only lifted her eyelashes at him.

"If you please," she said gently. Her eyes rested on him reflectively, and Evan turned away and strode out of the door into the deep cold dusk. It only made things worse for Jonathan, he thought, to have her so pretty. It would be very hard for a man to forget so pretty a woman. He walked fast, thinking with melancholy how this was the sort of woman who would demand every service of a man so that his life was consumed in trivialities. And he wouldn't even know it, he thought in a strange sort of terror.

He gave a great thump to Jonathan's door and walked in. Jonathan sat by his fire with a book in his hand.

"Well, Evan!" he cried.

"Judy's come," Evan said.

Jonathan dropped his book and leaped for his greatcoat. "I had a premonition, not ten minutes ago," he cried. He blew out the lamp and took the lantern from Evan's hand. "Here, I'll carry this."

"What sort of a premonition?" Evan set his stride to match Jonathan's.

"A queer soft feeling, as though something good had

happened, though what I couldn't think, for it's been a day like any other. How is she? Does she look well?"

"She looks well enough," Evan replied, so coldly that Jonathan was amazed.

"Evan, what's up!"

"Nothing."

"You're not telling me something, Evan!"

"There's nothing to tell," Evan retorted.

"Then why—"

Evan stood still. "I don't like her, and that's a fact," he said. They were talking in the darkness.

Jonathan lifted the lantern and saw Evan's stern face in the light of it. "You don't know her," he said.

Evan saw Jonathan—too young, too good, he thought. What he wanted to say was, "I knew her the minute I saw her."

"Maybe I don't," he said instead, and they went on.

But he did not enter the tavern again.

"Come in," Jonathan said to him.

"No, I've got a brief to write yet tonight," he replied, and then he added, "You don't want me and you know it."

Jonathan smiled at that and let him go. He could wait for no one, not with Judy in there waiting.

At the sound of his voice at the door, Mrs. Drear motioned Judy into the kitchen with her beckoning finger and came out and shut the door.

"She's in there waiting for you," she told Jonathan. Her red face was suffused with vicarious tenderness, and when Jonathan went in she sighed. "Let 'em have it," she told the men. "It'll never seem so good again."

"Hey, ol' lady!" her husband roared at her. He sat on a high stool behind his bar, stirring a spoon in a tin cup.

"No, it won't, Henry Drear," she said and, seizing a towel from the wall behind his head, she fell to mopping the bar.

Behind the closed door Jonathan and Judy stood for the least part of a moment. Then Judy put out her hands and lifted her head.

"Dear Jonathan!" she said softly.

And at the sound of her voice he stepped toward her and took her in his arms. "Judy—Judy!" he murmured. His lips were on her hair, her temple, on the smooth firmness of her cheek and then her full throat, and with every kiss his arms hardened about her.

"Why, Jonathan," she cried. She was a little frightened.

But the passion, deep and slow in his being, was stirring and waking, rising to the surface of his eyes and lips, new passion that had never stirred before. He crushed her head against his shoulder and held it there, his palm against her cheek, and then he kissed her lips and then again and yet again.

And yet in the end it was he who let her go, not she who withdrew herself. He loosed her, and he turned his head away and tried to laugh.

"What am I doing, Judy girl? But we're to be husband and wife, eh, Judy?"

"Yes," she whispered. She had been so surprised that she had not moved. Jonathan was just like other men, after all, she was thinking. Somehow she had not imagined he would be because he looked so calm and gentle and pale. But inside maybe they were all the same. . . . She drew away a very little and began to straighten herself in small secret ways, by a touch at her hair, at the lace fichu about her neck, the lace about her wrists. By means of these movements, so swift and slight that Jonathan scarcely saw them, she set herself right.

"Are you glad to be here, sweet?" he asked.

"I'm real glad," she said. Her eyes, lifted to his, were now full of a lovely soft timidity. It seemed to him the essence of all that was exquisite in a woman. He felt ashamed of his passion. He did not want to be a man like his father, God knows! He wanted only to be a strong, protecting, able man to meet this clinging, needful woman whose body was complete beauty. He took her hand.

"My very dear," he said, "my dearest dear!"

He drew her toward him gently, and when she was near was horrified to discern in the brown depths of her eyes a thing like fear, and in her hand a small reluctance.

"You aren't afraid of me, Judy!" he cried. "Why, nobody's afraid of me, my dear!"

"I'm not afraid, exactly," she said.

"What, then?" he asked. He had her very near again now, but passion was held back by this look and this reluctance.

"It's only—oughtn't we to go out now? They're waiting for us out there."

"I've waited a long time, too, Judy," he said.

"I know." She came of her own accord the last space between them and kissed him. He felt her kiss, soft as a snowflake on his cheek, and he said abruptly, "Reckon you're right, Judy. Let's go out."

With her hand in his arm he threw open the door into the tavern, and at the same moment noise broke like bedlam. The room was full. All of Median was there—no, not the Parrys, but everybody else—and not a soul without a tin pan or a horn or a cowbell to make a noise, and to noise everyone added yells. Judy hid her face against his shoulder, and he put his arm about her and stood in the doorway smiling as long as the noise blared. Then Evan leaped on the bar, beating Mrs. Drear's tin wash tub, turned over like a drum. When he caught Jonathan's look he beat the louder.

"Let's see the bride!" Evan yelled.

"Look up, lady!" a man's voice shouted.

"Give us a look, Judy!" Henry Drear roared.

"Look around for a minute, Judy," Jonathan whispered. "They mean the best."

And Judy, after a moment's coaxing, pushed back the curls from her face and lifted her head and every man in the room saw her. But Jonathan, gazing at her too, saw the direction of her eyes. They were fixed upward in soft appeal, and Jonathan followed as he might follow the path of a moonbeam and he found the end. She gazed at Evan, and Evan gazed at her.

24

STEPHEN PARRY PUT DOWN HIS TOOLS. HE WAS WORKING against deep winter on the schoolhouse, but winter would win, and now he knew it. The day had begun with a bitter wind, and by midmorning snow was glowing. From the north a smooth, even gray spread over the sky. The wind heightened, and he had to be careful lest he slip on the newfallen snow. By noon he gave up. He clambered down the shell of the house and found the lunch Sue had wrapped for him. He ate it, standing in a corner under the roof. The bread and pork was as hard as stone, and in the thick pottery jug the coffee was ice cold.

When he had eaten and drunk he plodded through the now driving snow to Jonathan's sod house and knocked at the door. A child opened it, and as he opened it the noise and talk and laughter of children at noon recess came out in an uproar. Jonathan stood mending the fire, and he looked up at Stephen, the tongs in his hand.

"Come in, Steve," he shouted. "That is, if you can. Shut the door, Melissa. Most of them brought their dinners with them today, and that's why all this hubbub. You see why I want to get them out of my house, Steve."

"Sure," Stephen replied. He hated to tell Jonathan, but it must be done. "Mr. Goodliffe," he said gently, "I sure do hate to tell you, but I ain't gonneh get that schoolhouse done before spring. I jest cain't."

He held up his hands. "I got frostbit today as it was, and if my hands are gone, I got nothin' to earn my livin' with."

The noise of the children stopped. It was not much to them whether the new schoolhouse was finished or not. Jonathan's house was comfortable, and it had become their own.

Jonathan's face tightened at the mouth. "I don't want you to freeze your hands, certainly," he said. He put down the tongs. "And I reckon you've tried to get help."

"Yessir, everywhere. But nobody wants to work in the open this weather. I'm fixin' to snatch any warm days they is and git the roof finished so's there'll be cover. But plaster would freeze before I could git it mixed. 'Tain't only jest labor."

"Well," Jonathan said, "I reckon it's not to be helped." He paused for a moment and then went on, his face with only its usual careful expression. "You'll make it the first job in the spring?"

"I will," Stephen said, backing toward the door. "I'm terrible sorry."

Jonathan inclined his head slightly and wet his lips.

"Well, good day, Steve," Jonathan said. "It's time for school to take up for the afternoon."

"Good-by, suh." Steve let himself out of the door and closed it.

"Pupils, attention please," Jonathan said calmly. The school shuffled back into its place, and Jonathan took up his pointing stick and went to the blackboard.

"The square of the hypothenuse of a right triangle," he said, "is equal to the sum of the squares of the other two sides, thus—" He began to draw his usual beautifully neat figures upon the board.

I shall have to compel Judy, he was thinking.

"I shan't give you a choice, Judy, sweet," he was saying to her. They were in her room at American House. She had made it comfortable and somehow pretty. She had curtained the bed off with Indian blankets so that the rest of the room was her own sitting room. There was a tin stove in it and a heap of split wood beside it. On the table was an oil lamp. He sat in the rocking chair by the fire but not rocking, because she sat on a hassock with her head against his knees. Every evening they spent together in this room.

She did not move her head from under his caressing hand. He loved her hair. It was not soft, as his mother's hair was. It was full of spring and curl, and no smoothing could make it smooth. He loved to feel it catch and curl about his fingers.

"You're marrying the schoolteacher," he said playfully, "and so you'll have to put up with my school."

"But where'll I sit all day?" she asked. "There's only the bit of bedroom. And winter's still here."

He had only thought of their evenings when, he had told himself, he would move the desks and stools into one half of the room. He had not thought of all the hours when she would be alone. Now he remembered, too, how cold the bedroom was.

"You can come and sit by the school fire," he said.

She smiled without answering. Her face was rosy and placid, but under it she was thinking of what she wanted for herself. But she did not speak.

"We want to get married quickly, don't we, dear?" Jonathan asked, his hands tender under the curls upon her white neck. "You and me together'll make the winter short. When spring comes the school will move out, and we'll have a fair house then all to ourselves."

She rubbed her head like a cat against his fondling hand. "I don't seem to care whether we're married or not so long as we're together," she murmured.

Jonathan laughed. "I believe you're too lazy to get married," he said. Her sweet softness of movement, her pretty dallying over anything she did, her long drowsy silences when they sat together, she like this or on his knees, he loved to call her laziness, but it was sweet to him because under his own calm he was so full of restless and nervous energy. He had never known rest, he often thought, until she came. But rest would not be complete until they had slept together, night after night. But he could not tell her that. She smiled up at him without answer. She had known since she was born that if she smiled she need not speak. She was a little irritated therefore when a moment later Jonathan pressed her.

"Shall we marry at once, Judy? Why not? Tomorrow. There's a preacher here now." An itinerant preacher had come to Median and, because of an infected hand, which Mrs. Drear was poulticing, he was delaying.

"No, not tomorrow," Judy said.

"Next week then," he urged. "Why not, dear heart?" He took her chin and looked down at her. "Judy, do you love me?"

"Of course." Her lips framed the words silently.

"Of course what?" he demanded.

"I love you—"

"Then it'll be next week—eh, Judy? On Saturday."

He held her chin so hard that it was uncomfortable and she could not escape.

"All right, Jonathan, but only if you'll make it two weeks."

"Why?" he persisted.

"I'm—not ready—next week," she said.

He felt himself flush. He knew enough about women to know there were times. He had plagued his mother with questions once because she looked so pale, until she had said impatiently, "Give over, Jonathan—it's only my woman's curse."

"What's that, Mother?"

"Eve's curse, I reckon. Once a month a woman's got to be ill a bit, and you may as well know, for you'll be marrying a woman one day, and she'll thank you to leave her alone then."

Now instantly delicate, he agreed. "Two weeks, surely, Judy—if I have to bribe the preacher." He let her go and lifted her to his knee. "That's my own wife," he said comfortably.

They sat together in the chair, the room warm and still.

Around the house the prairie wind howled, and in the tavern there was the clatter of pewter and tin cups and plates and men's voices. In the inner silence Jonathan heard the door bang and there was a roar of laughter.

"That'll be Evan," he said immediately.

He questioned, scarcely aware that he did, the sweet weight of Judy's body relaxed in his arms. In all these days he had not discovered what Judy thought of Evan or Evan of Judy. Neither mentioned the other to him. But there was not now the quiver of a nerve in Judy's flesh. She did not stir or move the direction of her eyes as she gazed into the open door of the stove.

"Everybody likes Evan," Jonathan said. He could hear men still laughing. Evan could always set laughter afire in any place he chose.

"I don't," Judy said lazily. "I hate him." She spoke without a flicker of intensity in the soft slow way in which she said everything.

"Why?" Jonathan asked. He was greatly astonished.

"I don't know," Judy said pleasantly. "I just naturally hate him."

Jonathan laughed with his delight in her. She was so lovely and so unreasonable, so adorable in all her foolishness.

"You mustn't say that, my Judy," he scolded with tenderness. "Why, Evan's my best friend, a wonderful chap and loyal as made. He'd stick to me through anything, and to you, too, for my sake."

"I don't like his eyes," she murmured.

"Why, he's thought to have uncommon fine eyes, so dark and flashing-like."

"He's conceited," she said.

"No, now, that he's not," Jonathan protested. "It's his great abilities—a natural-born orator, Judy, so that it's a treat to hear him argue a case. I've not seen him in court, but sometimes he's rehearsed a case with me for practice. His voice can be heard anywhere. It was in the paper once in Topeka that his voice could be heard all through the court-house when he was arguing a case for the railroad company."

"He thinks all he needs to do is to raise his right eyebrow at a woman," Judy said. In his arms she did not move.

"No, now, he lifts his eyebrow like that whenever he's about to crack a joke," Jonathan cried.

She sat up. "You like him better than anybody—better'n me."

He was deeply shocked. "Judy, shut up, my dear. Such things can't be said. He's my friend, but you're my wife."

But he thought to himself here was the seat of the coldness between Evan and Judy. They were jealous of each other with him. Only the other day it had occurred to him that he and Evan had scarcely met for days. It was his own fault. Every free moment he spent with Judy, and Evan in delicacy had not pressed himself.

"When we're married you'll see that Evan is your friend just the same as he's mine," he told Judy. He pressed her head back into the hollow of his shoulder. "Lie back, my sweet," he said.

Long after he was gone she sat without moving by the stove, her elbows on her knees and her hands soft fists against her cheeks. There were still voices in the tavern, and she was listening to them. Besides, what use was there in going to bed when she could not sleep?

It was nearly midnight when silence fell. Jonathan had gone at half past nine, tender of her good name. Now she rose in this first silence and went to the door and threw it open. Evan sat there alone at a table, a mug of beer in his hand.

"I hoped you'd gone, too," she said. "I want to sleep."

"I'm going," he said shortly.

She came in and stood by the table. "I'm marrying Jonathan on Saturday, two weeks," she said.

"Goddamn you," he answered, staring at her.

Mrs. Drear came in, her eyes bleary with sleep. "It's closing time, folks," she said. The words were easy, but her voice was sharp.

"I was just telling Evan that Jonathan and I have set the day," Judy said without moving. The purity of her face grew more pure, as it always did when she felt anyone was angry with her. "It's a week from next Saturday. The schoolhouse can't get finished, he says, so we may as well."

"I'm glad to hear it," Mrs. Drear said. She swept up an armful of dirty mugs.

Evan got up. "So'm I," he said heartily. "Jon's waited long enough for you, Judy."

"He shore has," Mrs. Drear agreed.

"I think so, too," Judy said. Her voice was tender with sweetness. "Shall I help you with the dishes, Mrs. Drear?"

"I don't care if you do," Mrs. Drear answered. Nobody could put a finger on Judy, she thought. The girl was always kind and willing. Then why did she feel queer about her sometimes? Jennet had been bad enough. Though Jennet was Henry's own daughter, there was no use pretending she had not taken more after her slut of a mother than she had after Henry. But Jennet was as open as a book. Mrs. Drear yawned over the dishpan and then sighed. Yes, Judy was good about helping. It couldn't be denied she was a real helpful girl. You would say she was a good girl if somehow you could be sure she was.

Jonathan in his bed lay awake with desire. He recognized it and was ashamed of it. Love and desire were two different things, and he meant to keep them so. I shan't be like my father, he thought. I shan't have my Judy growing into what my poor mother is.

He knew by now that his mother had had another child and lost it. Ruth had written him secretly one of her printed letters. Without wanting to be a murderer, he was glad the child was dead. Things were hard enough. Maybe he ought to have gone West himself to see how things were. But he had had letters, scanty as usual, from his mother. It was natural enough that she had not told him of the child. She never spoke of childbirth to him. The life was hard there, she said, but maybe it would be better, she always said. And he couldn't go now.

But desire for Judy ebbed out of him as he thought about his mother. He was going to make up everything to Judy. She shouldn't have babies unless she wanted them. And never, never would he persuade her against her will, and never make her afraid of his ill-temper if she did not want him. He lay thinking of his father with deep unyielding anger. He would be to Judy all that his father had not been to his mother. And then, strangely, having begun thus to think about his mother, he could think of no one else. She seemed to possess him. He had not for weeks given over his mind to her like this. He tried to recall Judy, but there was only his mother. He grew restless and at last sat up in his bed. If I believed in anything of the kind, I'd be wondering if aught was wrong with her, he thought.

He was not superstitious, but he sat listening and feeling through the darkness toward his mother. Coyotes were crying in the night. The wind had abated, and he could hear the wailing agony of their crying. But it was a sound common enough to the night, and he gave it no heed. He pushed his mind beyond through the darkness like a quivering, searching probe. Something was wrong, maybe, or for sure.

It was nearly an hour before he could lie down again. He'd write tomorrow. Once more he tried to think of Judy and could not. He fell asleep thinking only of his mother.

🌿 25 🌿

IN THE POOR SOD HOUSE IN THE MIDST OF THE WESTERN plains, Mary gave up her struggle. Beside her Clyde lay sleeping a hard snoring sleep. The harsh labor of his days had coarsened every part of him. His body, nerving itself to the day's work, indulged itself in food eaten quickly and roughly, in loud noise and quick temper, in a passion often savage in its demands, and then sprawling sleep. Mary, lying awake on the edge of the bed, away from his unwashed body, was crying quietly.

I s'll give up, she thought. It's no use. I can't die here with nobody but Ruth. It's too hard on her. Oh, Jonathan!

Such a yearning burst out of her for her son that she felt her head grow giddy. "Jonathan!" The name broke from her again in a low groan, involuntary, as though something had wrenched it out of her. Clyde woke.

"Eh!" he grunted.

"Clyde!" she whispered in the darkness.

"What?" He had no mind to wake.

"I'm going back to Median," she said.

That waked him. "What for?"

"I daren't stay the winter here again, with a new baby."

"But we're all right."

"I'm not. If I hadn't got caught again 'twould be different. But things aren't as they should be in me. I can tell."

"You're allays nervous when your time's near," he said sullenly.

"This isn't only that," she said. "I've had enough babies to know."

He flounced himself. "How can I go when I've got the sheep and the cows to care for? And it's the worst time of year for me to take such a journey. If there's a blizzard, who'll tend the beasts while I'm gone? Jamie can't manage alone."

"But Jamie can drive Ruth and Maggie and me," she said. "And you can stay with your beasts."

If she could only get to Median where Jonathan was, it would be almost like going home. And Mrs. Drear could help her when her time came.

"I'm going, Clyde, so it's no good your talking."

America had made her mean-tempered, but she could not help it. Everything was against a woman here. She had to fight for her life.

"Then I won't talk, if it's no good," Clyde said. He turned his back and jerked the covers. She knew he was full of fury and could not care. Plenty of times she had said to herself that he had it hard, too. He wasn't lazy, at least the way he used to be in England. In his way he worked hard, but he had no luck. The cattle strayed and were lost, however he branded them. And the cowmen in the next homestead were thieves, as everybody knew, but how to prove it? You couldn't expect a common chap like Clyde to have his word taken against an educated Englishman's, and he owned the ranch. Besides, there was Jennet.

Jennet had come and gone twice, and now she was back again. Ruth had told her that Jamie had seen her.

"I don't want to know about it," she had told Ruth.

She tightened her lips in the darkness. When she got back to Median she did not want to have to tell Mrs. Drear that Jennet had lived with the Englishman twice, once for three months and again for a month, and now she was back again.

She felt suddenly faint with nausea. But it was not the usual nausea of pregnancy. This sickness was mingled with pain in her lower belly, not sharp pain but one so vast and deep that it was as though it grasped some center of her vitality.

It's a wicked kind of pain, she thought anxiously and retched as sweat burst out of her. This, she thought in terror, was life or death. I'll set out tomorrow, she thought wildly, or it'll be too late.

Two days before his wedding Jonathan was shaving himself at twilight. For a fair man he had a rough, quickly growing beard, and he shaved evenings instead of mornings because he wanted his cheek smooth against Judy's. He was whistling and full of happiness. Everything was going right for him except one thing, and that maybe would, after all. Evan was not sure he could stand up with him at the wedding. He had spent half the afternoon today after school arguing it in Evan's office.

"Put the wedding off a few days and I'll come," Evan said in his offhand way.

Jonathan was deeply shocked. "A man doesn't put off his wedding."

Evan laughed. "Of course not, and I was only teasing you. What I say is, go on and I'll be here if I can, boy. It's bad luck this case had to be called right now in Topeka. Wait till I get Median the county seat. Will you let me do that, Jon, if you won't have it a cattle town?"

He had forgiven Jonathan, but he used their disagreement for teasing. Jonathan smiled without answer. Evan went on, "No, son, I've got to go. After all, I'm the corporation lawyer for the Santa Fe in these parts, and the claims for cattle killed on the tracks have got to be settled. It's getting to be the way a lot of unsuccessful cattlemen are growing fat. They drive their cows on the tracks—"

Evan's rich voice rolling along was befuddling in its ease. Jonathan stopped it.

"I won't have anyone else," he said. "If you don't come, I'll stand up alone."

"If it's humanly possible I'll be at your side," Evan retorted, "even if I don't approve the match." He made no bones about Judy.

"Is that the real reason why you don't want to come?" Jonathan asked.

"I don't like the woman, Jon, and you may as well know it," he said.

"But why, Evan?" Jonathan demanded.

"Too pretty," Evan said promptly. "A woman as pretty as that is thinking only of herself. You deserve someone who'll think only of you."

"You mustn't say such things. Evan."

"I must and I will if I'm to stay your friend."

Jonathan let it pass. He knew them both, he thought tenderly, and some day, when Judy was his wife, Evan would come to see her for what she was, and Judy would learn to appreciate his friend. He would wait.

"Well, I don't give up hope," he said with his wry smile.

"That's right," Evan said heartily.

When he had stopped a moment to tell Judy, she had looked strange, he thought.

"I'm glad he's not coming," she said. "He always makes me feel I've put my clothes on wrong, somehow."

Jonathan had laughed. "Oh, you two," he had said. He kissed her very lightly. "I'll kiss you hard later after I've shaved," he told her half-playfully. He was so happy these days that all his slight instincts toward mirthfulness were awake in him. And so he had turned homeward to make himself ready for her. He did not like to wear his work clothes when he went to her at any time. But these last two nights before their marriage were very precious. He wanted no slightest withdrawal in Judy from him.

He heard something. Razor in hand, he stopped to listen. The early dark beyond the windows was like midnight and the door was closed against the early cold. But a wagon had drawn up and stopped. He put down the razor on the shelf under the small mirror, and wiped the soap from his cheek. Then he threw the door open.

The light from the house streamed upon a sad-looking group of people. For a moment he could not believe his eyes. A tall boy and a girl were clambering out of the wagon.

"Jonathan!" a voice called faintly. He leaped forward.

"Mother, it's never you! Ruth—Jamie—why, what in heaven's name! Maggie, too! Where's Dad? Oh, Mother, whatever's wrong with you?"

Mary had raised herself out of the end of the old covered wagon, and he saw her sick face. He lifted her out, and then he saw what was the matter and he ground his teeth.

"Come in," he said, "come in quick and lie down in the bed. My God, Ruthie, to let her come like this!"

"She would come," Ruth said. Her old timidity had grown deeper in the long months upon the plains, and was as wild as a hare's now. She blinked in the light of the room and clutched Maggie's hand fast.

"Get me down, quick," Mary groaned. "Quick, and call Mrs. Drear, Jonathan. I mistrust it's my time. Dear God, how I've prayed to get home first! Well, for once He's let me have my hope."

She was sighing with pain, and she sat down on the bed and tried to pull off her shoes.

"Take 'em off for her, you, Jamie—or Ruth," Jonathan shouted. "I'll go for Mrs. Drear."

He rushed out into the darkness and ran over the clattering dry boards to the tavern. Mrs. Drear was sitting alone at the kitchen table eating her supper before she served up the food to others. He ran in upon her.

"Mother's come," he gasped. "And, Mrs. Drear, will you— she's going to—to—to—she needs a woman, fast."

"My soul and body," Mrs. Drear shrieked. She jumped to her feet and lifted a kettle of boiling water from the stove. "Henry, you'll have to dish up," she shouted as she passed the bar, and then she was gone.

Far into the night Jonathan worked at her side. He forgot Judy or where he was to have been. He and Ruth and Mrs. Drear fought together for his mother's life. He had never seen a child born before, and he was terrified at what he saw. Did every birth so devastate another's being? He was drenched with sweat and groaned aloud without knowing until Mrs. Drear bade him be silent. He rushed out for a moment and wept heartily before Jamie's awe-stricken face, and then rushed back again for fear she might die in the moment he was away.

The child was born at midnight, a girl, small and thin, but living, and less than an hour later, Mary died.

He had a strange feeling as he sat before the fire with the little newborn creature in his arms that somehow he had been widowed before ever he was married. The blanket curtain was drawn between the two rooms. The two rooms were very still. Jamie had gone to ask Stephen Parry to make the coffin. Ruth was moving in the room, tidying it, and crying quietly. No pupils came to school, for he had announced a week's holiday for his wedding. Mrs. Drear had stayed to make Mary neat for burial and then had gone home, taking Maggie with her.

"This one's too lively for you to have around now, I reckon," she had said. She hesitated, Maggie's hand in hers. "Jonathan, I'll tell Judy. It'll mean puttin' off tomorrow, 'course."

He had actually forgotten that tomorrow was to be his wedding day. Now he remembered and nodded.

"What to do with that mite—" Mrs. Drear's mournful brown eyes turned toward the hearth where in a wooden box the baby lay asleep.

"I don't know," Jonathan said. "I'll have to think about everything. I do thank you, Mrs. Drear."

"Don't mention it," she sighed.

So she had gone. The little baby began suddenly to wail and Jonathan picked it up and, wrapping his old coat about it, he sat down for the first time he had sat all night and held it. Some soothing quality in him flowed into the child, and it slept again.

It seemed to him that somehow it was his own child whose mother was dead. He was bereft of something beyond his own mother. He was responsible for more than a son's duty.

"We can't wait till Dad knows, can we?" Ruth's half-whispered question startled him.

"No," he said shortly. "How could we? I s'll just have to do what ought to be done." He controlled a strong trembling in his throat. "However did you not bring her home long before?" he demanded. He was thinking of his mother's body. After the baby was born it seemed to shrink into a wisp. She was such a small little thing even at her best, and now there was left of her only a handful of bones. A woman murdered, if ever there was murder, he thought somberly, and was glad that his father was not in this house.

"How could I?" Ruth asked timidly. "Besides, she always said as how things would be better maybe, and how could she leave Dad?"

"He didn't see, I suppose, that he might have brought her?"

"No, he didn't," Ruth said simply.

Jonathan looked at her sternly over the sleeping child. "Tell me the truth—was it terrible for all the time?"

Ruth nodded. "Yes, it was. She was always afeared. There was the snakes and she always would think Maggie would get bit one day—a mortal lot of snakes, there was, Jonathan, and they'd crawl in between the sod in the walls. And there was one on her bed, and she dreamed about it all the time after. And the water was bitter and hard. And Jamie swears something terrible now, and she minds his growin' up rough and ignorant-like. And Maggie never minds nobody and, oh, the wind, blowin' and blowin' night and day, used to drive her daft-like. Once she went outside and screamed and screamed, and after she cried a while she was herself again."

"Did Dad see nothing?"

"He's away all day and lots of nights, too."

"And were there no neighbors?"

"No, unless—no, you couldn't say there was neighbors. The Englishman wasn't a neighbor, and Mother never even wanted to hear tell of Jennet."

"Jennet?" Jonathan cried.

"She was there at his ranch sometimes. She was there when we left."

He sat with this news, thinking of it. "I thought she was in Frisco," he said.

"So she was—she's only sometimes at the ranch," Ruth replied.

"Don't tell the Drears," he said shortly after a while.

"I wouldn't nohow," she said.

"Anyhow," he corrected her. If he did not correct her now, there was no one to do it.

"Anyhow," she repeated humbly.

The baby began to wail again, and he wondered if it were hungry. There was no immediate need for food, he knew, but this one was such a wee thin thing maybe it would want food earlier than the others had. He hushed it and at last rocked it in his arms, but the child cried on.

"What'll we do?" he asked Ruth.

"Could I mix a bit of flour and water?" she suggested.

"That can't hurt, can it?"

"I reckon not," she replied.

But while they hesitated the door opened, and Sue and Stephen came in. Sue had a shawl over her head and a man's coat tied over her shoulders like a cape. She threw both off with one sweep of her arms.

"Give her to me," she said. She took the baby from Jonathan and hesitated a moment. Then she went firmly on. "Mr. Goodliffe, suh, do you min' if I give it mah breas'? My baby is six mont's, but I think it'll be fresh still, and I sho have plenty."

He stared at Sue for one startled moment and with her abnormal sensitivity she seemed suddenly to grow in stature before his eyes.

"If you don't want me," she said proudly.

His reason controlled him instantly. "I thank you very much," he said. "It may save the child's life."

But he left the room at the same moment and went into the other with Stephen and stood there while Stephen in sad silence measured the sleeping figure on the bed.

"Cottonwood timber's all I've got on hand jest now, suh," he said when he had finished. "But I can use pitch to make it tight."

Jonathan nodded.

"Sue's got some white cotton to line it," Stephen said gently.

Jonathan nodded again.

"I'll have it done tonight—will you want it tomorrow?"

"Yes," Jonathan said, and then remembered that tomorrow was to have been his wedding day.

🥀 26 🥀

"AIN'T YOU GOIN' RIGHT OVER THERE TO JONATHAN'S?" Mrs. Drear demanded of Judy. "He shore needs a woman to help out."

She felt exhausted this morning, and the sight of Judy, very pretty in a red wool dress with a red velvet collar and cuffs, somehow added to her exhaustion. She poured more milk into Maggie's cup.

"I'll go the minute I've had my breakfast," Judy said gently. She moved gracefully about the tavern kitchen, pouring herself a cup of coffee from the big granite pot on the range, and cutting herself bread and buttering it without giving a glance at the round-faced, red-haired little girl at the table in the middle of the kitchen. Mrs. Drear had waked her half an hour before to pour out the story of the night. She had sat up in bed, listening, her shining hair curling over her shoulders. Mrs. Drear, looking at her without liking her better, had nevertheless felt sorry for Jonathan because the girl was so pretty in her nightgown.

" 'Course you can't have the wedding tomorrow."

"No, of course not," Judy had agreed. That was all she said. But she had climbed out of bed and poured water into the porcelain basin on the washstand. Mrs. Drear had gone away then.

Whether she cares or whether she don't—she had been thinking the half-hour since as she fried salt pork and slabs of mush.

When Judy came in, in her red dress, her curls neatly pinned on her head, there was still no telling. Red, Mrs. Drear thought, wasn't suitable, either. But probably the girl hadn't thought. She sat there by the window eating her bread cut in little narrow strips. Mrs. Drear, glancing at her, saw Jamie go by the window with Stephen and Sue, and she ran to pound on the pane.

"Jamie!" she screamed, and when he turned clawed at him to come in. A moment later he was there at the door, a tall black-haired boy, his face cheerful in spite of what had happened.

"Come in and eat," Mrs. Drear ordered him. "There'll be trouble enough at your house without fixing breakfast for you. This hyere's Judy, your sister-in-law to be. You can take her along after you've et."

"Pleased to meet you," Jamie said. "Hello, Mags."

He felt embarrassed in Mrs. Drear's presence because he had seen Jennet a few days before he left his father's ranch. She had been riding with the Englishman, loping along at his side upon a chestnut horse, riding astride, too, wearing corduroy pants and high boots and a big cowboy hat. He had been herding sheep, and she pulled up when she saw him and stared at him, and when she recognized him she flicked his nose with the end of her whip.

"You don't know who I am," she had declared.

"I do, too," he had said so sullenly that she laughed.

"Then don't tell me," she had said, "for I don't want to know."

The Englishman came cantering up then, a long lazy sort of chap.

"Who's this, Jenny?" he asked.

"A boy I used to know," she answered mischievously.

Jamie had stared straight back at the Englishman's pale blue eyes.

"Ah," the Englishman had said at last, "then don't know him any more, will you?"

They had gone galloping off together then, and he had watched them go, until the prairie swallowed them into a mirage. But he had felt queer because Jennet looked so different from the way she had used to look in this kitchen—older, and not so pretty, and yet he had wanted to look at her.

He lifted his eyes secretly to Judy, met hers, and looked hastily away again.

"There." Mrs. Drear handed him a plate of fried mush. "Sit down across from Judy."

"Thanks." He took the plate and sat at the opposite end of the table. Her soft voice made him lift his eyes again.

"I'm ever so sorry—about last night."

He nodded and suddenly found his throat choked so that he could not swallow.

"Will you all stay here now?" Judy's gentle voice was at him again.

He forced himself to swallow. "I reckon I'll have to get right back to help Dad. One man can't hardly handle the sheep and cows, too. Don't know even as we ought to try both."

"Then the others will stay with Jonathan?"

"Reckon they'll have to," he said. "We couldn't hardly handle a baby out there."

She did not speak again. She sat sipping her coffee and eating her bread and butter daintily and slowly, and when she was finished she rose and smiled. "I'll put on my bonnet and go."

"Oh, Judy!"

Jonathan leaped to his feet and took her in his arms and put his face down upon her shoulder.

"I knew you'd come. It's been a dreadful night."

She put her hand to his cheek. "I knew it," she said. "So I came."

She saw a young dark-haired girl, and over Jonathan's shoulder smiled at her.

All these people, she was thinking, all to live in this house! Of course I can't be married now.

She drew herself gently out of Jonathan's arms, but she kept his hand. "Is that the poor little baby?" she asked. She went toward the box where the baby now lay asleep since Sue had left it fed. "It's very small," Judy said. "What's her name, Jonathan?" She gazed down at the child but did not touch it.

"I haven't—we haven't thought about that," Jonathan said sadly.

"Why not Mary?" Judy asked, "after your mother?"

Jonathan's eyes met Ruth's. "Why not?" he agreed. "You see, Ruthie, how Judy knows the right thing at once. Mary it is—she'd like that."

"But we named the baby that died Mary," Ruth said.

"All the more reason why this living one should take the name," Jonathan said.

He had not wept at all, but now with Judy's hand softly in his he wanted to weep, to tell her—

"Run outdoors a bit, Ruthie, there's a good girl," he said.

And when she had gone he put his head down on Judy's shoulder and let the tears well up into his eyes. He gave one sob.

"Can you marry a chap like me, Judy sweet—with all these here in the house?"

"Don't let's talk about it now, Jonathan," she said in her gentlest voice. So gentle was her voice that it could not tell him anything. "Only we mustn't put Ruth out," she said. "It's cold today, and she's no coat on." She gave him a little squeeze and went to the door. "Come in, Ruth," she said. "It's too cold outside."

So there was no time for him to weep, after all.

She stayed nearly all day in the sod house. With Jonathan she went into that inner room and stood beside his dead mother, lying in the bed that tomorrow was to have been hers. If she thought of this she said nothing. And when at noon, as she was helping Ruth to prepare the meal, Sue came in to nurse the child again, she let no surprise escape her.

"I didn't know what ever to do, and Sue offered," Jonathan said, half-defensively and ashamed of his defense.

"It's good of her," Judy said peaceably.

In the afternoon she sat down to mend a rent in Jonathan's

coat and looked so quiet and so beautiful that his sore heart took rest. He drew a three-legged stool to her side.

"Maybe we could manage after all," he said.

She smiled. "And put Ruth and the children out when we wanted to be alone?"

"Maybe we could all live at American House."

"And leave no room for travelers, besides the cost?" She shook her head and stitched steadily. She seemed so remote that he was frightened.

"Will you wait, Judy?"

She lifted her beautiful black eyes. "What do you think?" she asked.

He thought she would, but he did not speak. He took the pretty thimbled hand, the skin so smooth and white, and kissed the palm passionately.

"Dear heart!" he murmured.

She drew it back again to use. And after a moment she said, "Won't Evan be surprised when he comes back!"

He had not thought of Evan, or only to remember that he was in Topeka.

"What made you think of Evan?" he demanded.

"Only because he'll be so pleased," Judy replied, "because he doesn't want you to marry me."

The composure of her face did not break. He sat watching her quick hands, his heart clinging to her in his sadness. Not for a moment had he forgotten all day the quiet body lying upon his bed. And even now he could not forget. At sunset, Stephen said, he would bring the coffin.

"It's getting late," Judy said suddenly, glancing at the sky. "I must be going, Jonathan, if there's nothing else I can do. Ruth's so handy." She smiled across the room at Ruth, who sat holding the baby, her back turned carefully toward them.

And he thought, I must let her go. There's no reason why she should be here when Stephen comes. It'll be too hard on her.

So he let her go, wrapping her cape about her and tying her brown hood under her chin. He walked a few steps with her into the biting wind, and then he saw Stephen and ahead of him Sue.

"Good night, my true love," he murmured and tipped her head to find her lips.

"Good night, Jonathan," she said. Her face had never

looked more sweetly pure than now, in the pale evening light, and her lips were softer than a child's.

Mary was buried the day before the great blizzard. The wind as they stood about the open grave was bitter beyond any Jonathan had ever felt. Maggie had cried with cold, and Mrs. Drear had taken her back to the sod house to stay with Sue and the baby. Ruth was trembling against him with cold so that at last he whispered to Jamie, "Stand on the other side of Ruth."

Over the grave a traveling preacher was reading the Twenty-third Psalm, but the wind tore his big voice to echoes and left of the psalm only shreds. Judy, Jonathan had seen in a moment, was not here. He had postponed the funeral a few minutes waiting for her. Then Henry had shouted through the wind, "We'll all get frostbite, Jonathan."

"Where's Judy?" he had muttered.

"She was dressed to come, but we hadn't oughta wait," Henry had bawled against the wind. He looked up at the sky lowering over their heads. "It might break any minute."

So they had gone on with the sad little ceremony. Stephen Parry had dug the grave through a crust of earth already frozen. It was in the corner of the two acres that was to be the graveyard about the church that was not yet built in the town that would one day be Median. Jonathan and Evan together had planned it so.

" 'I shall not want!' " the preacher's voice roared like a trumpet in a second's abatement of the wind and was lost again.

But Jonathan had not dreamed that his mother would lie here first. And she had wanted everything in her short life. He made up his mind now that in the spring he would move little Artie from the hollow to here beside her.

" '. . . the valley of the shadow . . .' " the preacher's voice cried out, and the wind snatched the words away and flung them over the plains where there was neither hill nor valley.

Evan was not here, and Judy was not here. But everyone else was. They stood, a handful of drab-colored human beings in the midst of the wide emptiness about them. They were dwarfed to the size and shape of insects by the land and the sky. A few rods away was the flimsy shelter of Median. He looked at them all in a sudden terror because he too was one of them.

It's too big for us here, he thought, and longed with a sudden sickening longing for the smallness of England to be tight about him again. Now I'll never be able to take Mother back to England, he thought. The old age he had planned to give her when they left Dentwater he could never give her, for she would have no old age. There's nothing to go back for, he thought. And he would miss her in England if he were alone there without her. England and his mother were one.

No, he was committed now to this new country. Judy— where was she? He searched the roadway toward the hotel, but she was not there. And then, his gaze returning sadly, he met by accident another pair of eyes. They were Katie's. He had scarcely seen her for months. She had been away all the summer visiting her aunt in Topeka, Lew said. When she had come back he had not thought to ask. But here she was, a tall, somewhat gaunt-looking young girl, who had grown so much in the few months that now it seemed only her hazel eyes were exactly as they had been. They were as round and honest as ever in her plain face, and now red with weeping.

He felt grateful to her for weeping. She had scarcely known his mother; she was weeping, he knew, for him. And across the open grave he smiled at her, a small, sad smile.

" 'And I will dwell in the house of the Lord *forever!*' " The preacher's voice triumphed over the wind at last, and he clapped the Bible shut with a bang.

Judy, in good time for the funeral, had tied her brown fur-trimmed cape under her chin and then tied on the small fur bonnet that went with it. She smoothed the ribbons of the bow and glanced at the big clock as she passed through the empty tavern. It was exactly the hour at which she should have been marrying Jonathan, and in this very room, if his mother had not come home. Even if she had died out there in the West, the wedding would have been going on now because they would not have known it. But the children would have come home to Jonathan, and then it would have been too late for her to do anything to save herself. Now she was saved. Something always *saves* me, she thought solemnly. It must be God.

She stood for a moment looking out of the panes of the

tavern door. The wind was whirling in great coils of dust and snow.

I wish something would save me now from having to go out, she thought. The tavern was warm and sheltering. She hated winter as Joel did, and every winter of her life they had gone south for his preaching. "There's souls to save where the climate's good, too," he had always said.

If she had gone with him, she thought, she might have been now in the Sandwich Isles, a lovely spot, Joel wrote her, where only man was vile. If she had gone, probably she could have married there, too, and settled down.

She lingered on at the risk of being late. Everyone else had gone, and she was alone. If she said afterwards that she had been taken suddenly faint so that she dared not go out, nobody was here now to say she was not. But she waited a moment more for some salvation not of her own making.

And then it came again. The door of Evan's office next door opened, and he hurried out, wrapped in his great cape, his head bent to the wind so that he had to hold onto his hat. Then he had only just come back from Topeka, she thought, for less than an hour ago Mrs. Drear had said as she went out of the door with Maggie, "This is going to hit Evan real hard. He's that fond of Jonathan."

And no one has told him, Judy thought, watching him. So he will come here because he will think it's still the wedding. She instantly forgot the Sandwich Isles in the excitement of this present salvation.

She sat down quickly beside the big tavern table and buried her face on her arms and waited. When she heard the door open, when she felt the bluster of the wind against her, she did not move. She waited for his voice.

"*Judy!*" he whispered.

Then she lifted her head. Her lips were red and trembling and her eyelashes were wet. She had never looked so beautiful and so piteous.

"What on earth—why, what's—"

"There's no wedding," she faltered. "I'm not being married, after all. It's a funeral instead. Jonathan's mother came home and she died. There's a baby."

She turned her quivering face up to him, seeming not to think of him or to care who he was, but only to be full of her own trouble. "I was just—going to the funeral. And then it came over me that this was the very moment when if things had gone right, we'd have been standing up together—so I couldn't go—"

Evan was dazed. "Why, I rushed back—for Jonathan's sake—" He breathed out the words. He glanced about the empty room. "Where's—I suppose everybody's at the—the funeral."

She nodded and drew a little lace handkerchief from her muff and put it to her lips. Evan sat down on the long bench but not quite near her.

"But—you'll be married very soon, Judy."

"How?" she asked. "There's nowhere to live. The house is full of the children—and there's the baby. I don't know how to take care of new babies. Besides, Jonathan—he can't marry anybody. He oughtn't to—he hasn't a home to offer."

"You mean—you wouldn't marry him anyway now?" He was breathing in great sighs. "Is that what you mean, Judy?"

"How can I?" she replied in the gentlest voice. "There is no place for me."

"That—could be remedied." His lips were suddenly too stiff to speak. "If you—"

"Evan—oh, don't think me wicked," she said quickly, "but how did I know? The last few days have shown me—I don't love him. I couldn't have married him. God saved me, Evan. I might have gone on and been so unhappy. Now I'm saved."

He was leaning toward her, searching her face, drinking up her words. His black eyes were terrible in their burning blaze upon her, but she did not shrink from them. She wanted to throw herself into that blaze, to be taken with it, to be consumed. She flung back her head and stood up. And he leaped to his feet and snatched her into his arms and kissed her upon the lips again and again, and she who had so often turned cool under men's kisses was warm now. He's loved me all the time he was hating me, she thought with triumph. Never had a man been rude to her as Evan had been, nor flouted her so openly, and it was because he loved her like this. And yet as he kissed her he was groaning and frowning and she could see his face dark above hers, and she could hear him muttering, but not to her.

And all the time he kept kissing her, and she clung to him until at last she was exhausted and faint truly enough now, so that he had to hold her to keep her from falling at his feet.

"We can't help it," he groaned. "But who'll tell him?"

He put her down on the seat and wiped his lips again and again with his handkerchief, and she leaned her head against his thighs, as he stood beside her, and she shivered with chill and ecstasy and fear. Who would tell Jonathan, indeed? Who could save them now save her and Evan together? She looked at him in real fright.

"Let's run away," she whispered.

"In this storm?"

"Is it too bad? You came through it."

"Yes, but—because I had to see you once more before you were—lost to me."

"Is that why you came?"

"Yes."

"Evan, have you loved me always?"

"Yes, ever since I first saw you."

"I loved you, too," she said simply.

It seemed to her now that she had so loved him. At least she had looked at him that day and had known that he was a man she could love. She divided all men into those she could love and those she could never love, and now she knew that Jonathan belonged to those she could not. Oh, she had been saved again! She felt suddenly strong and happy and good, and she stood up.

"Let's go. I'm not afraid. Evan, we could go now, and no one would ever know you had come back. They will just find me gone. And I'll write Jonathan from Topeka that I've changed my mind. And then later, we can just—tell him we're married. You see, you wouldn't even lose him, that way. He couldn't blame you if, after I changed my mind, I married you."

She was so pretty, wooing him with her eyes and her voice, with her fingers on his cheeks and his eyelids and lips, and he was sure that she should not marry Jonathan. That, at least, he had always been sure of—

"You'd make him miserable," he muttered.

"I know I would," she said with her smile most gay, most coaxing. "You've really saved him from me."

He laughed grimly. "At my own cost, probably!"

"Ah, but I'll make you terribly happy!"

His head swam, and his blood burned. She was the sort he wanted, the opposite of his mother and his sisters, this earthy, passionate, sooty-eyed woman, with her cool ways and her skin as pale as cream, and her lovely soft voice, and that promise of heat within her which showed in the very way she walked across a room and in the most casual look from her eyes.

"And if Jonathan ever knows," she said in that sweet deep voice, "he's so good, he'd understand."

Yes, he could see Jonathan, could hear him almost. "Of course if he ever knew, he'd want this," he agreed. "But as you say, he needn't know."

"Never!" she whispered.

And without more words, his arms about her, they hurried out of the tavern, and she waited while he harnessed his horses to face the storm again.

27

MRS. DREAR WENT BACK WITH JONATHAN TO MAKE SURE that the baby was all right. Sue was nursing it and she had a slight start at the sight of that small pale child at the dark breast. But she controlled herself. All sorts of things happened, and one took them. But Sue, feeling that surprise upon the quick of her flesh, threw an end of her shawl over her breast.

" 'Twon't be long I has to do this," she said, her speech always the mixture of slave and master pronunciation. "I'm weanin' her a'ready on cornstarch and water and cow's milk. She's right smart at suckin' on a rag out of a bottle. I got one of them flat whisky bottles and washed it clean."

"You're doin' a good job, I can see," Mrs. Drear said politely.

Jonathan had gone straight into the bedroom, and now he came back in his old clothes, Maggie clinging to his hand.

For all the world like a widower, Mrs. Drear thought, pitying him. She thought of Judy, and her big nose itched as it always did when she was irritated, and she rubbed it. The minute she got home she would get after Judy hard.

"Do you have enough vittles, Jonathan?" she asked.

"Yes, thanks," Jonathan said. He could not mention Judy's

name, so deep was his hurt that she had not come to see his mother buried. But as soon as the children were fed he would go to the hotel.

"I'll bring you a loaf of bread tomorrow," Mrs. Drear said.

"Thank you," Jonathan replied.

She looked around on the family. Ruth was taking off her coat. It was her mother's old one, and she bit her lips and turned away to hide her tears. Jamie stood by the fire, warming his hands.

"Nothin' else?" Mrs. Drear asked.

"I reckon we can manage," Jonathan replied. He tried to smile and found it too difficult. "I may be up along a little later," he said.

"Do," Mrs. Drear answered heartily. "It'll be good for you."

She left them then and plodded her way through the heightening wind and snow. A smaller woman might have been swept from the boardwalk, but she had fought her way through too many blizzards to feed beasts and to care for sick human beings. She knew how to draw her shawl across her face and make a shelter for breathing and how not to shrink from the wind but to breast it. Nevertheless the hot liquorish smell of the warm hotel had never seemed more welcoming than now as she stepped into it.

"Pour me out a mug, Henry," she gasped. Her head swam with the warmth after the biting cold. A few men of Median were in the room—Lew and Sam Cobb, Jim White and Samuel Hasty, and two newcomers this year who, though not in Median properly, had the nearest farms. She knew them all and paid no attention to them.

"Where's Judy?" she asked truculently.

"Ain't seen her, hide nor hair," Henry replied.

Mrs. Drear marched toward Judy's room. "I'm goin' to tell 'er what I think of her for not comin' to the funeral," she cried loudly. Let her hear, she thought. She threw open the door of Judy's little room and glanced about it. Somehow Judy had managed to make it the only pretty room in the house. All her small belongings were there, the lace-edged bureau cover, the embroidered cloth on the table, cushions in the one old rocking chair, pillow covers and a spread over the bed, and ruffled curtains across the windows. They were the things she carried with her everywhere to transform, as far as she was able, the dreariness she found inevitably about her.

"Where's the girl hidin' herself?" Mrs. Drear shouted. Her black bonnet fell away as she hurried to look in the wardrobe. There hung Judy's scant store of dresses, all clean, all neat. "She ain't took nothin', so she must be around," she muttered. She turned to the men gaping at the door. "You reckon she could ha' got lost just goin' to the funeral?" she asked aghast.

"Looks that-a-way," Lew said slowly.

"Then git out, every man alive of you," she shouted. "This hyere'll about finish Jonathan." She paused. "But I reckon he'll have to be told. Henry, you go and do the tellin'," she said.

The search for Judy upon the plains Jonathan led with such fierce vigor that never afterward did the people of Median think of him as a medium-sized fellow with quiet ways and a gentle voice. He was a flame scorching them with his anger, a general driving them beyond their duty, a giant of endurance and anger.

"No, we'll not rest," he shouted at midnight when they staggered back to the hotel. His eyes burned at the bottom of their sockets, his lips were cracked and his face gray with cold. His pale hair was stiff with a fringe of ice under his cap. He drank off a cupful of whisky neat. "Shame on us, great men, if we can't stand the blizzard a delicate girl is lost in!"

Jamie, who had been about to speak, did not. He had taken his full part with the men and could go on again as soon as he was warm, though it seemed waste to keep looking. Mrs. Drear in her purple flannel wrapper and her braid screwed on her head brewed them coffee in grim silence and watched them go out again. Then she crawled between the gray blankets of her bed and lay waiting.

I can't think that Judy is in any real hardship, she thought. I can't think she'd get to any place of sufferin' without savin' herself before she reached it.

She half-expected Judy to walk in, her garments arranged as neatly as ever. But she did not. Long after the dull sunrise the men came back exhausted. She woke from a doze and climbed out of her bed, screwing her braid up again, and pinned an old black skirt over her nightgown.

"Any luck?" she asked Henry.

"Nope."

"I'll bet she ain't dead," she retorted.

He gave her a slow wink with a half-frozen eyelid. "I ain't bettin' against you," he said. The little icicles in his long moustache clinked in minute music.

"But Jonathan'll take it like sure death," Mrs. Drear groaned.

"He does a'ready," Henry replied.

In the sod house it was so still, so warm, that for a wild moment Jonathan thought, She's here! She had come, perhaps, and made this warmth for him. There was the smell of bacon frying and of boiling coffee.

"Sit down, Jamie," he ordered his brother. "You're beat out."

"No, I ain't," Jamie gasped. But he sat down. He'd have said he was stronger than Jonathan any day, but Jonathan had stood the night better than any of them. Thin-lipped, white-faced, he still moved with energy, and his pale eyes burned.

"I'll eat and go out again," he said.

"You're foolish," Jamie retorted. "It's comin' on heavier."

It was, and Jonathan knew it. But nothing could have kept him here while he thought of Judy, struggling through the storm. She must have been blown out of her way like a little ship at sea, he thought, groaning to himself. Great men were sometimes blown across the prairie miles out of their way.

"You ain't goin' out again, Jonathan Goodliffe!"

He jumped at the unexpected voice. Someone came out of the bedroom. It was Katie, the baby in her arms, and he faltered in his surprise.

"Katie! Why, it's—it's terrible good of you to be here."

"No, it ain't," she said in the prim childish voice with which she had so often contradicted him though now it came oddly from her new height. "I thought to myself that I brung the twins through when they was newborn and I cud be of use here, helpin' Ruth. Ma can spare me now, ours are so big."

She handled the child with brisk certainty which gave it content. It lay with its small face against her flat young breast, and looked at her and yawned. Jonathan had scarcely seen this child.

"How is she?" he asked.

"She's as good as gold," Katie said heartily. Her plain

brown face grew soft. "She sucks the sugar rag wonderful. You needn't worry a mite."

"I don't," he said bluntly. "I can't."

She did not answer this. But when Ruth came in at this moment with Maggie washed and dressed and her red hair in round tight curls, she gave her the baby and busied herself with breakfast. Jonathan ate, not wanting to talk further. Food choked him, and yet he knew he must have it. He tried not to hear the wind rising in howls about the house or to see the darkness growing blacker against the windows. The sun had risen but the day was not lighter for it. He would go, but he would not ask it of Jamie. When he had eaten the food Katie had set before him, he rose and put his hand on the block that barred the door. Only then did Katie speak. She called to him sharply from the stove.

"If you don't come back, what's to be done with the children?"

He had never thought of not coming back. If she had begged him not to go he would have pushed her aside, insisting on his sure return. But when she put the question thus baldly to his responsibility he stopped short. He might not come back, and then what would happen to these children, to Ruth and Maggie and little newborn Mary?

He flung open the door to test the storm before he answered and was blown across the room. They rushed together, he and Jamie and Katie, through a sheet of icy snow and forced it shut again and pushed the bar. And this he knew was the answer. He went headlong into the bedroom and flung himself upon the bed, and to the bitterest of death he gave up Judy.

Judy, in a little sod house less than twenty miles from Topeka, was sitting at breakfast with Evan and the owner of the house. She had slept fairly well upon a hay mattress in the bunk while Evan and Joe slept in blankets on the floor. The horses were in shelter on the leeward side of the house.

"Travelin' to Topeka, be ya?" Joe inquired.

"We are," Evan said.

He glanced at Judy's left hand. From somewhere, to his wonder, she had produced a plain gold wedding ring, and it was now upon her hand. Did she keep wedding rings ready for such need? He asked himself the question sarcastically and saw with unwilling eyes and a sullenly stirring heart how fresh she looked, and how neat, though she had slept in her clothes. He had been sleepless. Once, when the fire flared after fresh fuel, he had gone to look at her in the bunk. She was sleeping in such sweet silence as he had never seen upon a human being. It was impossible to believe ill of her, his love told his reason.

"You live in Topeka?" Joe asked. He was hungry for talk but he had to screw talk out of these two, he thought.

"Yes," Judy said. She had cooked the breakfast and made saleratus biscuits. Joe took his fifth.

"Shore is good to have home cookin' again," he said. "I don't wish you folks bad luck about the storm, but let 'er rip, says I!" He smiled through a snap of teeth at Judy, and she smiled back.

"I'll make an Indian pudden for dinner," she said sweetly.

"It's pyore luck the storm blew you my way, ma'am," Joe said.

But she was not quite saved, she thought. Everything depended on how she held Evan in this storm. If her sure instinct failed, if she could not conquer his remorse—no, fight it at its very root—he could leave her yet for Jonathan's sake. His love for Jonathan was stronger at bottom than what he felt for her. She saw it this morning in the coolness of his hand and the aversion of his eyes, and she accepted it without jealousy, though with wonder. What had Jonathan in him to make a man like Evan love him so well?

She busied herself in small slight ways all day in the wretched sod house, always shy and quiet, saying almost nothing to Evan, but looking at him often with large eyes that weighed him, he thought, feeling them upon him, in some secret judgment of her own. His pride was pricked.

"Not sorry, are you?" he asked when in the afternoon Joe fell asleep.

She gave him her wordless lovely smile and crept against his breast and waited. When she felt his heart begin to beat harder under her cheek, she took courage. She was going to be all right.

"I have no one in the world," she murmured. "I am all alone, except for you."

"No going back?" he asked.

"I can't," she whispered. She tightened her arms about him

and lifted her face. "Even if you should die, or if you should leave me—I'd never go back."

"Why?"

" 'Twould be wrong. I know it now."

He bent to lay his cheek upon her soft bright hair, and she put her hand to his lips. It was then he felt the ring.

"Where did you get that ring just when we needed it most?"

"It is my mother's. I wear it on a ribbon about my neck, ever since she died."

She was so right in all her ways, things came about so rightly for her that the belief in the inevitability of their love overwhelmed every other feeling in him again today as it had yesterday.

"You're sweet," he murmured, "you're perfect."

She smiled and swept her lashes downward and felt upon her lips his hot, strong kiss.

Now this will last, she thought. Anyway, until we're there.

🐬 28 🐠

IN HER OWN WRY WAY, JONATHAN THOUGHT HEAVILY, KATIE was perfect. At the end of the second day he knew he could not have lived out the storm without her. If he had been shut up in the sod house with Jamie, reminding him at every movement and word of Clyde, he would have come to quarrels with him. Maggie's incessant chatter, her meddling fingers and bustling ways, would have tried him sorely, for Ruth could do nothing with her, and besides Ruth was absorbed now in little Mary. And what would have made him most weary and angry together would have been the single sorrow of this family of his for their mother, a sorrow subdued in him to his loss of Judy. For that she was lost he was now convinced. Unless she happened upon the shelter of a farmhouse, she could never have outlived the storm. But he had visited every farmhouse near Median when they had searched for her, and beyond that she must have perished. True, other men hearing of her loss had pushed out beyond that, and there was the frailest of hope that when the storm had quieted, word would come in that she was found. But his native melancholy did not allow him to build upon this hope.

Through all his suffering and silence Katie moved serenely, managing everything well. She knew his trouble, but she did not once speak of it. It would have been intolerable had she spoken. But she spoke to him very little, and only of something she wanted done.

"Can you fetch in more chips, Jonathan? We mustn't let the fire down."

He felt his way around the corner of the house, grateful for the buffalo chips the half-breed children had piled there as pay for their winter's schooling. He disliked their ammoniac odor as they burned, and he seldom used them, but they burned and gave out warmth now, and he was glad he had not refused them as he had nearly done when the children brought them first. He had wanted to spare their feelings of being even poorer than the others. But Katie put the chips into the stove neatly with a bit of paper between her thumb and finger.

"They make a good heat for bakin'," she said.

Somehow she created order in the house and order in their sorrow, too. Her intensity in small activities, her very energy in cleaning and washing and cooking subdued the possibility of emotion; and Jonathan, engulfed in his tragedy, clung to this sharp and practical presence. Life had to go on, Katie made him feel. Eating and sleeping and washing and cooking and caring for children—they went on, though all else were lost. Slowly he began to take his share in the work while he waited for the storm to pass. And at last he was able to eat a little and to sleep fitfully and to plan in the night as he lay on a pallet before the fire that he would go out the first day that Henry Drear would let him have a horse and ask at every house upon the plains for news of Judy. And yet, he thought, perplexed, they would bring news in to Median, and would he miss it if he went? He might wait two days, he decided at last. That would give them time.

He steadied himself against that decision, and when the storm cleared he stuck to it though every bone in him ached for action. Then before the next day was over the first mail came in from Topeka. Jamie, gone to the hotel to ask for transportation westward, brought back a letter for him. Jonathan took it and saw upon it Judy's writing.

He stared at it and looked about for privacy. There was none anywhere in his house, and he went outside into the silent sunlit snow and, standing with his back against the wall, he tore open the envelope.

"Dear Jonathan." The thin paper crackled in his trembling hands. "It is best to tell you straight out that I went away because I could not marry you. It came over me like that when I was ready to come to the funeral. So I took a seat in a wagon that happened then to be going to Topeka. I will find some work here. Forgive me if you can, but whether or not you can, I know I am right, and it is kindest in the end to both. So I give you no address because I don't wish to be found. Judy."

He crushed the letter and held it in his hand and stood staring out over the endless snow. The sky was brilliantly blue, and the whiteness stabbed his eyes, but he felt nothing. He was beyond pain any more, having suffered to what he could endure. This was beyond.

She doesn't say why, he thought stupidly. But Judy never said why she did anything. And when in any letter she had ever written him had she told him anything? His mouth went dry, and he felt suddenly sick, as though his being must empty itself of everything. In the wrenching of his flesh he groaned and leaned his head against the house. Oh, if he need never enter that house again! If he could but walk on and on across that endlessness before him and in its final emptiness be lost!

But the door of his house opened, and Katie's voice flew out, "Jonathan! Dinner!" She thrust out her head and saw him. "What's the matter with you?" she cried. And he who had not wanted to mention his trouble to her, now felt that someone must know because he could not endure his loneliness otherwise. He put out his hand with the letter crushed into the palm, and she took it. He heard the faint crackling as he stared on into that blind white space, and there was silence while she read. Then he heard the sharp sound of paper torn to bits and felt his hand seized by her rough hand.

"You come right in and get your food while it's hot," she said.

Between Jonathan and Katie there was now this secret of his broken love. Neither spoke of it, but it was in each of them, though not by any jot of change in Katie could

Jonathan discern it in her. Every change was in himself. He was so bottomlessly lost in the emptiness in himself that all he did was useless, and he never stopped working from his waking at daylight to his sleep when sick fatigue compelled him to it. He brimmed over every moment, grateful to school children; grateful to little Mary, who must be fed and cleaned and put to sleep; grateful to Maggie, meddling everywhere at once. He managed somehow all this life under one roof, though how he would have managed it if Katie had not come morning and night to keep all straight was a thing he thought about. For Ruth was not good at doing several things together. With the tenderest heart and the softest ways and a will always sweet and ready to lend itself to another's, she seemed never to have anything finished. Work as she did, she would still by noon have not one full task ended—the dinner stewing, but half the morning dishes not washed; the floor swept, but a bed not made; Maggie fed, but her red mane of curls not brushed and her face unwashed. Yet Katie in an hour of energy could have the home docile and all of them cleaned and fed.

It was injustice to her goodness that, with knowledge of all she did, no one was grateful to her. But she could at the same time do a kindness with her hands and snatch it away with her tongue. A strange thing in women, Jonathan thought sorrowfully, that Judy who did nothing for anybody and who had wounded him for life he would love and long for because of her lovely looks and her sweet voice and her gentle ways. And though Katie was better than Judy, he was on certain days in agony until she was gone, though she was so kind always to him. He felt every edge in her voice and saw every abruptness of her thin sharply shaped frame.

"Ruth, why don't you do like I told you and save the scraps of fat for soap? Waste not, want not."

"Maggie, you're a bad girl. Don't poke the baby's eye."

"Jamie, there's plenty to do around here for everybody without you sittin' waitin' to go West. Hurry yourself and go out and hunt chips if nothin' else. I do despise laziness!"

When at last the roads opened enough for a horse to go through, she made no pretense at not being thankful to have Jamie gone. She disliked his carelessness and hearty appetite and the dirty feet he always forgot to wipe.

And yet she could not leave Jonathan alone either. If she

stayed to share the midday meal she often cooked, she was at Jonathan to eat when he could scarcely swallow. His wish for food had left him, and yet she made him eat.

"Now, Jonathan, you ain't goin' to sit there spurnin' good food. You eat that good boiled meat. Take a real slice of it. Here, I'll fix your plate for you."

His stomach, always too delicate for food when his mind was desponding, turned against the great plate she set before him, the slabs of yellow corn bread, the heaped potatoes and salt pork. He said once, "I could eat some of Mother's scones if she was here to make them," and Katie said, meaning only kindness, "Well, she ain't, and I'm sorry to say it but you'll just have to eat what you got!"

He must eat what he had. The words took on a sad symbolism in these days when he made symbols out of everything as he tried to know what he should do.

Should he not go to Topeka and look for Judy? But how, except to search from house to house? And who would teach school and who tend this house? And then he thought how Judy herself had cut him off.

Days passed and Evan did not come back to Median. Another blizzard came and went, bringing six days when he had no school and two days when even Katie could not come, and he fed the baby on thinned gruel for milk. It was a bitter winter for blizzards, and Jonathan blamed them when Evan delayed. At first he was glad that Evan was not there to prove himself right about Judy. Then he came to longing for Evan's comfort and his friendship and his talk. He could always forget everything in the talk he and Evan had together, and there was not another in Median who had such thoughts as he and Evan had. If Evan came I'd tell him everything and feel better, he thought.

But Evan did not come. February ended with a handful of mild days before March burst in, and then something began to trickle back to Median about Evan and Judy. A distant farmer, George Lacey, had gone to the city to set right a boundary to his land that the railroad had cut off, and the lawyer for the railroad was Evan. He went in the company offices but it was late and the lawyer wasn't there, so he got his address and went to his house. "It was a good brick house, square, and set back from the street, and his wife opened it, a soft-spoken woman she was, all dressed up like a lady," George said, around the stove at the store.

"Why, Evan ain't married!" Lew roared.

"He shore is," George Lacey said.

"Why, why in heck didn't he tell us?"

"Don't know," George Lacey said. "I didn't know him well—just saw him here maybe once or twice."

"Did you hear her name?" Lew asked. He was weighing a slice of store cheese, and his eyes were on the scales.

"He called her Judy or Julie, or suthin'," George Lacey said. The cheese was his, and he picked off a piece and ate it.

"Judy!" Lew whispered. "Did she have big black eyes?"

"Yep—I noticed 'em. Why, you know her?"

"Mebbe." Lew's mouth shut into a downward line between his flat, unshaven cheeks.

He took the news in to dinner with him. Katie was home that day. Though she could not have let Jonathan know it, he had hurt her in the morning by a chance gruffness. She had said, "Don't let them school children traipse in here with their feet all mud, Jonathan. There's no sense to it. I've tied some straw together for 'em to rub their shoes on."

And he, who seldom spoke at all, had answered quickly, "I have enough to teach their heads without bothering about their feet."

"You don't scrub after 'em—" she began, but he had not let her go on.

"Give over, Katie, do. There's things I care more for than scrubbin' and cleanin'."

So she had untied her apron and gone home then and there and, though he had shouted after her to come back, she had not come back.

"I've heard somethin' damned queer," Lew said slowly to his wife at dinner, staring at nothing while he chewed.

"Mr. Merridy, I wish you wouldn't swear before the children," Mrs. Merridy said.

"This is just plain cussedness I can't help swearin' about," Lew said. He looked at his wife solemnly. "Evan and Judy're married."

Mrs. Merridy choked on her tea. "They're never, Lew Merridy!"

"Shore as I'm born they are," Lew said. "And if Evan ever shows his face in Median again, I'll take a shotgun to him."

Katie said not a word. Into her freckled face there crept a deep color. She stopped eating and put her hands tightly clasped in her lap.

"Who's gonna tell Jonathan?" she asked.

"I dunno," Lew said. "It's plumb awful, that's what it is. Why'n't you tell him, Katie? You're there most every day."

"I couldn't—" Katie said, her throat tight.

"I'll go and see Drear," Lew said.

He lumbered over to the tavern after his dinner, and in an hour all Median knew except Jonathan, and nobody wanted to tell him, and then Jonathan himself came in, as he often did on a late Saturday afternoon, merely to see men's faces and sit and drink a little with them, and he made the excuse of a loaf of Mrs. Drear's salt-rising bread.

When he came into the room tonight silence fell upon the half-dozen men as though he were a stranger. Then they were too quick to greet him and their voices too hearty. And then Mrs. Drear put her head out of the kitchen to see who it was. Her face grew stern.

"You, Jonathan, come here," she said.

He went into the kitchen, and she shut the door. "Sit down," she said. "Now listen. You've got to know somethin'. It's terrible—"

"Nothing's happened to Jamie, has it?"

"No, it's what's happened to you. Judy's married Evan."

Her face before his eyes swam and receded, was lost and appeared again.

"Evan!" he whispered.

"Here—you drink this." She put her own cup of beer before him. But he did not see it.

"But—but—Evan—hated her," he gasped. "At least, no one could hate her but—but—"

"That's it, I guess he didn't," she said. "Now, Jonathan, you take it like a man. There's other girls as good and much better. It's a pity you had to see Judy first. Every man's got to see one woman first, and he thinks that's all there is. And they all see somebody like Judy. Look at my Henry. What does he do but fall in love with a low-down girl from the East on her way to Californy and she stays here and swears Jennet was his, and then runs off and leaves him with a month-old baby. Where'd he be if I hadn't took pity on him and answered his advertisement for a good cook and took care of the mother-

less child and married him and give him a home?" Her face
quivered. "But do you think he's forgotten how that slut
looked? No, he'll say, 'Jennet's pretty, like her maw.' He'll say
it till he dies."

Jonathan listened and heard nothing. Nothing that had ever
happened had anything to do with him. He rose to his feet, his
eyes on the ground.

"Thanks," he said vaguely, and then walked to the door,
and through the silence in the other room he went outside. He
stood hesitating, longing to be gone anywhere into the world
so that he was not here. But ahead of him and around him the
prairie lay purple under a purple sky. In the west there was
still a glow, but so dull that it did not dim the sharp stars.
There was nowhere to go. The prairie cut him off like an
ocean. He had only his house, and after a moment he
buttoned his coat and pulled down his hat and went the road
he knew the best.

At the door of his house he met Katie. When she saw him
enter the hotel, she had put her mother's old red shawl over
her head and run down the boardwalk to his house. She did
not want to meet him, nor have him see her; but she could
make sure, while he was gone, that everything was right in the
house and his supper cooked. As she ran through the store she
took up a tin can of fruit, peaches from the East, and planned
how she would open them into a bowl for a dessert. She
worked in furious silence to tidy the rooms for his coming and
fed the baby and put her into her box and then washed
Maggie after her supper and put her to bed, and last she
mended the fire and took a moment to whisper furiously to
Ruth, "You do like I said about them peaches—don't tell 'im
I brung them, but say they're from my pop."

"All right, Katie," Ruth said, bewildered.

All this had made her late, and so she met Jonathan at the
door when she opened it. He looked down at her face,
shadowy under the red shawl. In the twilight he could scarcely
see her features. But he could feel her sturdy presence, and he
knew her goodness.

"You've been in to clear me up again, eh, Katie?" he said
somberly. His hands were in his pockets and his collar turned
up, but the wind blew bitter over the plains.

"Nothin' much," she said, her lips dry.

"Yes, it is much," he said suddenly. "It's very much. It's

more than anyone in the world would do for me." He took his hands out of his pockets and put them on her thin, sloping shoulders. "So I ask you, Katie—will you be my wife?"

She stood under his hands for one brief moment, her breath so tight it caught in her lungs. Then she gasped and ducked and went running up the walk in the darkness and left him with neither yes nor no. And he stood looking after her.

Why not? he thought heavily. It doesn't matter now.

He went into his house and ate his food and knew where the peaches came from without asking. He was very gentle to Ruth and wiped the dishes for her, and then he said, "Would you mind if I left you a bit, Ruth?"

"No, not if it's not long," she said.

"It won't be long," he said gravely.

He lit his lantern and through the darkness plodded back to Lew's store and opened the door. It was Saturday night, and Median men were still there. Lew was behind the counter near the cracker barrel, but he came out and Jonathan drew him outside the door.

"Is Katie at home?" he asked.

"She's gone to bed," Lew said. "Came in a while back and said she felt bad."

"Then I won't disturb her, Lew. I must tell you—I asked her to be my wife."

"Katie?" Lew's thick jaw dropped. "See here, Jonathan, don't you go on a rebound. It'll shore be a mistake—"

"No—no," Jonathan broke in, "it's not that. You tell her, Lew, that I told you, and tell her I'll come tomorrow for her answer, and I hope with—with—all my heart, tell her, that she'll have me."

He bolted into the darkness and left Lew standing there. He was glad he had not seen her. It would give him time. There was all night ahead.

He spent a long evening with Ruth. It was unexpectedly quiet and good, in spite of the pain in his breast. That pain was for something over and ended. Pain might never end, but he was going on with life, whatever it was.

He mended the fire and drew the curtains his mother had made. No one drew curtains in Median, but tonight he wanted to shut out the prairie and shut himself in with these three of his own flesh and blood. He put fresh fuel into the tin stove and sat down in a rocking chair which Katie had brought one day for them to sit in and rock the baby. Though many houses in Median had rocking chairs, he had felt them foolish furniture.

"I can't sit swinging my legs like I was on a fence," he had always said.

This chair had a woven reed bottom, and Katie had put an old blue gingham cushion on it, and now it felt easy under him. He sat in it, swinging gently, and after a while he talked with Ruth as he had not talked since their mother died, asking her questions of those months when his mother had been away from him and piecing together the bits of her life that Ruth thought to tell. When he had gone to bed, for the first time in nights past he felt he could sleep. He had reached some sort of bottom to suffering. Nothing worse can happen to me, he thought. From now on it must be up.

He thought quietly of Katie and of how he would speak to her tomorrow, and then he was too drowsy to plan. It'll come natural between us, somehow, he thought without excitement.

After long sleep he woke, and after a moment's wild agony he remembered. He rose and washed himself and put on his second-best suit and then, happening to put his hand to his cheek, stayed to shave himself. My cheek'll feel as rough to Katie, he thought.

Without hurrying he ate and tidied up after himself, for Maggie had Ruth up long before; and then he put on his hat and walked slowly up the boardwalk. It was a forward day for March, and more like April. The air was clear with sun, though under the boards the mud was bottomless with melting snow. But he kept himself clean of it and went straight into the store and knocked on the door of Lew's house behind it.

Lew himself opened the door. He looked solemn. "Come in, Jonathan," he said and coughed behind his hand. "Lula, here's Jonathan."

Mrs. Merridy was sitting on the sofa in her best black dress. "Howdy, Jonathan, come in," she said.

They shook hands with him as though he were a stranger, and he felt strange and put an end to it.

"Is Katie here?" he asked simply.

"She's in the parlor," Lew said gently.

He went into the parlor, where he had never sat down in his life. It was the only parlor in Median, and there had been no occasion since his coming grand enough for its use. But Katie was sitting there now on the horsehair sofa, her hands clasped in the lap of her brown poplin dress. She looked at him wretchedly, two bright red spots in her cheeks; and, though she had brushed her brown hair smoothly into the coil upon her head and put a narrow collar of white lace at her throat, she looked as she always had. She was one of those women who, no matter what they wear, always look the same. The thought grazed his mind, and he let it pass. It did not matter. He sat down beside her and took one of her hands. It felt stiff and unwilling, but her fingers quivered when they touched his.

"Have you made up your mind, Katie?" he asked.

She nodded, and he saw that her face was white.

"I hope it's yes," he said.

She nodded again, her mouth too dry for speech.

He hesitated and in his bosom felt his heart give one last turn of agony. But that was all. In the deepest silence he leaned and kissed her cheek, and they sat a moment hand in hand. Then he said gently, "Shall we go and tell your folks?"

She rose at once and with her hand still in his he led her out.

"It's settled," he said to Lew and Mrs. Merridy.

They stood up and put out their hands to him, and he shook them, one after the other, and then they all sat down and Lew cleared his throat.

"Now that's over," he said, "and I—"

But Mrs. Merridy broke in sharply, "Katie, go and see what's burning. I declare, if I forgot to add water to the stew—"

Katie suddenly looked herself. "Oh, *Maw!*" she cried, and rushed out of the room.

But in the night, that second night, he woke to scarify himself. What had he done so quickly? He had rushed to his own crucifixion, without waiting to find even if it were necessary. He should have gone to Topeka and seen for himself whether the thing were true or not. He had not even asked Lew how the news had come. He should have found Evan and asked him if Judy was his wife. He lay writhing at what he had done to himself. It was too late. Was it not too late? If Judy was still free, if he could prevail upon her and bring her back to him—in the still night any madness seemed possible. But he could never bring her to Median. Median would stand by the Merridys and spew him out.

He thought on, sleep far from him. And the more he thought, the more inevitable it seemed to him that Evan and Judy were together. Their seeming hate was clear to him. They were trying not to call it love, he thought. In a small way, but the same, he had once hated Jennet like that.

Anyway, I'll write, he thought grimly. He sent a letter to Evan that day.

"Evan, where is Judy? Jonathan."

This was all he wanted of Evan.

In the time it took any letter to come and go, Evan's letter came back, many lines, written and crossed, in that fluent and familiar script.

"You must know, dear old Jon, that I did not take her until she had decided that she had made a mistake. I found her ready to run away—she insists that had she never seen me the results would have been the same so far as you are concerned— Believe me always unchanged—and eager to give you any help. Would you like a position in the high school here at a good salary? I might be able to secure it for you—"

He read the letter and put it in the stove and went out to find Stephen Parry.

"When are you going to finish my schoolhouse?" he demanded. "Winter's nearly over, and I want to begin everything new this spring."

"I'll git mahself right to work," Stephen promised.

29

JUDY WAS IN HER NEW HOME. IT WAS A HANDSOME HOUSE, spread to look its best in a lawn unusually wide, though not much deeper than the house as it stood back from the street. Four cottonwoods and two elms gave shade and dignity, and there was a carriage block. In the afternoons the colored man she had hired drove the carriage up to this block, and she stepped in, her small ruffled parasol open over her head, and drove down the street to Evan's office to wait for him at the curb. She had not usually to wait long. He came out briskly, very debonair in a frock coat, tall hat, and a striped gray waistcoat and trousers, and took his place beside her. Together they drove up the street, which was not yet paved, though it had sidewalks and small new elm trees.

At such times Judy's eyes were dewy with happiness. She was lovelier than ever to look at, lovely to be in love with, Evan thought to himself. He could not possibly have married a plain woman. Most—indeed, very nearly all—of the time he was delighted with Judy, proud of her beauty and prouder even of her quick instinct for rightness in any company. In a public place she was easily the prettiest woman, but she was more. She was the most quiet, and the other women were not usually quiet, and she was the most graceful among women who were framed to angles or heaviness.

When they were alone together in their new home, the fine details of which had cost him more than he cared to think about, she was no less lovely, no less perfect. Night or day she was amiable, passionate when he demanded passion and delicate when he did not.

He planned his first visit to his mother's home with no terrors. Judy, who could abandon her body to him without scruple, could in the presence of other women be as virgin as a young girl. He took her to New Orleans in May and bought her summer dresses that billowed about her little waist and great drooping hats under which her eyes were like dark pansies.

"Very nice," Mrs. Bayne said, surveying her. "I didn't think they could do as well in Kansas, Evan. Judy, your skin is as good as Laura's."

Judy laughed her fresh low laughter. "I wasn't raised in Kansas," she said.

"Where?" Mrs. Bayne demanded.

"Nowhere in particular," she said demurely. She made no pretense of her family, although she never spoke now of Joel. Had he not left her?

And Evan never admired her with more reason than he did in his mother's home. If she was not a lady, she played herself one so well that to the world there was no difference. There was mirth mingled with his admiration when he drew her behind the big cape jessamine bush in his mother's front yard, and when he kissed her there was still excitement in it. It was as exciting as though he stole the kisses when he placed the flowers between her round breasts.

But sometimes, in the night, in their own house, when she joined so cheerfully in his passion, he remembered how coolly she had put Jonathan away, how easily come to him. He loved her body and would have loved her wholly as well, if he could have forgotten altogether that she had betrayed his friend. But he could not always forget, and under their life together there stayed alive the thin and secret nerve that quivered with distrust of her.

But of this Judy knew nothing. She lay in his arms in the pleasant emptiness which was her happiness. Ahead of her the days stretched full of delight. Small changes in her furniture, flowers to be arranged in a new vase, lace to sew into her wine-red taffeta dress, the direction of the black woman Evan had hired for the housework—all were things to be done with joy and without responsibility.

"I wish Mama could see me now," she said suddenly to Evan.

"Not quite now!" he said teasingly. He tousled her curling hair loose upon his pillow, and when she laughed he gathered her into his arms in fierce delight. She had the trick of making herself so soft, so yielding when he did this, that even her bones melted. He felt only softness and clinging, and he smelled her faint perfume. Oh, she was good enough for him, he thought, or very nearly, having already asked himself the question and in one way and another answered it.

He found Jonathan's letter on his desk at the offices of the Santa Fe railroad company the next day. He had made the desk a permanent part of those offices because of his brilliant defense of the railroad's right to cross a man's land. "Progress, the right of the nation over the privilege of an individual." These were words he had dwelt upon ardently. Besides, was not the whole West open? A man could always move on if he was dissatisfied.

He walked gaily through the sunshine of the morning, twirling his cane and thinking of how Judy had looked in a cream-colored lace peignoir as she sat behind the silver coffee service that had been his mother's wedding present. In such a mood he had not been disturbed by Jonathan's letter for more than the moment it took him to read it. And the moment after he was thinking, half-pityingly and with not too much remorse to bear, of what he could do for him—a job, perhaps in the city school, and cash for pay instead of corn meal and buffalo chips and potatoes and black molasses. If Jonathan were here, he could help him in other ways, not to make amends, but to show him that a woman was not cause for change in friendship between men. There might be spice, even, he thought gaily, as years went by, in the memory that his best friend had once desperately loved his wife.

When Jonathan's reply came he shrugged and felt he had done all a man could do and had been refused.

Jonathan began the building of a new life that spring with zeal determined by his mind. What the heart had not, the head could supply. He told Katie, "We shan't be married until everything's the way we want it."

He told Lew, "I shall have everything for Katie the way I once planned it—for the other."

Lew, picking his teeth at the threshold of the store, threw him a look from under the bushy eyebrows that met over his big nose.

"That's only right, I reckon, and still I take it to be good of you."

"Katie deserves it more," Jonathan said.

"I reckon," Lew said peaceably. He ruminated a moment and then went on, "You don't have to say nothin' to me. You and Katie kin run your own show. A man's own marriage is all a man can tend to, and mine ain't done yet."

The Sunday dinners were begun again, and Jonathan and Katie sat in the parlor for a while, or if the day were fair they took a walk along the river. He talked a great deal at these times, his arm about her shoulder or her hand in his. He was always conscious until he fought it out of him of the difference between Katie's hand and Judy's. Judy's hand had curled into his with the angelic softness of a baby's hand, but Katie's was always stiff. He looked at it one day. "A good working hand," he said gently. "A useful, kind hand, always busy." He thought loyally that there was something here more firm than the pink and cream of that hand which he had once so passionately put to his lips. He never kissed Katie's hand and never would, perhaps.

But he talked to her as he had never talked to Judy. Judy had always put everything out of his head. With difficulty even had he thought of his school. He could only see how Judy's hair curled about her ears and how smoothly her throat shaped into her lovely bosom. But when he was with Katie, his mind built his plans and she, who always fell silent and shy at any hint of tenderness, replied quickly enough with good sense to all he planned.

The schoolhouse grew, paid for by bonds the townsfolk put out. There was not enough to pay for one of the newfangled basement stoves he had read of in a school magazine to which he subscribed. He wanted it sorely, for how would they keep a great two-story house warm otherwise? He had a little money in the Farmer's Bank in Topeka, saved to bring his mother home. But Katie would not let him use it.

"Once you begin usin' our money for the school, there'll be no end," she said, so definitely that he dared not disobey her.

He swallowed his pride and wrote to Evan, asking for a loan to buy the stove, he being willing to offer his own note for security. Evan replied at once with all his old gaiety. He was glad Jonathan had turned to him, though he had no money to lend. His own new house had cost him dear, and he had wanted Judy to have all she liked. But he could arrange a loan with the city bank, and he himself would give security.

Secretly he was glad to do this. He was in Jonathan's debt, and this put him out of it. "I want to help you in any way I can," he wrote Jonathan, and Jonathan wrote to thank him, making no mention either of Judy or of Katie. Thus the two were friends again, though very distantly.

By midsummer the school building stood finished, a square frame building on a brick foundation, two-storied and roofed with tin. Inside it were rooms with good windows, four rooms downstairs and four up. Jonathan kept the smallest near the door for his office. He had advertised for teachers in an eastern newspaper. A dozen letters reached him, and out of them he chose two, one a man and one a woman.

Without planning to delay his marriage, he did delay even when the schoolhouse was done. The sod house, he told Katie one Sunday, was too small and dark.

"When I come back out of my new office now, the sod house is like a cave," he said. "Besides, how will it hold us all, Katie? Ruth's a young woman nearly, and she and Maggie and little Mary should have a room for themselves. And we should have a sitting room anyway and a kitchen."

There was never any talk of not having the three children with them. Neither he nor Katie thought of living alone. The end of it was that he took out of the Farmer's Bank in Topeka the money he had there—and Katie was willing for this—and they bought from the township of Median a lot next to his school big enough for a small one-story frame house. He and Katie planned three bedrooms, a sitting room, a small kitchen, and a front porch.

"I'd like one of those newfangled rooms for bathing," he said. People in the East were beginning to have bathrooms, and in the catalogues that he had ordered for the school building he had seen pictures of heavy wooden bathtubs lined with metal and painted white.

"Whoever heard of such a thing!" Katie cried. "A whole room to wash in, when there's the kitchen, too? It's waste."

So he let it go for the present, having indeed all he could do to build the house. He helped to build it himself to save cost, and young Matthew Cobb worked with him and Stephen through long summer days and evenings. Matthew was nearly fifteen now, and as tall as he would ever be. He had settled into a plain-faced boy approaching young manhood, and he talked quietly of buying a farm somewhere not too far west when his earnings were enough. The boy's eye was true, and he could set a window frame into a wall without a slant. His fault was that all he did was done too carefully, so that in no day did he ever do all that he had set himself, and the knowledge that each day's work dragged upon the next made him always sober and anxious and pressed in mind; but that was scarcely a fault in a young man, Jonathan thought.

He came to know Matthew very well that summer while they put up the slender framework of the house and nailed the clapboards under the tin roof and lathed and plastered the inner walls. Lew told Katie to choose her wallpapers from his stock and, though what she chose were all too flowery for Jonathan's plain taste, he kept silence. He had a constant sense of some debt he owed her, as though he had done her an injustice, and more and more he let her have her way. Yet when he searched himself to find out what he did that was unjust, he could find nothing reasonable. He knew that no other man had asked to marry her. He knew that with him she was safe and that his kindness would not fail, and that her father and mother were grateful to him. It was on his wedding day, the last Monday in October before school opened, that he discovered why forever he would be in Katie's debt.   —

When he had dreamed of that other marriage, it was with impatience to have it done and over quickly and all guests gone and he and Judy alone forever. But now it was not that marriage, and he let Median have his wedding for its holiday. There was great talk about where it should be.

Mrs. Merridy cried out, "It's nothin' but proper that a girl should be married from her home."

But the parlor was small, and Jonathan insisted doggedly that all his pupils and their parents should come to his wedding. This, with what was left of Median, made the parlor a mere closet. His own little new home was no better. Besides, Katie would not have it there.

"I don't want to have a housecleanin' on my hands the first day after," she declared sensibly.

There remained the hotel, but it was crowded at this season with travelers westward and, besides, there were too many things to be remembered—his mother standing at the door with Artie in her arms, Jennet sitting at the table, her head upon her arms, and Judy the night she stood in the hollow of his arms—gazing at Evan, as he remembered now with the deep inward wrench that made him know pain was still alive.

Then he found the place himself, stepping into the empty sunlit schoolhouse one day in early September. Why not here? he thought, here, where my work is? There were no shadows in this house, no sadness. It was waiting for its life to begin. Let it begin, then, with him. The benches Stephen had made of pine boards shipped from the East smelled fresh and clean. By opening the doors between, the rooms were big enough. And they could make a pulpit where the desk stood. If it were too late in the year for traveling preachers, he would hire a minister from Topeka to come for that day.

He worked quietly at his desk until noon and then went home and on the way passed by to see what Katie thought. He found her in her mother's kitchen stirring cucumbers in boiling vinegar and sugar on the stove.

"We'll be married in the schoolhouse, eh, Katie?" he said.

She had on a gray gingham apron that covered her neck to floor, and her face was red with the stove's heat. She did not stop her stirring when he came in, nor when he spoke.

"That's a real good idea," she said.

Out of the passing flocks of travelers, Median caught twelve new families that year.

"It's the schoolhouse gets 'em," Henry said. "A woman with kids sees a school, and then heaven and hell and all her menfolk can't drawr her past."

He was cheerful because of a full house and the two teachers to board all winter, and for a long time had ceased to blame Jonathan that Median was not a cattle town. His hopes now were in the new railroad coming westward.

"Though we might find gas or oil like some of these-hyere places do," he rumbled through his beard. "A town's got to have somethin' besides a schoolhouse, Jonathan."

"Find it—find it," Jonathan said cheerfully. "School's my share to Median, and I'll stick to it."

There were already days when, ignoring moods, he thought his life solid and good. He grew anxious now to have his wedding over. When it was, a certain door would have closed behind him, and there would be no opening it. On the other side of it he and Katie would make their life. She loved work and so did he, and of work there was plenty.

He did little himself toward that wedding day. Women of Median went out into the prairies and gathered goldenrod and grasses, and Sue devised a silver-papered bell to hang over the desk made into a pulpit, and Katie baked her own wedding cake and cut and sewed a wedding gown, not of white, "for what else could I wear a white dress at?" she said. She chose a bright blue silk that Lew had in stock.

And Jonathan kept his eye out for traveling preachers and picked up by chance a small humpbacked man one day in the early fall, tramping westward with his clothes tied in a bundle. He was dressed in dusty black, and on his head was a wide black hat, and when he spoke he had a twist to his tongue that made Jonathan jump, it was so familiar.

"You're English!" he shouted to the man's good morning.

"Eh, what if I am?" the man had retorted.

He had been nailing a board to one of the trees in the square; and Jonathan, seeing it from his desk, had rushed out

to stop him. The trees were growing, and he was touchy about
them. He begged water for them in summer and shielded
them in winter with brush he had the big boys cut from the
river banks.

"What are you about?" he had shouted from the schoolhouse door.

"My Father's business," the little man cried back, and
Jonathan saw the board. It was smoothed and clean and on it
was painted in bold black letters, "Ye must be born again."

"Did you come all the way from England for this?" he
asked, smiling.

"I did," the man said. He had a strange, grim little
weazened face. "God sent me," he said.

"We're not heathen here," Jonathan said.

"Not only heathens are sinners," the man said.

"Are you a regular minister?" Jonathan inquired.

"Methodist, by God's grace," the man said fervently.

Jonathan laid hold of his crooked left arm. "Then I
reckon God did send you," he said. "Will you stay and marry
me to my young woman?"

"If it's God's will," the man said calmly. With no ado, he
dropped to his knees before Jonathan's legs and, screwing up
his eyes and moving his lips, he prayed silently for a minute or
two and then rose and dusted off his knees. "God says, do as
you like this time, Paul Higgins. So I'll stay and get rested up
a bit. I'm fagged with walking. 'Tain't every day I get a ride,
and I've mostly walked from Indiana."

"Paul Higgins, eh?" Jonathan said. He was quietly astonished at this small gnarled man who now chattered freely as
though God had given him permission.

"Christened Saul by my parents in England, but I was
converted ten years ago and changed to Paul. Ten years I
been nailing God's words to trees all over this country. 'Twas
on a tree Christ died, I figger, and to trees men must look for
their salvation. Though here I travel days on end and never
see a tree. Today I saw these trees stickin' up miles off, and so
I made for 'em. 'Ye must be born again' 's my favorite, but I
have others too."

He drew out of a sack other texts and laid them on the
ground. " 'God so loved,' of course, and 'Where will you
spend eternity' and 'Many are called but few are chosen'—"

"I like 'Ye must be born again' the best," Jonathan said, not knowing whether to laugh or be grave.

"Eh, well, it's suitable to all occasions," the little preacher said. "There's no one so good he can't be made better, is how I figger it out. Where'll I put up, mister? Will they be easy on me in Median, seein' I'm poor and a minister of the gospel and has only what God moves folks' hearts to give me, and there's plenty of hearts beyond even Him, I can tell you?"

"I daresay," Jonathan said dryly. "Come with me."

He led him to the hotel and found Henry Drear in his woodshed making corn whisky for the winter.

"Here's our preacher," he told him.

Henry stared and clapped the hunched shoulders halfway between his own waist and shoulders.

"Well, suds!" he cried. "How'd you come by him?"

"God driven," the little man said simply.

Henry's jaw dropped. "Well, I seen 'em all kinds," he said, and added his usual greeting to anyone who passed. "Come in and eat."

The strange little man married them expertly enough. He had a book in a torn cloth cover, but he did not read from it. Under the big silver bell he was grotesque.

"I learned the burial service and the marriage and birth by heart," he told Jonathan as he stood waiting for the ceremony to begin. "I was ready then, I figgered, for anything people wanted."

"Dearly beloved, we are gathered together—" He had a sweet and plaintive voice, as reedy and clear as a wild bird's.

Jonathan watched him, listened to him, and made his responses and heard Katie's. Her voice squeaked with earnestness when she said, "I do," and she put up her right hand and coughed behind it the polite two-syllabled cough that women make for apology.

He was being married, for better, for worse, as long as he lived, never to part from Katie until death parted them. But they were young, and life was long ahead. There was no use in thinking about death now except that it was the far end to any life.

"I pronounce you man and wife."

He turned with Katie's hand heavy on his arm. The rooms were bright with autumn flowers, and October sunshine poured into the uncurtained windows. It fell upon these patient people of Median, hard-working and good, and not one of them beautiful. He went silently and carefully down the aisle toward the door. He was one of them now. He had married himself into them, flesh to flesh and spirit to spirit.

At the door they stood and waited. Jim White fiddled the wedding march madly, and the people rose and came forward to pour out good wishes and shouts and congratulations and cheers.

"Eats is ready upstairs!" Lew bellowed, and upstairs they went, Jonathan and Katie leading the way, and behind them Ruth and Maggie, and Sue with Mary, her eyes enormous, clinging to her. That small creature, growing slowly and painfully through her first year, could always be quieted if Sue held her.

Laughter and loud good-natured talk and the clatter of children filled the rooms and streamed out upon the silent prairie. Jonathan went here and there seeing that all had food, pressing sandwiches and cake upon everyone. Ice cream was Lew's share, and he was not content until every saucer had been filled twice. There was no haste for any to be gone. The evenings were long and the hour set purposely early. And Jonathan and Katie were going nowhere except to step into the new house next door. He had no wish to travel with school so near its opening, and Katie was eager for the house.

"If we went anywhere I'd be thinkin' about the things waitin' to be done here," she had told Jonathan.

So he loitered at his own wedding and listened, smiling, to Lew and Henry telling stories to each other for the benefit of the newcomers.

" 'Member that young feller walked in one day with his scalp pulled down over his eyes?" Lew asked Henry. "Got away from Indians. Well, Jim White took a string off his fiddle and sewed it back again and feller got well again, 'cept he stayed crazy. Had to ship him back East to his folks."

"Indians was bad them days," Henry said gravely.

Samuel Hasty, always on the outskirts of any group of men, lifted his thin voice. "When I come here in sixty-five—"

"In sixty-three"—Henry's roar took the words and drowned him with them—"I was in Lawrence, and by Jiminy I slid out the night before with a bunch of wild horses I was drivin' east

and next day Quantrill and his gang bust on the town—left hundreds of people dead in the streets."

Jonathan found his pupils one by one and spoke a word to them and had his reward in Mrs. Drear's good-by.

"Seems as if the whole of Median got married and not just you and Katie," she said, leaning her head to his ear.

They lingered. There were so few times for merrymaking that when one came they held it as long as they could. There was no haste in Jonathan, either, only stillness. He stood listening, joining in the talk and forgetting a good deal that Katie was his wife and this their wedding day. Once, having forgotten, he saw her stiff young figure without thinking until he happened to see upon her finger the new wedding ring he had put there. He had chosen it from a dozen or so that Lew kept in stock for travelers west who met and married on the way.

My wife? he thought.

It would take time.

When they were gone at last and only he and Katie left, they closed the windows and went downstairs. Katie looked around the disordered rooms.

"This'll take a lot of cleaning," she said soberly.

"Don't think of it now," he said. "There'll be time tomorrow."

Tomorrow! There was the night between. But this was only Katie. She stood waiting for him, and he put her hand on his arm. She kept it there inert, and he thought again of that strange lack of relation between the quick energy of her body and her large, heavy hand. But he put his own hand over hers loyally, and together they walked across the little space to their house.

The sun had set with all the colors of the autumn in the sky. The prairie was dark and smooth, deep strokes of purple and black until gold edged the horizon. In the new house the shades were up, and Ruth had lit every light. She was watching for them and opened the door as they came. Mary was in her arms and Maggie at her side. "Welcome home," she said shyly. She had spent much thought about this moment and feared it. It's only natural they'd like to be coming home alone, she had thought. If it had been only herself, she could have gone back with Jamie. But there were the two small ones.

If there was any wish that they were not there, neither Katie nor Jonathan showed it. "Thanks, Ruthie," Jonathan said, and took Mary into his arms as he did every evening when he came home, and Maggie clasped his leg and laughed when he scuffled her along as he walked.

Katie came in briskly and shut the door. "It's cold," she said. "I wouldn't be surprised if there's frost tonight."

It was like any other evening, except that they were in the new house and everything was being done in a first-time sort of way. It was more like a house moving than a marriage night. After supper in the new kitchen he went to the door of the second bedroom and saw Maggie and Mary tucked into bed, Mary in her crib that he had painted a nice blue, and Maggie on a pallet.

"I shall get a bed for Maggie soon," he said, bending to kiss her good night.

"A big high bed," Maggie cried.

"For you to fall out of?" Katie said. "No, a little low bed."

"Maggie's a big girl," Jonathan said gently, seeing Maggie's full lips pout.

He kept Ruth with them without knowing he was doing so, talking of their mother and Clyde.

"We must write Dad about the new house," he said. He kept thinking about his mother and father and how once he had hated the night and how he had distrusted it because night took his mother away into a world he did not know.

Night lay ahead of him now. There was no postponing it. Ruth slipped away from them, and he and Katie were alone. Without looking at her, he wound the clock and put the ashes over the fire. She rose, and then he did look at her and saw what he had never seen before, fear cold in her eyes. Instantly pity made him calm.

"You mustn't be afraid of me, Katie," he said. "Nothing is changed, I'm what you've always known, my—my dear."

She could not speak, and he took her shoulders and turned her toward the door.

"You go in," he said. "I'll stay here for a bit."

He sat down then alone and thought to himself that he wished he smoked a pipe, though he had never felt the need of such a thing before. The house was very quiet—his home, of which he was now the head, and Katie was his wife. And then he was terrified. There was no stir in him of passion.

Now he knew why he was in Katie's debt and would be as long as he lived.

I've done a fearful thing to her, he thought heavily. I've married her without loving her. A mist of tenderness rose in his heart, and pity strengthened him again. He rose and blew out the coal-oil lamp and went resolutely toward the room where she waited. At least he could behave so she would never know, and at least she need never be afraid that he would be cruel to her because of love too strong.

She was in bed when he came in, her pale brown hair braided in two braids as she used to wear it. She looked exactly as she always had, and for a moment he felt the night impossible. But he undressed doggedly and put out the light and climbed into the big bed that had been her parents' wedding present. They lay awake, talking in fragments of one thing and another, each afraid of what they could not say.

"Jonathan, did you lock the door?"

"Yes."

And he, "Hush—is that the wind rising?"

And she, "If it is, there won't be frost."

But sometime in the night, he could not have told the hour, his virgin body woke to hers of its own accord and separate from himself, and so the thing he feared was done.

Out of that involuntary union his marriage took its shape. It was a wordless marriage. The fountain of his spirit was sealed. He marveled sometimes, remembering how in his love for Judy words had poured out of him, unconscious, as poetry. When he had Judy in his arms he had not been able to keep from murmuring as he caressed her. It was as though she had unstopped all his sources and his whole soul ran fluid in her presence, like silver made molten.

But there was only silence between him and Katie except when they spoke of his work and of their daily living. She could be voluble enough over a weasel in the henhouse or a snake under the porch, and she could talk endlessly, he thought sometimes when he was tired, over a rag of gossip in the town. But when they were alone together, when in the night the involuntary union took its place and became spare habit, she was silent and he. Their life together was scarcely different, he thought as time went on, from what it had been before they were married, except that Katie never went away from his house.

They were three years childless and then Katie conceived her first child. She kept her silence, in the reticent way of all prairie women, until she could not keep it any longer. Then, blushing her furious spots of red upon her cheekbones and her neck, she told him.

"Maw says I'm in the family way, Jonathan."

She blurted it out one night in spring when he sat figuring his school accounts and she sat mending. He looked up, not comprehending at first.

"What—Katie, you mean—" he stammered, and then he too began to blush. He felt the hot blood pour up from his body and drench the very roots of his hair. "Well," he said, and put down his pencil.

The silence fell on them again. He felt as though he had been given a blow, and familiar tenderness came creeping into his heart. It seemed piteous that a woman should bear a child to a man who did not love her, and at this moment his debt to Katie began to pile into a mountain before his eyes.

"My dear," he said gently, but not rising and not going to her, "I'd rather have a child than anything on earth."

She looked at him in her awkward shyness, and he thought he saw tears in her eyes. She put down her mending on her lap. "I pray it'll be a boy," she said in a low voice.

"Boy or girl is welcome," Jonathan said. He could figure no more that night, and he put the books away and sat watching her while she finished her mending, and then he saw his watching made her ill at ease and so he rose and wound the clock and set the house ready for the night.

The days went on, and their silence did not break. When the first deep snow fell in December, Katie laid herself down in her bed early one evening and before midnight his son was born. He did not go in until Sue Parry called him.

"The little child is bawn," Sue said softly. "It's a boy, suh." He had not gone in because he knew that Katie would have been shy before him. But now he rose and in dignity Sue stood and waited for him to pass her into the bedroom.

There in Katie's arm he saw a small form, a round black head, and he bent over it. For the moment he forgot her. He was so absorbed in this new being, his, as no other being in the world could be his, he thought with a rush of painful joy. He had his own at last.

Then he saw Katie's face, turned to look at him, and the heart in his breast gave a great and separate heave. One other could have been more his own—his child and Judy's. Had her flesh and his mingled, his fruit would have been perfected. He knew one instant of pure agony. He waited for it to pass, then he touched his boy's head.

"Thank you, Katie," he said.

He was surprised to see her little hazel eyes fill with tears. "You're tired, my dear," he said gently.

But she shook her head. "It's not that," she whispered.

"Then what?" he urged her. Her hand lay loosely on her breast, and he made himself take it and hold it. "What, my dear?" he asked again.

But she shook her head a little. "I don't know," she faltered. "It's me ought to thank you, Jonathan."

When his daughter was born two years later, he told himself that he would have no more children. His son he had named Jonathan, and Katie named their daughter Lula after her own mother. But he did not tell Katie that he would have no more children. The silence between them was never broken.

Part Three

✦ 30 ✦

"RUTH, THERE'S A TRAMP COMING IN THE GATE."

Maggie, a plump, pink-faced girl of fifteen, put down the dish she was drying and tiptoed to the window of the kitchen, her red braids bobbing up and down her back, and peeped out from behind the curtain. "He's got a big black beard," she whispered.

"Oh, dear," Ruth cried under her breath.

There were many tramps in this year of 1881. It had not rained well for two years, and from the western half of the state there trickled through Median a stream of ruined men. Those with families went on; but solitary men lingered until the town's patience was gone.

"Median ain't no Chicago," Lew Merridy grumbled. "We've got to scratch our livin' off the country, too, rain or no rain."

"I wish Katie wasn't over at the store," Ruth said. All her old timidity of the plains trembled in her. She thought of the two children upstairs whom Katie had left to her care while she went to help in the store. Lew had had a stroke last year, and Katie spent many of her afternoons there.

"Anyways, I wish she'd taken little Jonnie and Lula," she said.

"He's coming right to the door," Maggie cried.

Ruth's ready fear mastered her. "Run over to the school-house by the front door and tell Jonathan to come right over," she whispered. "I'll lock the door quiet-like."

She gave Maggie a push and slipped to the door and noiselessly turned the key. Then she stood with her back to the door. If the tramp looked in at the window he could not see her, and the kitchen would be empty. She stood there, and between her shoulder blades she felt the thump upon the wooden door of a powerful hand. Thus she was standing, dishcloth in hand, when Jonathan hurried in.

"Whatever—" he began.

"It's a tramp, a big one!" she whispered.

"Well, he can't eat you," Jonathan said shortly. "Move away from the door, there's a good girl."

He could never be impatient with Ruth's terrors because they had their beginnings in the years she had shared too young with their mother. Ruth's fears were his mother's fears, and sometimes it seemed to him he could see his mother over again in this girl's too-gentle face. But Ruth had not the final power of desperation that had made Mary strong. When no help came, Ruth was helpless against her own fears. Why else did she hesitate so long over marrying good young Matthew Cobb! She was afraid of marriage because she had seen marriage too close in that dugout on the western plains. It was one of his problems, and he thought of it every time he saw her, because it had somehow to be settled. Matthew was continually at him.

He pulled at the door. "Why, whatever—"

"I locked it," she said breathlessly.

He turned the key. "Really, Ruthie, it's very inconvenient for me. My history class is sitting there—" He threw the door open in spite of himself with impatience. There was no need to be afraid of these men wandering into Median and out again. If it would ever rain they would go back to being good farmers. "Good day," he said in a firm voice.

A burly bearded man stood there in dust-colored garments, his feet wrapped in rags and a bundle under his arm.

"Hello, Jonathan," he said. "You haven't forgot your dad, I reckon."

Jonathan stared at him. Clyde had grown heavier, hairier, browner. But his lips were as red as ever in his dark beard. "No, I haven't forgot," Jonathan said, "though I didn't think to see you like this."

But he had thought of it, as he had seen the stragglers tramping through Median. His father and Jamie, to whom he never wrote any more because they never answered his letters, he had asked himself, where were they in these evil times?

"Come in," he said. "Where's Jamie?"

"He's with an outfit as catches wild horses and breaks 'em in and sends 'em East," Clyde said, shuffling into the kitchen. "It's all right for a young chap, but I'm beyond it, though hearty enough for anything, nearly. Hey, that'll never be you, Ruth!"

He stared at Ruth and then slapped her on the shoulder blades. "Give us a kiss, girl! Eh, you're like somebody I miss sore to this day!"

He put his face close to hers, and Ruth felt the wetness of his full lips in the bristling cushion of his beard and shrank back. But Clyde did not notice it.

"Make me a bit of dinner, there's a good girl. I'm famished." He sat down and put his bundle under the chair and began unwrapping his feet. "I lost the last bit of leather from my soles a while back," he said.

"Couldn't you get a ride?" Jonathan asked. He was still standing. What would he do with this man? The house was too full already. If the times had been better he would have added a room to the house for his two children, but the times were bad and no sign of better unless rain came. Summer had passed and it was midautumn, and still no rain came.

"Folk don't give rides for nothin'," Clyde said. His feet were bare, and he sat up and looked about the kitchen. On the table Ruth was putting a cup and a plate, fork and spoon, bread and butter and sugar. He got up and went over to it and picked up the loaf and pulled at its end.

Instantly all the memory of his childhood rushed over Jonathan. The kitchen at Dentwater the day he came back to find Clyde set on America, pulling the end from an English loaf—here he was, a beggar still!

"You're very fine here, Jonathan," Clyde said. "A little bit of all right this is, I'd say." He stared around the room. "A coal cooking stove, too—and a pump in the kitchen—eh, Mary'd like that. What's the water, spring or deep well?"

"A well," Jonathan said shortly. He hesitated. Could he leave Ruth now or not? "My history class is waiting, Dad," he said, looking at Ruth. She nodded slightly, but he was not sure. "I'll send Maggie for Katie, and she'll be back in a jiffy, while you're eating your food."

"Where's Maggie?" Clyde demanded. "I'd like to see the little tyke."

"She's not little any more," Jonathan said, "and likely she's gone back to afternoon session now."

Clyde sat down at the table. "You go on to your job," he said, loud and cheerful before food. "I'll clean myself a bit after I've et, and be more civilized-like when your missus comes in."

"Very well," Jonathan said. "Make yourself at home," he added.

"I s'all," Clyde retorted. "You don't have to tell me that. Coffee, Ruth. Tea seems wishy-washy stuff to me now."

He was not changed, Jonathan thought grimly. He went out and then looked at his watch. It was too late to go back to his class. The hour was over. He would go for Katie himself. She would be what she always called "put out," but that must be got over with Katie when anything new happened, and once over, she knew what she wanted to do.

He walked quickly the six blocks to his father-in-law's store. They were proper blocks now. The old rotten board-walk was gone, thanks to his own insistence two winters ago, and the square was bordered with a hard-surfaced stuff a fellow named McAdam had invented. It made good streets except for being sticky sometimes under the summer sun. But he always suspected they had not mixed it just right, though he himself had read the directions out loud while the Hasty boys put the stuff together. Abram Hasty took up the road-building business after that and went everywhere in the state. But it was a good thing he had forced the road through Median before this drought set in. He glanced at the cotton-woods in the square as he did every time he passed them. Big as they now were, they would not last much longer. He had tried to persuade people living about them to throw their waste water to save them, but they wanted it all for the parched vegetable gardens at their kitchen doors.

If they die, I shall plant elms and maples and black walnuts, he thought. They're permanent.

He had reached the store now. It was not changed since the first time he saw it, even by a coat of paint. Inside Mr. Cobb was measuring striped calico for a solitary woman customer whom Jonathan did not know. That was how big Median was, he thought, so big there were now people here whom he did not know.

"Where's Katie?" he asked.

Mr. Cobb moved the tobacco cud in his cheek and wiped his chin with the end of his cotton tie. "Inside," he said. "Lew don't feel so good today."

He went on and, opening the door, saw Lew, now enormously fat, lying stretched on the couch, an old crocheted afghan across his stomach. Mrs. Merridy sat rocking sadly at his side, her thin hands clutched across her waist.

"Well," Jonathan said to them both. "Sorry you're not so well, Lew."

"My belly don't give me no rest." There was a rumble under the afghan. "Hear that? It's goin' again—clamorin' for food. And if I put anything like a square meal down, it sets up such a to-do I'm all wore out. I et canned corn for dinner, and this hyere's my result."

"You used to could eat canned corn like a hawg," Mrs. Merridy said sorrowfully.

"Well, I am sorry," Jonathan said. "Where's Katie?"

"In the kitchen bilin' up some pep'mint," Lew said faintly. "She thinks it'll help."

He went into the kitchen and found Katie scrubbing furiously at dish towels while she waited for water to boil. She looked up as Jonathan came in.

"I declare Maw's eyesight is gettin' so poor she can't see whether a thing is clean or not," she said.

It never occurred to her to come out of her world into his. He had always to wait until she had spoken herself out before he began.

"I'm sorry you have to do that much extra," he said gently.

"Well, I do," Katie retorted, "and there'll be more. The store's goin' to ruin. That Cobb's no good except to hand out something over counter when it's ast for. I declare, if he was all that Matthew was made outen, I'd say Ruth'd be sensible to say no."

He stood a minute, dreading to put anything more upon her.

"Anything wrong at home?" she asked. The tone of her voice made the question a dart.

"Well, yes, I suppose you'd call it that. My father's come, Katie."

"Your father!" she echoed. She paused, her hands in the scanty suds. "Why, what for?"

"He looks badly off," Jonathan said apologetically.

"You mean he's come to stay?"

"I don't know—of course he can't live with us, Katie, but—"

"As if there wasn't enough," she cried. She fell to fresh scrubbing. Flecks of soapsuds flew out and spattered his coat, and he wiped them off. "Is he sick?" she demanded.

"No, no, he looks fine," he said quickly. "He hardly looks any older, even. It's surprising."

She did not speak while she rinsed the cloths, emptied the dishpan, and piled them into it. "I'll hang 'em out and be right along."

"I'll help you," he said.

"No, you won't," she retorted. "I don't want people sayin' you've got to help me hang out my folks' clothes. You go on—I'll ketch up."

Long ago he had learned to yield to her on this pride of hers concerning him. She was bitterly independent. His position as principal of the school she made into a fetish, and only second to it was her determination to do her own work without help except what Ruth and Maggie could give her. "The men," as she called Jonathan and little Jonnie, were not to do women's work.

"All right, but let me carry the pan for you." He took it, and they went out of the kitchen door into the back yard, and then she seized it. He hesitated, as he so often did when he was with her, feeling incompleteness between them. "I'm sorry about my dad," he said.

"It can't be helped," she said. It was all she would say, it was what she always said, and he let it pass as he always did and went homeward. It had taken him a long time to realize that the phrase was neither bitter nor unkind, but merely a sign that Katie, after being "put out," was ready to make the best of a situation. He walked quickly through the dry October sunshine, deciding whether he could go back to his work or had better see how his father did. Then it occurred to him that the children might awake and be frightened, as he himself had used to be frightened when he was a little boy and his father rubbed his hairy face into his neck.

"I won't have that," he said sternly, thinking of his little son. He hastened into his house and then heard Clyde's laughter roaring out of the kitchen and went in. Lula was on his knees and Jonathan standing a little off, sucking his thumb!

"And then I says to the old bear, 'It's me as s'all have the honey, my lord, not you.' An' so in I dashes with my stick, an' the bear sees my beard, and thinks, 'Ah, that's a bigger bear nor I be, and mebbe I better go home.' An' that's how I had honey on my buckwheats next day's breakfast."

At the sink Ruth, washing Clyde's dishes, was smiling. No one saw Jonathan, and he tiptoed away. Never in his life could he remember sitting on his father's knee. But he remembered that in his way Clyde had been fond of Artie and Jamie, and that he had fondled Maggie roughly when he felt like play. Maybe he's changed, he thought.

He entered the schoolhouse, wondering for the first time in his life if his mother had made him unjust. Marriage belonged to women, and men had not much part in it, perhaps. He sighed and straightened his shoulders and, sitting down at his desk, he took up the paper he had put down when he left for his class. It was the copy of a bill newly passed by the state legislature making the selling of liquor illegal in the state of Kansas, and it was signed by Evan Bayne, the speaker of the legislature. He never saw that name without the old stir within his breast, and he saw it often now. All these years he had not been face to face with Evan, though they wrote when there was some matter to write about—he when Median had paid off the debt on the schoolhouse, Evan to congratulate him, and he again to urge Evan for his help in putting the branch railroad through Median southwest, and Evan to tell him it was done, and he again to ask Evan's advice about the new post-office building, and Evan to tell him what forms to send for and sign and what more to do; and now the post office stood on the other side of the schoolhouse, a small handsome one-story building of brick. And then last year Evan wrote to him begging him to fight this very prohibition bill he held in his hands now, and he had written to say he would not, though he hated as much as any man to put in government's hands the right to say whether a man could drink or not.

But there were six saloons in Median now, and the hotel was little better than a saloon, and he had his boys in high school to think of, the sons of farmers who came in to Median in wintertime to go to school. If they had been in their own homes, he would not have cared, but they lived where they could to come to his school, and he could not forget that woman who strode into his office last year and flung words at him like fire because in Median her son had learned to drink. He had taken it coldly until at last her anger was put out by her own tears, and she sobbed, "What's the good of learnin' out of books if he's to be a drunkard? And everybody talks so good about you I thought you'd be lookin' after him!"

He had looked after his boys ever since, and he had fought for this bill against Drear, stumping the county to do it all through the summer.

"I believe in man's independence, but I speak for those who are not yet able to be men," his speeches always began. When he and Henry met, he maintained his good humor against Henry's violence.

"Your own nose is too red, Henry," he said gently, "but that's all right with me. It's your nose. What I'm talking against is young Will Healey, tumbling out of your door at sixteen. He's one of my senior pupils."

"If we're goin' to run Median for babies," Henry bellowed, "I'll move out. Why, I can't make money on a hotel without a bar, and you know it, you blasted son of an Englishman! Yes, an' I wish your own father could see you. He liked his liquor as well as anybody."

"So do I—so do I," Jonathan said impatiently, "but tell me how to keep my boys out of your bar!"

The end of it was victory, made a little less sweet than it might have been for Jonathan, because Katie was so heartily for it. He was ashamed of himself, but it was true that he could fight more zealously for a thing if Katie were not on his side. She could not remain friendly with an enemy as he could, nor would she forget. It embarrassed him that still she would not speak to the Drears. He found in himself a perversity he wished to ignore when her very interest pressed her to question him.

"What'd you tell Drear when he said that?"

"I merely said that boys of sixteen were not babies exactly, and that they were important to the future of the town."

"If it had been me, I'd have told him a thing or two. He runs a gamblin' place in that hotel of his."

"Oh, I don't think so, Katie."

"Everybody says so!" This was her eternal retort, and he could not bear it.

"Everybody says so many things."

"Well, I know you never believe what I say, but there's our own children to think of."

"I think of all children," he said patiently. "Long ago I fought against Median being a cattle town because of children. I don't want the saloons here now." But he had felt goaded by her stiff figure, all its angles sharpened as she sat under the lamplight, one of his socks spread over her left hand, her right weaving the long needle in and out. "I don't want saloons, and yet I don't think it's right either that the state should tell a man he can't drink in a free country. It's a thing that has to be thought out, and I'm only doing this as a step toward that final thinking. Saloons have got to get out of Median, and I can't think of any other way to get that done for the time being except by prohibition. But maybe the next thing I'll work on is how a full-grown man can get a drink if he wants it."

She looked at him, her eyes round with indignation. "Shame on you, then!"

"All right, if you say so," he retorted and grinned at himself. It was his eternal retort, and he wondered if she knew it was. But such things they could not talk about, for she was humorless.

Then his irrepressible pity made him remorseful. She was so good a keeper of his home, scrupulously just to his sisters and carefully as kind to them as to her own children. And never had she let him know she felt a lack in him. His faults she might flare against, but then she made amends which he could scarcely endure because that way remorse compelled something beyond the power of his affection, and beyond he could not go.

But it was a marriage. It had become a marriage. Love was a single bond, but marriage could be a web woven of a thousand threads, none strong enough alone, but together as strong in time as love could be. He had come to believe that.

His eyes fell on Evan's name again. Evan's marriage had held by that single golden bond. At any rate, held—he had never heard a whisper of it, good or bad, and here in Median people had forgotten how Evan had found his wife. In his letters Evan always said, "Judy joins me in good wishes to you and yours." But that was all. "Judy joins me—" Evan saw Judy every day. As often as he saw Katie, Evan saw Judy.

"Pshaw!" he said aloud and folded the bill abruptly and thrust it into a drawer.

31

"WHAT SHALL YOU DO NEXT, FATHER?" JONATHAN PUT THIS question openly one day in early spring. Clyde had spent the winter with them, penniless and making no move to earn anything. He slept at night on a pallet in the sitting room and lounged in the kitchen all day if it stormed. Through it all Katie had not once been impatient with him. Clyde liked her tolerantly, never forgetting for a moment that she was plain. Privately he wondered how Jonathan slept with her. 'Tis no wonder I have such a few grandchildren, he thought wickedly. Damn it, I admire Jonathan's stren'th of mind. He longed for someone he could say this to and laugh, but there was nobody in Median who would laugh at Jonathan. He felt a little ironical about his son. Now Jonathan was fixing to build a church.

"I never knew you was religious," he said.

"I'm not much," Jonathan said honestly. "But a church is a good thing in a town."

"Eh, I reckon," Clyde said. "I haven't been in a church since I heard old Clemony in Dentwater. Last preacher I see was a humped little chap out our way as called himself a rainmaker. Give him a try, I did, but there wasn't no rain. Guess he hadn't the trick. Folks say some do make rain, though, with sulphur or somethin', but he only had his prayers."

"A humped little fellow married Katie and me," Jonathan said. "After he was gone I took texts off the trees like apples."

"Same chap, likely," Clyde said. "He was always nailin' up somewhere as how you had to be born again."

He went on talking and talking. He sat in a warm room and talked all winter long.

"I'm waitin' for somethin' to open up," he said.

He waited through the summer, through winter again, until the verge of another spring. Then rains fell and all that had been waiting in the soil sprang early into life, and suddenly one day he was ready to be gone.

"Guess I'll be goin'," he said, "if you can spare me fifty dollars, Jonathan."

"I suppose I can," Jonathan said, not looking at Katie. He drew it out of his small savings and gave it to his father, and with this in the suit of clothes Jonathan had given him, he took the train westward. "It'll be kind of good to see my own land again," he told them. "Well, good-by, all."

Clyde had trimmed his beard and parted it in the middle and pulled his hat over his dark eyes and let a red scarf Ruth had given him for Christmas fly at his throat. He waved to them gaily from the platform. He looked ten years younger than when he came—a young man still, Jonathan thought with disgust.

That night the house seemed full of room without his father's restless presence.

"A miracle you've been to that man, Katie," Jonathan said that night. "Don't think I haven't seen it all these months or that I haven't wondered at your goodness." He was somewhat dashed by her reply.

"Oh, I don't know, there's something about him I kind of like!"

But a strange good thing came out of Clyde's stay. Some terror went out of Ruth forever. She had been afraid of her father in memory for years because of the quarrels he had made in those nights upon the prairie, when she lay listening, because she could not help it, on the pallet beyond the blanket that curtained her parents' bed.

"Give over, do!" she could hear her mother's sharp whisper.

"Eh, what's the matter now? It's a headick or bellyache or somethin' every night—a sore toe, maybe, or a finger boil now."

"Be quiet, Clyde! You'll wake the children."

"Let 'em wake!"

"Clyde, for shame; what'll Ruth think?"

"She'll know, soon enough!"

But Clyde alone she grew used to through these months and no longer feared. He teased her and grumbled at her, and she came to mind neither.

"Eh, your hair's pretty, too, like hers was!"

"But Mother's hair was fair, Father, and mine's dark."

"Don't tell me what her hair was, for I know. I've wrapped them yellow braids of hers around my neck on a cold night like a muffler. When we was married she could sit in her hair like a cloak, and if I'd knew she was goin' to die with a child of mine I'd ha' let myself burn up before one of you was born, but a man don't think of it at the time."

She did not insist on what she knew, that her mother's hair had been as fair as Jonathan's, and soft and straight like his. Instead she laughed at him, and he made constant fun of her shyness with Matthew. When on Sunday afternoon Matthew came to see her, Clyde would open the door himself.

"Come in, lad! She's been waitin' for you all day. Couldn't eat no dinner, our Ruthie couldn't, and she's got on her best dress."

By now Ruth could not be found. Then he would shout at Matthew, "Sit down and wait, I'll find her!" He stormed through the tiny house, searching under beds and through closets, and from somewhere pulled Ruth out, half-crying and half-laughing, and pushed her by the shoulders and then shot her into the sitting room.

"There she is, lad!" he roared and banged the door upon them.

"You're terrible," Katie had said. But she had laughed, too.

And Jonathan, who could never have done the thing himself, knew nevertheless that it was what these two shy creatures needed. Behind that closed door Ruth would be blushing and wiping away tears and trying to laugh, and Matthew would have his chance.

He was not surprised when, the Sunday night after Clyde's going, Matthew came out of the sitting room to where he and Katie sat in the kitchen, his shoulders very straight.

"Mr. Goodliffe, sir, if you are willing, Ruth says she will have me."

Jonathan looked up from his paper and let his eyes twinkle.

"I've been willing all along, Matthew," he said. And then he rose and went into the sitting room to find Ruth alone, twisting a curl of her hair around her finger.

"Well, Ruth!" He kissed her crimson cheek. It was hot under his cool lips. "I'm glad you've come to this. It's the right thing."

"Do you really think so, Jonathan?" she whispered.

"Sure of it," he said. "Matt's a fine gentle chap, and he'll be good to you, and you to him."

To Katie that night he said, "If my old dad did this, I'll forgive him part of the nuisance he's been to you in the house—and to me always. A queer thing it took him to do it, though."

He put out his hand for hers in a gesture he did not often make. She quivered a little whenever he did it.

"There's something in him that makes folks easy-like," she said, and longed to tell Jonathan that she loved him. But between them those words had never passed.

Clyde trudged over the land, newly green, his big bundle on his back. The Santa Fe railroad came within twenty miles of his claim, and he got off at Garden City, a string of one-story houses along a wide unpaved street. He left it behind in a few minutes and tramped to the southwest. He was full of sleep and good food and restlessness and impatience. All of the old strength was in his blood again.

Everywhere over the land the firm, strong spears of buffalo grass were pushing up through last year's sod. The long drought was over. The earth was damp beneath his feet. It would have been mud had not the sod held it firm under its ancient roots. The sky was blue, but there were great white clouds rolling away to the Rocky Mountains. He had never seen the mountains, but they were there all the same. Some day he'd go to them, maybe. If farmers came cutting up the sod and planting their diddling crops, he'd go on West.

He yawned at the midday sun after he had eaten the bread and salt meat he had bought in Garden City, and then he lay down and slept for an hour. The warmth, the smell of the young grass, and the wet earth stirred him awake. He did not open his eyes at once. His blood rose uncomfortably.

Oh, I s'all have to get married again, maybe, he thought. When Mary died he swore marriage was a curse to man. But

later it had come to him that not all women were like Mary.
There were women who cared for men and not for whether
they had babies or not. If a man had one of them in his bed
every night, things would be different. He climbed slowly to
his feet, unable to bear the physical weight of his desire.

"There's no good teasing myself with thinkin'," he muttered. He shouldered his bundle again and went the eight
miles left. But the sun beat upon him warmly, and the stillness
could not take his mind off his need. He grew peevish with
himself.

Dang me if I couldn't have stayed in the town and come
home tomorrow if I'd thought of this, he thought angrily. He
had gone months in Jonathan's home with no violent need.
Everything there had made him think of Mary, and since she
had died he had thought of her as an angel and desire for her
was gone. Or maybe, he thought, it was the books in Jonathan's home. He never liked books about. They cooled him
down and made him feel ignorant. But here there was nothing, only him between earth and sky.

He plodded along angrily, aware of his body's need, and so
came to his own sod house. It looked like a lump of earth in
the midst of the green prairie, but it was still standing in spite
of two winters and rain. He hastened to it, and to his
indignation he saw the door was open.

"What son of a bitch has settled hisself here while I've been
gone?" he yelled. He threw down his bundle and tore off his
coat and made for the door.

Someone was standing at the stove where Mary used to
stand. It was a woman with a crop of red hair down her back.
She turned as he charged in.

"Hello, Clyde," she said.

He dropped his flailing arms, and his breath caught in his
lungs.

"Jennet! It's never you!"

"Why not?" she said. A spoon was in her hand, and she
licked it with the end of her red tongue. There was a great
bruise over her left eye. "I've been here off and on all winter.
Hope you don't mind."

She was not nearly as beautiful as once she had been. Her
face was pallid and her hair burned dry and carroty. Her
green eyes were still jewel-like, but the lids were tired. She put
the spoon back into the stew she was cooking and began to

braid her hair. She laughed a single hoarse note. "If I'd of known you was comin' I'd of cleaned myself up—maybe."

He was so dazed with the opportuneness of her presence that his head whirled. "I don't know anything as I'd rather have come home to than you, Jennet."

"You can make it permanent, if you want." She turned her back on him while he took this in.

"The Englishman'd split my head," he said.

"Reckon not." Her back was to him still. "I've left him."

"For good?"

She gave her short laugh. "For marriage," she said. "Is it the same?"

His throat was thick. " 'Twould be with me, Jennet."

"All right," she said indifferently. "But nothing don't begin before."

But in the night she yielded to him suddenly, and he cried out with happiness.

" 'Twill be fun to marry one like you," he panted.

Before the young minister Jonathan stood with Ruth clinging to his arm as she made her marriage promises. The wedding had waited through the spring until June before a minister stopped in Median. He was a young missionary on his way westward to the Indians.

But the long wait had determined Jonathan that the church must be next in Median. Upon the map he and Evan had once made together he had drawn a firm pencil line through schoolhouse and post office. These were done. He had the choice now between courthouse and church next. If the big county were to be divided, as there was clamor for, Median might be the new county seat. Courthouse, maybe, then should come first. Meanwhile they could go on having church in these two schoolrooms where he and Katie had been married, too.

But he liked this Paul Graham. There was none of Joel's fanaticism in his quiet gray eyes. He looked rugged and good. And since Jonathan never thought of anything near Judy without thinking of her, he wondered as he often had before, in some sad secret abstraction, whether Joel had put into Judy some of the shifting sand of his being.

Katie was gray rock, and Judy silver sand. He still saw Judy more clearly bright than he saw anyone. Katie's face, which he saw every day, was a blur when he thought of Judy's face, which he never saw and doubtless would never see again. He dragged himself out of the slough of memory back to this moment of another marriage.

Just now the young minister's face was flushed. This was his first wedding, he had told Jonathan, and he stammered over the words until Ruth was suddenly set at ease. He minds as much as Matthew and me do, she thought.

Matthew, she now knew, was even more shy than she. The discovery had given her a sedate pleasure, and she blamed herself at heart for what she called to herself her dilly-dally. Now, as Paul Graham pronounced the final words, she slipped her left hand from Jonathan's arm and her right into Matthew's and squeezed it gently. He had bought his farm, though it was heavy with mortgage, and had built a two-room house upon it, and they would go there tonight. Sue had put white organdie curtains in the windows for a wedding present.

The Parry family kept almost out of sight until something needed to be done, and then they were there. That was because Jonathan kept sending their letters for them to Beaumont in France. Jonathan did things for everybody. People came to him about their children from all over the county, and in Median nothing was done without him. He had been better to Ruth than anybody and had made his home hers. She thought she ought to take Mary with her anyway, but he was not willing.

"You'll have your own children," he said in his dry quiet voice.

Martha Cobb played the wedding march on the school organ, and Ruth stepped down the aisle. She felt the beat of her old shyness creep up out of her bosom as she faced the people. There were so many people in Median when they all came together.

"I shall miss you, Ruth, my dear," Jonathan had said, but he did not. Whatever Ruth had been, she had by her very presence kept Maggie a child. Now, without presage, or so it seemed to Jonathan, Maggie from being a fat little girl rose up from her bed one morning a plump young woman whose solid flesh had properly distributed itself into rounded hips and breasts and full white arms. By night, or so it seemed to him, as he looked back, every male under twenty-five in the county had known it.

For the first time there was quarreling between the women in his home, Katie scolding Maggie as she scolded all of them, but Maggie would have no more of it. Jonathan was abstracted from the discord because he believed it of no importance when women quarreled, and more because he had made up his mind that Median must be the new county seat. This decision he had come to because he wanted order in the new county, and because Median shopkeepers, headed by Lew and Henry, the old-timers, wanted business.

"And don't you look to gettin' the county by any of your peaceable means, Jonathan," Henry Drear said sternly. "Women ain't gonna be no use here. I'm sendin' East for two dozen rifles on my own hook. We'll need 'em sure. I know that there town of Ashbee."

"I'll get the money for the courthouse if you'll get the election for Median," Jonathan said.

To Paul Graham he put the matter plainly. "Here's Median wanting a church and a courthouse. Our souls need the church and our pockets the courthouse. Give us time and we'll have both, but sermons'll go down better if our pockets are fuller, especially after the drought. But I want you to stay here and hold down our souls till we're the county seat."

"But I volunteered for the Indians," Paul said. He saw in Jonathan a slender, shabby man who was neither young nor old, because he had never been young and would never be old. Jonathan was energy made human, a dogged power of a man who had Median by the nose.

"I never took much stock in Indians," he now said. "It was a good sensible thing to get them herded together so they can be taken care of. Every human deserves to live once he's born. But so long as there's the souls of folk like we've got in Median, it's folly to bother about Indians. Why, these people here are what the country's made of!"

"God sent me to the heathen," Paul said.

"Indians aren't solid heathen," Jonathan retorted. "They're what's left of something that's gone. Save 'em, of course, if there's enough salvation to go around, but why shouldn't salvation come first to us? You can preach in the schoolhouse, and when we get the courthouse, I'll put my mind next to the church."

"Median's a city whose maker and builder is you, not God," Paul said, his smile faint.

"When I ask you, I'm asking God to help," Jonathan retorted.

In the midst of all this to go home and find Katie and Maggie in quarrel was sore on his patience. He lay at Katie's side at night listening to her story of the day.

"I want we should get Maggie married as soon as we can. She's not like Ruth. She's like your old goat of a father, and her mind's full of nothing but men, though she ain't seventeen yet. And the way she answers me back—I slapped her face today, Jonathan, she'll tell you I did, and I want you should know how it was. Let her say what she wants, it was like this. I told her to clean up her bedroom. She don't do a thing she don't have to. Well, she didn't, and I did it myself, and there was a letter laying on the bureau, open. I didn't read it, but I saw the first page. She's going out at night from her window down to the drugstore, after she says she's in bed."

"She can't come to much danger in the drugstore," Jonathan said mildly. The new drugstore was kept by a Methodist from Iowa.

"But it's night!" Katie cried.

"Oh, all right, my dear," Jonathan said, sighing. There was magic in the night for some, maybe. "I'll speak to Maggie."

He spoke to her the next day, calling her into his school-room office, as he would any pupil who needed it.

"Sit down, Maggie," he said. He looked at her as he would at another girl and saw her young body bursting out of its faded gingham dress. "Seems to me you need a new dress, child," he said.

Her impetuous face brightened at every point, the blue eyes bluer, the full lips parting, her red hair seeming to crinkle. She had hair strangely alive to the rest of her being.

"Can I, Jonathan? I need 'em something terrible. I haven't gained weight, but I've just—*grown!*" She gestured toward her breast, and he saw a bright scarlet flying up her neck.

"You mustn't wear that one any more, anyway," he said.

"You've come to a place, Maggie, my dear, when you must be careful how you show yourself—that is, if you want to catch the right sort of man. And it's no good pretending you don't, for what every woman is set upon in her heart is how to find the man she'll marry, and every man is thinking about her whom he will—love. Don't behave so he can't see you when he looks at you because you've made yourself like somebody else."

Maggie's full young breasts began to heave, and her bright blue eyes were full of warm quick tears. She had not prepared herself for gentleness after what she well knew had been her impudence to Katie. But how could she explain the brimming of her being these days? Her veins were too full; she could not keep her voice low or her laughter soft. And she was alternately excited and frightened by the changes in her body which she wanted to hide and yet at other times to flaunt without knowing why.

"Katie'll think it a lot of trouble to fix me new dresses, though," she said.

"Katie has a lot to do," Jonathan said sternly. "She cleaned your room for you yesterday when you should have done it. There's no reason why she should make your dresses any more. Go to the store and pick out your cloth for two dresses and tell Lew I'll pay for it. Then after school take the stuff over to Parry's and tell Sue I sent you to be taught how to make them. Now go along and don't let Katie clean your room again."

"All right, Jonathan." She hesitated a moment as to whether she would not go over to him and kiss him. She longed to pour out her strong affections whenever she could. But she had never kissed her brother or seen him kiss anyone. He was familiar to her as no one in the world was so that she gave him not a thought, taking his presence and his absence equally for granted. Now, with the intensity with which she saw everything these days, she saw him, a quiet reserved man, whose hair and skin were sunburned and wind-bitten to the color of sand. Only his eyes were vivid. She longed to speak to him, to say something to show him how different she was now from the fat troublesome child she had always been. But she did not know how to begin, and then he glanced up at her from under his sandy brows and said in his decisive schoolmaster's voice, "That'll do now, Maggie."

"Everybody obeys my brother Jonathan," Maggie said proudly. She was having a chattering good time with Sue, who said little and listened well. The excitement of the green-and-red checked gingham skirt pinned to her knee flew to her tongue. But there was more than the new dresses. Yesterday when she went into the store a strange thing happened. She had a letter. Never in her life had she received a letter, and now she could not believe it.

"Come yesterday," Lew had said. He was well. "I thought I'd give it to Katie or somethin', but they don't keer a crumb about me onless I'm about to die. Got to have my ol' bellyache to get my family together these days."

"I'll take my letter," Maggie said and put it in her pocket. She could scarcely choose her goods for thinking of it, and when she had the stuff measured and folded under her arm, she walked away from the town toward the prairie, her hand in her pocket on the letter. When she was well away she sat down beside the dusty road and took out the letter. A big loose handwriting sprawled her name across it. She tore it open and read it slowly. It was from someone she had never heard of, a George Tenney.

DEAR MAGGIE:

You will be surprised to get a word from me as you will hardly rember me but ask your brother Jonathan does he rember George Tenney used to giv you brekfeast on the ship. Well Maggie now you are grown up nearly. I had it hard at first but struck good luck a year gone and am in clover. So thought of little Maggie I used to know. Is your hair still red I will come to see for myself one of these days soon.

Yours resp'flly,
GEORGE TENNEY

But she had had no chance to be alone with Jonathan. He was in one of his "jobs," as she called it. This one was to make Median a county seat. When he came home at night he told Katie what was happening, and they talked long after she had gone to bed. She lay with her letter under her pillow. She had once got up in the night, sleepless with moonlight and, putting on her clothes, crawled out of the window and gone to Hale's drugstore. It had seemed exciting, though no one was there except Mr. Hale himself, surprised to see her. While he mixed her a strawberry soda he said, "Does your brother know you're out, Maggie?"

She had lied and said something about studying late. When three men came in and banged their fists down for root beer, he had kept his eyes on her and at last he said, "You git along, now, Maggie. It's late."

But she did not need to crawl out of the window any more now. The letter under her pillow was enough.

Sue was ironing the sleeves of the dress with a potlike iron full of hot coals.

"I don't know about eve'body," Sue said. "I know I obey him on account of I can't pay back what he did for Beaumont."

"Who's Beaumont?"

"Beaumont's my son."

Sue set the iron on the stove and went to a bureau and opened the top drawer and brought out a package wrapped in white paper. She took from it a photograph of a young and foreign-looking man in a frock coat, with a narrow moustache curled upward. His hands, even in the picture strong and supple, clasped hat, white gloves, and a thin walking stick. In the buttonhole of the coat was a white flower.

"This is Beaumont," she said. "He's in Paris, France."

"What's he doing there?" Maggie took the photograph into her thimbled hand and stared at it. The young man scarcely looked black at all.

"He's goin' to be a brain surgeon. Not goin' to do anything else but just brains."

"He don't look like any of you," Maggie said, still staring.

"He ain't," Sue said. She put the photograph back into its papers, into the drawer, and went back to her iron. She wet her fingers and touched it and when it hissed she began ironing.

"Is he coming back here?" Maggie asked.

"I don't want he should ever come back," Sue said quietly.

"Then will you go over there?"

"I reckon I cain't."

"But you'll never see him again!" Maggie's blunt voice put boldly into being what Sue knew but had never spoken.

"I reckon not," she said.

Maggie sat silent for a few minutes. How would anybody behave to a man who looked like that when you knew he was only one of the Parrys? The Parry children had finished the grades in school, but then they had gone to work. Melissa hired out, and Pete helped his father, and next year Gem would stop school.

"I guess I better go home," Maggie said. Her letter crackled in her bosom as she stooped to pick up threads from Sue's rag rug. She knew every word of it, but she longed to read it again. "I'll be back tomorrow right after school," she said joyously. If he was coming any day, she must have a dress made and ready.

🦋 32 🦋

JONATHAN, THE SCHOOL CLOSED FOR SUMMER, TURNED heartily to the next work for Median. An idle day was beyond his endurance. His life was good enough when he came home at night after a day's work. But the small house was a cage when he did not get away from it. Katie's voice, not unpleasant in itself, carried a peculiar vibrating penetration that pierced wall and door so that every room was full of her presence. Without knowing, he was compelled to escape it.

From the empty schoolhouse he drew together the web of affairs in Median. Young Graham had gone to his Indians for a year of trial. That had been his compromise with Jonathan.

"Suits me just as well," Jonathan had said. "It gives me a year to get this county-seat business out of the way."

Actually he was resolved to do it in this summer. He set tasks for himself of heroic size and lashed himself to finish them.

Today, the third of July, the men he knew best were coming in to plan the campaign—Lew and Henry and the three Hasty men, Samuel and his two sons, Jim White and his eldest son Frank, and he had asked Matthew to come in if he could leave. They came one by one, these men whose faces were better known to him than his own—the old-timers, he thought, pushing chairs forward for them. They were solemnly silent before the idea of a meeting, talking with quieted voices of crops.

"Folks say there's grasshoppers to the west—"

"I 'member the hoppers in seventy-four, et up the fence posts even, and out in the cornfields the noise was like cattle chewin'. And I picked up a fork, I 'member, out in the barn, and they'd chawed the handle too rough to hold. But still the next year Kansas apples got a gold medal in Philadelphy."

"I was back near Salina then. Poor man's diggin's, it was."

They were waiting for Jonathan. He sat at his desk before his papers. He shot up his sandy brows at them.

"Well, folks, we better begin. First question maybe is where's the county line to be drawn. Shall it go thirty miles west of Median and take in Hyman, or do we let Ashbee have that?"

Matthew came in, but nobody spoke while they considered the map Jonathan held up.

"If we let Hyman go, Median'll be plumb in the center of the new county," Jonathan said.

Matthew coughed, but nobody paid him any heed. "I don't know as it means anything," he said mildly, "but my farm's just the other side of Hyman. Yestiddy I was ridin' after a colt that broke loose, and about five miles off I found him in a sinkhole—leg broke. But there was water in the hole, and the water was slimed with oil. Leastways it looked like oil." His voice sank into silence. The room was full of silence. A cicada outside the window sawed its two notes suddenly and ended in a long wheeze before anyone spoke.

"Anyone else know?" Jonathan asked.

"Not a soul," Matthew said.

Oil! The men looked at each other, their faces carefully skeptical.

"Couldn't have been planted, could it?" Henry Drear's voice was husky.

"I don't see how," Matthew said. "Besides, nobody's ever said a word. The man that owns the land himself don't know what's in that sinkhole."

"Wasn't he there to help you get the colt out?" Samuel Hasty asked. His meager little mouth worked.

"No, he wasn't at home yestiddy, his wife said. I borried some rope from her and got down in and roped the critter and crawled out again and hauled him out. 'Tain't but a young colt."

"Reckon we better draw the line west of Hyman," Lew said.

"The question is how far west?" Jonathan said. "Does the oil run east or west? We might cut the best part off, whatever we do."

"Put it ten miles west," Henry said.

"Put it twenty-five," Lew rejoined.

Jonathan was studying the map. "The river runs thirty miles west and south. Likely it's the boundary. Let's say thirty miles."

He glanced about a circle of nodding heads, and slowly he drew a firm pencil line. Then he put down the pencil and lifted his head.

"The next subject for discussion is the manner in which votes shall be collected as between Ashbee and Median."

Henry Drear grunted. "Jonathan, you let me tend to the vote-gettin'. Folks take their votes serious. It's a life-and-death business. You set the day, and I'll git me a gang and round 'em up."

Jonathan frowned impatiently. "I don't want Median votes got like that. Nobody'll be satisfied, and there's no luck to a thing when nothing but anger comes of it. Median's a decent place, and it's more important to have it so than to get the county seat."

Henry's chair came down on the floor. "If the world was half saints and half sinners, I would agree to that, Jonathan. But it ain't. It's full of sin, and I ain't pertendin' I'm not one of the sinners. I ain't converted. I never was baptized. I go to gospel meetin's, but I don't convert. I come out like I went in. You let me handle this-hyere votin'."

"What's the vote here?" Jonathan's quiet voice was steely with stubbornness.

Men looked at each other.

"I'm all for peace if you can get away with it," Lew said. "But I'd say keep the guns handy."

"My idea, too," Samuel agreed.

Jonathan waited. No one else spoke. After a moment he went on, "The next question is the date of the election. Ashbee wants it a month from today."

He waited again. The men were full of their own thoughts.

"Let 'em have what they want there, since they ain't gonna git nothin' more," Henry said. He rose as he spoke and pushed back his chair and spat into the spittoon near by. "I guess I gotta be goin'," he said.

"No, you don't," Lew said, his voice firm and his words slow. "We'll start fair."

Every man in the room, except Jonathan and Matthew,

rose and moved toward the door. But Lew's great body filled it first.

"We'll all line up outside the schoolhouse," he said. He drew a pistol from his pocket. "When I fire we'll start. It won't pay anybody to start first."

He heaved himself down the steps, the pistol hanging from his hands, and waited until the half-dozen men were in a line. He fired it, running as he did so, and down the main street of Median they ran, every man for his horse.

Jonathan and Matthew sat in their chairs. They had not moved. Jonathan arranged the papers upon his desk into their usual straight piles.

"Any reason to think there is oil on your land?" he asked.

"I don't know yet," Matthew replied. "There's no reason against it. The sinkhole ain't but about half a mile from my line post."

"Oil's a tricky thing," Jonathan said musingly.

He tried to imagine Matthew and Ruth rich with the sudden fabulous wealth of those who found the treasure of oil in their earth. What would these two simple people do with money? If he had money he would build Median a church and a hospital and himself a roomful of books and add a study to his house where he could be alone sometimes in the evening.

"Shan't you buy a piece of land around there, Jonathan?" Matthew asked.

"I haven't time to bother about getting rich," Jonathan said. He smiled faintly. "Reckon it'll be easier for me to get the money I want from other folks when they get rich."

But he couldn't ask anyone else for a roomful of books for himself. "Haven't even much time to read," he thought.

He stirred in his swivel chair. "Well, reckon we better get back to work, Matt."

"Ruth and me haven't had much luck yet," Matthew said. He stood up, a tall stooped young man with an Adam's apple so large that he looked like a crane. "One of the cows tried to jump the fence last week and tore her belly open. We killed her quick and made beef, but she was a good cow and just come fresh. It's too hot to keep meat now, and I couldn't get rid of much of it. Ruth's tried to salt it down, and I brung some to Katie today."

"That's bad about the cow, though thanks for the meat," Jonathan said.

"I've done some carpenterin' for Stephen Parry on a house, though," Matthew went on. His toneless voice was part of him.

"Well, it takes energy," Jonathan said briskly. "I don't believe much in luck."

"I don't know about that," Matthew replied with doubt. " 'Twasn't any energy put that oil in the sinkhole. 'Twon't be energy that'll put oil in my land."

Jonathan laughed. "You've got me there. Well, then, good luck, Matt!"

"Thanks, Jonathan," Matthew drawled and, gathering up his long legs, he went away.

Six men crawled down the slimy black sides of the sinkhole. Lew's face was purple veined with black. He had not ridden horseback in a year, and his heart was beating as though it would burst out of his breast. But he lowered himself down into the hole.

"Ain't no doubt about the way it looks," Henry said. He dipped his hand into the iridescent black water and smelled it. The water was foul and stagnant, but stronger than the foulness was the penetrating reek of oil.

They smelled it, one after the other, and then they examined the sides of the hole. The earth was damp but not with water.

"It's like putty, it's so full of oil," Samuel Hasty said.

Two men clambered out quickly and mounted their horses.

"Hey, there!" Henry yelled.

They clawed the slimy banks and pulled themselves up by the strongly rooted grass, each man thinking only of himself. Not one saw that Lew was left behind.

"Hi, Henry!" he shouted. There was no answer. He heard the clatter of horses over the hard sod. "Sam'l!" he shrieked. He scrabbled at the slippery earth, but his vast body it was impossible to lift. He made one last great straining effort and felt a strong hot fiery flash inside his skull. Thought and knowledge were wiped away in an instant, and he fell backward into the oily, rainbow-surfaced water.

"You'd ought to tell Hans you found that oil in his sinkhole," Ruth said when they were eating their dinner of beef stew and cabbage.

Matthew's mouth was full of dry salt-rising bread, and he took a gulp of milk to down it before he could speak. "Never thought of it," he exclaimed.

"We'd surely appreciate it if somebody'd tell us if 'twas ours," Ruth said with wistfulness. Dreams unfinished and suppressed were in her dark eyes and in the faint color on her brown cheeks.

If they found oil she would add a parlor to the house, and they would buy a buggy and a team of horses instead of the mules, and she would buy an organ and a big doll for little Mary and for Maggie new clothes and Katie a fur muff and for Jonathan a gold watch. She loved to give presents, but never in her life had she walked into the store and bought anything. By some overlooking, no one had ever given her money and let her buy with it. Her mother and then Jonathan and Katie had bought and given to her, and now Matthew went to the store on Saturdays. Even if she went with him, he did the buying. She never had money in her hand to exchange for what she wanted. I could have it if I'd only say so, she thought in her defending heart. But she could never say so, dreading to explain, to be thought silly.

"I'll go right away before I start the afternoon's work," Matthew said.

An hour later he and Hans found Lew's great bulk head and shoulders under the rich water.

Hans, a kind and melancholy German, groaned, "I'd do midoudt oil forever before it happens on my place."

The two men could only heave the head out of the water.

"I'll have to get Jonathan," Matthew gasped. "Can you stay here, Hans?"

"Sure," Hans said. He took the end of Lew's shirt and wiped the oil from his face.

Matthew climbed out and upon his mule galloped to Median and went to the empty schoolhouse. Jonathan was back at his desk.

"Lew's drowned," Matthew shouted. "He's in the sinkhole. It'll take a lot of us to get him out."

Jonathan leaped out of his chair. "They didn't go and leave him!"

"Must of."

"I wish you'd never found the danged stuff, Matthew. It makes men act like beasts."

"What'll I do, Jonathan?"

"Round 'em up. Get the hotel surrey and take the back seats out and lay a quilt down to put Lew on. I'll have to tell Katie. Then I'll join you. But don't wait for me. Get the others. My mare's fast. I may catch you anyway."

He strode out of the schoolhouse into the clear July afternoon. How would he tell Katie, and how comfort her? He longed to have love to aid him so that he could open his arms and make amends. But to begin a course so strange to them would only make misery for them both. He sighed and, entering the door, smelled cinnamon and the fragrance of baking cookies. He went toward the kitchen. She was there at the table, cutting the dough quickly into stars and hearts. Through the open window he could see the children playing together in the back yard under a tree. She looked up, astonished to see him, and he began to speak quickly before she could ask the reason.

"Katie, there's bad news, my dear."

Her mouth opened, and her round eyes grew rounder.

"Wait," he said. "Do you want to take the cookies out of the oven first?"

"I better," she said. "They're done, anyway."

He stood while she emptied the pan of brown hot cookies upon a clean towel. The watchful children ran to the window.

"Mom! You said we could have some!" This was Mary, who called her Mom as her own children did.

She picked up six and gave them two apiece. "Don't ast me for any more," she said. Then she turned back to Jonathan.

"Your father's—passed away, Katie."

She sank upon a chair. "Oh, Jonathan!"

"In a queer terrible way, Katie—"

He had not told her that Matthew had found oil. The fewer people who knew it the better, he had thought. But the real reason was that he did not want her to urge him to buy land. He was a schoolteacher, he had been thinking wryly when Matthew came in, a speculator in human beings, not in human wealth.

"Shame on those men," Katie cried. "That Henry Drear, too, that Pop always stood by!" She choked and lifted her gray calico apron to her mouth and held it there. Over it her eyes filled with tears.

He made a step toward her, feeling he must make some response to her sorrow for Lew's sake, too.

"I was fond of him," he said in a low voice. He patted her shoulder gently once or twice. "I'm going to miss him myself, Katie, a great deal. I've got to hurry, Katie."

She fumbled for the slit pocket in her skirt and found her handkerchief and blew her nose loudly.

"I'll have to tell Maw," she said heavily.

He tiptoed away, his heart thick with sorrow and pity which he could not express, because between them there was no path of communication. He could only use the common ways in which he would have helped her had she never been his wife. And yet he longed to come nearer to her in her need. He knew her, if not with the illumination of love, nevertheless with the sober knowledge of the days and nights they had lived together under the same roof. But that life had been bounded by what could be said and heard and done. All that lay beyond these boundaries they had not shared. He thought sometimes that only in himself was there the beyond, and that her complete life was in what she did and said as she kept the house and in the afternoons went around two sides of the square to the store. But there was no time now to think. He hastened away.

Two hours later he helped to lift the lifeless mass of Lew's dead body off the surrey and carry it through the store into the back room and lay it upon the couch. Sue was waiting, for it had become her service in Median to prepare the dead for burial. Mrs. Merridy was there, and with her the twins.

"Get Joe and Jack out of here," Jonathan said to Katie sternly over his shoulder.

But she had shaken her head. "Maw wants 'em to be here," she whispered back. She held her handkerchief to her mouth as they laid Lew down. Mrs. Merridy sobbed loudly, but the twins did not move.

But Sue had heard this command. "Go out from here, all of you," she ordered them, but her full soft voice made the words gentle. "I must do what I can before he gets his mortal rigors too set."

They tiptoed out as though Lew's deaf ears could hear. Katie held her mother's arm, but Jonathan put a hand on each boy's thin shoulders, as tall now as his own. They were pupils in his school and Katie's brothers, but he had never given them much heed. They were, he had always thought, commonplace boys, exactly alike, from dusty brown hair to bare feet. But now he saw them acutely as Lew's sons, robbed forever of Lew's hearty, happy presence.

"Come along over to our house," he said. "Jonnie and Lula and Mary'll be glad to have you." He turned to their mother. "Will you come, too, Mrs. Merridy?" He had never been able to call her mother.

"No, I want to stay here with Lew," she moaned. "Sue'll be here—I don't want nobody else."

So they had left her, and after supper the children played out under the trees in the square. Katie went out to speak to them sharply two or three times because they grew too noisy.

"Why not let them be happy?" Jonathan said.

"'Tain't decent, with a death in the family," she said indignantly. She was so exactly as she always was that he wondered how much she felt, or could feel.

In the night he thought he heard her crying. Something waked him, and it was Katie, sobbing. He moved from his side of the big double bed where he lay by long habit in a narrow stillness as he slept, and put out his hand. It touched her hair.

"Are you awake, my dear?" he asked.

"I been thinkin'," she replied. Her voice was firm. Perhaps she had not been crying, after all. He waited for her to go on.

"Jonathan, there's something I want you should do."

"I will if I can, Katie," he said gently.

In her fierce independence she had asked of him very little. He thought sometimes that it would have been easier for him if she had seemed to need him more than she did. A clinging, gentle woman might have wakened in him a deeper tenderness. But he was not a whit prepared for the stupendous act she now asked of him. Her voice came out of the darkness at his side.

"I want you should take the store."

His ears heard, but his mind refused belief. "I couldn't manage school and store both, Katie."

"You could give up the school."

"No, I couldn't!" His cry was sharp in the night.

"Why not?" she asked. "I wish you would, Jonathan. I've often wished you would. Even if Pa hadn't died, I've wished you would. It makes me mad the way you have to listen to the trustees and the way you're at everybody's beck and call, and you got to take what they feel to pay you. Last year they cut you a third, and you couldn't say anything. You haven't any independence—you belong to the town. But in the store you'd have nobody to be your boss."

"I couldn't," he gasped. He forgot that it had never been his thought to comfort her. She needed no comfort. It was he who would need strength to withstand her. He could hear in her voice the strong stubbornness that meant one of her ideas had taken her narrow mind in its hold.

"I do hope you won't push me, Katie," he said, trying to be stern. "For I won't be pushed in this. A man must do what he likes best to do, and schoolteaching is what I've always wanted. Why, even in Dentwater I used to plan a school. I never thought I'd have it here in Median, but now that I have, my life is here."

"Then you don't care if a bunch of men says they can't pay you what you earn," she cried angrily.

"No, I don't," he said, "not when I know it's a bad year and nobody's gotten what he earned."

"Well, it's me has to feed you all just the same," she retorted. "If you was in the store you'd get easy twice as much. Pa said last year was his best year. He laid by more'n he spent."

"I don't want more money, Katie," he said gently. "I can pay my bills. If I can't, Median folk'll trust me. Why, I don't even want to buy up land for oil. I just want to live the way we are. I'd rather put in my extra time the way I did to get the post office. If we win the election for county seat, I'm going to get us a courthouse this summer. I made it a promise to Drear that he could say Median would put up its own courthouse if it was chosen."

"You're ready enough to work without pay, but somebody pays!" Her voice was bitter. "I pay and the children pay!"

"But you have what you need, Katie!" he cried. "What would you do with more money?"

He asked it honestly. She did not read, she played no instrument of music, clothes could not change her or give her vanity.

"I'd like money in the bank," she said. "If anything happened to you—"

He interrupted her. "Nothing's going to happen to me. I shall live a very long time."

In the darkness of midnight he felt infinitely weary. In the darkness he and Katie must lie, side by side. It was a very long time until the day could break. They did not speak again.

🙚 33 🙚

AND YET EACH TIME WHEN THE DAY CAME IT WAS GOOD. Jonathan was a man born to enjoy small cheerful things. Good food, sunshine, the slant of the plains toward the sky that his eyes never failed to see, the welcoming solitude of his office chair, the papers on his desk, a book he bought secretly to add to his shelves, a schoolbook sent him sometimes, and this always flattered him though he knew it was sent to hundreds like him, the sight of his son Jon running out of the house to meet him at night—the days were lively with such cheer.

Lew's funeral was hardly over before Katie went at him again.

"What's to be done about the store, Jonathan?"

"It can be sold," he said firmly.

"Well, it won't be," she said. Katie's chin, of no particular shape, could look like a cliff under her plain mouth.

He did not answer. In his own quiet way, without being aware of it, he could be as high-handed as Clyde.

When after weeks he saw Katie would never sell the store and was trying with her mother to manage it herself, he said mildly, "I'll keep the books for you, Katie, and make the inventory and orders."

"That'll be a help," she said.

But she did not give up, and he knew she had not. Between her and her mother he felt a snare set for him, and he walked warily; and yet, though he did not know it, he had Mrs. Merridy to thank for what peace he had.

"Don't you nag Jonathan," Mrs. Merridy told Katie. "He's the kind that comes quicker without. Now Lew you could nag, for he'd do anything to git rid of you. But Jonathan goes his own way."

"It'll come around my way one of these days just the same,"
Katie said. "I shan't rest until he's in the store."

Outside of his house Jonathan gave no thought to the
submerged strife between him and Katie.

The dark rainbow promise of oil was being fulfilled. Fourteen great derricks had sprung up around the sinkhole in
which Lew had drowned. American House was jammed with
beds for men who had come out of every place in the country
where rumor had chanced to be blown. Even in the days
when wagons were going West there had not been so many
travelers. These were all men. If a woman came, she was an
oddity and she knew it. But the bulk of the oil land was not
for sale. The Sunflower Oil Company had bought it. No one
knew who were the men who made it. Hans Rourse said,
"Somebody comes to me after Lew is *todt* in my sinkhole—a
nize man knows Lew good, he sayed. 'Ain'dt it awful how
Lew dies,' he sayed, and he was Lew's friend. So I sayed,
'Yes, is awful, for sure.' An' he sayed, do I want to sell the
sinkhole and maybe ten-twenty acres around. He sayed maybe
is there oil there and if iss, I will get twenty-five percent. So I
sayed, 'Ya, I don't vant a sinkhole nohow a man drowns in
and maybe next my good cows.' And so I put my name on his
paper."

The same man came one day to Matthew's door at noon.
Matthew and Ruth were at dinner. They were eating their
first green corn, and Matthew had a great ear of it in his hand
when he opened the kitchen door.

"Good day," the man said. His dark eyes were soft with a
smile. "May I have a word with you?"

"Come in," Matthew said. "We're eatin', and you're welcome to jine in. That's my wife. Cobb is the name."

"How do you do, Mrs. Cobb," the man said. "I'm glad I
can speak with both of you. A man's wife is a useful partner.
I'd like to have an option on your land for oil, Mr. Cobb. I'll
pay higher than the usual terms—say, fifteen dollars a year,
and if we strike oil, a fourth of the proceeds are yours. Does
that seem fair?"

Ruth looked at Matthew. Others had offered them five
dollars a year, and eight and ten.

"I—it is more than we've been offered," Matthew said,
hesitating. "Won't you sit down, stranger?"

"Thanks, no," the man said. "I must be on my way. Then you will take it?"

Matthew looked at Ruth. "Can't do no harm to take the highest bid, can it?"

"I guess not," she said faintly.

"All right," Matthew said.

"Then will you sign this paper?" The man held a folded paper toward him."Read it first, please. I wouldn't want you to sign what you hadn't read."

Long legal words heaped themselves before Matthew's eyes. "I guess it's all right," he said. "I don't make much sense out of 'em, but I ain't puttin' out any money, am I?"

"Of course not," the stranger said quickly. "It's the other way. As soon as you sign that, I put out the money."

He took his purse from his pocket and counted fifteen dollars.

"And here's a pen," he said, "one of those newfangled ones that holds its own ink."

Matthew shifted his corn to his left hand and wiped his fingers on the seat of his jeans.

"Works, does it?"

"It's inclined to be balky." The man laughed a rolling gust of laughter.

Matthew signed his name and took the money and the man folded the paper quickly and put it in his pocket. Then he tipped his hat to Ruth and smiled his pleasant smile.

"Good day," he said and was gone. They saw him leap on a chestnut horse and gallop away across the plains toward the east.

Matthew looked dazed. "Did somep'n happen to me or didn't it?"

Ruth laughed. "The money's in your hand, silly! What was the name on the paper?"

"Damned if I know," Matthew said ruefully. "I ought to of looked, oughtn't I?"

"Oh, well," Ruth said easily, "it doesn't matter. We have the money. Oh, Matthew, suppose they should find oil on our land!"

"What'll we do with the money?"

"Matthew, could I have a piano?" she whispered.

"Shore you can!" He stooped to kiss her and then sat down. "It's silly when I can't play," she said.

"You can learn, can't you?" he retorted. "We'll have to move if they find oil. Might buy us a house in Topeka. You could get a music teacher there."

"What'll you do in Topeka?" she asked anxiously.

"Might go into making furniture," he said slowly. "I always did hanker after woodwork. Something I could smooth to the grain."

They sat in silence a moment, the fifteen dollars he had in his shirt pocket the kernel of all their hope.

"Seems like we ought to share all this with somebody," Ruth murmured, looking out of the window.

"Jonathan ought to buy, but he won't," Matthew said. "He don't want to bother with gettin' rich."

"Then let's tell Jamie!" Ruth's brown eyes lifted.

"Good idea," Matthew said largely. "You know where he's at?"

"He's still at the Big Four Ranch, his last letter said."

"Then shore," Matthew said. "I guess we can afford a stamp now, cain't we, Ruthie?"

"I reckon!" she said and laughed. "Oh, Matt, ain't we lucky?"

"Wonderful," he said.

At the Big Four Ranch, lying on the grass at noon hour, Jamie folded Ruth's letter and put it into his shirt pocket and stretched himself. Who would have thought of oil in Median? He was taller than either of his brothers, taller now than Clyde, and blue-eyed and black-haired. Hard riding against sun and wind had made his skin coppery as an Indian's. His hairy young hands were as strong as steel traps.

"Quickest way in the world to get rich," he muttered.

He had a contract with Big Four to stay until winter, but he made up his mind now that he would break it. No contract had ever held him beyond his wish when all he had to do was to jump on a horse and lope across the prairies. He had the finest horse that he had ever had, chosen out of the wild horses that he had lassoed by his uncanny skill with the rope. The horse did not belong to him, but that did not trouble him. He took care to keep it in the height of condition. If I have me a good horse, he often thought, it's my freedom.

A man came to the door and yelled at him. "Hey there, you! It's a long way from quittin' time!"

Jamie grinned, rose, and, pulling his wide felt hat over one eye, sauntered toward the door.

"You round up them horses you finished off yestiddy," the foreman ordered him. He was swallowing the last gulps of a tin cup full of black coffee. "They're due to be shipped by the four o'clock. Got a rush order today from Indiana."

Jamie did not answer. He changed the direction of his saunter from east to southeast to stop at the bunkhouse. It was empty. All the men had gone back to work. He went to his bunk and opened the end of the straw tick under the blankets and drew out a small wad rolled in oilcloth. In it were his summer's wages and all he owned except for an extra shirt under his pillow. This he drew out and stuffed inside the one he wore. Then he went out again.

If I'm goin', I'll git started, he thought. He quickened his easy loping gait and came to a small fenced-in lot full of horses pushing and nudging each other.

"Come here, Lady!" he called. He had a fine voice, Clyde's voice, but rich and young.

A bay mare thrust her head against him, and he led her out by the long black hair of her mane.

"Stand there till I fetch the saddle," he ordered her. Scarcely a trace of England remained upon his tongue.

He came back almost instantly to the obedient mare and flung across her back a saddle so handsome that half a year's pay had gone for it. The mare quivered, but he buckled the girth without paying any heed and tested the stirrups. Then he leaped on her back. The instant she felt his weight she sprang forward and across the sod.

Within sight of the ranch house, he headed seemingly for the corral. But before he reached it he turned sharp east. Then, leaning low, he gave the horse her head. If he kept her to her speed, he could reach the homestead by sundown. His heart lifted as the wind sang in his ears. This was what he loved best in his life, a horse flying beneath him, and he headed for a new life. . . .

He did not think of his mother from one day's end to another, but for one moment his heart jumped when he stooped to enter his father's door. There was a woman sitting by the stove, her chin on her hand as Mary used often to sit in the last days of her life. He saw a thick braid of red hair swing over her shoulder as she turned her head to him, and instantly he knew her.

"Hello, Jennet," he said.

"Hello, you," she said without moving. "Where'd you come from?"

"I better ask you that," he retorted. He came in. "I belong here in a manner of speaking, but what about you?"

She laughed suddenly and held out her left hand. A wide shining gold ring was on the third finger.

"Meet your step-maw," she said.

"You're lying!" he said slowly. Anger and admiration mingled in him for a moment, an anger vaguely for his mother's sake that Jennet, whom she always disliked, should be here, and rueful admiration of a man as old as his father who was able so to persuade a young woman. Then he laughed.

"Why, Dad's a reg'lar old geezer!" he cried. He sat down on the end of the table without taking off his hat. "How'd you come to leave His Highness?"

"I got tired of being chucked out when he thought he didn't want me," she said. Her mouth, which had been beautiful in sullenness when she was a girl, was now coarse. "I decided I'd show him. I'm a respectable married woman, now."

"Does he come around?" Jamie asked, staring at her.

"Your paw took his shotgun to him the only time he did," Jennet said. They looked at each other and broke into common laughter.

"Dad's an old goat," Jamie said and spat on the earthen floor. "Nothing downs him."

"He's talkin' about runnin' for land when they open up the new territory," Jennet said with a fresh burst. Her laughter was unchanged, the same hard, clear laughter that even in her childhood had carried no music in it.

"Why, he can't run with that game leg!" Jamie cried. "And he's never learned to sit his horse right."

"He's rigged himself up a seat on the back wheels of an old wagon," Jennet said. "And he's training one of the colts into a race horse."

Across the grassy landscape they saw Clyde limping briskly toward them. Jamie leaped from the table and went to meet him.

"Hi!" he shouted.

Clyde squeezed his favorite son in his arms. "Where'd you

blow from?" he inquired. Under his torn hat of Indian straw his hair flew in curly gray strands, but his eyes were as sharp and black as ever, and a red handkerchief was knotted about his throat. He looked younger than he had in years, and full of impudence.

"I'm goin' East," Jamie said. He pulled Ruth's letter from his pocket and held it out to Clyde.

Clyde spat in the grass. "You tell me what's in it. I don't read much any more. Haven't the time."

Jamie put the letter back in his pocket. "Oil's been struck."

"Never on their land!" Clyde cried.

"Next door," Jamie said. "And they're lettin' 'em try on their land."

"Dang me if I won't go that way instead of the Territory." Clyde limped faster to match his son's long even gait. "Beats all how opportunity fair crushes a man here. Oil spouts out on one side of him, and there's free land on the other. I'm all in a maze."

"How's things here?"

"Good so far as they go, but I haven't enough land. Three hundred and twenty acres don't go far. A man's got to think big here in this country."

"But how'll you manage land there and here?"

Clyde shot a look at his son. "Thought maybe you'd give your old dad a hand. You was always the one I count on, Jamie."

"But I'm goin' in for oil, Dad."

Clyde scratched his fingers into his beard. "Eh, well, I'll manage," he said stubbornly.

Without knowing it he had decided for land and against oil because Jamie would not help him. "I can do for myself," he said with such complacency that Jamie looked down at him and then followed the beam of his father's eyes. They fell on Jennet standing in the doorway, the sun shining on her red hair as she shaded her eyes to look for them.

Jamie's white teeth shone. "I should say you can," he said. "A reg'lar billy goat, ain't you, Dad?"

"Well, I'm hearty," Clyde said, and his red lips were smug in his beard.

✣ 34 ✣

In his office Jonathan sat with three other men counting ballots steadily, stacking them into packages and slipping rubber bands about them. The box on the floor to the left of him was Ashbee; on the right was Median. Outside the midsummer sun of an August afternoon beat upon a crowd of men and horses and wagons. The horses were stirring against the flies, and men fanned themselves with branches they had picked from the trees in the square.

Jonathan stopped counting and leaned out of the window. "Don't you chaps break those young hardwoods!" he shouted. "Cottonwoods don't matter, but I sent East for the others to plant around the courthouse." He pulled his head in as they guffawed and went on counting.

Henry Drear waited patiently, a rifle across his knees. "Ashbee's goin' to declare the election's illegal if we win," he said.

"They can't do that," Jonathan said, his lips still murmuring numbers.

"Ashbee can do anything," Henry retorted. "But I've got 'em fixed."

Jonathan paused. "Median isn't going to do anything illegal, now, Henry."

"You git along with the countin'," Henry said.

Jonathan went on counting.

"Say," Henry said, "some of the folks want to change the

name of the town when we git to be the county seat. Median sounds kind of common."

Jonathan stopped again. "How can I count if you keep on with your dangety ideas? I won't have the town called out of its name. Median it was when I came, and Median it'll be when I go. It's a good sensible name that don't pretend to be big."

"They want to call it Mecca," Henry said doubtfully.

"Mecca!" Jonathan repeated. "Why, that's the name of a city in heathendom!"

"They say it's a place everybody wants to go like to heaven."

"Who wants everybody coming to our town?" Jonathan's voice was querulous. "I've a good notion to stop this whole business right here."

"Now, Jonathan, don't get cantankerous. I swear for a man your size—" He sighed and spat.

"Don't let me hear any more silly talk about Mecca, then."

Jonathan's look was so gloomy that Henry took alarm. "Don't it look good for Median?"

"Too many handwritings alike on some of the ballots."

"So long as they all say Median—"

Jonathan banged the table with his fist. "Danged if I'll be party to a fraud," Jonathan cried. "Looks to me like your handwriting, Henry. See here." His square dexterous hands sorted a dozen or more ballots of the same large irregular writing. All of them were for Median.

The men roared with laughter. Henry was not abashed. "Don't look alike to me," he said.

Jonathan swept them together and threw them into the wastebasket. Henry chewed the straggling brown ends of his long moustache.

"Look hyere, you can't—"

"Then we'll declare the whole election fraudulent."

"Oh, all right," Henry grumbled. He had risen, but now he sat down heavily and took off his felt hat and wiped his forehead. "But if Median don't git it, I'll turn the hotel into a whorehouse to spite your damn pigheadedness, Jonathan."

"Median's getting it," Jonathan retorted.

"Even without my votes?" Henry shouted.

"Even without your many votes," Jonathan said.

But Henry did not notice irony. He leaped to his feet and rushed to the window and fired into the sky.

"It's Median!" he yelled. "Median's got it. Median—Median—Median—hooray!" and throwing his gun on the floor he jumped out of the window and ran round the schoolhouse while the crowd yelled.

But at his desk Jonathan picked up a letter. It was very short:

DEAR JONATHAN:

I shall be glad to see you for any cause. Shall we say on Saturday the eighteenth? Judy joins me in regards. I am yours as ever,

EVAN

At the end of the letter Evan had scribbled in his own handwriting, "Come to my house, Jonathan."

Upstairs in her big bedroom, Judy hid behind the rose satin curtain and looked out the window. The house was the same into which Evan had first brought her, but a new wing added to each side had made it into what the Topeka newspapers called "a mansion." Judy herself had taken on stateliness. Her hair was brushed high and lay in curls over the top of her head. But above the lace collar of her dress her creamy nape was still as soft as a child's. Her hands clasping the curtains were strangely childish, too, in their shape, and her lips had kept their purity, and her eyes were as dark as ever above the wine-red taffeta of her wide-sleeved dress.

"Do you mind if Jonathan comes here?" Evan had asked her last night.

"Why should I mind?" she had replied, lifting her lashes at him.

He was no longer disturbed by this sight of long lashes sweeping upward like the wings of dark butterflies. He knew the movement was meaningless because she used it to delay the necessity for thought before speech.

"No reason whatever, my dear," he retorted. "All the agony is over, and it seems a little ridiculous now."

Judy did not answer. But had someone been there who loved her, he might have seen timidity in the look she gave her husband. She was afraid of him because she loved him and because he did not love her. Where it was in their life together that Evan had ceased to love her she did not know. Much of the time when she sat alone in the strange stillness which was now her life, she pondered this matter, searching over the years to discover at what moment the thing had happened.

"I haven't changed," she murmured often to herself.

She was even as beautiful as ever she was. She examined her hands, her face, even shyly her body, alone before the mirror. No, she had not changed, and did not know that in this very fact lay the secret of Evan's change.

For it was Evan's curse that he had a gentleman's conscience, and that he had in his way loved Jonathan more than he had ever loved any human being. Never except with Jonathan had his mind met the mind of another human being. Even now, when he and Jonathan had been years separated, he found himself remembering the hours of talk with him, when as two young men they had told one another everything, had argued and quarreled, but always had trusted one another. With Jonathan he had been himself, his good self, large and honest and free. Jonathan had been his foil and his inspiration. He had whetted himself on Jonathan, handsome because Jonathan was plain, gay because Jonathan was sober, a tempest beside Jonathan's calm. He had continued to love Jonathan because Jonathan alone of all the people he had known made him his best. And he knew that he was at his happiest when he was also at his best. He laughed at his own tricks but despised them. He could not enjoy dishonesty.

As for Judy, he had ceased to love her when he understood that he could never hope for more from her than the beauty of her body. He enjoyed her beauty especially when they were in public places. Alone with her, its satisfaction was swiftly over. There were no depths to it. He found himself wishing often that under the lovely face he might also have found an exciting mind.

"Unreasonable," he thought now, looking down into the lovely face. For he had taken her in his arms suddenly at this moment in a quick shallow burst of passion, stimulated by the thought of Jonathan's coming.

"You're not sorry you ran away with me, Judy?" he whispered.

She closed her eyes and put her white hand against his lips. "Never, Evan—if only you love me!"

He kissed her swiftly. "Of course," he said, and let her go. What perversity not to love a woman more because she loved him so much! But Judy was in perpetual surrender, and he loved excitement.

He kissed her once again, lightly, his passion gone in a whirlwind as small and useless as a toss of leaves in the middle of the road on a summer's day. He smiled, pulled her little ear, glanced at himself in the mirror, and went away.

Her eyes followed him with their large dark gaze, and when he was gone she went to the window as she always did when he left her. If he left the house she watched him, and when he did not, she stared out into the street. Behind the curtain her childish hand held from her face she now saw a slender sand-colored man step from a hired hack and pause for a moment. He lifted his head and looked at the house and the look seemed to fall upon her, direct as a beam from a lamp. She shrank behind the curtain and hid her face in her hands.

"Oh!" she murmured. "He's just the same!" She sat down on her rose-colored taffeta chair, and waited to see whether Evan would send for her.

Downstairs in the library, Evan and Jonathan looked at each other after many years. Evan saw Jonathan, but between him and Evan Jonathan saw Judy. Evan was Judy's husband. This was Judy's home. Through these rooms she moved every day. Her hands perhaps had arranged the bowl of roses on Evan's desk. A large silver photograph stood beside the roses, and he could not see the face it held, yet doubtless it was hers.

"Well, Jonathan!" Evan filled his voice with heartiness. He had risen to shake Jonathan's hand and then had sat down again behind the desk. He had planned to be formal and full of business, but the sight of Jonathan in his usual gray garb, sitting quietly before him, moved him to an impulsiveness he did not often feel in these days of his increasing success. He saw governorship clearly ahead of him.

"We'll take up where we left off, Jonnie." His fine smile made his face young enough for Jonathan to recognize him. His first thought had been how much Evan was changed. The even, early gray in his dark hair made him strange.

" 'Tisn't for anything past that I've come, Evan," he said calmly. "It's for a thing I want now."

Evan withdrew his smile. "What can I do for you now?"

"I want quite a lot of money, it happens," Jonathan said firmly. "It's for Median and not me. Looks as though we'll get the county seat unless Ashbee protests the election, and if they do, it'll help us to say we have funds for the courthouse."

Evan's smile glimmered. "You wouldn't let me have a cattle town. I might take my revenge now, Jonnie. I wouldn't put it above my doing."

"A county seat's a dignified, respectable thing," Jonathan said, "very different from a rumbling, tumbling cattle town. A county seat'll bring churches into Median and law and order of all kinds. The people that buy lots in the town'll be the better sort as have to do with such things." He looked steadily at Evan with his cool gray eyes.

He's forgotten Judy, Evan was thinking. He's an odd, cold chap, but I'm fond of him still, somehow, though he'll never be anything but the principal of a small-town school.

"Still building Median, Jonnie!" he said aloud. "How far have you got on that map we made together?"

"Schoolhouse is up, post office, and after the courthouse I aim to start the church. I've got a young chap in mind for the preacher, though just now he's out among the Indians. But I'll draw him back maybe with the church."

"Do you have children?" Evan's question was a thrust.

"A boy and a girl," Jonathan replied.

"Ah, you're luckier than I am," Evan said significantly. "Judy has never had a child."

The name fell between them like a stone, and Jonathan was struck to silence. For a moment he could not speak, try as he did. His heart, so carefully hidden even from himself, pounded under his gray coat; and Evan, watching him, saw a dull red creep into his colorless cheeks.

He still thinks about her, Evan thought with cool pity. He turned the big photograph frame on the table abruptly to face Jonathan. "She's changed very little," he said carelessly.

Jonathan did not move by a hair. His hands upon his knees he held there. But with all his heart he gazed upon Judy's face. She was very beautiful. In the richness of her evening dress and the jewels about her bare neck, he saw her as infinitely handsomer and more stately than he remembered her. How ill she would have fitted his small plain home, he thought suddenly. No, Katie was the sort of woman anyone would expect to see come out of his door, a busy housewife of a woman, her face clean and brown, but not one to look at twice.

"What's past is long gone," Evan said. He laughed a little. "I used to think Judy might be a bit skittish, Jon, as pretty girls often are. But she settled into marriage like a cat by a fire. Never has a thought outside the house, apparently."

He felt himself seized by an absurd desire to tell Jonathan that somehow his marriage had been a disappointment to him, as though disappointment were expiation of the betrayal of his friend.

"Judy's a strange woman, Jonathan," he said abruptly.

"Indeed," Jonathan said stiffly. He did not want to hear Evan talk about Judy. No, nor did he like to hear any man talk about his wife.

Evan saw the pale plain face grow stern. There was to be no expiation there! He laughed uneasily. "You're thinking that I made my own bed."

"I am thinking only about my business," Jonathan retorted. "Will you do what I ask?" But his heart was pounding all through his body. How dared this man be disappointed in his love? But had Judy indeed repented of what she had done? Did her coldness come from deep within her? "Does she still remember me?" his heart demanded. He gripped his heart with his will and choked it into silence.

"Well, Evan?" he asked and made his voice as dry as rustling winter cornstalks.

Evan put the picture back. "What's your proposition?"

"Ten thousand dollars, at six per cent, the new town lots to be security."

"Can you sell them?"

"In time we can."

"What time?"

"Ten years."

"What's the population now?"

"Three thousand two hundred and ten."

"That include niggras?"

"Why shouldn't it?" Jonathan's pale eyes flashed a cold spark, and Evan laughed.

"Still think a lot of niggras, eh, Jon?"

"No more than of anybody else, but as much."

Evan leaned forward. "Say, what's become of that boy you sent to France?"

"He graduated last year from the Academy of Surgery in Paris, France. He's married a young Frenchwoman."

"You don't say! But the French are *white!*"

"I believe so," Jonathan said very coldly.

Evan drew in his breath. "Well, it couldn't happen here."

"Beaumont himself rather proves it can."

"What do you mean?" Evan demanded.

"Beaumont's father was white."

"Come now, Jon—that's different, and you know it."

"I do not know it."

Jonathan's thin body was erect with embattlement, and suddenly Evan laughed. "You haven't changed a hair of your head, Jonnie!"

"I hope I have not on this subject at least," Jonathan said severely.

"Well, you haven't, and let's shut up. Now, about this money. You shall have it. I don't mind saying I wouldn't think of laying out that much for Median if it weren't for you, Jonathan. Median's not my kind of a town. Now, here in Topeka we've just issued bonds for the new trolley-car system, and that's a sound investment. Trolleys will be wanted as long as the city stands. But I doubt Median ever grows to the point of needing them. In fact, there's no real reason for Median to grow."

Jonathan broke in. "I have no desire to see Median grow only in size. What kind of people live in Median means more than how many there are. And we've a good kind of folk there now. They're honest—barring an old-timer or two like Henry Drear, who sees things always off the end of his gun the way it used to be when the country was wild. You needn't be afraid your money wouldn't come back out of taxes."

"As long as you're alive, I'll have my security," Evan said. His good smile made the words very warm.

"Thanks," Jonathan said. He rose. "I aim to live a long life."

"I hope so," Evan said. He pressed a bell and, when Marcus appeared, rose and followed Jonathan to the library door. "Good-by, Jonathan. I'm glad you came."

"Thanks, Evan."

The two men clasped hands for a swift instant and parted, each aware that they were not brothers as they had been, and so they were not sorry to part.

In the hall, Jonathan put on his coat quickly and took his hat from the Negro. He wanted to be away out of this house, and yet he could not keep from glancing about him and up the stair. It was so silent a house. Not a sound could be heard from the carpeted and curtained rooms. From all that ear told, it might have been empty. Marcus opened the door and bowed; and Jonathan, nodding his head, went out. Behind him the door closed softly.

But he stood before it with a strange hesitating clairvoyance, as though the closing had not been final. Was this all or not? He wanted to go, but he did not feel free to go yet. And even as he stood, the door opened again suddenly, and Judy stood there.

The moment he saw her he knew that this was why he had come, and that he could not have gone away without it. She was more beautiful than his deepest memory had remembered. She was a woman of cream and roses beneath her softly piled curls, her red dress a vase for her beauty. In her little ears were pearls, and on her white neck a fine gold chain, and he saw everything about her—every color and tint and shape, the deep sweet corners of her red mouth and her glorious eyes and her upflung lashes. He had never seen a pretty girl until he saw Judy, and he had never seen a beautiful woman until he saw her now.

She spoke at last. "Jonathan, I couldn't quite just—let you go."

He was speechless, gazing at her, and she put out her hand to him.

"You aren't still angry with me, Jonathan?"

He shook his head and felt her hand in his hand that was trembling in a palsy at what it held. She looked this way and that and whispered, "I often think you loved me best, after all, Jonathan."

He could not speak. He put her little hand to his lips and then knew what he did and turned himself and ran down the steps and into the waiting hack. Then he took one backward look at the door. She was standing there, the hand he had kissed against her mouth.

"Get on," he groaned to the hack driver. As the vehicle

clattered down the street, he bent his head and shielded his face with his hand, full of horror at himself. I'm not fit to be trusted near her, he thought. I love her still.

"Did you get the money?" Katie's voice, her face across the supper table, the children between them to be served and fed, were what he had every night. Nothing was better, nothing worse.

"Yes, I got it," he said.

Katie stared at him. "You ain't sick, are you, Jonathan?" she asked. He looked more than usually pale, and he had eaten almost nothing of the fried liver and potatoes.

"No, I'm—tired."

"I thought maybe a day in the city would liven you up," she said.

He smiled faintly at this. "Do you feel I should be more lively?" he inquired.

He had entered his home tonight under the fresh shadow of his strong debt to Katie. He owed very much to this hard-working good woman who belonged in his house and made of it a place suitable for a man like him. Judy would have been a bird of paradise, and what would a plain chap like him have done with her?

"I'm sorry I'm dull, Katie," he said gently. "I did hear some interesting things. There's to be trolleys in Topeka—"

"Just so's you ain't sick is all I care," Katie said.

But in the night, lying sleepless in the bed beside her, he suddenly longed to confess all his heart to Katie. It would ease him to share the weight of his love, to tell her that because he had loved another woman and today knew he still loved her and would now love her always, he would make eternal amends to her for having married her. He put out his hand, and then he drew it back and lay in long self-examination. Why should he want to tell Katie a thing too great for her to bear? She would never comprehend it. So long as she lived she would stagger under the knowledge.

Another man would leave Katie, he thought bitterly, but I can't—I wouldn't. I care too much for what I've built up here in Median.

Yes, he was the sort who could love a woman with all his power and agony, and yet he would not give up what he was to that love. He could not forsake himself even for love. He lay on, sleepless through the night.

But I'm never to be left alone in the room with Judy, he thought. If ever we meet again, it's never to be alone.

He rose early before Katie stirred and stole into the kitchen and lit the fire for her and put the kettle on and then made himself a cup of tea and set the table for breakfast. She came bustling in while he was busy and cried, "My goodness, you don't have to help *me*, Jonathan!"

But he knew it was her wry way of thanking him.

"Dad's married to Jennet," Jamie said in the manner of one who makes a joke.

Jonathan looked up from a pile of architects' plans he was spreading over the dining table. An hour ago Jamie had come riding up to the kitchen door.

"Jamie, what are you saying?" he cried.

"Sure, Dad's married Jennet Drear," Jamie repeated, grinning.

"He's never!" Jonathan said.

"That Jennet!" Katie shrilled.

"Seems she was there when he came in one night, and so it kind of—happened," Jamie said.

"How'd she come to be there at all?" Katie demanded. She remembered Jennet as one who was a plain little girl remembers an older and pretty one, with a prickling of old envy.

"Well, she came over from the next ranch where she lived for a while," Jamie said with the proper deceit before women and children. Later he might tell Jonathan the truth. His old childish admiration for his father made him laugh now at Clyde's marrying again.

Suddenly Jonathan gathered up his papers and stalked out. He wanted to be alone that he might comprehend why he was so angry with his father. He stepped through the shadows and moonlight upon the grass and went up the steps of the schoolhouse and into his office and lit the oil lamp on the desk. He threw the roll of plans upon the floor and sat down and, thrusting his hands deep into his pockets, stared across the room.

A map of Europe hung on the wall, and he saw off in one corner of it the small oblong that was England. His mother would have been alive now if they could have stayed there.

She had died because his father was impatient of work and steadiness and all that which Englishmen knew was righteousness. And now even as an old man he had not the decency to stay a widower for her sake, who lay so small and forlorn in her little grave in these huge plains!

"Oh, my poor wee!" he cried silently. In the spot upon the map he saw the green isle where she belonged.

But, no, his father must marry a red-haired woman who had wandered in and out of western towns and mining camps and who knew what else?

And then in his fearful honesty he went deep into his hatred for his father and found its roots. It was that once again, as gaily as a boy, Clyde had taken the woman he wanted, a thing he himself could not do.

I'm a wicked and deceitful man, he thought, pretending I'm crying for my mother's sake! It's Judy I'm thinking of again— and always will, I reckon.

He sat a moment, his lips pursed together, and then he stooped and picked up his plans.

🐦 35 🐦

IT WAS NEARLY SIX O'CLOCK OF A SUMMER'S DAY OF THE next year when he heard footsteps upon the cinder path which led from his own house to the open door of the schoolhouse. He had been uneasily conscious that Katie would be sending for him at any moment to come to supper. She divided her day into the three crises of meals, and nothing disturbed her more fiercely than to be ready to "dish up" and he not there. He yielded to her in such small tyrannies, though now he delayed.

He thought for a second before he looked up that the step was Maggie's plump footfall. But this was not Maggie. He looked up, and a strange man stood in the door. The late afternoon sunshine of a summer day falling through a dusty western window showed him a tall man, broad-shouldered, strong-legged, his face shaven as though he were young and yet lined enough to show him not young. He was dressed in a new gray suit, which fitted him ill, and his step had been the heavier for his new yellow leather shoes.

"You Jonathan Goodliffe?"

The man leaned arm and hand against the door jamb.

"I am," Jonathan replied. He showed his cautious English origin. Anyone else in Median would have cried to the man to come in, but Jonathan waited.

"You don't know me," the man said.

"I can't say I do," Jonathan answered.

"Ever see me before?"

Jonathan examined the sunburned face before him. "Can't say I have."

"Ever hear the name George Tenney?"

Jonathan stared again, and now the face seemed younger and familiar. "You were on the ship coming from England."

"I was, and I gave you my name and you never sent me a word about Maggie, though you said you would."

"I didn't take that serious," Jonathan said, smiling.

George Tenney stood, his arms still stretched across the door, and gazed at Jonathan. "I'd ha' known you anywhere," he said at last.

"I daresay I don't change," Jonathan said calmly. "Come in," he added.

But now there were Maggie's footsteps, hearty and hurrying.

"Jonathan!" Her clear loud young voice shouted through the silence of the evening. "Supper!"

"That's Maggie," George Tenney said.

"How did you know?" Jonathan asked.

"I know Maggie," George replied. A shy peculiar look came over his face and he looked over his shoulder. Then Maggie came near and stood staring with young severity at the big man in the door.

"Well?" she inquired tartly.

George Tenney's blue eyes smiled down at her. "Walk under my arm and let me see if you're the right size," he said slowly.

Maggie took quick offense. Girls were valued and indulged in Median, being too few.

"I don't see as my size has anything to do with you!" she cried. The curly ends of her red hair sprang out about her face in the wind.

"It's got a lot to do with me—I'm George Tenney," he said.

He could not have asked for more than the vivid red that rushed into Maggie's face.

"Did you get my letter?"

She flung up her head. "What letter?"

"You didn't answer it, so I came to see for myself."

"I don't answer strangers," she cried.

"I'm no stranger," he said in his slow deep voice. "Walk under my arm, Maggie." She did not move, and he repeated the words, but now they were not a command. His eyes smiled at her.

She stood rebellious and unwilling and shy. But she was struggling to fit to this man the vague man behind the letter which she kept all these months. She kept the two for a moment, and then the real man grew strong beside the conjured shadow, and suddenly, without bending her head, she walked under his arm. He dropped his hand to her shoulder.

"You're just the size I wanted you should be," he said gently. With his hand still on her shoulder he turned to Jonathan. "I'll come and take supper with you, Jonathan, seeing as I'm to be one of the family."

"Maggie's too young for you, George," Jonathan said.

Throughout the meal he said almost nothing, while the children were there. He simply watched George Tenney as he ate and drank and made friends with one child after another, and deferred to Katie with "ma'ams" and "thank yous." He was pleased that to each child this man made a gentle new approach. To little Jon he spoke of work as gravely as he would to a man.

"Cattle's my business," he said. "I herd 'em up from Texas by the thousand. It's a mean job while it lasts, but the pay's good. But I don't aim to stay in it. I've got other irons in my fire—a ranch, for one thing, with hosses, and if your pa'll let you, I'd like you to come out and give me a hand some summer. You can take your pick of the colts."

"Can I, Father?" Jon asked, yearning. He was a stocky, strong boy, more like his grandfather Lew than his own father.

"Maybe," Jonathan replied.

George teased Lula about her blonde curls.

"Store curls, I'll swear," he said. "They don't grow on your head. You've bought 'em and stuck 'em on with glue."

"I never!" Lula cried happily, pulling her curls to show.

"And them pink cheeks are painted on and real eyes ain't blue like yours. You're just a store doll-baby."

"No—no—no!" Lula screamed, laughing. "I'm real!"

"Come here and let me feel your sawdust," George said gravely. He pinched her little arm. "No, damn if she ain't real, Jonathan! I wouldn't ha' believed it. She looks like a store doll, but she ain't."

And while he was talking and teasing, his arm was about Mary, small and quiet and dark. He did not tease her or notice her overmuch, and she stood contentedly in that large shelter. Jonathan liked it that through the evening George was content to be with them all, and that he did not hasten to be with Maggie alone. There had to be talk between them before he would leave Maggie alone with this man almost old enough to be her father. Maggie was more quiet than she had ever been in her life, and no one could tell what she was thinking. When the younger children went to bed, she rose, saying to Katie, "I'll make the bread tonight, Katie," and went to the kitchen.

So the three of them were left alone; and Katie, her mouth set, took up her mending basket. Jonathan would speak, but she would listen and uphold him. She wanted Maggie married and out from her care, but only if this was the man Jonathan wanted in the family.

"I am old for Maggie," George Tenney admitted, "but still not old as men go. I'm forty to Maggie's eighteen. But I'm a young forty, and she's an old eighteen. Girls are women early out hyere. And I don't want somebody snappin' her up. I've thought about Maggie as mine a good many years now."

"It doesn't seem possible a man could remember a baby," Jonathan said.

" 'Twasn't a baby but Maggie I remembered."

Jonathan pondered a moment on Maggie's life, a troublesome healthy child, a troublesome healthy girl, but to him no more. "You'd find her a handful," he said.

"I've broken hosses aplenty," George Tenney said. "Always by gentlin'. I never took a whip to one. And I'd rather do the breakin' than leave it to another—never liked a hoss in my life that another man broke."

"I don't like the cattle business."

"Nor I, and I'm gettin' out of it into hosses. I've got my ranch, and I own half a gold mine that's got pay dirt. I aim to give my wife a piano and her own carriage if she wants."

Katie looked up from the sock over her hand. "Maggie's that headstrong," she said.

"Yes, ma'am, I can see she is," George replied, with deference. Jonathan's wife was the respectable, managing, housekeeping woman common to the country, salt of the earth, he thought, liking her, and plain as all git out. He thought of Maggie's round pink cheeks and blue eyes and firm round body. He liked women to have body.

Katie, catching Jonathan's eyes, rose. They said as plainly as speech that he wanted her to go, and she went. When the two men were alone, Jonathan cleared his throat.

"George, in a manner of speaking, I stand in the place of father to Maggie."

"Your old man passed on?" George's hearty voice was full of respect for death.

"No, but he doesn't give heed," Jonathan said. "And for my dead mother's sake I must ask you if in your own opinion you're fit to marry a young pure girl. If you were her age I wouldn't ask it. But a cattleman's had—temptations. And you have had twenty years of it."

"Of temptation?" George bellowed out laughter. "Well, if I have, I've resisted most of the time. I won't say I'm a virgin, Jonathan, for I'm not. You couldn't hardly find a man that was—west of the Mississippi, that is. But I'm clean, if that's your trouble, and now that I've found my girl, anything else is over. There ain't but two kinds of women in the world, good and bad, and the bad uns are only temporary in a man's life."

He spoke with confidence in the simple God who had created woman and therefore knew his material, and Jonathan did not contradict him. Katie was the good. Jennet was the bad. And what was Judy except herself? But perhaps there was no other like Judy in the world.

"Well, I still say you're old or she's young, one or the other. But I reckon Maggie'll have to make up her own mind," he said unwillingly.

"I'm agreeable to leave it to Maggie," George said. He rose. "Will I go out to the kitchen?"

"I can send her in here," Jonathan said. He felt a faint

repulsion toward the excitement he saw creeping into George's eyes.

"I'd rather go and find her in the kitchen," George said.

"Good night, then," Jonathan said abruptly.

Upstairs in the bedroom he shared with Katie he undressed himself and placed his garments in the careful order habitual to him.

Katie was already in bed. "You goin' to let him have her?" she asked.

"Maggie'll do what she likes," he said. He blew out the light and, wrapping his nightshirt about his knees, he climbed into bed and stretched his slender body and sighed. He was tired of love and all its ways. He had other things to do, and he would put this far from him. But he was glad to have Maggie gone early from his home. He could not cope with passion.

"You all right?" Katie inquired. She reached through the darkness and put her hand on his forehead. "You don't feel bilious, do you?"

"No, I don't think so," he said mildly. He felt suddenly grateful to her. "You're too good a cook to make a man bilious, Katie," he said.

"Oh, get out," Katie replied, but he could feel her happiness.

She fell asleep quickly after that, but he lay long awake, aware of what was in the kitchen beneath this room. He was not disturbed, but he fell into pondering on the distances that lay between man and woman. That abyss he would never cross. Never so long as he lived would he know what a woman really was. For into that heaven, too, the gate was narrow and the way strait. Not through many women did a man come into it, but only through one. And if that one were denied him, or if he denied her, then heaven was closed.

But perhaps other men were not like him? He considered this a moment and put it aside. I've no reason to think myself anything but an ordinary man, he thought.

He fell asleep at last, long before those two in the kitchen had parted.

George Tenney sat in the old kitchen armchair that was padded with plaited rags and held Maggie upon his knee. The range was hot with wood he had thrown in.

"We might as well be warm," he had said when he came in.

Her bread was made, and she was waiting. Then he had drawn Maggie into his arms. "I'm glad you've growed into something hefty, my girl," he said. "I never did like little bits of kindlin' wood."

Maggie's cheeks were scarlet, and she laughed loudly. "I'm too big," she said.

"Not for me," George said.

"I've outgrown everything," she said proudly, "so my brother Jonathan told me to make myself two new dresses."

"Did you make this one?" he asked. He smoothed the bright green stuff over her round thighs. He was going to be very gentle with this young thing. She was hot as fire, he could see, and heady for any man, because she did not know herself what she was. Better for that kind to be married quick and young and to a man old enough to handle them! He was right to come before another man had begun the job. His smoothing hand crept up over her waist and her young breast. She caught it back.

"Don't!" she said sharply, and tried to rise from his knee.

But he held her firmly. "Wait," he commanded. "I'll never do that again if you don't want I should. I've talked with Jonathan, and he says you're to do as you like. So—will you have me, Maggie?"

She quieted. "I don't hardly know you."

"You know me, but you don't remember."

"But you only came back today!"

"Did you keep my letter I sent you as you didn't answer?"

She hung her head. "It's here," she said, and put her hand on her breast.

"Was that why you pushed my hand away?"

She did not answer, but her ready blood was beating. She was trembling into love with him. He was handsomer than any boy in Median, a handsome man, the sort of man she liked, with big shoulders and sturdy legs, and strong hands and a voice you could hear across a field. And she was only a girl, and sometimes she feared not such a very pretty girl. Her body began to ache, and she looked at him. And suddenly she hid her face on his shoulder.

He held her as though she had been three. "There," he murmured, "there—there—there! I ain't goin' to hurry, or force you in any way. You shall come along as you want to, my little Mags."

But she seized his hand and pressed it against her bosom where his letter lay.

"That's where it is," she whispered and held his hand hard upon her hot young flesh.

In a month there were left in Jonathan's home only the three children, his own son and daughter and his small sister Mary. George Tenney went away and came back twice, and the third time he and Maggie were married. The marriage was right. Jonathan liked the man better each time he came, though he had little learning and never in his life had read a book from beginning to end. But few men had in these parts, and Maggie herself was no great reader.

In that month she grew into a woman ready for marriage. Her nature was defined by love. She was prudent in spending the little money Jonathan could spare her, and she did not once quarrel with Katie. Instead, she busied herself with recipes and ways of cooking, learning willingly all that she had rebelled against before. Katie was generous and taught her and helped her with advice and bade her choose what she liked from the store. Maggie exclaimed warmly over this kindness to Jonathan one day as he weeded the vegetable garden.

"Though there isn't much there," she added practically. "The store's gone down something terrible, Jonathan."

He looked up from his beets. "Has it?" he said sharply. "How, Maggie?"

"Well, the stock's poor," Maggie said, "and Mrs. Merridy isn't there much, and the boys take what they want to eat, and old Mr. Cobb is real lazy. He only works when Katie comes in or Mrs. Merridy."

"I'll have to talk with Katie," Jonathan said. He deliberately did not talk about the store with her, feeling upon him the uneasy knowledge of her wish that he would return to it. But maybe he owed it to Lew. Besides, Median wanted a good general store. He put it off until after the wedding.

The wedding was in the new church. The small wooden building had been finished a few months ago under Stephen Parry. It now belonged to all the denominations alike, the Episcopalians who were few, the Baptists and Presbyterians who were more, and the Methodists who because they were most had two Sunday mornings out of the month. But Jonathan had seen to it also that a strange sect from Russia had the church to themselves once a month, too, though in the afternoon. They were Mennonites and farmers, and they had come to Kansas bearing in their hands little bundles tied in kerchiefs. These held their most precious possession, the seed of a hard red wheat.

Traveling preachers held the meetings of the denominations, but in his heart Jonathan dreamed of a church where one man would be the minister for all, and that man Paul Graham. But Median was not ready for it. He had sounded out the people and had been hotly accused of believing in state religion, in the English fashion.

" 'Tisn't that I believe state and church should be one," he denied, "it's that I don't see the good of waste. What's it mean but that our folk will build six churches and struggle to pay half a dozen preachers and all the time they're worshiping the one God?"

But he gave up for the time and satisfied himself by inviting Paul Graham to come and marry Maggie and George, and advise him about uniting Median's souls. He liked Paul more than ever, a pale, grave, slender young priest. Then he was startled because he saw Paul's eyes on his sister Mary, who was still only a child. He was so put out by this that he let the matter of church unity rest. Might it be better not to have Paul living in Median? He was perturbed on the day of the wedding because Mary looked so pretty and grown up in her long bridesmaid's dress, and he was so cool to Paul that the sensitive young man was alarmed.

"Have I offended you, sir?" he asked before the ceremony. He was gowned in his ministerial robes and waiting with George and Jonathan in the little vestry.

But Jonathan was unable to put his irritation into words. It was beyond him to say to Paul, "My sister is too young for a man to look at her as though she were an angel."

"Of course not," he said shortly, and decided that he would not press Paul to stay on after this wedding day. So the matter of Median's unity in religion was put off into the future by so human a thing.

Median was too big now to come entire to a wedding, and Maggie had invitations printed, the first that Median had ever seen. A new little paper was sweating its way into print once a week, and this was its first wedding. The editor was the boy whose mother had accused Jonathan of paying no heed to drunkenness in Median. Jonathan had discovered in him an aptitude for words, and out of it had grown the boy's wish to make a newspaper.

"Why not?" Jonathan had replied. "Median's big enough now for its own paper." He talked gravely about type and headlines and what news was, and now every day or two the freckled young editor came loping down the street.

"What'd you think of today's paper, Mr. Goodliffe? How'd you think I handled the new populist trouble?"

Yesterday he had said solemnly, "I'm going to cover your sister's wedding myself, sir," and all during the ceremony he wrote feverishly upon a pad on his knee. Jonathan, walking up the aisle with Maggie's hand on his arm, saw a bent brown head look up and stare and bend to scribble again upon the pad.

He went on to the slowly pacing wedding march Martha Cobb was playing on the little organ. Someday he must find time to think about a big organ for the church. It was a pretty church. What would his mother think if she could know that there was a church in Median? Or if she knew that the fat, naughty little girl whom she had so often scolded and sometimes slapped had grown into this young bride? But Maggie had changed very little. All she had been was simply increased in quantity. He felt the vague stirring of his dry humor and repressed it.

After the wedding was over and they were all in his house for cake and lemonade, he took George aside.

"My mother used to say Maggie needed smacking once in a while. Don't be too gentle with her."

"Don't you worry," George said, grinning. "I can keep the upper hand, at my age."

He saw them out of his door and on the puffing noisy little train that was to carry them westward. There were no more wagons these days. People went West from Median on trains, though Jonathan had never set foot in one of them. He put a ten-dollar bill into Maggie's hand as she kissed his cheek, and then she put her arms around him and kissed him again.

"You've done too much for me as it is," she whispered.

"Take it," he said. "What's it for but to use?"

"But you could use it!"

"I have what I need, I reckon." He pushed her away a

little, not knowing he did so. The smell of her warm body, perspiring freshly, was sweet enough, but not for him. "Good-by, good-by," he said, and turned back to his own home.

Because he knew that we would never leave Katie he was glad when this earthy pair were gone from his house. He and Katie were a commonsensible pair, and both of them had been faintly ashamed before one another while George and Maggie had been in the house. The two could not hide their frank passion and their eagerness for marriage.

Yet when he opened the door of his house its stillness smote him.

One by one he was sending them away from him, the children his mother had left him, and soon it would be his own children, he thought. Then he and Katie would be left alone, with no one between them for a shield. When that day comes, I'll be old, he thought. Then he put old age far from him. I've a lot to do first, he thought grimly. He glanced at the courthouse in the middle of the square. They had had to take away some of his trees when the foundations were laid, but he had let only the cottonwoods be cut. The hardwoods he had transplanted.

They're permanent, he always thought when he passed them. Whenever he planted a tree now, and he had the school children plant them somewhere in Median every spring, he always planted hardwoods.

🥀 36 🥀

THE SUNFLOWER OIL COMPANY, JAMIE DISCOVERED, WAS Evan Bayne, the new candidate for the governorship of the state. Jamie had been living these months in Ruth's house. He slept there at night and spent the days on his horse examining every acre of the surrounding country. He bought three hundred acres and options on three times as much before his savings ran out. Then he cast about for resources, and Matthew told him of the Sunflower.

Without capital to offer, he went to Topeka to find the manager and to proffer himself for a job in the company. None of his land had produced oil yet, but it might at any moment. For a young man his assets were good, even if he had no cash.

Evan, taking shrewd stock of him, thought so too. A handsome fellow, this brother of Jonathan's! There was no trace in him of Jonathan's mild English look and ways. He was tall and bold-looking, his closely cut black hair was rough with a curl that could not be shorn, and his mouth was firm. It suddenly occurred to Evan that his sister Laura was coming to visit him, and that the last time she had come she had declared that if he did not produce at least one eligible young man, she would come no more. She had no time to waste, she had said. . . . Was this young man eligible?

"I rather think I might be able to do something for you," Evan said. "I'm very fond of your brother." He shot his eyebrows up, watching to discover what Jamie knew about that.

Jamie's face did not show him. "Of course I wouldn't want you to do anything for me because of Jonathan. I'd expect to stand on my own feet."

"Of course—"

A young woman came into the room. She was dressed in the new mannish shirtwaist and skirt, and her intensely black hair was pompadoured about her pale face. She was not pretty, and when she was not introduced Jamie dismissed her. But as soon as she spoke he looked at her again. She had a voice as deep and soft as the heavy string on a fiddle. It went to his spine.

"Did you ring, Mr. Bayne?"

"This is my secretary, Miss Power," Evan said. "Rachel, when's Laura coming?"

"Saturday, sir."

Evan frowned a little. Why not? If both birds were killed with one stone, or if neither, no damage was done.

"Come along to my house Saturday night," he said to Jamie. "We dine at seven. Afterwards we can talk. Rachel, be sure I have the last figures on Sunflower before then."

"Yes, sir." Again the deep, sweet voice.

"Suits me, sir." Jamie rose.

The dark girl held out a card upon which she had been writing quickly. "Your memorandum, sir."

His spine quivered again, and he looked down into a

narrow, clever face, still not pretty, but wise enough to confound him.

"Th-thanks," he stammered. He went out, sweating a little. Gosh, I'd hate to have her around me all the time, he thought. He looked at the card. Upon it in the neatest clearest script he had ever seen was all the information he could imagine, name, address, and hour for Saturday's engagement. In small bracketed letters she had even written (Dress).

"Well, damn it, does she think I'll go naked?" he wondered. He thrust the card into his pocket and took it out again. There was something queer about that bracketed word. He sauntered along and went into a men's clothing shop and accosted a man who wore striped pants and a long coat and a high collar.

"What do you make of that?" he demanded, presenting the card.

The man took it and read it. "I should say it was a dinner appointment, sir, to be attended in evening dress."

Jamie grinned. "My evening dress is my nightshirt."

The man grinned. "This isn't that."

"Show me what dress you've got for a man," Jamie demanded.

In less than an hour he was fitted to garments he had not only never worn before, but had never seen or heard of.

"Nifty," the man murmured.

"I kind of agree with you," Jamie said, looking at the young man in the mirror.

Too handsome, Laura was thinking. Would I dare?

She was older than this man, perhaps by a year, perhaps by three. But she was small, and he so big. Besides, she did not want to marry anyone she knew.

"I hate oil," she said aloud. "It smells."

Over her white shoulder she smiled into Jamie's face. Not quite a gentleman, she was thinking, but then all the men she knew were gentlemen, and they tired her.

"It smells," Jamie agreed, "but how it pays!" His brown face broke into a shimmering smile, and she laughed.

"You don't mind money, do you!" she said.

"It's what I'm lookin' for most," he said.

"More than anything?"

"When I get it, I'll look for a wife," he said impudently.

This girl made him feel like his dad. She drew the billy goat out of him as no nice woman ever had done in his life. He must be nice because she was his boss's sister. But he felt bold. He had not been here ten minutes before Evan had told him there would be a place for him in the company if he could agree to certain financial details.

"You bet I'll agree, Mr. Bayne!" he had said. Then he saw that dark girl again at his boss's elbow, and he heard her deep voice.

"I have the memoranda ready, but you won't want to talk until after dinner, will you, Mr. Bayne?"

"No—in the library, Rachel."

She had slipped away, but at the dinner table she was at Evan's elbow again, her seat at his left. Jamie looked down the table at Judy.

Tonight when Evan introduced them she had bowed her head a very little in answer to his bow. He remembered when he had seen her last, but he did not tell her so. Now he wondered what she thought of this dark girl at her husband's elbow, whose violin voice, so seldom raised, was always heard when it spoke. Anyone could see that it was to her that Evan turned when he wanted anything. No use pretending that a man could have a girl at his elbow all day and not grow to depend on her in all sorts of ways—not that it was any of his business, now that Evan was his boss!

"Can anything good come out of Kansas?" Laura's pretty insistent voice was at his ear.

"Me," he said promptly.

"I thought you were English?"

"If I ever was, it's been forgotten."

"I met your brother once—he was very English."

"Yes, Jonathan's pretty much what he always was. He's stayed in Median. All the rest of us have scattered. Why, my old dad's just run for new land and almost got it, by Jiminy!"

"Not quite?"

"He has a game leg and his wagon broke down, or he'd have made it."

"And Jonathan's not going in for oil?"

"No, he's a schoolteacher. He doesn't want to be anything else. Median's grown all around him, but he goes on just the same."

"I'd like to see him."

"He looks the way he always has."

"Not like you?"

"You'd never know we were brothers."

"Maybe I'd like him better than you."

" 'Twould surprise me, but he'd be even more surprised."

She laughed her quick, falling laughter. "I like you rather well," she said. Her great coquetry was to seem guiltless of any coquetry.

Jamie leaned toward her. "Like me as well as you can, will you?"

"Why?"

"Because some day I might fall in love with you!"

"You are too quick," she murmured. "We haven't reached dessert, yet."

"Out where I come from we hurry," he said.

Katie at the sitting-room window looked at the clock. It was six o'clock of the November day, and the sky was already black. Across the dead lawn the light in the office of the schoolhouse burned. Jonathan was still working. It used to be that she could see him through the curtainless window. Then one day he said the light from the window was too strong, and he had moved his desk so that now she could no longer see it.

"Mary!" Her voice rose high to the last syllable. "Oh, Mary!"

"Yessum?" Mary's light and childlike voice floated through the floor from her room upstairs.

"Go and call your brother to supper!"

"Yessum!"

Katie sighed and put down her sewing and went into the kitchen. She wanted supper over because there was something she must tell Jonathan. She had to tell him because she was sick and tired of holding her tongue when people complained about the way he was running the school. Today in the store she had had her fill, with fat Mrs. Tenber wanting her to ask Jonathan why he didn't let her Theodore pass the sixth grade.

"Three times he's been through the same grade, Mis' Goodliffe, and still Mr. Goodliffe don't let him pass it!"

"I reckon he'd pass if he was fit to pass!" she had said.

She was not afraid of any Mrs. Tenber, but it made her sick to think of all that Jonathan did and yet anybody who felt like it could criticize him. Schoolteaching was a thankless public job. And at the last meeting of the trustees they had made it plain enough that Jonathan could never get a raise in salary, not if he lived to be a hundred. She had quarreled with Jonathan over that, not because she wanted more money, but because they had hurt him. He was so gentle, so careful to explain to her why they had felt as they did, that she knew he was deeply hurt.

"It's perfectly natural that now, with all these young chaps getting out of universities in the East, they wouldn't much want a chap like me, Katie. I can see it."

"With all you've done!" she cried. "Every child like your own, and you slaving away summer and winter, Saturdays and vacations and everything!"

"They don't ask me to do that, though, Katie. If I wish to do it, I can scarcely expect to be paid for it."

"Ain't experience anything?"

He knew she stormed at them through him, and so he could be patient with her. "While I've been getting experience I've been getting older, too, Katie."

"What I hate is folks thinkin' they have the say-so of you, because you're paid out of taxes. A miserable little pay, and it's not your own when you've got it! I wish you was in the store. Then you'd be beholden to nobody."

"I can't quit my rightful work, Katie."

Neither of them mentioned the money for its own sake, she because she did not want him to think she could not manage, and he because he felt uneasily that he was deepening that vague great debt to her of his marriage. Would it make it up to Katie, he often wondered, if he could provide her with more comforts? But how could he give up his school?

In his office now he was preparing again for the quarterly meeting of the school board. Times had changed very much from those days when as a young schoolmaster he had simply gathered together his pupils. Subscription school, it had been then, paid for by parents who wanted their children taught. Now the schools were public. People grumbled at taxes and then expected everything from the scanty dollars they paid. He loved teaching, but the sinew of his life now could not go into it. He had to spend himself upon this grinding down of every expense to meet an appropriation too small. In the sod house there had been so few books that each had been precious. He had scarcely thought of the possibility of new books. Now there were so many books required that they were no longer precious, either to study or to possess. There were too many new ones for every school term. Children came and went to school loaded with books and caring for none of them. But he was still angry when he found a child defacing a book with scrawls and drawings.

"A book is a treasury," he always said. "You must learn how to find the treasure. That is why you come to school." This was really the soul of his teaching. But it was getting out of date, his sort of teaching. People were wanting a lot of new things that should not be in a school. Girls could learn them at home in their mothers' kitchens, and boys could apprentice themselves to blacksmiths and carpenters. School was a place to acquire learning out of books which were the fruit of man's knowledge and thought. So he believed.

"Supper's ready, Jonathan."

He looked up and saw that Mary had run out of the kitchen in her cotton school dress. He spoke quietly.

"Mary, why do you disobey me again about not putting on your cloak in this weather?"

She looked astonished and then frightened. "Honest, I forgot!"

She was so stricken that he smiled at her. She looked so like his mother in these days of her new adolescence that he could never scold her. It always seemed when he did that he was scolding the dying creature who had found her way back to him. "I notice you never forget anything Katie tells you to do," he grumbled.

"She keeps after me," Mary murmured.

"And I don't, eh?"

"You're more peaceful-like."

He went on smiling without hearing her, his mind on his determination to refuse the demand of the trustees for a course in manual arts in the high school. It would come to a battle, but he would fight it and win it. He wanted the money for a new teacher of history. People here did not value history. The newspaper was all they wanted—yesterday was far enough away, and only today was important. But how could man measure himself if he did not know the history of his kind?

"I'll be along, Mary." Then he remembered her and tossed her his old mackinaw. "Here, put that around you."

"But you?" she asked.

"I haven't on a thin dress." He saw her face for the moment framed in the coat she put over her head like a hood. A prettyish girl, he thought, too fine-featured, perhaps. At least among the sturdier girls of Median she looked puny. He must think to notice how she ate. She was small, as their mother had been small, but she must not grow up delicate.

He waited for her to be gone, then he rose, turned out the gas lamps he had just had installed with all of Median beginning to use gas, and strolled into sharply cold darkness. There was a smell in the air of frostbitten lawns and flowers, and it struck into his memory so sudden and sharp that he recognized it instantly. This was the smell of the night years ago when he had been dreaming of his marriage to Judy. But he had forgotten, surely he had forgotten by now.

Katie said, "Don't raise the window yet, Jonathan. There's somethin' I've got to talk about."

He hesitated, his hand on the window that had once been a quarrel between him and Katie until he had removed it by simply refusing to sleep in a room in which the window was not opened at night. Love of air he had learned in England, and he was stifled unless he felt it fresh and cold upon his face. "Jonathan ain't happy without he's sittin' in a draught," Katie said so often that he had ceased to hear it.

"I'm fair tired tonight," he remarked, but he sat down on the bed instead of getting into it. This room, meant for quiet sleep, was in reality the storm center of his life. It was the only room where he and Katie were ever alone. Children, growing and gangling, noisy and clamorous, trailed and galloped and lounged in every other.

He knew before she began what it was she wanted to talk about. It was another battle in her long war against the school. Depending upon his mood and physical state, he was able to be quietly humorous in his defense, parrying and delaying, or else he was abrupt. He was not sure tonight which he would be. He watched her as she slipped her full cotton nightgown over her head. In all these years she had never undressed except under this great evolution of white stuff. She was writhing, screwing herself out of garments underneath it now, and there were small clicks and pulls of sound.

THE TOWNSMAN

"Jonathan, Mrs. Tenber's awful mad again about that boy of hers not passin'."

"Is she?" He suddenly felt he would not be humorous.

"She's goin' to complain to the trustees."

"It'll do her no good. The boy is a fool. I told her she ought to put him to work in the machine shop or livery stable."

"Jonathan, you didn't!" There was a small crash of steel-stayed corset about Katie's feet.

"I did."

Katie stood an instant imagining Mrs. Tenber's state of mind. "I reckon she thinks if she pays taxes she has as good a right as anybody else to send her boy to school."

"Just because the country's a democracy is no guarantee that none of our citizens are ever born fools," Jonathan retorted. He felt he wanted to be angry and he became so. He pulled the sandy moustache he had decided to grow last year.

"The trustees can't realize it, either. Instead of facing the truth that men may be born free but they are never born equal, they propose to meet the problem of fools like this Tenber boy by putting a machine shop and a carpentry shop and what-not into my school. The town's full of such places, but, no, fools have to think they're getting an education while they are tinkering with their hands though they've got no brains."

He was so angry now that he was chewing the rough ends of his moustache. "This isn't just one boy, Katie, it's a situation—a battle—and I'm going to win or get out."

"Then I'll be glad if you don't win," she retorted. "School-teachin' is a poor thankless business."

"Teaching is the highest job a man can do," Jonathan said firmly. "But they don't let me teach any more in these newfangled days. When I began in the sod house I was able to teach. I could put my whole mind to it, and I turned out sensible people from the raw ignorant boys and girls I got. Now I'm supposed to supply mechanics and carpenters and blacksmiths instead of scholars and civilized people."

He rose and flung open the window, and the cold air hit him like a wave of sea water. Upon such a night his mother had come home, and all his life was changed. The wind had been cold that night. He turned to Katie. "Here's a promise, Katie. If I can't have the kind of school I want, I'll give it up."

"And take the store?" She was braiding her tight brown pigtail of hair.

"And take the store," he said.

But he had no intention of letting it come to that. He was full of stubborn zest for his own way. He got into bed and lay very stiff and straight as he summoned before the tribunal of his mind one after the other of his school trustees.

Abram Hasty owned the mill now that old Samuel had died of apoplexy—a curious way for that wire of a man to die, but his veins were petrified with the whisky he had drunk for years instead of water. Abram had grown into a stolid pigheaded man who made a good thing out of the mill by putting in machinery. But Abram still remained nevertheless one of the stupidest of his pupils.

I can down him, Jonathan thought.

He ran his mind hastily over the others. Faience, the president of the new little Median Farmer's Bank; Riggs, the postmaster; Baker, the head of the livery stable. Not an educated man among them, Jonathan thought triumphantly. Not one who knows a Latin verb!

By his side Katie sniffed as she breathed. She suffered with hay fever and, though the hard frost had cured its cause, she kept for months the habit of sniffing.

"I hate your being at the beck and call of every taxpayer," she said.

"I'm not," Jonathan said flatly. He hated Katie's sniffing, but not for anything would he have mentioned it. Instead he said suddenly and inexplicably, "Put up or shut up!"

"Why, Jonathan Goodliffe!" Katie cried.

"I say that no more for you than for me," he retorted. And without further explanation to her or to himself he turned his back on her and went to sleep.

🌿 37 🌿

WHEN JONATHAN SAW THE HACK STOP IN FRONT OF HIS house, he recognized it as one of those that stood usually behind the railroad depot. Then he saw his brother Jamie leap out of the hack and turn and put out his hand to help a slender woman step down. They went into the house, and after a moment Katie came out of the door, her apron over her head, and he hurried from his office and met her halfway.

"Jamie's brought his girl," she cried. The wind twisted her skirts about her thin legs and big feet.

"I didn't know he had a girl," he shouted against the wind.

"I reckon it's only just happened!" she shrieked. "It's a Miss Bayne—Laura!"

He caught the name like a blow and set his teeth. Evan's sister, that fierce child of a girl he had seen years ago! Yes, she would be grown and not too young—older than Jamie. But why did she want Jamie? He stepped into the little hall.

"Smooth down your hair," Katie said. "You look wild."

He smoothed it down hastily. . . . But would this marriage bring him nearer to Evan? He did not want that.

"Howdy, Jonathan!"

Jamie was at the door of the sitting room. He was dressed in new city clothes from head to foot. Jonathan surveyed him, delaying. "You're looking very fine, aren't you?"

"I've struck oil," Jamie said, grinning. "A good deep well of it. Queer thing is, it ain't a hundred feet from Ruth and Matthew's cow pasture. I bought next to them."

"They never struck any."

"Not a drop. I've been all over their land myself. It's the dangdest thing I ever see."

"Hmph." Jonathan pulled his moustache. "Maybe the rest of you are draining it off of them."

"Maybe, but if we are, it's all legal." Jamie's bold blue eyes were calm. "Sure is bad luck for Ruth. I wisht it wasn't my own sister."

"Bad luck for anybody," Jonathan said dryly. Then he heard the rustle of a taffeta skirt and braced himself. Laura came to the door.

She put out her hand to him. "You don't remember me."

"Yes, I do." He took a long slender hand into his for a second.

Jamie grinned. " 'Tisn't only oil I struck." He pulled her other long slender hand into his arm and patted it. "Laura and me are going to be married, Jonathan. That's what we came to tell you."

"I came to see Jonathan," Laura protested, with her pout that was still girlish enough to be pretty. "You made an impression once on a certain young thing, Jonathan. She was smitten for a while with a grave young Englishman—long enough to look twice at his brother."

"Hey! Which one of us is the lucky man?" Jamie inquired loudly. He was proud of her being a lady.

But he was proud of himself, too, these days. Luck was roaring around him. Money was pouring into his bank account, and Evan was talking of making him a vice-president of Sunflower, so that if he himself should be elected governor, Jamie could take over the company.

"Come in and sit down," Jonathan said. He was master of himself now, and he led the way into the sitting room and nodded when Katie went out to fetch coffee and cookies. "Well!" He looked from one face to the other. "When's it to be?"

For in this moment his mind had leaped ahead to their marriage day, where he and Judy must meet. Not once had he yielded to any imagination which would have made possible his seeing her again. But that his brother should marry Evan's sister was beyond imagination.

"After Lent," Laura said. "I have to go home and tell Mamma and get my trousseau."

"Your mother still living?" After Lent was a long time away, but the longer the better.

Laura gave a little scream of laughter. "Mamma would be furious if anybody thought she was dead!"

Jamie shouted, and Jonathan smiled dryly. "Give her my respects," he said.

He had a strange wry tingling of the blood at the relationship between these two because somehow it brought closer the separate orbits of his life and Judy's. Then he recognized this as the cause of his secret excitement and put it sternly away. Even if he met Judy face to face, what could it mean to him? He turned abruptly to Jamie. "Tell me about Ruth. Is she taking it hard that they don't find oil?"

"Ruth feels it right smart," Jamie said.

Laura was thinking, He's so handsome, and when we're married, I shall teach him manners and I will throw away that suit he's wearing. It was patterned like a checkerboard. But he was growing handsomer every day. The city was grooming him. She had taken him home and paraded him before her friends, complacent when they chorused their admiration. "I declah, honey, he's just beautiful!" "Laura, *how* did you—" "Laura, he just makes my haid *swirl!*"

Her mother, seventy-one years old, had stared at Jamie for a long time. "A very pretty man!" she declared at last. Her voice was silvery with age and self-will.

Laura took out her fencing weapons. "A man's a man for a' that," she said lightly.

"I suppose so," old Mrs. Bayne said. She had blinked her old eyes once or twice. "But what are you going to *do* with him when you've married him, Laura?" She behaved as if Jamie sitting not ten feet from her were cardboard.

"Keep him," Laura said sharply.

"My child, you always were ambitious," her mother had said. . . .

"I got the better of Mother," Laura thought and gazing at Jamie, her eyes grew liquid with love.

Jonathan caught that look and was as uneasy as though he were eavesdropping. "Excuse me," he said. "I'll step out and help Katie."

Neither of them noticed his going.

"Come over here by me, Jamie," Laura commanded. She still had to tell him when she wanted him to kiss her. He rose, shyly, very tall and full of beauty, and came over to her and took her in his arms. She gave herself up to the breathless luxury of giving herself up. "Love me?"

"Sure do."

"Are you a one-woman man, Jamie?"

He grinned down into her face on his breast. "How do I know?"

"Your dad sounds an old rake."

He laughed, and she dug her nails softly into his neck. "Feel my claws?"

"Like a tiger cat's!"

"I'll dig them into you if you ever stop loving me!"

"I'll remember that."

"Even when I'm an old woman and you're still a handsome young man, you'll have to love only me—oh, Jamie, you'll always be a handsome young man as long as you live, and that's what I've got to face."

He laughed again, not knowing quite what else to do, and she wrenched herself out of his arms.

"I wonder if Jonathan still loves Judy? I wonder if that's

what is wrong with Judy? Even if she doesn't love anybody, if he loves her, and she knows it? Love is such a *poisonous* thing when it goes on and on after you want it to stop! It poisons lover and beloved."

He had not the slightest idea what she was talking about, and she knew it.

"Oh, well!" she said and threw herself into his arms again and closed her eyes. He was male, bread to her heart and wine to her body. What a curse to a woman was intelligence! How unnecessary and useless and unwanted in the life of man and woman! At this moment of her passing youth, it was the only life she wanted.

The door opened. Katie was back with the cookies and coffee. Behind her came Jonathan, his eyes cold, his lips set. With him were his children. He had brought them here to keep beside him, and when he sat down, he held them in the circle of his arms.

. . . Weeks later Laura ordered Jonathan to come to her wedding.

He smiled faintly. "Well, Laura, I'm a very plain chap, and Evan's a great man now."

"Nonsense! Evan doesn't forget his old friends. There's such a snobbishness about men like you! You're always thinking you're too good for people who are what you call 'great'!"

Jonathan knew she was baiting him, but still there was truth in what she said, and he was always confounded by any atom of truth.

"Maybe you're right at that," he agreed. He examined himself. "Reckon maybe I do like plain people because I feel good enough myself when I'm amongst 'em."

"Ah-ha!" she cried, shaking her pointed forefinger at him.

"Leave it to you to drag out my innards into the open air," he said good-naturedly. He liked Laura now and marveled at her folly in marrying Jamie. She read Dante in Italian, and he had never been able to persuade Jamie to read anything.

"I haven't finished," she said impudently. And then she leaned forward and dragged out his heart and stared at it thumping and leaping in her hand.

"You do love Judy still," she said.

"Reckon I'll always love Judy in a curious sort of way," he answered in a low voice. Not to another soul than to this impetuous, clever woman could he have said it. But once the thing was in words, he felt relief. There it was, out. His heart suddenly lay still in her hand. She took pity on him and put it neatly into his breast again.

"Dear Jonathan," she murmured. "You needn't come to my wedding, if it hurts you."

" 'Tisn't the hurt," he said. "It's just—the uselessness of hurt. But I'll come."

. . . That was it—the uselessness of even looking at Judy. And yet he looked at her quietly and freely all the time Jamie and Laura were being married, and in all the city church full of people he saw only that beautiful woman standing by Laura's side. She was dressed in some sort of soft stuff the color of cream, and she wore a big black hat against which her pallor was pure beauty. He knew that all she wore cost a great deal of money, more than he earned in a year; but for that he cared nothing. He wanted simply to look at her, without memory of the past, without thought of the future, without passion or possession. And as he gazed it came over him that she was as much his life as she had ever been. Whatever she was and was not, the mysterious form that the elements had taken to shape her being was the one form that he loved or could ever love.

He became aware of the small snifflings and twitches at his side that were Katie's sign of being, and he turned to his daily wife.

"There's a terrible draught!" she whispered.

He glanced about the church. "I can't see where from. Everything's shut tight."

"I feel cold."

He lifted her coat from the back of the pew and held it for her to put on. At the same instant the wedding march burst into pealing music, and the bridal party turned and paced down the aisle. The instant was near when Judy must pass within very reach of his hand if he should put it out. Surely she would see him. He felt sick and giddy. If she should look at him? . . .

He kept his eyes on her approaching face. Her head was bent, but just before she reached his pew she lifted her head suddenly and gazed straight ahead, seeing no one. He saw her face foreshortened and still so innocent.

So the moment passed. She did not see him. Light went with her, the music faded, and people began to stir.

"Well, it's over," Katie said half-aloud. She wiggled her foot into the new shoe she had slipped off.

"Yes, I reckon it is," he agreed. "Let's go home."

He was very gentle with Katie that night. She complained of headache and cold, and he made some ginger tea and heated a brick. It occurred to him as he put the brick to her feet that she was very thin. It was so seldom that he noticed such things that he was ashamed now.

"Aren't you all right, Katie?" he asked.

" 'Course I'm all right," she replied.

She looked away from him, and he said no more. Between them the primary silence had never yet been broken. But that night he lay, long awake, astonished at the passing of life. Katie, whose small adolescent breasts had seemed shocking to him so short a time ago, this Katie had been his wife for all these years, and now she had reached the end of youth. He thought of Judy, changed only to greater beauty. He put out his hand and felt Katie's shoulder blade through the yoke of her nightgown. At his touch she woke.

"Did you lock the kitchen door?" she asked.

They had never locked doors in Median until recently. But since the panic in the East, panhandlers had come westward on freight trains and on foot, and there had been robberies everywhere. Even in Median people were beginning to lock their doors.

"I think I did, but I'd better make sure."

He climbed out of bed, fumbled for his carpet slippers, and lit the candle. Upon the stairs a cold small wind folded his nightshirt about his bare legs. The door must have blown open. He went on, shielding the candle with his hand. A good thing he got up, he thought, for the door stood wide. He peered out for a moment into the darkness. But there was nothing to be seen except the trees in the square, ghostly in the corner street lamp. When he had planted them they had been saplings. He shut the door and locked it fast and went back to his bed.

✖ 38 ✖

"You can't go against the times," Abraham Hasty said.
Then he added, "sir." Jonathan had all but beaten the word
into him years ago.

It was the last meeting of the school year, and the question
of manual arts, long argued, always delayed, had come to
crisis.

"You're such a practical man, Goodliffe," Faience said
courteously. Faience had come from Virginia. "I don't know
anybody the town owes more to than you. Why, folks tell me
you have started pretty nearly everything we have that's any
good. But your attitude on the new education astonishes me."

"I've been a schoolteacher long enough to know what you
can educate and what you can't," Jonathan said. "A schoolteacher's job is to sort, and sort more clearly as the grades go
higher. Everybody ought to read and write, we'll say—though
I don't know even that does everybody good. But not everybody ought to go on to higher mathematics and Latin."

"Exactly," Faience said, "so the manual arts allow education to those who shouldn't. It gives the right emphasis to
education in a great democratic country. It says to the
common man, 'The work you do with your hands is as worthy
of a graduating degree as is the learning of books.'"

Jonathan put doggedly aside the river of words. Faience
was the new mayor of Median, and everything was practice
for speeches the mayor must make. "But manual arts are
better taught where they're really practiced. Makin' little

396

useless things that don't sell, that aren't wanted, that's not education for anyone. It's unreal."

"Still, seems as if fellows ought to have a chance at a diploma even if they can't memorize things outa books," Abram Hasty said.

Jonathan turned a pale sand color. His eyes glittered, and his blood was icy around his heart. Pure anger always made him cold. There was no rise in the level of his voice.

"Very well, I'll tell you what, gentlemen. I offer my resignation if there's to be carpentry and blacksmithing and basketry in the school. It'd be dishonest of me to stay."

"Now, Mr. Goodliffe," Abram protested. He was a big, hairy, coarse-fleshed man, but he had always been afraid of this slender, firm figure. He had secrets in books that Abram could never learn. Even money had not been enough to free Abram from distrust of the learning he had not been able to acquire or use. School for him and for Sam had only taught them enough to make them afraid of an educated man.

Jonathan rose and pushed his chair under the desk. He held his head high, and from under the sandy shelf of his eyebrows his eyes were agate-colored and full of cold light.

"I'll withdraw, if you please, while you talk it over. I'll hand in my resignation if it's decided against my opinion as a schoolmaster. Good day!"

He stalked out, his shoulders stiff, and so went across the lawn and into his own house. In the quiet of midafternoon in May it was empty. The children were at school, and Katie was at the store. He stood a moment not knowing what to do. Then he turned and went out again, down the street and toward the store.

Upon the single main street of Median which ran into the square and around it, a colored boy was selling newspapers. Jonathan stopped. It was Parry's youngest boy.

"Link, why aren't you in school?"

The boy's face was framed for impudence, but now he looked alarmed. He shifted the papers under his arm and wet his full lips. "I just got to earn me some money, Mr. Goodliffe."

"What for?"

"Circus comin'."

Jonathan gazed at him sternly. "When?"

"Sat'dy, suh."

"You know I ought to punish you for truancy?"

"Yessuh!"

Jonathan kept the moment long and miserable. "Give me a paper," he said at last, "and keep the change."

He gave the boy a dime and hastened on, shutting his ears to thanks. Circuses! So Median was big enough for circuses to find it worth while to stop. The town was getting too big— nearly six thousand people by the last count. He unfolded the front page. The smiling dark eyes looked at him from under the handsome silver-gray hair. "Evan Bayne for Governor," the headlines shouted. He stared at them. He was neither sorry nor glad. All that the words meant was that Judy was going farther away.

No, I'm danged glad, he thought.

It separated him, sent him deeper into Median. Here in Median was his life. If the school were taken from him, he had the store. He'd make it a good store. He folded the paper and marched to the door of the store and went in, seeing it for the first time as something possibly his own. It was empty. He called, "Katie!"

She came out of the back room, two pencils stuck in the knots of hair on top of her head. "Jonathan! Why, what're you here for this time of day? We're taking inventory—"

She looked tired, and his heart, quivering in his bosom, leaped to her. This faithful woman was his home, his dwelling place in Median. Her good and honest face, her plain figure and working hands—these were his possession. His, too, her being, framed for loyalty and devotion and forgetfulness of self. How could he ever repay her all he owed to her? He knew. He held her reward in his hand.

"Katie, I've as good as resigned from the school."

"Jonathan Goodliffe!" She clasped her hands together with one loud clap. "Oh, I hope you didn't do it for anything I said!"

"No. They're going to put carpentry and blacksmithing and stuff like that into my curriculum. That's not school."

"Oh!" She sighed. Her hazel eyes were suffused. "If you knew how I've prayed!"

He had seen her by their bed every night, praying, her nightgowned figure kneeling, her head bowed on the counter-pane. The soles of her large bare feet were repulsive and pathetic to him, but he always stopped any noise he was making until she rose.

"Well, here's your prayer answered," he said. A faint smile was upon his lips for a flickering second. "Though I've never thought of myself as able to give the answer to any woman's prayer!"

She laughed because she knew he meant to joke.

"I might as well begin," he said, and went behind a counter. He might just as well, for he had nothing else to do. To Katie now he paid his debt in full.

For the first time in his life he put much thought upon the matter of his marriage. It could have nothing to do with love, for what people thought of as love was certainly not between him and Katie. But other things were.

There were the children. He had made up his mind that they were ordinary children without a glimmer of the flame that was in Beaumont. But he did not blame them for that. He had not found it in any other child of the hundreds he had taught. And why should he think there was any source of it in himself or in Katie? Judy might have transmitted it from something Joel had. But others had not given it to Katie or to him.

I'm a common chap, he thought, and it would take something very uncommon to make my children anything else.

They were all the same, good and common. In church every Sunday he saw Ruth and Matthew, faithfully worshiping God in spite of disappointed hope. He had ceased to ask them whether they still had hope of oil. Matthew went on farming, and Ruth kept her house.

Once a year Maggie came home with George. In two years she had had two children, but they had not changed her. She was still impatient and high-tempered, but George kept her in bounds. They were well off, although they took care not to talk about it before people. Maggie was shrewd and a manager. She liked good clothes and good food, and she had both. George had put off leaving the cattle business until Maggie nagged him to it by complaining of the way he smelled. The crisis came one night when she climbed out of their bed and flounced herself into the spare room.

"And here I stay until you quit smelling like a farm hand," she said.

George had got himself a job in insurance the next day, for he was perpetually infatuated with the vigorous, plump-bodied, red-cheeked girl he had made his wife. Now she wanted him to move East, and sooner or later he knew he would do it, though he loved the West.

Yes, they were all good plain people.

Jonathan found that he even enjoyed the store once he knew it was his fate. I've shopkeeping blood, he thought, remembering his mother's small and fragmentary shops. Not that I wouldn't have enjoyed something else more if I could have had it the way I wanted.

Denied that, he was cheerful, and he arranged everything the way he liked, and this was pleasant. He asked no one anything, and that was good. If he had none of the high moments of the spirit that once had been his when he looked down into scores of young faces waiting for him to speak, he had solid moments of content. He liked to search out the thing he had to fill a need. When someone came in to ask for anything he liked to say, "I have it." He liked to think he had everything in the store. To a woman coming for a dress, a child for candy, a man for a scythe, boys wanting rubber to make slings or string for kites, he wanted to be able to say, "I have it here." It was his ambition to have in the store what anybody in Median could want and to have it before it was asked for. He had wire screening before people thought of flies as anything but inevitable, or of any preventions for them except a branch broken from a tree and waved over the dinner table. He had rubber hot-water bottles, and hot bricks and warming pans slowly disappeared from homes in Median.

At American House, Henry Drear was growing too fat to walk and Mrs. Drear had colored men in the kitchen which she had made into a new dining room. Rows of rocking chairs stood on the porch now, and Henry Drear was always in one of them asleep. People passing took for granted his great body, hands folded across his belly, and head rolling on his shoulder.

At night Jonathan locked the store and went home and talked over the day with Katie. When he had been in the school there had been little to talk about with her. But now there were the things she had known all her life—the price of cloth and ribbon, the quality of carpets and the brands of groceries, the colors of hats and curtains and the styles of dresses, the quantities of furniture and underwear and overalls and shirts and haberdashery and hardware and the vegetables and baked goods that women brought in to sell. These home products were his bane, but Jonathan wanted to sell food, and he could not refuse to take eggs when a woman had no money to pay for a dress she needed.

In all this Katie's instinct was needle-fine and sure as money in his pocket after a sale. She was so average that she always knew what the average wanted, and he trusted to her completely when he ordered his stocks. They disagreed on two things only—wallpaper and books. He disliked wallpaper, but Katie said they must have it because it was coming into style. People were building little bare frame houses that wanted paper on the thin walls. So against his will he did his share to put upon Median walls the large flowery patterns that offended his sense of decent quiet.

"Stands to reason it's silly to paste up sprawling ribbons and flowers and scenes to stare at all day," he told Ruth sternly when he found her lingering over the table of wallpapers. He put it in the back of the shop, and time and again he told people, "You don't want that stuff." But they did and so did Ruth, and at last he said, "Well, have your way in your own home." But in his own he had plain limed walls and was firm with Katie except for the new parlor he put on the house that year.

There was no doubt that storekeeping paid him more money than teaching. The only thing in the store that never paid at all was books. He kept a small stock of them, old writers and new, on the chance that they might be wanted. But they seldom were. Even Charles Dickens, whose stories his mother had loved so well, was dead upon his shelf in Median. Jonathan read a volume sometimes, snatching a few pages when on a rainy afternoon the store was empty for an hour or so, but not in months did any other hand than his touch those books. He kept them, wondering why he had spent so much of his life in teaching people to read, and where they were whom he had taught.

And so in this life he and Katie grew together. It was her life, and he went into it. And the long unspoken friction between them was gone at last. She was jealous of no one and nothing now, for she and he were together in the store. She approved of him fundamentally at last, and he found peace in this approval. It made him free. He had done something he ought to do for her. He had done what she wanted him to do more than anything else. And so, his love expiated, he found his marriage better than it had ever been, a solid, everyday comradeship in which he and Katie took common share of the sources of their money and food and goods.

The store was a success and, because it was, it made all his life seem successful. He put a bathroom into his house, though it did not occur to him yet to take away the outdoor privy. But the women no longer used it. It became private to him and to Jon. This was a relief, for it had always been horrible to him to meet, coming to or from that small apartment, Katie or Lula or Mary. He ignored them as though he had not seen them. Now he merely ignored Jon, and he did not need to pretend to be examining the blight on the old lilac that screened the privy.

Median made a Chamber of Commerce the fourth year he had the store, and he was its first president.

🐝 39 🐝

ON AN AUGUST DAY IN A HOT SUMMER JONATHAN SAT IN the office. It was early afternoon, people were still loitering over noonday dinner, and the store was empty for the moment of customers. The mixed odors were strong, of pickles and cheese and dry goods, for he had ordered doors and windows shut against the heat. Behind the counter old Cobb was checking stacks of calico.

In the silence he heard the street door open and shut, and then Jon's voice.

"Where's Pop?" Jon demanded.

"Here!" Jonathan called. "And don't you call me Pop. It's no way for a boy to call his father."

"Want me to sweep the store, Dad?"

Jonathan looked up from his ledger. He wore small steel-rimmed spectacles to which he had fitted himself from the gross or two he kept in stock.

"If you get clean behind the counters better than you did last time."

"Didn't I?"

"No, you didn't." Jonathan's voice was kind but dry.

"Well, I will." Young Jonathan took the broom from the corner of the office and lingered. "Dad!"

"What, Jon?"

"Would you mind if I joined the Navy?"

Jonathan snatched off his spectacles. "What're you talking of, boy?"

"I'm sick of this little town."

Jonathan's eyes were upon his son's eyes, exactly like his own. "Why?"

"Everything's always the same here."

"No, it isn't. Every day is different. I've been here over thirty years, and no day has been like another. When I think of Median as I first saw it when I was your age and now, it's like a different world. Even the prairie is different."

"Everything's the same to me." Young Jon's eyes were hostile, but they did not drop before his father's and Jonathan liked that.

"Where do you want to go?"

"Manila."

"Manila!" Jonathan cried.

Upon Jonathan's earth Manila had of late been a place well defined because it stood for the chief cause of an inner discontent. He seldom discussed politics. He had early discovered that men were as irrational about politics as they were about religion, and he hated irrationality. But of all that he had disapproved in his time he most disapproved the push west across the Pacific. "West, west," he would mutter to himself, "as though heaven were there!"

The Sandwich Isles he had considered the ultimate folly of a people with already more land than they could conquer. Now these other islands were being talked about.

"Whatever has Manila got to do with you?" he asked, his voice so chill that young Jon longed to answer nothing. But he had the stubborn English blood in him, too.

"I'd like to travel a bit," he said quickly. "You came across the sea when you was my age, Dad. But I've only been to Topeka a couple of times."

Jonathan considered his son. He loved him, but the boy was not altogether his own. Half of him was Katie's, and he never forgot that. It was a strange piteous thing for which he could not blame his children that he knew still that he would have loved them better had Judy been their mother. He was the more carefully just to them.

"Do you want the Navy or only to travel?" he inquired.

"I don't feel any real call to the Navy," young Jon answered, considering. He suddenly noticed his bare feet and maneuvered the broom in front of them. "I'm just tired of Median."

"Tell you what I'll do," Jonathan said. "I'll give you a trip to Washington. I'll go with you. I've always wanted to see the capital of this country. That's what you want to see—not some place on the other side of the world that's none of our business as Americans."

"I'd like Washington all right," young Jon said cannily. "But what if I still want to join the Navy when we get back?"

"You shall go," Jonathan said. "It'll be against my judgment, but if you're going anyway I'd rather you went with my yes than with my no."

He was aware for the first time that this son of his had grown too big for him to command. How strange it was that merely by passing of days a small creature too helpless to feed itself should grow into a man! In his mind's eye he saw Jon always that little creature. But he was mistaken. Jon was a man in size and will. His eye moved over the broad-shouldered, brown-faced, sandy-haired boy. Then he saw his feet, and Jon trembled. But instead of being angry Jonathan smiled.

"Here I was thinking how quick you'd grown into a man. But those bare feet comfort me. You're still a little boy, and in a way I'm glad."

A scolding Jon would have taken and rebelled against it silently, but this kindness undermined rebellion and made him furious. He began to sweep the floor, his young mouth set. He was no child, and he would go barefoot no more.

And Jonathan, not knowing that he had ended his son's childhood, went back to his neat rows of figures, that by care and calculation showed always a profit, a reasonable, righteous, earned profit.

He grew quietly excited throughout the next month about going to Washington. He bade young Jon come to the store, and he fitted him to a new blue suit and brown shoes, and himself to a new gray one. Out of his stock he took two new suitcases, some socks and shirts, and two ties. Secretly he was troubled by young Jon's choice of the gayest design. Left to himself, he would have stocked only ties of small and sober patterns, but this Katie would not allow.

"Men have to have fancy ties," she always said. "Don't know why, but Pa used to say a man always feels he can let himself go on his tie. So we got to have all kinds on hand."

Jonathan chose the quietest for himself. Without knowing he did, he estimated the men of Median by their choice in ties. Faience he distrusted because he liked flamboyance in ties. It was not suitable for the president of a bank. He had often considered putting his account into the state bank in Topeka.

That night before he and Jon went to Washington he inquired of Katie as they lay side by side in bed, "Has Jon a kink in him somewhere, would you say?"

"What kind of kink?" Katie asked.

"Wildness or something."

"Not as much as most boys, and you ought to know it," she retorted. "When I see the way women worry over their sons going to poolrooms and saloons, I'm thankful for our Jon."

"Ah, well," Jonathan said mildly.

They started to Washington on a September morning the day before the opening of school. He had planned the time to be away because he could never see the children crowd into the school without a quiver of his heart. He had planted a quickly growing hedge between the house and the school, and every day he walked around the square rather than pass the schoolhouse. But nothing could shut out the rising of their voices when in the custom which he himself had set they sang, "My country, 'tis of thee . . ." After they had sung, he used to stand looking over the great roomful of children, healthy and eager and restless. It had been the most exciting sight his eyes could fall upon. And he had always said the same thing. "We begin by singing our national anthem. That is the way we should begin, for America gives you this school. Boys and girls, America treats you the same. America built this house and gives you books and hires teachers to teach you how to learn and how to grow into good men and women. That's all your country asks in return for all you are given—"

On the day school opened this year, he and Jon were on the train, rushing eastward. He sat by one window and young Jon by another, and across the space he talked to Jon of this country and for the first time of what he could remember of England.

"A different feel to it there, and when first I came here, Jon, I felt let loose and lost, and I didn't like it. In England everything was close around you, and you knew where every path went. But when we first came to Kansas there wasn't so much as a path. Sky and earth, and wherever you were it went on the same forever. Now I'm used to the size, and I doubt I could go back to closeness. I'd feel it too tight, maybe."

Young Jon listened politely. England was a name and no more.

When they reached Washington, Jonathan bought a guide-book at the hotel desk and marked what must be seen, and at the end of each day checked what they had seen. What effect the city had on his son he was not able to tell. Young Jon's sunburned face, always darker than his hair, showed no change. But neither did Jonathan's. Seen together, anyone could have told that they were father and son, and could have told, too, that they came from the West. Their voices had contended against wind and dust, and when they spoke their consonants were hard, as they must be when human voices contend against the wind and call across distances. Jonathan still carried the echoes of England in his speech, but Jon had the plain Kansas burr. They talked of what they saw, without communicating what they felt. They walked miles over hard pavements and up and down stone and cement stairs and floors and grew footsore as they had never been in their lives. They stared until they saw so much that nothing had any meaning, and still they kept on going, buying their food hastily wherever they happened to be and dropping into their cheap hotel beds at night too tired to speak. Jonathan had had ideas of teaching young Jon something of history and govern-ment, but he was too busy to teach or Jon to learn. They crammed their minds through their eyes.

They left Washington on a rainy night at midnight. Young Jon curled himself upon a seat, but Jonathan could not sleep. He sat upright and thinking.

He knew now that his was a great country. But he had known it in Median. There was never a day when he walked down a Median street and looked beyond it into the endless prairie that he did not know his country great. Washington had showed him a great nation as well, a vast civilized nation. Handsome buildings, great libraries and art galleries, magnificent streets, embassies and hotels and gardens and parks, and at the center of it, in a plain white house whose beauty was its plainness, there sat a plain American. They had seen the President by the merest chance on the day they went to visit the Senate. A heavy-set, square-faced man in a frock coat had passed through the hall, his silk hat in his hand. Whispering flew from mouth to mouth. "The President!" "Is that the President?" "That's the President."

He and Jon had stood gaping like everyone else. Afterward Jon had said, "He looks like anybody, don't he, Dad?"

And Jonathan had answered, "That's the glory of him."

He went back to Median proud of all that he had seen. Yes, it was a great country, and he was part of it. Men like him chose a common man and bade him go to Washington and run the nation for them, and so long as they willed, he obeyed them. When they willed, they sent him home again, and he went back to some little place like Median and was no more than anybody else. It was a glorious idealism, its only weakness the weakness of the individual.

He talked about this to Katie the night he came home, without expecting her to know what he was talking about, but having to talk.

"It was a beautiful sight, that city, but terrible, too. It made you take thought who you sent there. Only the best is good enough. And how'll we find the best in a country as big as this and people living so far apart? What is the test of a man when there's no guidepost to where he is, no class to define him, no standard of birth or race or religion to measure him by? Is democracy too big?"

Katie waited for him respectfully. This was men's talk and beyond women. She wished young Jon could hear his father. It was so educational when Jonathan talked like this. When she was sure he was through and not going to say anything more, she remembered something she had had on her mind.

"The long underwear stock is kind of low, Jonathan. I was pickin' out two new suits for you today, and I noticed we don't have enough."

"I'll order some tomorrow," Jonathan said. He was back in Median.

But he kept his word to Jon. A year later Jon went to his father on a Sunday after church, in that empty pleasant hour after worship and before food. He had grown much in this year. There was no possibility of bare feet now. He would have been more shocked than his father.

On this Sunday, at this hour, Jonathan was walking among the trees in the square. He made it his business to examine them and keep them sound. He was searching down a borer in an elm when he saw his son coming through the shadows. Jon had on his Sunday suit of dark blue, and he was a sturdy fellow. Jonathan was proud of him and pretended not to see him.

"Hello, Dad."

"Hello, son. That you?"

"Yep. What you doin'?"

"Chasing a borer. Got him, too."

Jonathan took out his pocket knife and opened a small winding tunnel. Young Jon watched him find its end and dig out a fat white worm and crush it carefully.

"That's the end of a nasty thing," Jonathan said.

"Dad!"

The sound of Jon's voice made his father wary. Something was about to be asked.

"Yes, son?"

"I'd like to remind you of something you promised me."

"If I promised, I'll keep to my word."

"Remember you said I could join the Navy?"

Median rocked a little about Jonathan. The boy hadn't forgotten!

"Yes, I remember."

"I don't want to join the Navy now, but I want to go away."

Jonathan kept on walking and looking at the trees, sharply aware of his son at his side.

"I want you to be anything you want to be, Jon. It's the beauty of America that a man can say that to his son. You don't have to be a storekeeper because I am one. It doesn't matter what you're born. It doesn't even matter how much money I've got. You can work up to anything. Have you thought of that?"

"I'd like to get away from Median, Dad."

"You can go anywhere you like to college." There was a blight on a chestnut, and he took a leaf apart to examine its disease.

"I don't want to go to school any more, Dad."

Jonathan dropped the leaf. "You don't want to go to *school!*" he repeated. "Why, I never heard that before!"

"I didn't want to tell you, because you set such store by school," Jon confessed. He was very red and afraid.

"I can't imagine it," Jonathan said slowly. "When I think how in Dentwater I longed and ached and suffered for school—and here it's free!"

Jon did not answer because he did not know how. Why was it that the old, in their youth, were so different from the young? He waited.

"If you don't want any more schooling," his father said, so coldly that he knew he was angry, "I reckon it doesn't matter what you do. A farmer, a sailor, a blacksmith—"

Jonathan pulled his moustache. Common folk were common folk. It was the one weakness in the democratic idea which no one heeded.

"I want to go to Nevada," Jon said. "Reckon I'll go to the gold mines."

"Go where you like," he told his son shortly, and knew that it would do him no good, whatever Katie had for Sunday dinner. He would not be able to eat it.

The desolation he felt when he saw the train carrying his son to a new West was broken before it was two days old. Clyde came back to Median. Jonathan in the hurly-burly of a Saturday morning heard the news from Mrs. Drear, running into the store with her apron about her head.

"Jonathan, you come over to the hotel quick. Jennet's come back and your old man!"

Everybody knew long ago the story of Jennet and Clyde, but no questions had been asked after Mrs. Drear had said flatly, "I'm thankful to any man that's put a wedding ring on Jennet's finger."

That it happened to be Clyde Goodliffe was strange, but she was still grateful. Besides, Clyde was now respectable in Median because he was Jonathan's father.

"Whatever!" Jonathan leaned across the counter to whisper, in his hand a slab of cheese. "I'll be over. Is he all right?"

"Looks the picture of a hearty, wicked old man," Mrs. Drear said and laughed.

But Jonathan did not even smile. "I'll be over." He filled a basket hastily with packages and called to one of the twins who were now clerks in the store.

"Joe! Carry this out to Mrs. Johnson's buggy!"

Then he hurried across to the hotel. His father had not written to him in years. Twice a year he wrote out of duty, but he had long ceased to expect an answer. What news he had of his father was from Jamie, to whom Jennet sometimes wrote. He went into the hall of American House, now called a lobby, and to the bar made over into a desk space. A young, smooth-faced man stood there. Jonathan knew him as a boy he had taught in fifth grade.

"What room has my father, Hal?"

"The room over the kitchen—twenty-eight, it is."

The rooms in American House had in recent years been numbered, but more often than not they were still called by old location.

Jonathan mounted the stairs and went down a narrow carpeted aisle and knocked at twenty-eight.

"Come in!" Clyde roared.

He opened the door upon his father and Jennet. They were sitting in rocking chairs, each of them, and a basket full of yellow oranges was upon the floor between them. Oranges were beginning to come in from California, but they were still a luxury. Try as he would to accept it, he was shocked by Jennet in his father's room. And yet he saw at once that every trace of girlishness had left her. She was a woman of middle age. What had been willful on her face was changed into firmness; what had been wistful was gone; and what had been gay was now only humor.

"Well, Jonathan!" Clyde leaped to his feet and seized his son's hand and shook it. And in that moment Jonathan saw that his father had dyed his hair and his moustache. They were blacker than they had ever been, and he had cut off his beard, and under his chin his neck was corded. For the first time in his life Jonathan saw his father's chin. It was not at all the chin he expected. Instead of being bold and jutting beneath the bushy beard, it was narrow and receded a little; and in this instant, beholding it, Jonathan lost all fear of his father forever.

"Hello, Dad," he said coolly, and to Jennet, not shaking her hand, "How are you?"

But Jennet laughed, and her laughter was not changed. "You don't hold it against me that I'm your stepmother?"

"Certainly not," Jonathan said with all his dignity. But he knew he would never forgive his father. Mary's little ghost came creeping to his side and stood looking with disdain at this red-haired woman in a golden-brown taffeta suit, cut too tightly across her bosom and her thighs.

"You're looking well," Jonathan said to his father.

"Never was better," Clyde said. He sat down and nodded at the oranges. "Help yourself."

"No, thanks," Jonathan said. Then he asked, "Are you staying long?"

Clyde peeled the skin in strips from the ripe yellow flesh of an orange. "The rest of time," he said. "Jennet and me've sold out and put the money in the bank. We made out well. And we've come home to help out the old folks."

"You mean—"

"Pa and Ma need help," Jennet said, "and Clyde and I are going to take over American House."

"Ah?" Jonathan said. He was suddenly glad that young Jon was gone. It would have been too hard on a decent boy to have this rakish old man for his grandfather. I needn't stay long, he thought, there'll be plenty of time.

But there was very little time, after all. For Clyde in his restless old age after two weeks of Median decided suddenly to go back and see what England was like now.

"There's all that money in the bank, and it's now or never," he said.

Jennet was willing because she was tired of him. But she was always good-humored with this man who had made her a wife.

"Good idea," she said, and saw to it that he set off with what he needed in two new carpetbags.

He reached England. This they knew because Jennet had a letter which Clyde told her to show to Jonathan to save him the trouble of writing another. And Jonathan, reading it, saw for the first time how little educated his father was. A child might have written these large, uneven penciled words. There was neither spelling nor punctuation. But still Clyde made himself plain. He was full of disgust because nothing was changed in England. The only news was that Edward and Millie had six fine children, to whom, it seemed, he preached the greatness of America until he had them all discontented. He ended the letter with a smack on Jennet's lips. "A fond kis as you no wat I like my girl."

Jonathan folded the letter abruptly on the words and handed it back to Jennet across the same counter over which he had once sold her a red dress, and she laughed.

"He's having a wonderful time, but he always does, doesn't he?"

"So it seems," Jonathan said dryly.

And then they heard no more and months passed and Jennet had time to turn American House over and over with paint and wallpaper and a new quick lunch counter, and still there was nothing from Clyde. She began coming over to the store every few days to ask Jonathan if she ought to do something about Clyde, and then suddenly one day in January Katie brought a letter to the store because it had an English stamp upon it and an unknown handwriting. It was Edward's handwriting. Jonathan read it behind the meat counter. It was high enough to hide him, for he had just this year put in ice refrigeration beneath the meat.

DEAR BRO. JONATHAN:

I take my pen in hand to tell you the Sad news. Our father passed away the sixth of December. Walking on the railroad track. Though we had warned him it is not safe as trains are frequent here, but he was used to America and an unmanageable old man. Said English trains was so slow he could run faster than them. He met his Sad end by a train and was mangled very bad. We buried the remains in Dentwater churchyard. Old vicar is gone, but the new vicar did the burial nicely and Millie says tell you everything was done.

We are all well. Business fair to good. We have four sons and two girls the eldest married and two boys in business. Millie sends her best and so does

Your aff. brother
EDWARD

He handed the letter to Katie, and she read it. He met her eyes.

"Dad would be the one to go back to England and get himself buried safe in Dentwater churchyard," he said bitterly. And he thought of his mother and of her little grave here in Median that he kept tended carefully. Now all he had done was not enough.

"I'm going to put up a new tombstone for my mother," he told Katie, "one with an angel on it."

He stood before the angel on his mother's grave a few months later. The angel was very nice, a pretty thing of Vermont marble. But he was not excited by it. Indeed, he did not know what was the matter with him this April. He had been ill in March with a heavy bronchitis that left him tired and thin, and had gone this morning to see the doctor. He had been proud that he could go to a doctor in Median and had entirely pooh-poohed Katie's anxious suggestion at breakfast that he go to a doctor in Topeka.

"It's a pretty pass if a man doesn't trust the doctor in his own town," he had exclaimed.

His temper was distinctly not as good as it used to be, and he knew it. But there was no one in the house any more except women, Katie and Mary and Lula, and being the only man gave him some privilege.

So he had listened to young Dr. Peter Hall, and he took pride in the shining new offices. Very gravely he had breathed in and out under the stethoscope and had allowed the young man to thump him soundly.

"You need a rest," Peter Hall said affectionately. When he had first come to Median he had been told to go and see Jonathan Goodliffe.

"No use your figurin' to settle down here in Median withouten he likes you," the postmaster had chuckled.

"That's so," men had agreed. They were hanging about waiting for the mail to come in.

"Rest!" Jonathan now exclaimed. "What from?"

"Well, sir, you're not as young as you were," Peter hinted.

Jonathan did not answer this. Secretly he had been dismayed for some time at the new feeling he had nowadays that life was passing, and he had nothing more ahead except one day after another. This feeling had returned upon him heavily as he buttoned his clothes and waited for the prescription.

"A month off is what you need," Peter Hall said.

"A month!" he had exclaimed. "Doin' what?"

"Play," Peter had said smiling. "Indulge yourself, Mr. Goodliffe."

Play! He had come out of the office feeling that he was sentenced.

"Danged if I want to go home and look at Katie, though," he muttered into the warm spring sunshine and was aghast at his wickedness. Remorse had led him here to the cemetery and the comfort of looking at the new angel on his mother's grave.

"I would like to indulge myself," he thought solemnly.

But what would such indulgence be? Was there really anything more that he wanted? Median had grown into a handsome town. It would be easy enough now for the citizens to go on and put in what they wanted. There was talk of a park and a swimming pool. Some of the young fellows had wanted a race track but he had put his foot down on that in town meeting.

"Racing brings in a lot of trash," he had declared. "I fought once against Median's being a cattle town for the same reason." When he had finished what he had to say, the council had voted against a race track.

"Don't know why I shouldn't indulge myself a little," he thought. "I'm not needed any more like I was, I reckon."

And then into his heart crept the old small serpent of desire. The angel on his mother's tombstone began it and the fragrance of the violets in the grass at his feet went on with it.

"It's Judy I'm still thinkin' of," he murmured. "Judy, my dear!"

Yes, this could be the only indulgence he craved, the delight of seeing her again, of talking with her and perhaps holding her hand.

" 'Tisn't as if I'd want anything of her," he thought. "Except to hear from her own lips—"

Except to hear from her own lips why she had run away from him that dreadful day, except to know if Evan treated her well, except to find out, once and for all, how she was!

He lifted his face in the sunshine and closed his eyes and standing so, with his hands clenched behind his back, he felt tears burn under his eyelids.

"I've lived mortally alone, Judy!" he murmured.

Then struck with fear lest someone had heard, or seen, he opened his eyes and looked around. Nobody was near. The little cemetery lay, a place of peace, beside the church and shielded from the street by trees. The quiet graves were all his company. He wiped his eyes and felt better. His heart loosened, as though something tight had slipped away from it.

"And I don't see why I shouldn't go to see my love just once," he thought. "It wouldn't hurt Katie if she didn't know."

But it was impossible to break in a day the habit of years. He would have to get himself ready for it, think about it for a few weeks perhaps, dream of it, plan it.

"I shall just put Evan aside, too," he thought. He was walking slowly homeward through the streets. It was noon and Katie would fret if he were late to dinner. "And if Evan comes in, why, I'll just tell him the truth, that it's due me after all these years, to hear her voice." He lifted his head as he thus made up his mind, and hastened his step.

It was at this moment he heard Lula's piercing voice shriek at him down the street.

"Dad—Dad—where've you been? We couldn't find you nowhere!"

"Why, Lula girl—" He broke into a little trot to meet her.

"Dad—Dad!" Lula sobbed. "Mother's fallen on the kitchen floor!"

He hastened down the street, Lula's hand clinging to his, and pressed her with questions. But she knew nothing of how it had happened. She had been upstairs in her room, "reading with my ears stopped with my fingers so I wouldn't hear nobody call," she sobbed remorsefully, and Mary had come and pulled her shoulder.

"I heard somebody crash down, like, in the kitchen," Mary had cried.

"We ran downstairs together and there Mother was lyin'," Lula sobbed, "and she don't know anything."

He dropped her hand, hurried to the back door and into the kitchen. Katie lay on the floor, and Mary was kneeling beside her. She had put a cushion under Katie's head and an old afghan over her, but Katie knew nothing of it. The dishes she had been carrying clean and ready to put away lay smashed on the floor around her. Lula began picking them up, still weeping.

But Jonathan stared in horror at Katie's closed eyes, and at her thin face, dark with blood.

"What in God's name—" he gasped.

He stooped and lifted her inert body, and her heavy hands fell like weights to her sides. He carried her into the sitting room and laid her on the couch.

"Mary, telephone the doctor!" he flung over his shoulder.

Now he lifted Katie's hand that had slipped from the couch and put it on her breast. And then, because he could not bear the torture of her gasping breath, he went into the kitchen and pumped a basin full of cool water and found a clean towel and came back and bathed her hot, dark face. It was the most intimate service he had ever given her. The peculiar independence which was her being had taken its pride in doing everything for herself as well as all she could for her family. Now, as he sponged her forehead and her cheeks and wiped her twisted mouth, he felt awkward and shy and touched to tears. Poor Katie, who never in her life before had been helpless!

"Dear wife," he whispered. But she could not hear him now.

"My God," Peter Hall exclaimed, "her blood pressure—"

His mouth clamped shut, and he began his examination. He knew the signs so well. These swift, hard-bitten, thin-bodied women, driving themselves under the whip of their own restless energy, intoxicating themselves with their own ferment! He was fond of Katie, and he liked the kindly lash of her tongue. His own mother had been just such a woman, a prairie woman, lean and hard and direct as the prairie wind.

"Stroke," he muttered.

"You mean, she'll be helpless?" Jonathan whispered.

"If she lives," the doctor said.

He rose, and they stood looking at Katie. Mary, standing behind them, put her apron to her face and began to sob, and the doctor turned.

"You'll have to take her place, my girl. This woman'll never work again."

"Then I know she'd rather die," Jonathan said.

"Yes, but maybe she can't, after all," the doctor replied, "and I doubt she'll ever so much as lift her own hand again."

Jonathan's mouth was dry. "What'll I do?" he asked.

"Put her to bed and feed her, care for her, like she was a baby," the doctor said sadly. "It's all a man can do except to wait and see what nerves and muscles may come back. I'll help you lift her to her bed."

He put his hand beneath Katie's arms, and Jonathan took her stiff inert feet. One of her slippers fell off. Only this morning he had seen her thrust her feet into the carpet slippers she wore around the house in the morning and had thought to himself that she needed a new pair, and he would give them to her for Christmas. It was always hard to find things to give her. She needed so little, and now she would not need even slippers. They laid her on the bed.

"Mary can put on her nightgown, can't you, Mary?" Peter Hall said.

Mary nodded, and they left her. Out in the sitting room they sat down.

"Did she never tell you she felt badly?" he asked.

"She never talked about herself to anybody," Jonathan said faintly. He felt himself trembling, and his throat was dry. He kept asking himself, now what was he going to do? If Katie was going to be like this, what would he do? What would any of them do without Katie?

The doctor coughed. "I ought to tell you, Mr. Goodliffe, as your family physician, that I'm afraid your married life is over."

Jonathan stared at him, not comprehending. Then he understood and blushed as he had not for years. "Th—that's all right," he muttered. "Th—that's the least of it."

"Well, I'm glad you take it that way," the doctor said solemnly. "It's not that way with most men. You're a decent man, Mr. Goodliffe."

He wanted to tell the doctor that it wasn't that he was decent—though I hope I am a decent man, he thought to himself in the silence. But how could he say that what he had spoken was the truth and yet make the doctor realize how good his marriage was and how fond he was of his wife? Marriage was a manifold thing, he thought gravely, and in the variety possible between man and woman he had been happy with Katie in his way. By her conquering goodness Katie had made him content.

"It's just that we had much more," he said firmly.

The doctor bowed his head.

"You've had a real marriage, Mr. Goodliffe," he said.

"Maybe I have," Jonathan replied.

Night and day, thinking of a thousand small and sorrowful things, Jonathan watched beside this silent and inert woman. He moved the couch in from the sitting room, and on it he lay through the long hours of the night, listening for the slightest movement from the bed. But there was no movement, only Katie's breath, coming and going, catching, unsteady, and going on again. Sometimes he rose, conscious of a change in the direction of the endlessly blowing winds of spring outside the house, or in the warmth and cold of the April air, and he changed and adjusted the covering over her according to the need of his own body. In the morning he rose and while he was alone with her he washed her face and hands and brushed her dry mouse-brown hair that had as yet no gray in it.

But the bathing of her body and the changing of her garments he left to Mary and to Lula. He could not bear in her unconsciousness to see the nakedness her painful burning modesty had always hidden from him. If she had known, she would have suffered because anyone must see her, but even so he felt that she would choose the girls rather than him. So he went into the sitting room and waited and came back again and sat beside her and waited.

She might be conscious again at any moment, the doctor had said. When that moment came he must be there. He did not leave the house for an instant. Unwillingly even did he leave the room where she lay to answer a knock on the door and the many inquiries of neighbors. Hour after hour through the days and the nights he waited.

On the fifth day, at three o'clock in the morning, the moment came. He leaped from his couch at the sound of her louder breathing. He turned the wick high on the oil lamp on the table by the bed, and he saw her eyelids lift, and then in her eyes he saw the rising terror of her awakening mind. For the first time in all their life together he bent and gathered her in his arms and held her.

"You're going to be all right, Katie," he said in a loud clear voice, so that she might hear. "I'm going to see that you're all right, my—my dear. You needn't be afraid of—of anything. I'm here. I'll take care of you, night and day."

This he kept saying with the tears streaming down his face and into her hair that was against his lips, when suddenly she died.

He laid her down and looked involuntarily at the clock on the mantel. A lifetime was finished, and he felt it was his own.

🌿 40 🌿

THE BRIEF HOUR BESIDE THE ANGEL ON HIS MOTHER'S TOMB-stone was now nothing but a dream. He thought of it some-times and felt it as heavy upon his conscience as an actual sin.

"If I hadn't been dreaming in my own mind that morning I'd have been at home, maybe," he mused over and over again, driving remorse into himself until he felt himself bleed within. At least, he would have been at the store where he could have been found. For an hour the girls had let Katie lie, searching for him before they went for the doctor.

He had made sure Katie's death was not caused by the delay. "Still, that doesn't excuse me," he thought with gloom.

He knew what the sin was. He had been dreaming of Judy. Nothing else would have delayed him. To have pursued the dream now was no longer possible. It was over again, he told himself.

He went grimly back to his life in the store, and Mary and Lula kept the house for him. He sat down at table with two women instead of three, that was all. And he slept alone in his bed.

The summer dragged by, full of heat and drought. It was a year of grasshoppers. Business was bad and he had much idle time. Without missing Katie he was lonely. Then in August he had a letter from Jon.

"I'm here, Dad, and I plan to settle in San Francisco. Got myself engaged to a very fine girl, Isabel Dent, and we hope to marry next month. Her father will give me a job in the railroad business."

Jonathan wrote back with some bitterness. "Why shouldn't you come and help me in the store? You can have it, if you wish. I'm thinking of a holiday."

He had not thought of a holiday, but as soon as he said it, he knew he still wanted one. Jon wrote back promptly. "Why didn't you say so before, Dad? Sure we will come, if you'll come to the wedding."

But he did not want to go to the wedding. He was done with marriages and lovemaking. He wanted to go away alone.

"Where'll you go, Dad?" Lula asked fearfully when he spoke of it. She could not imagine this house without him, nor the town. It was impending catastrophe.

He felt his imagination grow reckless. He'd go as far as he could, away from everything.

"Where do you want to go, Dad?" Lula pressed.

"Go?" he repeated, searching his heart for its longings. "I'm goin' away off—I'm going to England. And maybe I'll never come back."

"Oh, Dad!" Lula wailed. And across the table, Mary, his mother's child, looked at him with sad dark eyes.

But he shut his lips and gave them no promises. If he did not do what he liked now, when would he? The image of Judy framed itself before his eyes and he stared at it.

"Not you," he thought, "not you!"

For he had begun thinking of her, to his shame, even at Katie's funeral. He had stood aloof in the midst of his family, solitary in his being. He was free, and he was afraid of freedom.

I'll have to get out of this, he had thought, looking down into Katie's grave. "I'm acting out of something that's not the man I am. I'll go away for a bit and get my own nature in hand again."

It was then that he had thought suddenly of England. But there had been delays, one after the other. Paul Graham came to Median as the rector of the new Episcopalian church. The churches in Median had been built as Jonathan had foreseen. There were now four of them. But Jonathan had grown more tolerant of men's souls. "There is only one God," he had said to Paul one day, "but men do not know it yet. You'll have to tell 'em, Paul."

He liked the older Paul better even than he had liked the young missionary, and he made no objection when early in the autumn Paul told him frankly he had come back to Median because he wanted to marry Mary, and Mary wanted to stay here. Mary was long ready for marriage, a fragile fair girl with his mother's tenacity under her fragility. But this wedding had been a cause for Jonathan's delay. It was not decent to have a marriage so soon after Katie's death, and yet he was not willing, out of his sense of duty to Mary's mother, to go away without seeing with his own eyes how happy she was with Paul. He had given Mary to Paul on a February day at a quiet wedding in the small new rectory and had felt the last duty to his mother finished.

It had been difficult to arrange his own affairs. Martha Cobb and the twins could manage in the store, and after some thought Jonathan had invited Matthew and Ruth to live in his house with Lula. It would do Ruth good to come to Median away from that lonely, heartbreaking farm, set like a dry island in the midst of a sea of rich oil.

But the real reason for his delay, month after month, after Mary's marriage had been none of these things. Judy, only Judy had held him. And yet he could not blame her, dear soul, since she knew nothing about it.

In May, only a month after Katie's death, Laura had come to him. She and Jamie had been in New York at the time of the funeral. Evan had sent Jamie there to put some new stocks on the market. But as soon as they came back to Topeka, Laura had come flying out to Median in a new bright yellow automobile, with Jamie driving. They had been kind, too kind about Katie, and Jonathan had soon wished them gone. And then Laura, in one of her commanding moods, had sent the others away, declaring that she must and would speak to Jonathan alone.

He had dreaded what she might say about Katie. Instead, she had leaned forward in her low chair in which she sat and clasping her ringed hands about her knees, she had said abruptly, "Jonathan, Judy is most unhappy."

He had given a startled cry. "Eh—is she?" He was ashamed of the cry the moment it came hurtling out of his mouth.

"You still love her, God bless you," Laura had exclaimed. "Now, Jonathan, you must tell me what to do for her."

He had sat motionless in his old Windsor chair, his eyes upon Laura's pretty, painted face. She talked with impetuous shrugs and rustlings of her taffeta ruffles and little frowns and grimaces, her hands clasping and unclasping.

"I'm furious with Evan, Jonathan—but it's really that Rachel Power's fault. She's inveigled Evan into making her his mistress. It's been going on for years, so long that he doesn't even deny it. They're together all the time in his office. Oh, dear—Mamma used to say when he first took that woman into his office that it would end this way. Mamma said Nature always took advantage of such a situation—"

"Wait!" Jonathan had commanded her. "You're saying a serious thing."

"Do you think I don't know it?" she cried.

"Is there proof?" he had asked.

"Everybody knows—"

"Everybody doesn't always really know," he had insisted.

"You wait," she had commanded him in return. "Don't forget, Evan is my brother. I'm not afraid of him. I asked him, and he wouldn't deny it. Do you know what he said? He shouted that he'd dare anyone to let it make a difference in the way they treated Rachel. He's simply going to carry it off with his usual high hand, forcing her down all our throats as his secretary."

"What does that mean?" Jonathan asked, and his hands gripped the sides of the Windsor chair.

"It means that Rachel will stay in his office all day and go with him on all his trips as his secretary and sit at his table in his house. And no one can say a word, least of all Judy."

"Why is she helpless?" he asked sternly.

"She seems to have no close friends, except me," Laura replied.

"Has he been cruel to her?" he asked. He thought of Judy as he had first known her, young, gay, at ease in the world, pouring her music into the old accordion.

"If you mean beating—no," Laura said. "But Evan is cruel. He thinks only of himself."

"Many men do that," Jonathan said. His lips were tight, and his eyes were pale and bright.

Laura leaned forward again. Her small, intense face was burning. "Jonathan, of course men think only of themselves. Jamie's a selfish man—don't I know it? But there's a place where even Jamie has the sense to know he has to think of me, for his own sake. Well, Evan hasn't that sense. And Judy can't talk with him. Judy never talks with anybody. She's like anything lovely—she simply *is*."

He quelled the rush in his heart. "This—this other woman—"

"Rachel Power—"

"She's different from Judy?"

"Different as night from day. She's as selfish as Evan, smart enough to use her love. And he needs everything she says because she's so smart."

"I'll have to go and see Evan," Jonathan said.

Laura laid her narrow hand on his. "He'll listen to nobody else, Jonathan. I know my own brother. He'll listen to you maybe because he's never confessed even to himself that once he injured you."

He had not answered this, and he had drawn his hand gently away.

But Evan had not listened to him, either. When that brief, hard interview was over, Jonathan knew that he and Evan would never meet again. The words they had spoken to one another were an end.

"I come to say something direct, Evan, for the sake of what's past."

"Say what you like, Jonathan."

They were in Evan's office. Rachel Power had been there, a tall, dark handsome woman in severe clothes, and Evan had sent her away. She had returned Jonathan's look with quiet arrogance and then had closed the door softly behind.

"Evan, I am told that Judy is unhappy."

He had thrown this at Evan, and Evan had hid his surprise behind a quick smile. He tilted back in his chair. "Now where did you hear that?"

Evan was successfully rich, but the signs of disappointment were upon him. His handsome eyes had hardened and his lips sneered through the smiles. He had run twice for governor and had been defeated, the first time by the Populists, and the second time no one quite knew why. He had flung away politics then and had devoted himself to making money. Now he held the reins of half a dozen utilities and industries in his hands.

He's like a man with a lot of horses tearing away and nowhere to go, Jonathan had thought shrewdly, looking at him.

"Don't matter how I heard," he had said aloud. "It's this I want to say: What's gone is over. I've had my life and I'm content. I'm goin' to England now."

"To stay?" Evan broke in.

"Maybe," Jonathan said. "So, Evan, I want you to remember you owe it to me—to—to keep Judy happy. That's all."

Evan sat still. "Why, damn you, Jonathan," he said slowly. "I don't owe you anything." He rose and leaned over the desk on his hands. "I owe no man anything—nor any woman!"

Jonathan rose, too, a slight medium figure in his new pepper-and-salt suit. "When you marry a woman you take on a debt, Evan—if you're a man."

"Judy has had everything she wanted," Evan said.

"You can't be sure of that until death do you part," Jonathan then said gravely and took up his black felt hat and went away.

He came down early one morning a year later to make his own breakfast. Since Katie's death he found himself in the habit of waking just before dawn. He lay usually until daylight, listening to the twitter of birds in the ivy that climbed about his window. When the day silenced them, he rose, washed, and dressed and went down. It was six o'clock and he heard Bill Hasty, Abram's boy, throw the morning newspaper on the porch and go whistling on his way. He opened the door and reached for the paper. The wind had unfolded it and great black letters leaped at him. EVAN BAYNE KILLED BY WIFE'S INSANE FATHER. He gripped the paper in two hands and stood staring at the news, and the cool autumn wind blew his thinning hair.

In an instant he had it all as clearly in his mind as though he had been there. Old Joel had been sent home from Honolulu to his daughter. He had been found wandering on the streets, a beggar. Joel had been in Judy's house less than a week and yesterday he had walked into Evan's office, had shot him and killed him instantly.

Jonathan took the paper into the house and burned it in the kitchen stove. Then forgetting he had not eaten he went upstairs and put on his best suit and told Lula to get up.

"I'm going in to Topeka," he said. "I don't know when I'll be back. Evan Bayne is dead."

The black butler opened the door but Laura was there instantly, rustling out of the drawing room in her black taffeta.

"Oh, Jonathan, how I prayed you would come!"

"Where's Jamie?" he asked stolidly.

"At the office, looking after things. Jonathan, it's so terrible." She seized his hand and pulled him into the drawing room. "Sit down—let me tell you. It all happened in a minute. I can't get Judy to move. She just sits there in her music room staring at her hands." She glanced at a closed door. "And her poor old father—crazy as a loon. They have him in a padded cell in the hospital, waiting trial."

"They'll never prosecute," Jonathan said.

"How can they?" she cried back. "He's just an old ghost. And he keeps telling everybody God made him do it. Nobody even knew he was in the building. He just walked into Evan's office."

"Nobody with Evan?"

"That Rachel Power, of course. She says he tried to shoot her, too. But she grabbed him—he's so weak and old."

He did not speak. He was listening beyond Laura's voice. She saw it and said, "Dear Jonathan, you want to see Judy."

"No, better not," he said indistinctly.

"I will send her to you," she said and went away.

And in the next moment the door opened. He saw Judy standing there in her soft full black skirt. "I knew you would come, Jonathan," she said.

"Of course," he said and took her hands. They were as soft as ever and crushed so easily—how he remembered!

"I didn't want to go away, Jonathan, because I knew you would come as soon as you could."

They sat down on a satin couch, and he went on holding her hands.

"Poor Papa," she said gently. "He thought he was doing right. You know how he is, Jonathan. He told me over and over, 'I did God's will, Judy, and God helped me.' He was so pleased with himself, poor Papa. They won't kill him, will they, Jonathan?"

"No, Judy." She was so beautiful in his eyes, so frighteningly beautiful! Her lovely bright hair, shining about the black frock, her creamy skin and the dark sweetly lashed eyes!

"And you, my darling dear," he said with unutterable tenderness, "how are you bearing it?" He had her hands at his breast, fondling them, kissing them. He could not help it, after all these years. And she did not pull her hands away nor turn her eyes from his face. But large clear tears came rolling down her pale cheeks. "I loved Evan so," she said. "It never mattered what he did—I loved him."

She spoke with such innocent honesty that he felt his blood stop. He put her hands down gently on her knees.

"Did you, Judy?" His voice sounded small and weak in his ears. "Then, how can I help you, my dear?"

She gave a sob and leaned her head against his shoulder. "Oh, be my friend—please, Jonathan!" He longed to put his arm about her, but he sat rigid.

"That I will, Judy, always. Count on me for that, my dear," he said and forced false cheerfulness into his voice.

And she lifted her head and wiped her eyes, and he sat rigid while she talked softly, sobbing now and then. "They sent poor Papa back from Honolulu, Jonathan. They sent him back because he was destitute. He was begging in the streets, they said—begging and preaching. Jonathan, I want him to come here and live with me, and I'll look after him. I haven't anything else to do, now."

"We'll have to see, my dear," he said. His voice was trembling again, but he mastered it. "It'll depend on others, I fancy—not on you and me."

Distress flushed her sweet pale cheeks. "But, Jonathan, you tell them."

"I will, my dear," he promised and suddenly could bear no more. "I'll go now, Judy, and see your father and find out how things are."

"Oh, thank you, Jonathan. I feel safe again, now you're here." She dried her tears with a wisp of lace and muslin she took from her belt.

He went away without touching her hand but she did not notice this, and seeing her absent eyes when he said good-by he felt a shock that chilled his heart. The brief flame kindling out of the old smouldering fire of his love died suddenly to its final ashes. He knew, in the instant he closed the door, that she had never loved him. If she had loved him even when he was young, she would have come into the sod house with him in the days of his grief, and she would have stayed with him.

"As Katie did," he muttered bleakly.

Instead she had run away with Evan and all these years she had been Evan's wife. Today when Evan was dead, even when it was plain that Evan had ceased to love her, she still had no thought for him whom she had left so lonely long ago.

"Though I've loved her faithfully," he thought with stark bitterness.

No, Judy had come to him even today counting with simple unthinking selfishness upon the faithfulness of his love. But he understood now that she had thought only of herself. Well, he would help her and go away.

"I'm cured, I hope," he thought.

But he felt a wound within him, a bottomless loss, a grief for something that never was except inside his dreams.

"Best to know," he told himself.

He buttoned his coat and plodded down the street to fulfill his last promise to her.

At the city hospital he asked to see Joel. "I'm a friend of Evan Bayne's, and Mrs. Bayne asked me to come," he said simply.

A male nurse led him into a barred room, and there old Joel sat bolt upright in a wooden chair in the middle of it. He lifted his head at the sound of the door and rose when Jonathan came in and stood tall and spare in his rusty black suit, taller than Jonathan remembered him, his white hair hanging to his shoulders.

"You don't remember me?" Jonathan asked.

"I do not, I am sorry to say," Joel replied in a resonant strong voice. The bright mad eyes did not look at him. "Are you sent to me from the Lord?"

Jonathan smiled. "Perhaps I am," he said. "I'm Jonathan Goodliffe. I was a lad in Median when you came there to preach, years ago."

"The Lord sent me there," Joel declared with energy. "The Lord has sent me to many places." He stood towering over Jonathan, his eyes fixed on space above his head.

"And the Lord told you to kill Evan Bayne?" Jonathan asked quietly.

The vague blue eyes glittered, wavered, and fell to Jonathan's face. Joel put up one hand and clutched his hair. His hand, thin and fine as a shell, was crusted with dirt. "The man wouldn't let me see Judy—he wouldn't even tell me where Judy was." Joel's voice was suddenly weak and childish and all the resonance was gone. "I was coming home to be with Judy, and the man behind the desk said, 'Put the old fool in the asylum.' "

"And what did you do, Mr. Spender?" Jonathan asked. His voice was quiet and kind, and Joel answered at once.

"I hastened out of that room, and the woman outside the

door put a pistol into my hand, and I listened to the voice of the Lord."

"What did the Lord say?" Jonathan asked.

"She said, 'Go and kill that man!' "

Joel drew himself up to his full height and thrust out his hands as though in invocation. "Blessed be the name of the Lord!" he shouted.

"Mr. Spender, sit down and rest, sir," Jonathan said. "I will try to take you to Judy."

Obediently as a child the old man sat down. Jonathan took this strange conversation to the nearest police station, and in less than half an hour he stood listening, with a police officer, to the dark handsome woman locked behind the mahogany doors of Evan's office.

"He wouldn't marry me," she said sullenly, in her deep and strange voice. "He loved me, but he wouldn't marry me. He said it would ruin him if he divorced his wife and married me. People wouldn't trust a divorced man with their money. He said I had to go on as we were. He made me sit at his table, obey him, work for him. He used me like a servant. I'd bought that pistol weeks before. When that crazy old man came out talking about God—I took the chance."

"Take her to headquarters," the officer commanded his men.

So Evan's life had ended, a bitter frustrated history, Jonathan told himself sadly. But he thought most of Judy.

I can understand my poor dear, he told himself. In some queer way, I still love him, too.

But he made up his mind to go to England at once.

The ship ground against the wharf, and the gangplank was flung down, and people pushed ahead of him. It was the habit of his whole life to let them pass him and go on. Then, as he was about to move forward, he felt his shoulders strongly grasped and held.

He looked up astonished and saw looming above him a tall, dark-faced man and knew him instantly.

"Beaumont!" he gasped. "However?"

"Mother told me to meet you, sir, and here I am. This is my wife, Michelle."

He felt his hand taken between two soft ones, he smelled a

delicate perfume, and a woman's pretty face under a little lace hat leaned forward impetuously and kissed his cheek.

"Ah, Mr. Goodliffe, you who are so good—now I can see you!" Her warm woman's voice spoke with an enchanting accent. He was too bewildered with surprise and pleasure to speak.

The more he looked at them, the more shy he was. They were so beautiful, their garments rich, their faces happy with the careless happiness of those who have no secret cares of their own. They took his arms and bore him away between them; and a porter, unseen until now, seized his bags. Protesting and pleased, together, he was carried off to a hotel which he saw from the very flunkeys at the door was an expensive one.

"I say," he remonstrated, "I can't stay here, Beaumont. It's not my kind of a place."

"You're our guest," Beaumont cried with joy. "To think I have the chance!"

They swept him along with them into an enormous mahogany-lined lift and then along wide halls into a suite of rooms facing the sea. Beaumont threw open the door of a huge bedroom, and the bellboy put his bags down, and Beaumont gave him a tip from which Jonathan averted his eyes.

"We'll have lunch in twenty minutes," Beaumont announced, "and we'll wait for you in the parlor. We have everything to talk about—not a moment must be wasted, *mon cher!*"

Jonathan understood not one word of the French into which these two fell as naturally as they breathed, but he understood them. He had never seen two such glorious creatures. In the cab he had sat between them, looking from one face to the other, silent while they poured out talk, and thinking that Beaumont had fulfilled his whole promise as he could have done only in the air of a country where he was free as France could make him free. Jonathan thought with sorrowful contrast of Stephen and Sue in Median, living out their lives humbly under the shadow. But upon Beaumont no shadow had fallen.

I got him out in time, Jonathan thought with thankfulness.

And Michelle had dispelled even the chances of memory. She was a lovely creature, her auburn hair curled about her pretty vivid face and her violet eyes dancing and gleaming with light. The love between her and Beaumont was open, and neither thought of hiding it.

He stood alone in the huge bedroom and caught a sudden sight of himself in a great panel mirror behind the door. He had never seen himself from head to foot all at once, and he was startled and abashed. What did that brilliant pair see in this middle-sized, common-looking chap that was he? He turned away from himself and tiptoed about the room. Everything in it was big and solid, nothing was makeshift. On this little isle people built to last for eternity. Centuries could not destroy such stuff. He thought of the makeshifts of Kansas, the quick wooden buildings thrown up in a few days, the shoddy furniture of mail-order catalogues.

It's because America is so big that folk can always move somewhere else, he thought. Here they know they've got to stay.

Beyond the bedroom was a bathroom so immense that he was struck with admiration. Even America had no such bathroom. The tub was enormous, built upon the floor like a monument, the plumbing massive and too firm to admit of improvement. This bathroom would endure as it had been installed, let invention be what it might.

He inspected everything, gazed out of the window, and then inexplicably changed his tie. He had put on a plain gray silk tie in the ship's cabin this morning. Now he took it off and put on the gayest one he had, a narrow maroon satin stripe. Then he opened the door into the other room and stood there smiling at them with love in his heart.

An hour later, in the great orderly hotel dining room, he told himself that this could never have happened in America. He had hesitated half-fearfully at the dining-room door, between Beaumont and Michelle. Beaumont looked prosperous and proud, a man obviously of the upper classes. But there was no need for hesitation. The steward had hastened forward.

"Yes, sir—Dr. Parry, please, your table is reserved."

They had followed him and seated themselves at a table where a high window gave toward the sea, and he had eaten the best meal of his life, English food, roast beef from a hot service wheeled to the table and carved by a white-capped, white-aproned cook—Yorkshire pudding and gravy, mashed potatoes and boiled cabbage, a green salad and plum tart. His heart was warm toward this country of his ancestors. He felt foundations firm under him. People knew where they were. Every man had his place.

And all the time he listened to this pair. They made a duet, wanting to tell him everything at once. Yet he could scarcely listen for looking at them.

"I wish your mother could see you, Beaumont," he interposed.

"I wish we could see her," Beaumont said eagerly. "We've thought often of going back to America, just for a visit. I'm still an American. We think of that often, eh, Michelle?"

"How often!" Michelle echoed. "I long to see my dear good *belle mère* and my good *beau père* and the brothers and sisters. Gem—it is such a sweet name!"

"We will talk of it later," Jonathan said quietly.

They did talk of it later, but he had first to hear of Beaumont's great achievements as a surgeon of the hospital where "he reigns supreme," Michelle said proudly. She put her white hand on Jonathan's arm. "I must tell you what he will not—that he is a *vairy* great surgeon. Oh, people come from everyw'ere—only for the brain, you know. Last mont' a prince from India, dying of the tumore, and my Beau cut it away and mended the brain again, and the prince grows well. If he liked, my Beau could be a great musician, but he chooses to do what helps so many people!"

Beaumont laughed, his white teeth shining in his dark face, and his dark eyes tender upon his wife.

"It is my turn, Michelle," he said, and then he told Jonathan in a few deep words what Michelle had meant to him.

"We loved each other so soon after I came," he said. "How it would have been for me without her I cannot imagine. She was my home, my love, my security, my refuge. She comforted me when I was discouraged, praised me, scolded me. I was not lowly or alone because of her."

Michelle's eyes were wet. "And was it nothing for me to have you, too, all those years?" she said.

In the presence of this love Jonathan's heart began to bleed from the old heart wound. Ah, he had always known that love was like this, even if it could not be for him. "I thank you, my dear," he said gently to Michelle. "And you, Beaumont— you've grown to your height, my son."

Yes, this great brown fellow was his son, the son of his spirit. He looked at the big, dexterous, life-saving hands. "You must never come back to America, Beaumont," he said slowly. "Never—never."

Beaumont's face quivered. "Is America the same?"

Michelle was suddenly quiet. Her luminous eyes moved from one face to the other. Ah, these two, Jonathan thought, so happy, so rich in one another, they knew the shadow over there across the sea! They did not live in it, they were free; but they knew it was in the world with them.

"America has not changed in her heart," Jonathan said in his quiet sad fashion. "The body has grown. How the body grows! You would never know Median, Beaumont. The courthouse, the churches, the post office, the fine school—I'm not the schoolmaster now, you know—"

"I can't imagine you not a schoolmaster," Beaumont said. The tenderness in his deep, gentle voice broke over Jonathan's heart.

"I tend the store now," he said. "But I daresay your mother's kept you up in Median news."

"Yes," Beaumont said simply.

They were still thinking of the shadow over there. In silence Beaumont leaned forward, his hands hung between his knees, his head drooped. It was an attitude of unconscious memory, the memory of Stephen, his stepfather, and of Sue his mother.

"If America doesn't change," he said—with somberness—"if her heart doesn't grow to comprehend the brotherhood of man, she'll be torn in two when the big war comes."

"The big war?" Jonathan repeated blankly. He had not thought of war for years. That minor splash in the Pacific had been soon over, and Admiral Dewey had come home to be made into a hero of clay and then broken into dust again by a childish people.

"There'll be lesser wars first," Beaumont said. His voice was the prophetic tolling of a bell. "There'll be a war in Europe in the next five years, but it'll be a lesser war. Maybe there'll be a couple of wars like that. But the big war is coming, the war for the brotherhood of man."

He had dropped back into the speech of his childhood. Michelle looked frightened. "Beau, what are you saying!" she cried.

Beaumont shook his great head. "No, we won't go to

America, you and I, Michelle. We'll live in the sunshine of France. But I'll never see my mother again."

They stayed together four days, talking a little less each day but feeling closer together. In the evenings Beaumont went to the piano and played, and sometimes while he played he threw back his head and sang. When that great rolling voice poured into the room, Michelle slipped her hand into Jonathan's and squeezed it. "You see why I adore him," she whispered, and Jonathan nodded. Most of these songs he had never heard, but sometimes, a few times, Beaumont sang the slave songs of his childhood, and tears came into Jonathan's eyes. Ah, Beaumont must never come back!

On the morning of the fifth day Beaumont was summoned to Paris by cable. The only son of a cabinet minister had been caught in a motor accident, and his skull was crushed. There could be no delay.

"Come home with us, sir," he begged Jonathan, and Michelle's soft hands clasping Jonathan's pulled him toward France.

But Jonathan refused. "No, I came back to see England, and it was rare luck to be met by you and Michelle. I'll never forget these days. In a way, they're better than any of my life."

"We'll meet again," Beaumont said.

Jonathan smiled and did not say what he knew, that such meeting could not be sure. Once in a lifetime it was lucky enough.

🐝 41 🐝

IT WAS NOT MANY DAYS BEFORE HE KNEW HE DID NOT WANT to stay in England. He found no such companionship again as Beaumont and Michelle had given him. The great hotel was too fine for him left alone. He took the train to Blackpool and was met at the station by Edward and his two eldest sons. He saw the three medium-sized, soberly clad figures and knew them at once. Edward had settled into thickishness at the waist, and his long gray moustache was yellow at the fringes.

"Well, Jonathan," Edward said, and they clasped hands.

"Well, Edward," Jonathan replied.

"This is Tom, my eldest, and this is Ed." Edward pointed his stick at his two sons.

"Fine lads," Jonathan said heartily.

The men took his bags, and the brothers walked ahead. "We'll take a cab for once," Edward said.

"Don't for me," Jonathan replied.

But they crowded into a cab and rattled off and stopped in front of the store. Nothing was changed. Jonathan knew the rooms as soon as he stepped into them, and knew Millie, too, stout and middle-aged as she was. The younger boys were apprenticed at shops, but the house still seemed full of Edward's children.

But after the first day it was hard to talk. Edward and Millie talked while he listened, and he saw the picture of their lives—the petty troubles with rival shops, the competition of too many people trying to earn their bread in the same spot, the careful watching of tiny profits. It was a decent life, but how small! His own life in Median, he now saw, had been filled with immensities.

Of that life, to his amazement, they asked no questions. When he spoke of it, Edward lit his pipe and let his mind wander and Millie said, "Well, I never," her eye on her knitting.

Once she stared at him and when he paused she broke in, "Jonathan, remember Connie Favor?"

Jonathan blushed against his will. "Yes, I do—just."

Millie smiled. "She was sweet on you—she'd have gone to America for the asking."

"I was only a lad," Jonathan said stiffly.

Millie laughed. "Ah, well, she married a chap as went to Australia—lives on a sheep farm now."

He gave up talking of Median after that, and in a few days he had had enough.

England was small, too small for him, and he knew he did not want to stay in it. All against his will America had stretched his soul. He thought much of Median, in the narrow streets of Blackpool, and he longed for the wide plains and wider skies of Kansas. There's room to grow there, he thought.

On his second Sunday he tramped off to Dentwater. "Don't expect me until you see me," he told them.

He took the familiar road along which he and Edward had climbed into the coal cart when they went to see Clyde off to America. Nothing along the road had changed. He came to Dentwater, and saw it had not added a house or changed a chimney. England's a damned finished kind of place, he thought, looking over the village. He tramped to the cottage that had been his home and stared at it and did not ask to enter. A surly old chap tilled the garden plot and looked at him suspiciously.

"I lived here once as a lad," Jonathan said to excuse his presence.

"Eh, you're not the only one," the man retorted. "It's changed hands often, this place has. Chimney smokes."

"I don't remember that," Jonathan said. "But I do remember that from that window up yonder, if the day was fair, I could see the sails of ships upon the Irish Sea."

"Attic's full of stuff now," the surly man said.

He left the cottage then and walked down the street to the school. It was no longer a school. Two ancient and withered old men sat on a bench outside the door into which he had gone so eagerly every school day.

"What's this place?" he asked them. One of them was deaf, but the other took his pipe out of his mouth and said, "Dentwater Almshouse," and put the pipe in again.

"It was a school in my time," Jonathan said and had there been answer he would have asked next of his old schoolteacher. But there was no answer, and he went on and took his lunch at the small public house which had been such a cause of quarrel between his mother and father. The faces were strange, and he did not remind them of Clyde Goodliffe. He drank his glass of ale and ate his cheese sandwich, and when this was done he went down the street and into the empty church and sat a while. A young curate came in, not yet out of pimples. "Anything I can do for you, sir?" he asked.

"I came to this church as a lad with my mother," Jonathan said. "The rector was old then, and his name was Clemony."

"He's in the churchyard," the young priest said. "Maybe you'd like to see his grave?"

"If you please," Jonathan replied.

He followed the fluttering robes along the mossy churchyard path and stood at the foot of two narrow graves. He remembered as clearly as though he had been in church this morning the old vicar and his flying white hair, preaching the brotherhood of man. What was that old Clemony had said about the blacks in India? Jonathan could only remember that tears had streamed down the prophet's cheeks as he cried out to the staid and wondering people in the little village of Dentwater. . . . Beaumont and the big war! Against the vague trouble of his own mind Jonathan saw the face of Stephen and Sue Parry, dark with sorrow.

"Where's Clyde Goodliffe's grave?" he asked abruptly.

"Here, sir," the curate said.

And in a moment he stood beside his father's grave. It was hard to believe that under this still green sod lay the restless bones of that wild-hearted man.

"You knew him?" the curate asked.

"Yes," Jonathan said and shut his lips.

"He'd come all the way from America, and his family is mostly on the other side—one son in Blackpool, I believe," the curate said.

"Aye," Jonathan said and turned away. He was glad that he had not brought his mother's dust here into this shadowy old churchyard. Let her lie where she was in the bright western sunshine.

He put some money into the church box, thanked the curate, and went away. He knew now he could not live in Dentwater, and if not in Dentwater then not in England. Yes, England's made and finished, he thought, and hurried his steps along the road he had come. A man can't do anything here but live out his time and die.

He took passage within the week for America.

On the ship crossing the ocean he found he could not sleep for eagerness. He rose at dawn and went on deck where he could feel the ship's speed and see the parted waves flow from its sides. And while his body was carried forward to its home his mind roamed backward over the years and to his first voyage over these same waters.

"I ought to thank my dad, I reckon," he told himself, thinking of the unwilling lad he had been. "I'm glad now he pulled me up out of Dentwater. I wish I could tell him so."

He had been pulled up out of a small place and set in a

large one. He thought with joy of Median. It was the core of all his being.

"It's the kind of a town I like," he thought fondly.

In a queer way his father had been right about life and his mother wrong. No, they had both been right in their own ways. But they had never been fused. Not all their passion toward one another had fused their eternal difference, he the wanderer and she the homekeeper.

"Reckon I'm the mixture," he thought with some astonishment. For was he not the fusion? He stared down into the clear green waves and pondered himself. Homekeeping he was, and he had made a town his eternal home. But the town he had set in the midst of land as wide as any sea.

"A love of a town," he thought fondly, and knew when he said the words that Judy had lost her power over him at last. It was not Judy now who drew him, but Median, the creation of his being.

He found himself hungering for the first sight of it. He could not bear a moment's delay between ship and train, and seated by the window in a day coach of the first train westward out of New York, he watched the rugged hills of the East shorten and smooth into the plains and his heart began to beat fast. He knew better than he knew any human face the outlines of his town, the comfortable solid shape, rooted in the prairie and open to the sky. He was glad that Median would never grow into a city. He had protected her from the ravages of cattlemen and had forbidden her to the coarse men who might have spoiled her with gambling dens and racecourses. Median was now what he had planned she should be, the seat of a prosperous farming county, a town where laws were made and enforced without cruelty, a center for homes and a place of rest for the old. All around her, except to the south where the oil wells stood, the wheat grew unbroken, green in spring and yellow at harvest, the fine hard red wheat brought from Russia by peasants. It made the country's finest flour.

His mind dwelled with rising love upon every aspect of his town. He was proud of his own neat white house with its green shutters and of his good store. Jon was there now looking after things. His son's children would be born there in the town, too. Median was a good town for children, just as he had always planned.

He was to reach there in the midafternoon of a Saturday and he had told nobody of his coming. Again and again he had imagined his homecoming. He would get off the train casually, and say hello to old Jackson, the ticket agent, and then walk down the street to his house and go in. Maybe the children would all be out somewhere. They'd come home and find him. "Hello," he'd say. "Well, I'm back."

When the train passed the last station, he reviewed all this in his mind and found his heart beating so hard that he was alarmed. He walked down the aisle and poured himself a drink of water. It was stale and lukewarm.

"Next time I drink it'll be from my own well," he thought. That water was the best in the world, clear and cold and pure.

But his heart kept on beating hard and he had to bear it while the train pulled in at the station. He fumbled over his bag and forgot his hat and hurried back to his seat for it. He got off finally and for a moment stood bewildered. He was the only passenger for Median, and almost immediately the train shrieked and went on again. The sun was so bright he was blinded. He had forgotten how bright the sun could be in Median. He stood uncertainly, looking about him. Then suddenly he heard voices cry out.

"There he is!"

And down the platform a host approached him. He stood smiling sheepishly, recognizing them all. Why, it looked as if the whole town had turned out to meet him!

"How'd you know I was coming?" he demanded as they drew near.

"We cabled Uncle Edward," Jon said proudly. "He told us the ship and of course we knew you wouldn't waste time in New York. We have met every train anyway."

He was in a mist of happiness. The whole town wanted him back!

"I was going to slip in and surprise you all," he said.

"You're the one that's going to get the surprise, Dad," Jon said.

"Where's Isabel?" Jonathan asked. He began to suspect some extravagance of welcome and to guard against his heart melting under it, he looked severe.

"At home, getting ready enough cake and ice cream to feed the town," Jon said joyously.

But there was no more time for such talk. They were pressing around him, all wanting to shake his hand. Faience, who was still the mayor, took his bag.

"I can carry it," Jonathan said. "I've carried it a couple of thousand miles."

But no one answered anything he said. They were full of a superb secret. Jackson locked the railroad station and came with them and they swept up the main street, the young people singing and yelling and the children blowing whistles.

"I never knew there was so much noise in Median," Jonathan cried.

"Never was before!" a voice shouted back at him.

Up Main Street they went, beyond the courthouse, beyond the church.

"Where are we going?" Jonathan asked.

"Never mind," Faience said, laughing. "We're just going!"

They crossed the street, swarming around Jonathan, treading on his heels. Then they paused and he stood still. There in a big empty space where years ago he had planted hardwoods on the edge of the town he saw the foundations for a big building. Walls had been laid to the level of the ground, but only in one corner had they reached above the level.

"What in time—" he began.

"Hush!" said Jon.

He stood silent and the crowd drew back from him. He looked down and saw at his feet a great white marble stone, cut square and polished smooth. There were letters on it—he read his name.

"The Jonathan Goodliffe High School."

He began to tremble and he felt his son's steadying hand on his arm. The mayor stepped forward and drew a paper from his pocket and began to read and the people listened.

"Friends and fellow citizens of Median," the mayor said in a loud voice. "We are gathered today to perform a most significant act—"

Jonathan stood rigid, his eyes on the stone. There upon the eternal marble, he went on reading—*"named in honor of Jonathan Goodliffe, the man who more than any other made and shaped the town of Median into a goodly home for us and for our children."*

The mayor's voice rang out through the trees. "We have

laid these foundations for our new high school, the school which we dedicate today to Jonathan Goodliffe, the man whom we all delight to honor. We deliberately choose to express our love and gratitude now, while he is alive and active among us. We want him to know today how Median feels."

Median had made a monument for him! His heart dissolved and he would have wept had he not fixed his eyes sternly upon the shadows dancing over the mayor's bald head and shaven cheeks. A bird sang shrilly in the hardwood under which they stood and a boy threw a stone into the leaves and it flew away. Of course he did not deserve all these things Faience was saying. He had simply lived in Median and done his duty.

The mayor was finished. He stooped and picked up something and put it into Jonathan's hand. It was a shining silver trowel.

"Will you lay the cornerstone of our new school, Jonathan?" he asked, his voice natural again.

"Yes," Jonathan said. "Of course—yes—"

But the big white stone blurred through his tears. Two men stepped forward—his son and Steve Parry.

"I saw Beaumont," he muttered to Steve. "I want to tell you—"

"Later, Mr. Goodliffe, sir," Steve whispered.

They heaved the stone up before him, and Steve took the trowel and filled it with mortar, and put it back into his hands again, and somehow he smeared the stuff on the wall and together Jon and Steve placed the stone.

"The cornerstone is laid," the mayor announced.

It was over. They were all gazing at Jonathan. He looked away, but wherever he looked, he met the eyes of Median warm upon him. Unutterable shyness rushed over him. He tried to smile and felt his face stiffen.

"We talked over a dozen things we wanted to do for you," Faience said tenderly. "Some of the people wanted a bronze statue."

Jonathan felt his tongue unloosen. "Nonsense, that," he said sharply. "Waste of money and for what?"

They roared with laughter, and he smiled and felt his blood begin to flow again. He flung his hand toward the foundations and tried to make the gesture careless. "The school's the thing," he declared. His eyes twinkled. "I shall plant some ivy at this corner and let it grow. I'm a common chap—no reason why my name should be on the school more than anybody's."

They shouted laughter again, they hugged him and all but smothered him with their joy in him.

"He's just the same!" they cried to one another. "Jonathan Goodliffe, you haven't changed a bit!"

"The same old screw," he agreed. "Why not?"

They carried him down the street in the heart of the crowd and Jon went ahead to tell Isabel he was coming. But Jonathan turned his head and looked back. It was odd to think that his name would be there upon the cornerstone, forever! Long after he was dead and buried, his body dust, his name would be carved solidly in the midst of Median. Generations of children, coming and going, would read—*Jonathan Goodliffe*.

"It's queer how I like it," he thought. "I like it wonderfully well."